Arthur William Upfield is well known as the creator of Detective Inspector Napoleon Bonaparte (Bony) who features in 29 crime detection novels; most are set in the Australian outback. It is not well known that he also wrote about 250 short stories and articles, mainly based on his experiences in the bush between 1911 and 1931.

Up and Down Australia Again is the third published anthology of Upfield's short works. Kees de Hoog has selected another 34 short stories, and has added a radio play and the first five chapters for an unfinished Bony novel. Five stories and the play are published for the first time in this book.

Some stories and the play are based on Upfield's personal experiences in the Great War. There are also adventure stories and comedies set in the outback, and historical stories based on what really happened when Australian Aborigines and immigrants crossed paths during the years of European settlement and expansion.

Kees lives in Australia, and has been reading and researching Upfield's life and works in his spare time since 2001. *Up and Down Australia*, the first selection of his short stories, and *Up and Down the Real Australia: Autobiographical Articles and The Murchison Murders,* are also published by Lulu.com.

Up and Down Australia Again

More Short Stories

by

Arthur Upfield

Collected, Selected, Edited and Introduced by

Kees de Hoog

Published 2009 by Lulu.com (Lulu Enterprises Inc, Suite 300, 860 Aviation Parkway, Morrisville, NC 27560, USA.)

Rights Owner: Kees de Hoog, Australia.

ISBN 978-1-4452-2984-3

ALSO BY ARTHUR UPFIELD AND PUBLISHED BY LULU.COM:

Up and Down Australia: Short Stories
Up and Down the Real Australia: Autobiographical Articles and The Murchison Murders

The front cover is a photograph by Oz Photo of a windmill in Central Australia.

Contents

Contents

Introduction

Arthur William Upfield is well known to aficionados of crime detection novels as the creator of the Australian Detective Inspector Napoleon Bonaparte (Bony) who appears in twenty-nine novels written over forty-two years from 1924 to 1966; most are set in the outback. It is not so well known that Upfield also wrote seven other published books, as well as many short stories and articles that appeared in magazines and newspapers in Australia and other countries.

He was born in 1890 into a family of drapers at Gosport on Portsmouth Bay in England. An avid reader of boys' adventure magazines, at school he did well only in subjects that interested him – history and geography. Apprenticed to a firm of estate agents, auctioneers and surveyors just before his sixteenth birthday, he was more interested in writing novels and other, more daring, escapades. He once claimed his father sent him to Australia in despair, saying "it is so far away that you will never save enough money to return,"[1] but it is more likely he wanted to go and see the world.[2]

Soon after arriving in Adelaide in 1911, Upfield went to the outback where he worked in a variety of jobs including fence building, boundary riding, droving and opal digging. He quickly developed a lasting passion for the Australian bush that laid the foundations for the rest of his life, and eventually "carried his swag"[3] to all the mainland states and the Northern Territory.

On the outbreak of World War I in 1914 he joined the Australian Imperial Forces, and later served in Egypt, Gallipoli, England and France. Returning to Australia in 1921 with a wife and son, and probably still suffering from shell shock, he "went bush" again soon afterwards as he could not tolerate working in a factory and missed the outback lifestyle.

Upfield had continued to write desultorily, and in 1924 was

---

[1] Hetherington J, *Forty-two Faces*, Melbourne: Cheshire, 1962, p21.
[2] See Upfield A W, "The Land of Opportunity, Part 1," *The Wide World Magazine*, vol 61, No 365, August 1928, pp 363-374.
[3] Walked; travelled.

persuaded to "have a go" at writing professionally, drawing on his experiences in the bush.

While working on the No 1 Rabbit-Proof Fence in Western Australia in 1929, Upfield developed a way to dispose of a body – the perfect murder – for his next Bony novel, *The Sands of Windee*, with the help of friends and acquaintances. Fact and fiction collided when a friend, Snowy Rowles, used that method when he murdered one person in 1930, and probably two more in 1929. As a consequence, Upfield was almost charged with criminal offences, and was summoned to give evidence at Rowles' trial in Perth in 1932. Rowles was found guilty and hanged.[4]

After four novels and a number of short stories and articles had been published, he left the bush in 1931 to live in Perth with his family and write full time. Two years later he moved to Melbourne to join *The Herald* newspaper, but resumed freelance writing after about six months.

His output of short stories and articles was most prolific between 1931 and 1940 as he sought to supplement the income from his novels. Of about 250 short stories and articles I have found, about 180 were first published during those years.

Upfield joined Australia's military intelligence as a censor during World War II. With much less time for writing, he sent some Bony novels to a United States publisher in 1943. The books proved very popular and most of the earlier Bony novels were published there within a few years, as were those he wrote later. The extra sales allowed Upfield to live comfortably from writing mainly Bony novels until his death in 1964.

For this anthology I selected thirty-four short stories written by Upfield – none are in my first anthology of his short stories, *Up and Down Australia*.[5] I added a radio play, "Love and the Leopard," and the first five chapters for a Bony novel that was never finished. Five of the stories and the play have not been published before so far as I can ascertain.

The known sources for all the stories are listed at the end of

---

[4] For more details see "The Murchison Murders", in Upfield A, de Hoog K (Ed), *Up and Down the Real Australia: Autobiographical Articles and The Murchison Murders*, Lulu.com, 2009 at pp 169-202, and Walker T, *Murder on the Rabbit Proof Fence*, Perth: Hesperian, 1993.

[5] Upfield A, de Hoog K (Ed), *Up and Down Australia: Short Stories*, Lulu.com, 2008.

this book. I also listed the sources for the stories in *Up and Down Australia* following several requests for those details from other Upfield enthusiasts.

One theme in this collection is war – the carnage and futility, as well as the lighter aspects. Another is the uneasy interactions, often friction, between Australian Aborigines and immigrants during the years of European settlement and expansion. And Upfield again demonstrates his versatility by writing in yet another genre – historical fiction.

This anthology is a companion volume to *Up and Down Australia* and *Up and Down the Real Australia*, my anthology of autobiographical articles by Upfield.[6] For those I classified stories as biographical if an element of the plot is in his unpublished autobiography, *Beyond the Mirage*,[7] or his official biography, *Follow My Dust*.[8] I adopted the same approach with this selection.

The stories are presented in four groups. The first group is based on Upfield's experiences in World War I, particularly at Gallipoli. "Little Stories of Gallipoli" is a collection of very short stories describing events at Gallipoli. All but the last little story were originally in one or both of two similar, but not identical, series of little stories published in different newspapers in 1916. If a story was duplicated I selected the later version as being more polished. In an introduction to the later and longer series Upfield wrote:

> The collection of storyettes . . . are in the main true and occurred during my visit at the now famous Anzac Cove on Gallipoli Peninsular. . . Many of the happenings related were personally witnessed and the remainder were told me by men whom I have no reason to disbelieve; while the scraps of conversation I have endeavoured to put on paper are in nowise imaginary. The language may be blunt; it is at least honest.[9]

The last little story, "All Must Pay," is the earliest published work by Upfield I have found to date.

While the little stories may be historical fiction, that may not be the case for "Under Shell-Fire at ANZAC." In his biography of

---

[6] See footnote 4.
[7] Upfield A W, *Beyond the Mirage*, National Library of Australia, Manuscript, MS9590, c1937.
[8] Hawke J, *Follow My Dust*, Melbourne: Heinemann, 1957.
[9] "Storyettes of the Great War," *Hampshire Telegraph and Post*, Portsmouth, UK, 7 April 1916, p5.

Upfield, Milnor notes it is far more personal than Upfield's other articles documenting the horrors of Gallipoli, and suggests it tells the reader much about why Gallipoli had such an effect upon him.[10]

The second group consists of six adventure stories, all clearly fiction. "The Water Witch", first published in 1917, and "A Desert Flower," first published eighteen years later, have similar plots. Putting aside those in the first group based on Upfield's war experiences, "The Head of the Revolution" is the only story I have found that is not set in Australia. It was written in England after the war before he returned to Australia. "A Murderers' Home" is clearly an early version of *The House of Cain*, Upfield's first published novel.

Next is the radio play, *Love and the Leopard*. The manuscript is not dated but it appears to have been written in 1934 or 1935. It returns to the war theme, particular the futility of war and its repercussions, not only for those who actually served, but also their families and friends left at home.

The six stories in the third group are historical fiction squarely on the theme of the interaction between indigenous Australians and immigrants during the period of European settlement and expansion in the eighteenth and nineteenth centuries. These stories were first published as a series in *The Australian Journal* in 1937 and 1938, and introduced with the following words:

> The short but eventful panorama of Australian history contains scenes as strange as any conceived by the imagination of the fiction writer. In this new series of stories the author . . . retells in striking narrative some of the fantastic tales he has unearthed in old letters, ancient documents and forgotten diaries. Curious as they may seem, these things HAVE happened.[11]

The fourth group consists of seven comic stories. The last five, all feature Joseph Henry with his poorly-educated narrative style, who also appears in nine rural comedies included in *Up and Down Australia*. The context of these stories is Henry's army service during World War I, and returns to the war theme albeit in a lighthearted way. It is noteworthy that "Miss Oo-La-La" was

[10] Milnor A J, *Arthur W. Upfield: Life and Time of Bony's Man*, Newcastle: Cambridge Scholars, 2008, p67-68.
[11] *The Australian Journal*, Melbourne, vol 73, pt 860, 1 November 1937, p1477.

rejected by the ABC[12] Weekly in 1941.

In *Up and Down Australia* I included most of the first chapter of a *Breakaway House* conversion into a Bony novel begun in 1962 but never finished. I later discovered Upfield had actually written the first five chapters so, for Bony enthusiasts, I added all five at the end of this book.

The themes, settings and characters in this selection generally have little in common with those in my earlier anthologies of his short works. The exceptions are some of the stories in the second and fourth groups, but even the Joseph Henry stories are set in different contexts and locations.

These articles reflect the attitudes and the ways of talking about women, Australian aborigines and migrants that were common in the early decades of the twentieth century. By selecting them for this anthology I do not endorse those attitudes and opinions.

I am grateful to the late Arthur Upfield for writing the articles in the first instance, and to Bonaparte Holdings Pty Ltd, the Baillieu Library at the University of Melbourne, and Rob Blackmore for their kind permission to publish them. I thank Pam Pryde at the Baillieu Library, Travis Lindsey, Stuart Mayne, and Joe Kovess, as well as staff of the Battye Library in Perth, the National Library of Australia in Canberra, the Mitchell Library in Sydney, and the Central Library of Portsmouth in England, who helped me to find them.

And last, but not least, I thank my wife, Margaret Robertson, for her advice and encouragement throughout the search and the publication process.

I hope readers enjoy these articles as much as I did collecting, selecting, editing and introducing them.

Kees de Hoog
Perth Western Australia
November 2009

---

[12] Australian Broadcasting Commission

Little Stories of Gallipoli

I

Able Seaman Craddock was steering his boat towards the shore. He had often steered boats ashore, but never in such circumstances as upon this occasion. It was four o'clock in the morning – dark and clammy – yet his whole being was filled with a fierce excitement of expectancy.

His boat was full of soldiers. Some faced him as he pulled at the oars – for they had just been cast off by a destroyer; others sat on the gunnels; and still others upon the thwarts nursing their rifles. Ahead of them loomed a dark mass of cliffs and bluffs, ahead of them lay Gallipoli Peninsular. Craddock belonged to Hampshire, and the others came from Australia.

A desultory crackle of rifle fire broke out from the beach, and one man said "Hell!" before he slid to the bottom of the boat. Over the water, on their right, came the dull boom of a gun, followed in a couple of seconds by the ever-growing wail of metal in rapid transit though the air. The wail ceased suddenly in a flash of light, like summer lightning, when the shell burst, and discharged its bullets in and around other boats on Craddock's left, going in the same direction, and upon the same errand. The rifle fire had ceased as suddenly as it had begun, about thirty seconds before Craddock's boat grounded upon the stony beach. For the first time Craddock spoke:

"Now then you – Colonials, op it."

Some of them had already "opped it," and were up to their arm-pits in water. Carrying their rifles above their heads, they waded ashore and shouted thus:

"It's blasted cold" "Where's Bill? . . . Come on, Bill, – you!" "'Ere comes some more shells." "Oh – blank this pack!" "Bill. Where the 'ell is Bill?" "That one has got me in the chest, by gum! 'Ere, give me a hand ashore, I feel giddy!" "Where's them – Turks?"

And so on. Craddock's orders were to take that boat back. For a moment he hesitated. Dawn was breaking over the tops of the bluffs. His boat-load of men were ashore, flinging away their packs – that is barring the man who lay in the bottom of the boat dead, and another propped up by the gunwale, equally dead.

To the devil's music of bursting shells, the seaman snatched up a rifle, and ran over the thwarts to the bow of the boat, off which he jumped into the water that reached his middle. With a yell, he raced the Australians up the bluff. Orders he had forgotten. What of it? He had a bayonet on the end of an empty rifle, and the Turks were ahead, going up the hill for the lick of their lives. Objects began to take shape, but nevertheless he ran into prickly bushes which tore his clothes and his flesh, and tripped over roots.

Without engaging a single Turk, he and his companions gained the top of the cliff, and paused to get breath. Directly below them lay the beach, and Craddock wondered how he had got where he was, for in places the cliff face was almost like a precipice. Boatloads of men were still coming ashore, and on them hung jagged-edged balls of white smoke, marking the shell bursts. Away out the fleet exuded stabs of flame and clouds of black smoke, and sent tons of metal where it was exactly wanted to go.

A few moments' respite and then away they went over the top of the bluff, which was flat for five hundred yards. The ground then dipped suddenly into a gully. And on the further side of that gully they saw the enemy scrambling up the opposite bluff.

Leaping, slithering, and sliding, they fell rather than scrambled down. When they were nearing the bottom a man below Craddick uttered a guttural sound and expired. A sniper had got him in the back of the neck. The rest were intent on the gentlemen ahead.

Now they were tearing up the further side of the gully. A bayonet flashed out from behind a bush. It missed its intended object, as the man had leaped aside just in time.

The man's "cobber," however, settled the Turk, and then exclaimed: "By Jove! it's like sticking a fork into a haystack."

A little later Craddock bellowed like a bull when he saw one of the enemy dive head-first, despite the prickly leaves, into a bush and with a mighty lunge he drove his bayonet into it.

Now, somehow or other, the bayonet guard got caught in the bush and all Craddock's efforts could not disengage it. The seaman swore, and while he swore, he saw the soles of a pair of boots. Leaving the rifle, he grabbed the boots and hauled away. He hauled out the Turk. Craddock, working his six-foot body and his twelve-stone weight, whirled the enemy round his head and smashed the man's skull against a stone. The body suddenly grew limp, and he cast it back into the gully. Then he turned slowly round and dropped silently over the bush in which his rifle had stuck.

Over the edge of the bluff he had just come down an enemy sniper moved back the bolt and jammed another cartridge into the breach of his rifle. The bullet from the empty shell had killed Craddock during his first charge.

II

Achi Baba viewed from the north of the Peninsular looked nothing more than a gigantic mole-heap with gentle sloping sides. At that time it was a mole-heap and the moles – and there were thousands – got about on two legs, used picks and shovels, and loosed quantities of flying metal.

One peaceful afternoon, however, a battle-ship, intent upon a little gun-practice, came up from Cape Helles way, and slowed down to the westward of Achi Baba. While the destroyers danced the tango round the battle-ship, various things began to happen.

Almost instantaneously there were five or six great tongues of flame, immediately preceding five or six greater clouds of smoke. Upon the side of Achi-Baba there suddenly sprouted five or six gigantic mushrooms, composed of the hill-side and human moles. When the mushrooms had nearly subsided, there came the roar of five or six guns, followed by the whine of five or six lumps of metal attaining great velocity in the air.

Thereafter there were countless tongues of flame and much smoke, the continual roar of many guns, and the shriek of passing metal. Quite recently Achi-Baba had looked like a quiet and peaceful mole-hole; it now looked something like a pot full of boiling water. The scenery on that hill never for a second remained still for half an hour and ten minutes.

An Australian remarked in flowery and picturesque language something to the effect that "he was glad it was the British Navy that was kicking up the dust."

III

Private Scaddon met one of his many friends walking along Anzac Beach one afternoon. The friend was an officer, who in normal times was an overseer on a large station at the back of Queensland. Scaddon owned that station.

While they were discussing the many delightful people they had met in Cairo, there came to their ears the low, faint wail of an arriving shell. When they first heard it, they knew they had just two seconds and a half to get to cover, and the nearest cover was a stack of bully-beef, just thirty feet away. As many shells had "lobbed" just where they stood, they estimated that this one would "lob" there also.

A bee-line was made for the bully-beef stack. Scaddon was the faster of the two and was leading by five yards when the shell dropped at his feet. Together with stones and sand, he rose in the air to a height of seven or eight feet, and then flew in pieces.

The officer was knocked down but immediately got up again, with his clothes torn to ribbons and smelling of fire. He staggered along the remaining distance to the bully-beef stack. There he fell for the second time and vomited violently. He died half an hour later from shock.

IV

It was about mid-day. In the minds of many the weather brought memories of enjoyable days spent with ladies at regattas. The light breeze merely rippled the surface of the blue water that reflected the light of the warm sun. The hills of Embros looked blue and mysterious. Everything was quiet and peaceful, and there was very little murder being done.

But it had not been quiet and peaceful all day. Up to within an hour two battleships had been exercising their guns to the disadvantage of some Turkish batteries. Those battleships were evidently satisfied that their guns were in good workable condition, as they were steaming away towards Embros Island, when a huge column of water shot up into the air on the port side of one of them.

She stopped very suddenly, and the other didn't wait to inquire the reason of that column of water and the sudden stop. She went like a greyhound.

From the pinnace-boats moored to the various piers at Anzac Cove there arose much shouting and hooting of sirens. Trawlers that were anchored a little way out pulled up their anchors as they never came up before. The pinnace-boat crews spoke thus:

"Cast off there, 'Arry. . . She's submarined." "Hurry, – you!" "Go astern, Bill." "Look out, blast you!" This to a rival coxswain: "Go a'ed, Bill, and tear 'er guts out!" "Gawd – she's going over!" "My sister's bloke is on her, too."

A Naval officer spoke through a megaphone: "Are – you – men – going – to – stay – there – all – the – blank – blank – day? Do – you – think – you – are – a – blank – blank – windjammer?"

And while the trawlers and the pinnaces raced out to the stricken ship, with men stoking up below and flames leaping out of their funnels, an Australian fatigue party conversed.

"Gawd, strike me dead, Jim, she's torpedoed!" "The blasted swine!" "They've got her alright." "Look, she's going over!" "What about them poor – down below?" "She's going right over." "Look at them destroyers coming up from Helles!" "By hell, they're shifting! They must be doing forty." "And 'ere's two more coming over from Embros, and another down from Sulva way."

And while destroyers and pinnaces and trawlers raced from all points of the compass to that majestic battleship, she slowly – very slowly – heeled over. What occurred on board only those know who were there, but the watching Australians saw the water seething white as her funnels and upper works struck the water. Thereafter they saw her red bottom only, for a few minutes, and then – never again.

One man – a six-foot giant – stood outside his dug-out and looked at the swarm of small craft that clustered in a heap near by where she had disappeared. Tears ran down his face as he said:

"Gawd! I never want to see nothing like that no more."

V

It was Private Anderson's visiting afternoon – or rather one of three afternoons of every week which he devoted to visiting his friends in the trenches at Anzac, and incidentally, doing a little shooting. It is to be inferred, then, that as his "cobbers" were in the trenches, he himself did not reside there. That is correct. He had a "burrow" a little way up off the beach. He belonged to the Army Service Corps.

His work – that of issuing supplies – was done in the hours of darkness. At about four in the morning he would crawl into his "burrow," and sleep till noon, innocently, and undisturbed by the explosions of falling shells. After luncheon on his three visiting days, he would leave the empty bully-beef can outside, to be buried later, make sure of his supply of tobacco, and set forth, if there were no shelling; and if there were, he would wait till it was over.

When luncheon was finished, upon this particular day, and the beef-can heaved out, Private Anderson strolled along the beach and up along Dead Man's Gully. After prolonged consideration, he had decided to visit his "tart's" brother, who was then engaged in the delightful work of sniping.

He accordingly made his way towards a certain section of trenches and by many devious roads, at length reached his friend's little "nest." It was more like a fox-hole than anything else, and was reached by means of a tunnel, that entered the "nest" at the back. The front was sand-bagged up to within three feet of the roof, and the sand-bags were painted green on the outside. Near the front entrance the space between roof and floor was just sufficient to allow a man to kneel, while further back a man could stand upright and move about in a chamber six feet square.

When Anderson arrived his friend greeted him with a bayonet, which was held four inches from his chest. Recognition caused the weapon to be stuck into the wall, and the A.S.C. man was asked to come right in. This, of course, he did, and then proceeded to unload his person that had carried two tins of milk, and several tins of meat extract – stolen.

"How yer doin'?" asked Anderson.

"Oh, not too dusty. How's things on the Beach?"

"Pretty hot-like, now and then. Any lice up here?"

"Tons," said the sniper. "They breed as fast as I kill 'em."

Receiving permission to look out, Anderson did so. He did not stick his head out over the sand-bags. Oh no; he wished to live a few more hours at least, so he looked out from behind the bags. It was then he realised that the nest was situated on the slope of a sandstone bluff, and that a gully separated him from the opposite bluff, which was six hundred yards away.

"You see that white patch on the other side a little to your right?" queried the sniper.

"My oath," answered Anderson.

"Well, just below that there is a Turk who is a mighty good marksman. If you'll stop here a couple of hours and try and get him, I'll go down to the beach and 'ave a bathe."

"By Jingo, I'll blank well stop here," agreed the A.S.C. man. "Only if you're going down there, you mind them blasted shells. So long."

Left alone, Anderson took up a position which allowed him to sit with his back to the wall, and gave him as well a good view of the enemy sniper's "jossie." With his rifle sighted to a yard, and lying across his knees, he waited for a shot.

He was still like that when his friend returned. Only he was quite dead. The enemy had fired into the hole on the chance of hitting something. The one chance in a thousand odds had favoured the Turk, for bullet had got Anderson through the head. The Ottoman never knew it, however.

VI

In civil life Ted Slayton was a bookmaker. When Anzac was in full swing, he was a gunner in a howitzer battery. It was some time in August when he and his "cobbers" were doing some excellent shooting at a target they could not see that the thing happened.

The gun section to which Slayton belonged were far too interested in the attainment of accurate shooting to heed such things as "arriving shells," and when one did arrive most of them never had time to realise it.

It was two days later when Slayton woke up, to find himself on a hospital ship on its way to Alexandria. The right half of his body was burned terribly, but he did not think much of it then, because he was so amazed to learn that all his mates at the gun were killed. You see, he is positive that when the shell burst he was nearest to it.

VII

Bill and Jim were "cobbers." They had been "cobbers" for many years, and the years had made them indispensible. In New South Wales they had carried their swags. In Melbourne they had "flashed their dough" on barmaids and had taken them out to tea. South Australia had seen them punching bullocks along its northern tracks. The Giza pyramids witnessed them being turned into soldiers, and Anzac saw them scrap, and was proud of them. They were always together, but they cursed each other picturesquely always, morning, noon and night, and had done so for years.

They were bathing one quiet morning off the beach, when Jim suddenly went under, and Bill found himself swimming in blood-stained water. Bill dived instantly, and succeeded in grabbing his mate. Other men, seeing him struggling with a man, swam out to him, and after a while they got Jim ashore. But Jim was gone. A stray bullet that had probably travelled twelve hundred yards had pierced his heart.

They took him to the hospital, and he stayed there that day – upon the roof, under a tarpaulin. Bill went back to his job, and one did not dare to look into his eyes.

Two weeks later Bill received a nasty shrapnel wound. Four days after that occurred he left the hospital ship he was on and joined Jim, who was pretty certain to be waiting on the farther shore for his life-long "cobber."

VIII

Corporal Houghton was in a machine-gun section. Before the war he was a sort of sky-pilot. Funny thing that a man should point out to other men the roads to heaven and the other place one year, and then the next be engaged in sending them along those two romantic roads of ancient folk-lore. However, it was so.

It was in the early part of the operations at Anzac that one fine morning he found himself looking over the sights of his gun and gripping the handles. Many loaded belts were laid out neatly, just handy to another man, who was to jamb them in when required; and they would soon be required, as many millions of Turkish gentlemen were charging them at the double. Houghton was with his section in a fairly rough trench that was occupied by plenty of men who were just then inactive, as they had been ordered not to fire until a whistle blew. The machine-guns and rifles were sighted at four hundred yards.

To the Corporal those long lines in massed formation seemed to be coming nearer very slowly, but at last the whistle blew and the shrill blast was repeated by other whistles up and down the line of trenches. Hundreds of rifles, fired continuously, kicked up a devil's tattoo, and to it was added the murderous cackle of the machine-guns.

Houghton saw those dense lines of advancing humanity literally wither under the rain of bullets. Men flung up their arms and dropped; others spun round and fell down backwards; while yet others were seen to stagger from the effect of one bullet, and to drop quietly after being hit with a second bullet.

They went down, and disappeared under the boots of others that still came on. Their running, however, was slowing down into a walk; and when their advance came finally to a walk, Houghton could see the expression upon their faces distinctly. And as he gripped the handles of his gun, that poured out its hundreds of bullets per minute, he shivered – not with terror, but with horror at what was before him.

Fear, uncertainty and hopelessness were written as plain as twelve-foot letters upon the faces of that yet advancing mob. They went down in scores, and the horrible sounds they made as they went down could be heard even above the cackle of the Corporal's machine-gun. No sooner had Houghton fixed his eyes on a certain face than it disappeared. Sometimes a face, white as a sheet, with two black discs for eyes, became in a second a bloody pulp which would sink never to rise again. The world was full of horror-distorted faces to Houghton, and he wondered dimly where all the hills and gullies had disappeared to. The air was full of shrieks, yells, curses, and cries of exultation, that rose even above the predominant rattle of the rifles. And then the faces seemed to dwindle in numbers with exceeding rapidity. The enemy had halted one hundred and forty yards from the defenders' trenches.

For an instant they hesitated. Then the idea of retreat, the idea to run and escape those awful bullets, seemed to pass along those lines from man to man, like the flames leaping from trees to trees that grew in the path of a forest fire.

They turned and ran, and fell as they ran; they leaped over comrades who had fallen before the main body had turned to flee. After a while there was no man there who stood upon his feet. The sun looked down upon men who were dead; upon men who withered in the agony of their wounds to die slowly from loss of blood and thirst, while the great god Mars exclaimed: "War? This is not war; this is murder!"

The men in the attacked trenches cheered and shouted to each other, but Corporal Houghton leaned against the back of his trench and sobbed like a woman.

IX

Steep-sided sandstone bluffs, and cliffs over which a man could drop for two hundred feet sheer in some places, and in others where a cat could not climb. The whole covered in small, stumpy, holly-like bushes; innumerable holes made by man, and thousands of sandbags built into walls that formed dugouts and trenches. Thousands of nearly naked men toiling in the sweltering heat, making roads and gun emplacements and transporting rations and materials of war. Such was Anzac Core, a pin-prick of land a little to the north of the promontory known as Gaba Tepe, on the western side of the peninsular of Gallipoli.

To an aeroplane observer looking down from an aeroplane two thousand feet high, Anzac and its unusual human activity must have reminded him of an ants'-nest just recently disturbed with a spade. Only in this case the "ants" worked harder during the night than during the day.

It was about an hour before sunset that the Colonel came out of his dugout, and placing his hands on his hips, looked upward into the clear sky overhead. For a few seconds his eyes wandered, and finally – being directed by a loud buzzing sound – became fixed, as his gaze rested upon a small bird-shaped machine. It was an aeroplane with peculiarly shaped wings and a bird-like tail. Upon the bottom side of each wing was painted a large black cross. A

German Taube aeroplane.

The sight of that sinister shape was not an unusual one to Anzac or to the Colonel, but at this instant it looked to the man to be directly overhead. And every second that 'plane hovered over the Australian position, there might be let drop a high explosive bomb.

Now the Colonel, like every other man, was not akin to the heroes in the magazine illustrations, wherein tailors' dummies are seen rushing at the enemy with swords and things. He was just like an ordinary man, but he had had a long military training. Hence his job at Anzac.

When, therefore, he looked up and saw that aeroplane directly overhead, when he heard the ciss-zip . . . ciss-zip . . . ciss-zip of a bomb that was dropping earthwards, he did not rush about waving a sword and calling romantically to his men. No, he stood still and waited. What use to run? He might run into the explosion. What use to get inside the dugout? No dugout there would withstand an aeroplane bomb, unless it had twenty feet of solid earth over it. While the "ciss-zipping" sound grew louder and louder as the bomb neared the earth the Colonel lived one year to every second. The relief to his nerves when the bomb burst two hundred yards away could be likened to the relief that cocaine, injected, will give the owner of a raging toothache.

X

Sergeant Sawyer had been under fire more or less severe – it was generally severe – for nearly fourteen weeks, when a bullet hit him in the neck. The circumstances were rather sportive, and also somewhat accidental.

Through a loophole in the trench he was occupying he was endeavoring to shoot an enemy who was rebuilding the parapet of his trench, and who in so doing occasionally showed himself. Two men of his acquaintance were similarly occupied. A wager had been made wherein the first man to hit the enemy was to receive two packets of cigarettes from each of the other two.

Unfortunately for Sawyer, however, some interfering ass in the enemy trench spoiled the show. He put a bullet through the loophole a fraction of an inch above the sights of Slayton's rifle.

The lump of lead passed through the Australian's neck, and smacked into the rear wall of the trench. Result – stretcher and bearers and a journey to the Base Hospital.

"A holiday at last," he managed to gasp, as he was being temporarily bandaged. With his back-bag he was removed.

Half-way to the hospital, at the lower end of a deep gully, a shrapnel shell intended for the beach burst prematurely and cut short his life. The stretcher bearers were unharmed and continued on their way. It was only when they reached their destination that they realised they had brought in a corpse.

XI

Mr. Henry Trotley, alias Private Trotley, No. 219, alias 'Enery, was reckoned to posses the safest dug-out on the peninsular, bar none. It was built deep down a natural "cut" in a cliff, that in the rainy season was a water-course. The cut opened out upon an artificial flat on which were stacked various rations. The rations and the cut were not many yards from the water's edge at Anzac. Shells fell all around those stacks, and horrible things occurred daily, but 'Enery in his dug-out felt quite safe. It was a haven of refuge to men seeking cover hurriedly, and 'Enery was therefore much put out when he and his company were moved to an advance depot. The day following 'Enery's evacuation there landed a Colonel, who immediately took up his abode in the empty dug-out. The Colonel had been settled just four hours when the impossible happened. A shell dropped accurately upon the roof of "the safest dug-out on the Peninsular," and the Colonel was designated "Killed in action."

XII

Driver Simpleton of the A.S.C. had a sense of the grotesque; he also had a revengeful disposition as shall be shown. Being an ardent photographer, he occupied all his spare time in snapping shell bursts and dead men.

At one time an armistice was arranged for the duration of one day. That day was to be spent, not in bringing up reinforcements, but in burying the three weeks' accumulation of Turkish and

German dead.

By systematic lying and scheming Driver Simpleton arrived at the burial ground with a small pocket camera. He had taken three scenes that would have given most men a perpetual nightmare, when an officer demanded the film.

The photographer was mightily displeased, retired from the operations – under orders – and made many judicious inquiries before returning to his duties. At 10 o'clock that night he visited the too officious officer's dugout, and did a little annexing himself.

"Exchange is no robbery," he murmured, as he totalled up the spoils. "Five tins of milk, four tins of cocoa, two pocketfuls of sugar, three tins of meat extract, and one tin of tobacco; but, after all, that lot is not worth the film he destroyed. I must go back next week."

War is a great educator. It teaches men self reliance as well as values.

XIII

To the Australians there came one day many generals and staff officers, and admirals and orderlies. They called unexpectedly when the Australians were taking their daily ablutions in the sea, which, of course, was inconvenient.

One hundred yards out from the jetty the conveying State barge began to collect many hangers-on, who clung to the fenders suspended round the sides, and were dragged through the water in a lather of foam. Upon arriving at the jetty the naked escorts were so numerous that they completed a ring all round the craft.

Without a word they looked up and over the gunnel into the faces of the generals and staff officers, and admirals and orderlies, who without a sign stepped up onto the jetty. Four other men were about to dive off the jetty when the "heads" arrived, but instead they came to attention. With perfect I'm-a-good-little-boy countenances they saluted, with not a shred of clothes upon them. One officer remarked, "If the enemy cannot tone 'em down, what hope have I of doing so?"

XIV All Must Pay

Private Rayton was on outpost duty one very dark night. He was lying flat upon his chest out on No Man's Land, where most of the drama of war is staged and the actors play with their lives. While there he began to think, and to think is bad policy.

What he thought about was his life, and to him it was a most engrossing subject. It had not been a brilliant one, or in any way different to millions of others. His childhood had given him many pleasant memories, and he was beloved by a good father and mother. He had many good friends, and he had learnt and followed a trade in which he was interested. And – he was engaged to one of the best girls in the world. Many are like him, and have found life very good. Years of happy youth remained to him, and all the mysteries of life waited for him to solve.

"Very well," he said. "I have many things to live for. Life has given me many pleasant memories. It has given me the best girl in the world, and it offered me the cup of happiness. Then why am I here, where my life is not worth a halfpenny, and where at any moment a violent death may come to me? Why? The agony of death is really nothing, the mere giving up of life is a little thing. The thought of losing home ties, friends, and the one little girl in all the world for me gives me the fierce desire to live. Then why am I here, when at any moment I may lose all that in death, or may become a living mangled wreck who has only his dreams? Why?"

A voice answered him: "It is because of the good things of life and for the retention of those good things that you must risk your life. Nothing is ever gained in this world without payment, and people have to pay. Even the look of a loving woman has to be paid for. All that life has given you has to be paid for, and you are squaring the account now."

"But why," he asked, "should I pay for the rightful and natural things of life with my life when thousands upon thousands like me refuse to pay? Am I not a fool?"

The voice spoke again: "Because you are paying the price in the most honourable way, you are paying a reduced price. Doing your duty reduces the purchase price. Those others who are afraid of the method of your payment will pay in other ways, the ordinary cost plus heavy interest. They will pay in loss of respect, loss of human sympathy; they will pay with sneers and insults; they will pay with the everlasting stigmas of the shameful word 'slacker' which is akin to 'coward.' All this they will pay, and it will be extra to the ordinary cost. Never fear, old man. They will pay."

So ran the thoughts of Private Rayton. The bullets hissed over him, some low down and others high, and when day was just breaking over the eastern ridges he crawled back to his trench calmer and more ready to pay Fate her dues.

Under Shell-fire at ANZAC

There are no two men alike, and consequently there are no two nervous systems alike. James and Henry may be like the proverbial peas yet when war comes, and they are sent into the proverbial firing line or in the immediate vicinity of it, it is more than probable that one of them will "break up" much sooner than the other." Shell-fire will affect one man sooner than the other. A man, therefore, in ill-health cannot continue long under a bombardment, and retain his reason; yet while his nerves do stand the strain, he may win forty Victoria Crosses in a day. Cowardice or bravery is a matter of will-power, and will-power depends on nerves, and nerves to a certain extent depend upon health.

Men will cower down under shell-fire, but, with a laugh, will face a hail of bullets. Why? Either will cause death or mutilation. An approaching bullet will make no sound; an approaching shell will whine, shriek or hiss. And therein lies the answer. Noise, uncertainty, imagination. A shell is heard coming; wonder is aroused as to where the shell will explode; and the imagination is excited by the horrors that have been seen. And as time goes on the imagination becomes keener and becomes a mental torture that in the end will derange the mind.

We therefore come to the fact that imagination plays a very big part in the stability of a man's mind. Murphy, the famous Anzac donkey, had many narrow escapes from being blown to pieces by shells. A shell would explode fifteen feet from Murphy, and he would not look up from the grass he was feeding upon. Why? He had no imagination. Some men are like that animal. Their imaginations are dull, and they are therefore better able to stand the horrors of war. Other men's imaginative powers are so keen that it is only by exerting strong will-power that they prevent an outward show of cowardice. A man who says he is unafraid of shells is a liar, or devoid of all imagination. And a man's imaginative powers are not the outcome of education or pedigree, blue blood or green. It is a gift or a curse – as you will.

Let us take an example. We will call him Smith. Smith belonged to the despised A.S.C., and when he was towed ashore on a barge the enemy tried to hit him with shrapnel. He had no previous experience with shrapnel, and consequently when the first shell burst he was much interested in the effect the bullets had upon the water when they struck it. When the second shell could be heard coming – he had five seconds' warning – he tried to burrow through the floor-boards. The effect of the first shell had excited his imagination as to what would be the effect of the second shell upon him. His imagination then dominated his brain. He could no more help trying to get under cover than not to try to run if a tiger chased him. When the third shell arrived, his will commanded his imagination and forced him to play the man. His nerves then were in good order.

As time went on and he was working in his depot ashore, the daily effect of shells taught him what shells were liable to do. At first the humourous attitudes of men diving for cover on hearing the approach of a shell gave him cause for much mirth; but after a few days the things that happened shook out his imagination outfit, and he did not tarry in the open. But even then he would laugh at his own actions. His nerves were still good.

But very slowly they weakened. At first certain places where shells fell mostly he began to avoid as much as possible. Then his keenness for his daily bathe grew less, and he bathed only every two days, and at last only at night. He became real glad when opportunities afforded him the chance to visit the trenches that were seldom shelled. Temporary security was to be found there, as bullets he spurned, security; that is, during the day.

The continual witnessing of horrible scenes kept his thoughts continually occupied with them. When a shell dropped at a man's feet and blew him up like a rocket, he vomited badly, as he did when another man's leg was blown off.

When he heard the whine of an approaching shell, his imagination instantly recalled those incidents to mind, and during those seconds that he waited for the shell to drop the beats of his heart increased a hundred per cent. That would not occur once a day, but dozens, and each time it would be imperceptibly worse than the previous occasion.

Noise was affecting his imagination, that was excited by seen things. His imagination was affecting his nerves, and his nerves his health. His appetite fell away, and he vomited often. Still, his will-power forced his body to do its duties, and will-power was based on pride. But life had become an exquisite agony, and his brain suffered torment.

When he was lying inside his dug-out one afternoon reading a novel, a shrapnel shell burst a little above him. Half the shell-case flew through the roof, and he was covered with two inches of earth. Nothing impeded his movements, but he was quite unable to move. Matter in the end had failed to respond to the mind. It was twenty minutes before the mind regained control over the body. He had then been under daily shell fire for over three months.

Ordered to Alexandria for a rest – a matter of weeks would have sent him insane – he slept five days and five nights, being wakened for meals by the nursing sister.

Drafts for Haig

"Draft arriving at eight to-night," remarked the captain, as he took his seat in the orderly room. "Send a guide to the station to meet them at 7.30. Hut accommodation fixed up?"

"Yes, Sir." The orderly-room sergeant laid a list of numbers and names on the table. "Here's the nominal roll of Over-seas Draft all signed up. Inspection at seven. Move off at 7.15 to-night."

"Very well." The officer's voice sounded tired. Drafts always provided a strain on the staff of the Nth Training Depot. The order from headquarters to hold a draft in readiness on a certain day is instantly followed by the selection of fit men required, with a few spare men in case of sickness at the last moment. They must be medically and dentally examined, passed through the quartermaster's hands, and paid. Numberless nominal rolls have to be made out.

"Fall in the draft," roars a voice on the parade ground. "Look slippy, now. Leave your kits. 'Shun! Right dress. Number."

The C.O. passes down the ranks followed by the adjutant, sergeant-major, and quartermaster, and the N.C.O. in charge of the draft. There are three minutes yet to spare. Good-byes are exchanged between those going over and those remaining.

"Good-bye, Bill. If you see Ted over in the 3rd tell him I'm still with the mob."

More orders are given. The draft for France moves out amid the cheers of the crowd. The music of the band grows fainter. The men have gone to meet their destiny.

Later

"Here they come," murmurs the C.O. to the adjutant. "Wonder what sort of crowd they'll be?"

"Oh, the same old sort, I expect."

The number of men now about the parade-ground is not so great. Friendships have to be made. A column of men march into camp and are lined up by the waiting sergeant-major.

"How's old Australia getting on?" someone yells.
"Oh, she's still alive."
And another: "How's the food here?"
Still they come. And still they go.

The Miracle

At the station homestead, half a mile up river, the thermometer that day had recorded a maximum of 117°. The instrument hung from a nail driven into the bole of a giant pepper-tree, and in consequence was always in deep shade. In the ordinary shade cast by thin-leaved mulga, needlewood and pine growing beyond the river flats, the temperature must have been some degrees hotter.

The soft yellow rays of the setting sun fell obliquely on the red gum-trees bordering the river Darling, scintillating on the gummy contusions marking old storm wounds. A cadmium sky and a faint odour of burning grass told of a bush fire devouring potential wealth in the far west of New South Wales.

Old Joe Avery lay full length on his unrolled swag within a few feet of the steep river-bank, an ancient pipe held to his still firm lips by a hand gnarled with age but still imbued with strength. The ringing cadence of his voice belied his eighty years of crowded life, whilst he told the story of Donald Macdonald.

I could understand the present-day scoffer of miracles had he lived sixty years ago (began Joe), because then I was a scoffer myself. We all in those days scoffed at the imaginative writers and their flying-machines, horseless carriages and iron monsters which moved along over endless iron belts. To scoff now at apparent impossibility, in these times that produce fresh miracles every day, is to betray a shallow mind. The onrush of human progress since the steam-engine was invented causes any thinking man to admit that nothing is impossible, and that those things he formerly would have called the fantasies of a mad brain possess to-day at least probability. I am thinking that when you have heard the story of Donald Macdonald you will not be so quick to call me a liar as your grandfather would have been at your age.

The smell of fire in the air these last few days has kept me reminded of the time I worked on Windsor Station, a run having a frontage on the "Gutter" above Wilcannia, and bounded on the west by the township of White Cliffs and Torbay Station.

I first went to work on Windsor in '98. Donald and I were

boundary-riding for eighteen months from a hut on the west side of the Parroo River. We became firm friends, in spite of living so much in each other's company.

The morning he pulled out promised a snorting hot day. The sun rose behind a blood-red mist of dust and the north wind blew as though straight from hell. From looking at the sun and sniffing at the wind, Donald turned to me and says: "Joe! Damn boundary-riding! Damn the bush! Damn this damned station! I'm going into Wilcannia for a spree."

In five minutes he had his swag rolled and his water-bag filled. In ten minutes he had disappeared in the scrub, walking across country to the homestead to get his cheque. That is how the bush always "gets" a man. In a second he will come to hate it so fiercely that he could run amuck. He can stay in it no longer. He feels that he must get into a town and go all out with Mister Booze.

By nightfall he had reached the homestead and drawn his cheque, which amounted to fifty-five pounds and odd. A young feller like you would consider a fifty-five pound cheque slave wages for eighteen months, but in those days a man could get drunk and keep drunk for three weeks on that cheque; whereas to-day a bend of that duration would cost three times as much. In '98 booze was booze, and not a fifty-fifty mixture of tobacco-water and arsenic. You don't get drunk like a gentleman these days – you get paralysed like a nigger.

Donald reached Wilcannia the following evening, having got a lift in a squatter's buckboard. The "Bushman's Welcome" being the first shanty he sighted, he went in and asked for six pints of beer as a starter. Knowing Donald for many years – knowing, too, that he must be "chequed up" – Mum Savage filled twelve pint pots, which she set in a row before him, six of them being emptied when she set the last one down. She started on the empties again; but Donald was minded to have a smoke, and cutting tobacco between swallows delayed him a bit.

"Are you going to give anything for Mabel Dark?" says Mum Savage, laying a subscription list in front of him.

"Mabel Dark! Who's she?" says he.

"Miss Oakes, that was," says Mum Savage. "You knew her. You went to school together."

"Yes, I know Mabel Oakes. 'Course I do. Good sport, Mabel. But why the list?"

"Lor! Have you been dead?" says Mum Savage, with bulging eyes and a toss of her frowzy head. "Mabel married Bill Dark the bullocky, this time last year. You know that, stupid. You know, too, how Bill Dark was gored to death by a young steer he was breaking-in last month; leaving poor Mabel and a six-weeks' baby with not a penny to bless herself with. We're getting up a subscription to pay her fare and expenses down to Melbourne, where she has an aunt. What are you going to give?"

"Put me down for a fair thing," says he. "I'll pay you in the morning. Where's Mabel to be dug up?"

Mum Savage looked hard at Donald. She couldn't understand the sudden look in his blue eyes. She couldn't figure it out why Donald did not pass her his cheque for her to tell him when it was cut out.

"Where's Mabel to be dug up?" says he again.

"She's living with Mrs. Dooley," she says.

"Is she? Well, I'm going along to see her;" and Donald walked out, leaving eleven full pints on the counter, and Mum Savage so surprised that she went into hysterics and had to be bounced about by her daughter Edith.

Leaving his swag on the shanty veranda, Donald went down to Mrs. Dooley's slab hut on the river-bank and asked for Mabel Dark. When she came to the door, holding aloft a lamp, he says to her:

"Evening, Mabel! You remember me?"

"Of course I do, Donald," says she, smiling 'spite bereavement and adversity.

"I'm glad of that," says he softly. "Because I want to have an honest-to-goodness talk with you. What about coming a little along the river for a walk?"

Mabel agreed, putting the lamp back on the table and calling to Mrs. Dooley to mind her baby. She and Donald wandered among the gums in the half-light of late evening, he talking about the weather and the river and finding it hard to come to the point of explaining his sudden resolution. Presently, stopping and laying a hand on her arm, he looked at her squarely and says:

"I've heard of your trouble, Mabel, and I'm sorry about poor old Bill and the rest. Seems to me that you're right up against it, Mabel; and, seeing as how Bill and me used to rob the Chinaman's garden together, it is up to me to stand by his wife, ain't it?"

"It is good of you to say that, Donald," says she, her eyes suddenly misty.

"Maybe – maybe not," says he. "Any way, I've a proposition to make which sounds good. We haven't seen each other much these last few years, but you know me for an ordinary bloke, neither angel nor devil. Mabel, what about us getting tied up? I'd be a good husband, bet cher. They would give me a job back on Windsor and would welcome my wife. Working for you would keep me off the booze. If you married me, you wouldn't have to accept charity. Say the word, Mabel."

Looking at him with steady eyes, her mind raced. Memories of girlhood days and of Donald Macdonald, who was her champion, intermingled with pictures of life with her aunt, herself a poor and hard-working widow, and of the time when her baby would be growing up to demand education and clothes. She was sure Bill Dark would not mind. She knew Donald for a good man. She felt that she could trust to her influence over him to stop his yearly or bi-yearly sprees.

"All right, Donald," says she. "When you are ready."

And when, a fortnight later, they left for Windsor Station, Donald was perfectly sober and had thirty pounds of his cheque in a bank. The people were surprised at Donald taking out a wife; they were astounded at his leaving sober and returning with thirty pounds unspent. A bushman had never been known to do such a thing.

Old man Winterton, the owner of Windsor, was delighted to have Donald back; for Donald was a good sheepman and a reliable boundary-rider. He sent them to a comfortable house built at the foot of the Penanga Hills, paying Donald the usual wage and paying his wife a good wage, too, to keep a room always ready for either himself or the overseer, who might chance to spend a night or two at that part of the run.

It doesn't always follow that a hasty marriage turns out bad. In their case Donald's motive for offering marriage was to serve, and was entirely unselfish, which cannot be said of any love marriage. There is, I think, a lot of good in the old-fashioned arranged marriage, which chiefly was a matter of hard cash. Donald and Mabel liked each other when they were married; they loved each other twelve months later.

Donald thought no end of Bill Dark's baby-girl, and no less of her when Mabel presented him with a baby-boy during the second year of their marriage.

From that night he proposed to his wife Donald never looked back. Mabel was a good woman, patient and true. Neither ceased to respect the other. As for Mister Booze, he had to take a back seat; and no longer when in Wilcannia did Donald call for a row of pints.

About the time young Donald saw the light of day, his father was made boss musterer; and when, a year later, the overseer got a manager's job up in Queensland, Donald was again promoted. That was the year when thousands of square miles were devastated by a fire which started somewhere near Tibooburra and was only stopped by the old "Gutter" [river Darling], which happened to be running a banker.

Every available man was hurried to the north-west corner of the run to burn a fire-break, one hundred yards deep and twelve miles long. We had just completed it when the fire, with a frontage of ten miles, swept against the break and stopped. But a sudden whirlwind, rushing east at the moment of victory, carried blazing wisps of grass over the break, and started it again on Windsor country in a dozen different places.

It so happened that Donald and I were the only men at that point; and we were less able to stop the blaze, fanned by a twenty-mile-an-hour wind, than you and I could stop this river. In less than ten minutes it looked as though the whole world was going up in a gigantic mushroom column of smoke.

I saw Donald look up at the crimson disc of the sun through the whirling smoke-clouds and take note of the direction of the wind. Almost unconsciously, I did likewise. I saw the colour of his face turn grey, and his black eyes grow wide and glittering, which turned me cold. He was thinking of his wife and the children living at what was called Deep Well.

"Lend us a hand, Joe," says he in a kind of whisper. "The wind will take that blaze direct to Deep Well. You know how things are, dry grass two feet high almost to the veranda. We must beat the fire to Deep Well. One of us might do it. Will you take it on?"

"Of course," says I. "Let's start."

Without wasting time on further jabbering, we ran to the horses hitched secure among a clump of mulga on the south side of where the whirlie passed over. They were good mounts, but none too fresh.

Now, though the wind was taking the fire south-east, it was spreading fanwise, and when we set off at a loping gallop we were forced due south. It was a toss-up whether we would gain on the fire and circle back to the north, or whether the fire would press us back again to the fire-break.

We used to reckon that the distance from the west boundary to Deep Well was not less than fifteen miles. The curvature we were forced to follow would probably make it twice as far. As we rode neck to neck with the fire on our left, behind and in front of us, and constantly pushing us further west, I could not agree that Mrs. Macdonald had one chance in a hundred.

Every man being on the boundary, there was not a soul anywhere near Deep Well to assist her. For sure there were several horses in the horse-paddock; but, when she realised that the fire was coming her way, there would not be time enough to get them into the yards and put a couple of them into a buckboard.

Even the well offered no safety. There was a pump staging one foot above the water, but the bottom third of the well was always full of foul earth gases, which would kill in less than a minute. If she lowered the children down half-way in the windlass bucket, and, chocking the drum, climbed down to them, the fire biting at the rope would part it and let them down.

Gradually Donald drew closer to the fire, his mouth a thin white line across a smoke-blackened face, hatless and coatless, crouched along his horse's neck, easing his weight as only a born horseman knows how.

Billowing grey-black clouds fled in the direction we were travelling. I was gripped by dread when, beneath smarting eyelids, I noticed that the smoke was travelling faster than we. My horse almost fell when a fox – there were few about in those days – streaked across his fore-hoofs.

Above the roar of the flames we could hear the pines splitting like a million cannon during a battle. Nearer and ever nearer Donald and I edged towards the conflagration. The smoke-clouds enveloped us, catching our breath and burning our lungs as though we breathed hot cinders.

Time ceased to have any meaning. Only by a miracle did we escape the low branches of the clumps of mulga and the pine-belts through which we galloped. How it was our horses avoided the rabbit-holes is to this day beyond my understanding.

I was beginning to think that like pygmies opposed to a giant we were doomed to defeat, when I noticed that the smoke was slanting across us. That meant either the wind had shifted to the north, or that we were gaining on the fire and were rounding to the east.

Donald noticed it at the same tine, for I heard the whisper of his shout. If we were circling the fire, we presently would be travelling north, when we should be ahead of it, and able to strike due east and race it to Deep Well.

How we were to save Mabel and the kids when we got there never crossed my mind, which was occupied almost solely by the tremendous desire to get there. Every minute now increased the danger to ourselves. Taking a swift glance at the sun, now the colour of an old penny, I saw that we were in the direct path of the fire. A fall, the collapse of a horse, and either of us was as good as dead.

We pulled our mounts to their haunches at a fence, not daring to put them at it in their wearied condition. Of course it had to be a new fence, with new wires strained like violin-strings. Jumping to earth and handing Donald the reins, I tore at the posts to loosen one and bear down a panel. The roar of hoofs and the sound of a thousand frightened bleats told of a stampeding mob of sheep seeking an opening in the fence which entrapped them. Sparks dropped about us like rain. The smoke was like a fog. Donald fought the maddened horses, whilst I grappled with a post and with frenzied strength broke it off at the ground. I laid on the wires as he got the horses over. And then once more, with the fire less than two hundred yards from us, I was again in the saddle, tearing over the almost invisible ground.

A mile, two, three miles, we rode like madmen. We lashed the poor horses, but our lashes were as nothing to the lash of terror. Their agonized breath screamed from gaping, foam-flecked jaws. Donald was ahead of me. Only a few yards. Then his horse fell dead. There was no time to avoid them. My horse crashed into the dead horse and somersaulted. Something hit me, yet I felt no pain. On my feet, I saw that my mount was done. Not even terror could make him get up. Donald was either unconscious or dead.

How the gods must have laughed when I picked Donald up in my arms, and, laying him across my shoulder, started to run. How they must have jeered and cried the odds against me without meeting any takers! And I only had a quarter of a mile start.

Somehow I retained a glimmering of sense. By the mercy of God, I stumbled on a large clay-pan, hard as iron and clean of herbage. In the centre of it I laid Donald down, ripped off my shirt and placed it over his mouth. Then, flinging myself down beside him, I buried my face in my arms and waited whilst the fires of hell passed by.

Whilst Mabel Macdonald washed the breakfast things at the kitchen sink, she could observe through the window the smudge of smoke on the north-western horizon.

Little Doris clung to her skirt, cooing the tune of the song she was singing, and young Donald crawled about his crib like a lion in a cage testing the strength of the bars. It being bread day, Mabel punched down the dough when she had tidied up; and when, an hour later, she went again to the window, the smoke out west was higher in the sky, and darker in colour.

Even then the thought of danger never occurred to her. The fire was a long way off, and the men had been confident of stopping it at the boundary. It was about eleven o'clock when she donned her hat and picked up a basket to gather eggs, because the crows were bad, and the hens laid anywhere.

On the veranda she stood aghast at the picture of smoke, now an appalling, terrifying sight. From the near mulga scrub halfway to the zenith a writhing, bulging, whirling wall of dense smoke, stretching from north to south, seemed as though it would fall upon the house and obliterate it. It was so near that the top of the mulgas glimmered red. Like the coming of a cyclone, the racing fire roared its song of destruction.

A pet sheep, bleating fearfully, tried to get on the veranda through the wooden gate; a mob of white cockatoos fled eastward screaming with fright; a milking cow in a near-by paddock bellowed loudly and was answered by a mate. All living things sensed the danger; but it was the horses, the cows and the sheep that were entrapped by the wire fences.

With horror writ large on her bonny face, Mabel dropped the egg-basket and stared fascinated at the coming terror. Like the large animals, she and her babies were also trapped. She thought of the half-dozen horses then galloping with frightened whinnies about their paddock, and almost started to run out to drive them into the yards; when numbing realisation swept over her that such a course was hopeless.

The spear-grass and wild oats, such a pleasurable sight but a few months before, surrounded the house and cane-grass sheds, looking like swathes of unbleached calico. The wind carried to her ears the sinister sound of the splitting pines above the ever-increasing roar.

The well! There lay a chance, a slender chance, their only chance, of life. It was one hundred and seven feet to the water, seventy feet to the asphyxiating gas. She was aware of that fatal measurement.

Quite suddenly Mabel became cool and fearless, a real chip of an old pioneering, fight-the-world, parental block. Re-entering the house, she filled a canvas water-bag, and, fetching the egg-basket, filled it with cakes. With bag and basket she ran to the well, and, pulling on the two-inch rope, unwound it from the horse whim-drum and re-wound it on the drum of the windlass, till the big thirty-gallon iron bucket was an inch or two below the windlass, when she chocked it with an iron plug. That done, she fled back for the children.

With Donald in one arm and a pile of cushions in the other, with Doris hanging to her skirt and the pet sheep bleating at her heels, she again hurried to the well. The fire was now little more than a mile distant, and travelling at the rate of twenty miles an hour. The advance smoke-clouds already were passing overhead, almost touching the whim structure.

Dropping the cushions into the bucket, she lowered young Donald down on them, and, without a trace of the dread showing on her face, says to Doris:

"Now then, dear! You get into the bucket, too. You and Donald play hide with mummy."

Lifting the little girl into the bucket, the mite's head barely reached the lip and there was no possibility of either of them climbing out of it. Mabel gave the food basket to Doris, with the injunction not to let young Donald eat too many of the cakes. The water-bag she fastened to the inside of the bucket in such a position that Doris could draw water from it into a cup.

Then, slipping out the catch-pin, Mabel lowered her babies till they were half-way down the well, when she again chocked the windlass with the pin, leaving them gently swinging at that level.

The woman knew that the whim-timbers would fire; knew also that the rope would burn apart and send the children hurtling to the death below. She dared not re-cover the top of the well with the dust-boards, for fear that blazing splinters would fall down the well.

She tied a cloth over her mouth and nostrils. She picked up a corn-sack – and waited. For she was resolved to protect the windlass and the rope from the bite of the fire whilst life remained to her. If only she could beat out the sparks which would grow into a blaze till the first blast had passed, it seemed to matter little if she died in the stifling atmosphere which would follow.

She saw five horses in the paddock beyond the sheds race houseward with the fire licking at their flying hoofs. Without feeling, without emotion, without sense of living, she watched the monster sweeping towards her, lurid tongues of flame curling in and out of the smoke. The pet sheep looked up at her and shivered. A rabbit dashed past and a snake seeking refuge in the well was crushed by the heel of her shoe, as determinedly as though it were a beetle.

Then she heard Donald's voice at her shoulder, and, swinging round, saw her husband, hatless and coatless, his face blackened by sweat and smoke, but his mouth curved into a smile of assurance.

"Slide down the rope to the bucket, Mabel, quick," she heard him say.

"Donald! Oh Donald!" was all she could cry, fear and terror overwhelming her the moment she realised there was some one she could lean on.

"Don't waste time, Mabel," says he. "Down the rope now. Give the children a kiss for me."

"But you, my dear! Oh, I couldn't live without you!" she moaned.

"You must live for the children," says he, giving her a smile, his old smile she loved to see. Then his voice became hard with determination to be obeyed. The cane-grass sheds were now alight.

"Go down!" says he. "I'll be all right. The fire can't hurt me."

So she lowered herself down the rope to the bucket, there to pacify the children and listen to the whim structure crashing to earth – to hear the howling, hissing roar of the fire sweeping about the mouth of the well. Looking upwards, she saw the circle of light darken and lighten, redden and pale in the fiery tempest. But never a tongue of flame touched the windlass or the rope.

Mabel was not strong enough to climb the rope to the well-mouth when the fire had passed and cool, clean air drifted down to them.

Amazed that the well-head, the windlass and the rope remained unblackened amidst appalling desolation, old Winterton and I jumped out of his buckboard seven hours later, and pulled them up. Mabel's eyes were swollen with tears. Young Donald slept peacefully in her arms. Her voice quavering with dread, she says, looking about her:

"Donald – where is my husband?"

"Donald!" says I, and like a fool blurted out the truth.

"He and I were riding to get here before the fire. His horse fell. Donald's neck was broken. They're bringing his body, along in the buggy."

"Oh God!" she cried softly, very softly. "He said the fire couldn't hurt him."

The Water Witch

Dave came to a halt and "hoosked" his four camels down upon their knees but a few yards from the door of a corrugated-iron hut. It was not a large hut, neither was it artistically built, but one does not expect to see a mansion in that particular corner of the earth. It was situated at the edge of a lake, a good many miles west of the Parroo River in New South Wales, and it was there Dave lived for days when he passed that way.

In the nearest township, at least two hundred miles east of the lake, David Thorne was known to be a man of quiet, scholarly habits when sober, which was not often during his visits, but a mighty wielder of the crimson paint-brush while under the influence of whisky. His occupation did not breed conversationalists; it certainly reared many self-taught, clever men.

Dave at that time was keeping in repair a one-hundred-and-sixty mile section of a seven-hundred-mile fence. The fence was built of wire netting, and its purpose was to keep out the vermin that would otherwise have come in upon the many millions of fine scrub and grass plain country which produced thousands of bales of the very best wool.

Sometimes he met a white dog-trapper, and with him would converse for a day. Occasionally he fell in with a civilised black fellow out hunting for stray horses; but these meetings were very rare, and six and seven weeks would pass in absolute solitude. Only a man with a very evenly balanced mind could stand the awful loneliness for any lengthy period, even though he were born and reared in the bush.

Along the fence, at intervals of ten or twelve miles, wherever water-holes or surface dams favoured, he had established permanent camps, but the hut near the lake was his most favoured camp. Besides being the only one on his route, it was near abundance of water and good wild-fowl shooting. He would stay there sometimes for a month, shooting and reading, knowing that his fence was in order and required no attention.

The sun had gone down three hours ago, and a full moon shone upon the water which was as an unbroken sheet of glass, when Dave pushed off in his light duck punt and propelled it from the shore with a single oar. Brushwood, to a height of two feet, had been fixed round the fore part of the punt in order to conceal it and the man from the ever suspicious birds. He sat in the stern, sculling quietly and slowly, while a forty-two Winchester lay across his knees.

He was not a handsome man, though he stood six feet high and was broad in proportion. His constitution was of iron, and his muscles of steel. A man unafraid of any living creature, yet a man who dreamt dreams.

The night was magnificent. Fleecy clouds floated slowly across the sky, and sometimes hid the glory of the moon; not a breath of wind disturbed the water, and the air was fresh and bracing. Soft, strange bird-cries, some mournful, others full of music, came across the surface of the lake.

The man in the punt ceased sculling and allowed it to drift. He picked up the gun and waited. One duck he would get with his first shot. Two more would fall as the mob rushed along the water before taking to the air. In the moonlight he could see them – black spots upon a sheet of silver. Instead of sculling to them he waited for them to come to him. Curiosity would draw them as a magnet attracts iron-dust. He had but to wait.

Imperceptibly the birds and the punt drew closer together, while Dave sat and nursed his gun. Gradually he became surrounded with ducks. He selected a little bunch of them upon his right, where the moonlight fell full upon them. They were eighty feet away. Five minutes later they were but fifty. Dave decided that his moment had arrived. He raised his rifle and the foresight covered a bird upon the extreme left of the bunch. Before he could pull the trigger the bird disappeared.

It did not dive, neither did it fly. Where there had been a duck, there was now no duck. Dave lowered his gun and frowned.

A second bird disappeared as suddenly as the first.

And then the stillness of the night was broken by wild cries of astonishment as the whole mob of birds rushed with flapping wings through the water, to rise in the air and disappear skyward. Perplexed and annoyed, the man lit his pipe. But the pipe went out.

Up from the water there slowly rose a human head; a woman's head upon two shoulders. Long, dark hair fell from her in waves and floated like seaweed in the water. One hand brushed back the hair from a low, broad forehead; in the other were two drowned ducks. And she was white – pure white.

Dave drew in his breath sharply. The face, every feature of which was plainly visible in the moonlight, was wonderful in its marvellous beauty – beauty such as the man had never dreamt of: dark eyes – he couldn't tell their colour; a mouth that parted and showed pearly teeth as she endeavoured to regain normal breathing; shoulders as white as snow, and arms as shapely as – Dave remembered a picture called "The Birth of Venus."

The man stared, and his breath came painfully. At the risk of upsetting his frail craft he stood up. He held out his hands and called, but a look of surprise and terror came into the woman's face. As mysteriously and as silently as she had appeared she sank down into the water and left but an ever-widening circle to mark the spot where she had been.

A cloud sailed before the moon. Frantically Dave sculled his punt to the place where she had disappeared. His brain afire, he threw off his coat and boots and dived into the water. He dived repeatedly for half-an-hour, but he did not find what he sought.

At dawn of day David Thorne was sitting upon a packing-case before a log fire in his iron-built hut. He had dried his clothes, and was smoking the inevitable pipe. Over the fire hung a billy-can full of water, while upon his knee purred a small black cat – Dave's only companion. The hundreds of wild-fowl out upon the lake had now settled down once more and were noiseless. The only sound that came through the clear air was the tinkle of the bell hanging from the neck of one of his camels. Direction and sound told him they were feeding upon a patch of pig-weed from which they would not stray until it was eaten bare.

The man sat watching the flames and brooding upon the strange happenings of the night. A peculiar unrest stirred his soul and wondering uneasiness dominated his thoughts. Until that night no power had ruled his life – a life free as the birds and as careless; but now he felt some power which he could not define, a power which was leading him along unknown paths.

Cold, analytical reasoning disproved any idea of phantasy or imagination. What he had seen he knew to be real. It was no spirit, no ghost, but a warm living woman who had come up out of the depths and had sunk down into them again.

The method of catching ducks by swimming under water for a long distance and pulling them under by their legs was, as Dave knew, much in vogue among many tribes of blacks. Blacks – yes; but this woman was white, as white as he was.

When it was sufficiently light he would walk round the lake to look for tracks. If he found them they would perhaps lead him to some camp, and to her. His heart increased its beat when he remembered her face, her shoulders, her arms.

Breakfast over Dave made his way down to the lake's sandy foreshore. Turning to the right he walked by the water and beneath the box and gum-trees that grew along its edge. Occasionally he was obliged to make a *détour* round a large thicket, but he always came down to the water again, for there upon the sand would the tracks be most clear.

A little over two miles had been covered when he came upon such a thicket. Upon the farther side he pulled up short.

He stood upon the edge of a clearing surrounded upon three sides by dense brushwood and upon the fourth side by the lake. The trees threw out their branches, and the mass of foliage, shutting out the rays of the sun, formed a leafy roof. In the centre of the sandy floor lay a big, dead branch, and sitting upon this branch was the woman Dave was searching for.

Dressed simply in a sleeveless garment made of rabbits' skins that fell only to her knees, she looked as if she belonged to the Stone Age. Her feet were small and bare. Her dark hair fell in rippling waves nearly to the ground. She sat facing the lake – a specimen of perfectly built womanhood. About her feet three fat little pups rolled and gambolled. At them she laughed, and picked them up in turn and kissed them. Laughed! A very melody of sound fell upon Dave's ears and caused him to suck in his breath.

Standing at the edge of the clearing, he watched her for fully three minutes, with his heart thumping against his ribs and the blood surging to his head. Then across the soft, grey sand he walked to her. No sound came from his tread, and he stood at her back within a yard of her, and she was not conscious of his nearness.

Still laughing and playing with the pups, her every action spoke of freedom – the freedom of the birds on the lake and the animals that played about her.

Then slowly she became conscious of his presence. The silvery laugh died away and the smile fled. Springing to her feet she faced round upon him like a startled fawn but stood her ground unafraid.

She was not more than twenty years old. Her face, oval and full, almost stopped the beating of Dave's heart. Perplexity and astonishment showed in her lovely eyes. Fear? No. With one hand clasped to the bosom of her dress, she looked him up and down, and saw six feet of muscular manhood good to look at. Seconds passed and neither moved nor spoke.

She seemed slowly to realise the meaning of the expression which filled the man's face, and the blood showed from beneath her skin in a glorious flush. Dave, the thin cloak of civilisation thrown from him, stood there before her, the natural man. He held out his hands to touch her, but instantly she stepped back. His breath rasped through his nostrils. With a cry he sprang and she was in his arms.

She did not struggle; she did not even move. She merely threw back her head and looked at him with her big, blue eyes, the eyes of a wondering child. Slowly the man bent his head and kissed her upon the lips.

"Who are you?" he cried. "A goddess?"

She answered him, but in the language of an aboriginal tribe.

Dave shook his head and unconsciously spoke in pidgin-English.

"Me no savvy. You no speak English?"

But she could not understand.

Again Dave bent his head and buried his lips in hers – red lips – lips that asked to be kissed. Even while he kissed her, her eyes were open wide – blue, blue as two sapphires – and the man sank into their depths and was conscious only of them.

Then a pair of hairy, black arms slid about his neck and locked themselves like the jaws of a trap. Dave released her from his embrace. A knee was forced against his spine and instantly he was upon the ground, fighting three hefty blacks, each of them bigger than himself.

Grass ropes were passed about his body and within a minute he was bound and helpless. The blacks stood up and jabbered excitedly; but of them Dave took no notice, for his eyes were searching for the woman he had had in his arms. She was gone.

The bushman was lifted up and carried a quarter of a mile farther round the lake, and eventually put down upon a grassy spot inside a blacks' camp.

It was very evident that his captors were members of a nomad tribe, for the few humpies there were very badly and roughly put together. Branches from trees had been lopped away and placed slantwise together, forming a hollow triangle with the ground, upon which dead leaves were scattered. These humpies were arranged in a half-circle facing the water, and between them and the lake was a big heap of hot, wood ashes, which smouldered still and sent a thin spiral of blue smoke up into the tree-tops.

There were no more than two dozen men and fifteen or twenty gins, while a dozen children played with and splashed each other in the water. To them, however, the arrival of Dave furnished a new attraction. They clustered round him and looked at him with big, round, black eyes. The three natives who had made Dave prisoner stood excitedly jabbering at a furious speed with much gesticulation, while the remainder surrounded them and interjected grunts and savage cries. One of them, a small man, stood with folded arms, and sometimes nodded as if ticking off the accusations as they were made against Dave.

Dave watched them. He felt exceedingly surprised to meet even such a small tribe, or part of a tribe, so far south-west, for the Darling River blacks had migrated years ago to the central districts of Australia. Certainly in various places there were one or two of them who lived with their gins and children, but invariably these were semi-civilised and generally camped near a station homestead.

To him it was quite evident that these were wild, and he rightly guessed that the prolonged drought in the Northern Territory had forced them to leave it for more fertile pastures. Who was this white woman, and what was she doing with them?

Nearly an hour passed, and then the little black fellow came over to him, and, squatting down upon his heels, said in broken English:

"What for you catch Min?"

Dave glared and roared:

"Catch who, you black swine? Loose these ropes!"

But the black merely shook his head and repeated the question. Dave saw the uselessness of bullying.

"Me no savvy," he said. "I catch no phellor!"

"Black phellors find um white phellor in um arms!" the little black man cried fiercely. "She no phellors' gin. She never your gin. She black phellors' boss."

Dave whistled softly. He began to understand a little. He questioned further and learnt much that he wanted to know. Min, as the blacks called the white woman, was the daughter of a squatter's wife who, twenty years previously, had been carried off by a marauding tribe. The husband, away out on his run, returned in the evening to find his home in ashes and his wife vanished. All efforts to find her proved futile.

The tribe, who had a definite object in capturing the white woman, made her their queen, or, as the little man said, their "boss." But six months of terrible privations and strange surroundings told upon the poor woman's constitution, and she died upon giving birth to Min.

Although not of their colour the child grew up to be one of the tribe. She thought like them, and spoke no other language but theirs. Never before had she seen a white man until she met Dave in the clearing. She could throw a boomerang and swim with the best of them, but never did they allow her to cook or to carry as they expected their gins to do. To the tribe Min was queen only in name. They looked upon her not as a ruler or leader, but as a charm, the possession of which would give them influence over other tribes, and bring them luck. And now the white man had come and would have carried her off – would have taken from them their boss and made her his gin. But by the tribal laws, made when Min was a child, no man could be her husband.

Such was the gist of the little black man's conversation; broken and sometimes unintelligible. Dave asked what they intended to do with him.

"White phellor die," came the simple response.

Dave shivered. He knew the aboriginal methods of disposing of enemies, and those methods were artistic to a degree. Buried to his neck and left to die of thirst in a scorching sun? Pegged out near an ants' nest to have his bones picked white? To the blacks both procedures were favourable. Which would they apply to him?

At noon they gave him a cold leg of baked duck and a drink of water. Through the long afternoon they left him severely alone. The sun slid down the burnished dome of the sky, and throughout the hours Dave called to Min; but neither sight nor sound did he get of her. He worked at the ropes which bound him, but not a fraction of an inch would they give. The confinement of his limbs caused him dreadful agony, but as the hours passed his body slowly grew numb and dead to pain. He knew that he could expect no mercy from the tribe whose queen he had dared to touch. He gained a little comfort from the belief that the beautiful, uncivilised creature would have come to him had she been free to do so. The belief helped him to bear the torment he was in.

The sun sank down behind the scrub and left but a fiery blaze to mark the place. The wind, too, had died down and the leaves had ceased their rustling. The wild-fowl out on the lake woke up and sent their cries over the still water.

About seven o'clock the gins came out of their humpies and proceeded to cook a large number of ducks. To Dave they appeared to be countless. He watched the gins and the humpies and wished with all his heart that he could get even a glimpse of the woman he now knew he loved with all his heart.

Half-unconsciously he watched the women. Their culinary efforts were simple. The ducks, still feathered, were plastered all over with mud. They were then placed in the hot ashes of the fire and left for an hour, when they were raked out. On becoming cool enough to handle, the mud, which had caked dry, was broken away and with it came the feathers, leaving the flesh perfectly clean.

At eight o'clock Dave was placed, still bound, in the very centre of the camp. The men formed a complete ring round him and squatted upon their heels, while immediately behind them likewise squatted their gins. The children were sent into the humpies, where they remained. Round the inside of the circle heaps of baked ducks lay at intervals upon clean gum-leaves, and from these heaps the men helped themselves. Biting off the choicest parts they handed the remains over their shoulders to the gins behind, who squealed their thanks for such morsels from their lords.

Glutted with meat and half-drunken with the awful fire-water made by the little, semi-civilised black, the men suddenly sprang to their feet and whirled round, keeping their circle, with terrific yells. The gins became infected a little later. Old and young, they leapt into the air with screams and squeals, and followed their circle round in the opposite direction to that of the men. For hours they kept it up without a stop. Some frothed at the mouth and fell exhausted. Others performed horrible feats; and the more they danced the more mad they became.

And in the centre of the two revolving circles of insane humanity lay Dave, bound and helpless. The logs upon the fire within the circles threw golden, fitful light upon the horrible, glistening faces and naked bodies, while high above the filth and madness sailed the moon, calm, cool, and disdainful.

A little after midnight the blacks lifted Dave up upon their shoulders and, still yelling hoarse cries, bore him away into the bush. Dave could have screamed with the pain of the movements to which his numbed limbs were subjected, but his pride of race made him forbear.

Half-a-mile or more they carried him beneath the trees and to the top of a sand-dune. Here they pegged him out like a starfish and sprinkled the blood of a rabbit over him. With shouts and jibes they danced away, leaving him within fifty yards of two large bull-dog ants' nests, confident that when dawn broke and the thousands of ants came out in search of food they would smell the blood and do their hideous work. One bite and the man would fight. The rest would immediately attack, and in five minutes he would have disappeared beneath those inch-long, red bodies.

The touch of the man's lips had awakened Min's soul. Kind called to kind as the fox howls across the waste to its mate. To her brain, the powers of which were still on a level with the niggers whose queen she was, came the decision that no longer should she remain alone. She would go to this man and crave his permission to become his gin.

Thus it was that Min eluded her vigilant subjects and followed the tracks, by the light of the moon, that led to the man upon the sand-dune.

Only gradually did Dave realise that someone was looking down upon him – that the someone had long, dark hair, and small, white feet, which were shoeless – that it was the woman he had held in his arms twenty hours ago – the woman upon whose lips he had wrung out his very soul. He raised his head; it was the only definite movement he could make.

"Min!"

The name was spoken softly, but a very world of longing was in the tone. With a low cry of sympathy, she fell upon her knees and dragged at the wooden pegs which kept him down. Her small, sinuous body swayed backwards and forwards as she loosened them. With her teeth she untied the knots that bound him to them, and then tried to induce the blood to re-circulate in his limbs.

For three or four minutes she would rub furiously at his arms, stopping suddenly to listen with raised head, knowing full well that sooner or later her absence would be noticed. The blacks would track her surer than bloodhounds. Her hair sometimes fell across Dave's face, and he trembled like a child who is frightened. After a while he staggered to his feet and held out his arms to her, but she drew away from him. Not quite recovering his strength he fell upon the soft, red sand. She helped him to his feet again. With her finger upon her lips, dumbly entreating silence, she nodded towards the direction of the blacks' camp.

It was then that there came to Dave realisation of the full danger that he and the woman were in. He flung an arm about her bare, white shoulders, and together they stumbled down the sand-dune and went in the direction of his hut and the camels. The touch of her shoulders thrilled him. Dave's strength was slowly returning, and the crawl merged into a walk. But he could not yet run. The blacks could. Even now they might have discovered Min's absence and be coming silently along their tracks. They had his gun, certainly useless to them in their ignorance of fire-arms, but they possessed boomerangs and could use them with deadly effect.

Dave thought of that and broke into a run. The woman ran

also, adapting her speed to his. With the true instinct of a bushman he headed straight for his hut, and, true to the gambling habits of his class, made wagers with himself as to whether the camels were still feeding upon the patch of pig-weed or had wandered away in search of fresh food. If they had and he was unable quickly to find them, then indeed their chance of escape was small.

Then came faintly through the tree-tops a piercing yell.

Ah! The chase had commenced. Dave ran faster, and the woman, with no apparent effort, kept by his side. As he ran he decided upon his immediate plans. He would go to the hut first. There he would procure his long, iron riding-saddle and a nose-line. He and the woman could carry the saddle to the camel upon which he generally rode, and which should be feeding not more than five hundred yards from the hut. God grant them time!

A few minutes later Dave heaved a sigh of relief. Through the trees the silvery light of the moon was reflected upon the iron roof of the hut. One minute more and they halted beside the pack-saddles which had been neatly placed, one upon the other, just outside the door.

The man tore them down and dragged out the riding-saddle. Min picked up the heavy iron thing as though it were a feather. Dave shot an admiring glance at her and selected the nose-line. With a movement of the head he commanded her to follow him. The tinkle of the bell hanging from the neck of one of the camels came to their ears through the still night air. With the saddle upon her shoulders the woman raced past him to the four camels. Dave staggered to his riding-beast and attached the nose-line to the little wooden plug in one of its nostrils. He jerked upon it.

"Hoosh Hoosh!" he hissed, and obediently the animal fell to its knees. A gasp from his companion caused him to turn his head, and there, not three hundred yards away, he saw through the trees the dark, flitting forms of their pursuers. With a curse he flung the saddle on and hastily buckled the girths.

Catching up the woman quickly but gently he placed her straddle-ways on the front of the saddle. He leapt into the hack part and viciously heeled the camel to its feet.

It was then that Min screamed, not at the boomerang which sang through the air above their heads, but because of the strange animal she was upon. It was the first camel she had ever seen in her life, and a camel getting up from a kneeling position is not gentle by any means. The scream frightened the beast, which broke into a trot. Another boomerang flashed through the air. Dave leant forward and did his best to shield Min's body with his own. The third missile merely touched his arm, but it smashed the bone to pieces.

He gritted his teeth in pain. The blow from the boomerang, together with the exertion of the past half-hour, combined with the nearness of this wonderful wild woman, set his brain in a whirl. Yet the one predominating thought was that he must at all costs of pain and fatigue keep his senses. He kept them enough to guide the animal along the track to the station homestead, and soon they had the satisfaction of hearing the savage cries of rage grow fainter and fainter.

Never slackening in its speed, the camel kept to its long, loping stride, until they reached the first fence some five miles on their way. Here, by a trick Dave had taught it, the beast raised one leg up and over the four wires – the other followed in the same way, and the two hind legs came over together.

Mile after mile was covered thus, until some thirty lay between them and the blacks. Then Dave halted the beast beside a surface tank full of water and weakly "hooshed" the camel down upon its knees. The woman slid from her seat to the ground and faced him, as fresh as when she rescued him. Dave also slid from the camel's back, but fell to the ground in a dead faint.

Cool, delicious water splashed upon his face brought him to his senses again. His arm, broken and useless, throbbed with pain and all his body ached. The smell of burning wood was in his nostrils. The camel was quietly eating the leaves from a mulga-tree and a human sigh came to his ears – the sweetest music he had ever heard. He scrambled to his feet and looked with his soul shining through his eyes at his woman – his love!

Slowly, very slowly, her lips parted in a smile. The blood came to her face in a radiant flush. Then her right hand rose and the forefinger pointed to her lips; her lips made the movement of a kiss.

Dave lives with his wife in an iron-built hut similar to that which stands by the edge of the lake, and the township knows him no more.

The Death Heralds

Over the track which ran for hundreds of miles beside the River Darling in New South Wales rode a solitary horseman. The river was low – so low, indeed, that it had ceased to run, and only in the deep holes was water still to be found – while the country through which it meandered was a desolate, blasted waste.

It seemed to the man riding slowly northwards that years had passed since it had rained. Months ago the grass and herbage had disappeared and left but the brownish, reddish sand, which never lost its colour. The young mulga and belar trees were dying then, that is, those of them that had not been felled to feed the sheep which had died in hundreds of thousands, and dotted the earth with their bleached bones. Dying scrub, sand, and bones – evidence of a prolonged drought.

The road ran near the river at points in its great sweeping bends, and it was at one of these places the horseman halted and unsaddled beneath a giant gum-tree which grew upon the river bank. He sighed regretfully when he remembered that his horse would not find a single blade of grass within a hundred miles, and forty remained to be covered to reach the little township of Louth, where fodder might be bought.

Together – man and beast – they scrambled down the steep bank to the river-bed, and after a while found a deep hole full of water. The water was thick and dirty, for countless fish had been left by the receding waters, but thirstily they drank, after which the man filled his canvas water-bag and a small billy-can. With the horse following him like a well-trained dog, the man went back to the gum-tree, where he had left his saddle, and there he gave the animal two double handfuls of corn from a small calico bag.

"Guess we shall have to push on, old girl, and mighty quick, too," he drawled. "We could run a railway engine along them ribs of yours without fear of its getting off the lines. This country is absolutely the devil!"

The horse whinnied, and the man stroked her neck with

affection. Then he "shooed" her off, and lit a fire to boil his billy. Upon one side, the dry, empty river; on the other, a sandy, desolate waste – waterless, grass-less, lifeless.

Jimmy Clayton was travelling in search of work. His chief occupation was erecting lines of fence, but fences were not wanted then, for there were no sheep left to keep inside the pasture paddocks – not even a rabbit or a bird far away from the "Gutter of Australia." Two hundred miles south, he had received a cheque from his ruined employer, and laughed good-naturedly when the bank declined to cash it.

"I reckon the old man is hit harder than I am," he had remarked to the cashier.

Jimmy was twenty-eight years old, possessed average height, and was slightly, although muscularly, built. Dress, of course, did not matter a great deal. A wide-slouched hat, a brown shirt, open at the neck, grey moleskin trousers, and elastic-sided riding-boots completed a wardrobe that, of necessity, was never large. Two blankets, quantities of flour, tea, and sugar, in separate calico bags, together with a few odds and ends, made up his swag, which he took every care to keep as light as possible.

The water in the billy having arrived at boiling-point, Jimmy scooped off the gathered scum with a spoon, and made his tea. That, with a piece of damper and the pickings from a mutton bone, made up his luncheon menu. He had all but finished when he saw approaching him an old man with his swag slung over his shoulder.

Jimmy looked at the remains of the meal ruefully, and hoped that the old chap had had his dinner. He was seventy if a year, and Jim Clayton pitied him when remembering the dreadful state of the country. The times were hard even for him; much harder, therefore, would they be for this old bushman.

"Good-day-ee, mate," he drawled, stroking his white beard.

"Good-day," responded Jimmy. "Have a drink of tea?"

"Thanks, I will, if you've any to spare."

"Where did you camp last?" asked Jimmy as his visitor produced a tin pannikin and filled it from the billy. He loaded and lit his pipe before he received an answer.

"Just come up from Bundip Creek."

"Bundip Creek. Never heard of the place. Where is it?"

"'Bout five miles down the river – in a bend." The old man indicated with his thumb where the river took a sharp turn to the east. Jimmy looked in that direction.

"But that is right off the road," he remarked; "what's down there, anyway?"

"The Death Heralds."

"The what?"

"The Death Heralds. Ain't yous ever heard on 'em????"

Jimmy reckoned he could place the old swagman. There are many harmless lunatics wandering about the mighty, silent bush, and assuredly this was one.

"What's down there besides them?" he asked, and added, "Have a pipe of bacca?"

"Thanks. Oh, nothin' there much but a pub."

"Do you know if they've got any horse feed?"

"Yep. A little."

Jimmy considered. Then:

"I think I'll go there this afternoon. The mare is crocking up, and I can't afford to lose her. Bundip Creek! Been up and down the river dozens of times, but strike me if ever I heard of the place!"

"Well, you'll find it about five miles down them cart tracks that joins the road here, and, by cripes! if yous stays there long you'll be a better man than me. Ugh! Just to 'ear 'em turns a bloke's blood inter water." And the old man shivered.

"What do they sound like?" Clayton asked sympathetically.

"Sound like? I carn't tell yer properly, but I never wants to 'ear 'em no more. Every time they wails someone's sure to die. I believe it's me this time."

"Get out!" said Jimmy cheerfully. "Anyway, I'll go to Bundip Creek when the sun gets a bit lower, and I hope I hear these Death Heralds of yours."

"You'll 'ear 'em all right, never fear," prophesied the old man. "I'm going up the river to a big hole I knows on. So long!"

With a friendly nod of the head he rose stiffly to his feet, and, swinging up his swag over his shoulder, slowly walked along the river bank.

When the sun was within half an hour of setting, Jimmy gathered up his culinary utensils and placed them inside a saddlebag. He had dozed away the afternoon, and now he was sorry he had left the start so late, for the weather, which had not changed for ten months, looked exceedingly bad. A bank of jagged-edged clouds ranged from south to north-west, while above them the sun, a gigantic ball of blood-red fire, was about to disappear.

Clouds – the first the man had seen for many months. Jimmy studied them. Edged with black, they were brown in colour, and became dark red near the horizon. By no means were they healthy-looking, and their appearance told of a sandstorm that was probably approaching at seventy miles an hour.

The saddle was flung across the mare's back and the girth buckled up. After glancing over his temporary camp to see nothing had been left, Jimmy vaulted into his seat, and, a few minutes later, upon coming across the waggon tracks the old bushman had spoken of, rode slowly along their winding way.

The heat was still terrific – a dry, fierce heat which made one perspire freely. The scorching, shrivelling wind had died down into a stupendous calm that could actually be felt. It was as if every living creature in all the world were dead; as if Nature itself had expired upon close contact with the sun.

The horse jogged along the track made by the waggon wheels; the rusty brown clouds drove along the darkening dome of the sky and engulfed the sun with lightning. But the silence still reigned supreme – all living creatures were quiet and afraid of the coming storm. Higher and higher rushed the jagged edge of the cloud range, and deeper and more red became the sand and dust beneath it.

"The devil will be out to-night, little woman, and there will be something doing, I'll bet," remarked Jimmy. "I reckon we ought to sight that shanty in the next act, and then for a good feed and a good drink, and, it's to be hoped, a strong roof over our heads. Looks as if the drought is going to break up, and then fresh grass for you and more money for me."

It may have been that the stillness accentuated the sound upon human ears, or it may have been that his surroundings were depressing, but there came to the horseman from the river, which was two hundred yards upon his left, the most horrible cry he had ever heard.

Very low it commenced – like the bubbling gurgle of a man who screams for help as he sinks beneath the surface of the water. Then, in increasing volume, it rose up the scale into a piercing howl, which broke off suddenly and ended in dreadful, gasping sobs.

The horse stopped and its body trembled. The man sat frozen in the saddle, stiff in very horror. The sobbing cries died away, and it seemed that the four corners of the world echoed them. A minute passed. Then, about a mile farther down the river, there came an answering cry, equal in clearness and horror to the first.

"Good God!" muttered the man. "The Death Heralds!"

Undecided whether to go on or to return the way he had come, Jimmy remained immovable. Dreading it, he yet strained his ears to catch the sound should it be repeated. He shivered. He wanted to go back, but it was too late, for the storm was not many miles away, and a sandstorm, followed probably by floods of water, was no time for a man to be out in the open.

"Hang it, I believe I am as frightened as you are, old stick-in-the-mud! We had better go on, although I don't like the place. I wouldn't care to meet one of those things in the dark, and I reckon in half an hour a man won't see a hand before his eyes."

The mare snorted through quivering nostrils, but trotted forward under the pressure of the man's heel, while with every step she took the storm swept nearer to them by a hundred yards. Yet the air never moved a leaf among all those trees.

It was growing dark. Suddenly the track sharply ascended a low hill, not more than two hundred feet high, and through the trees which grew thickly upon its slopes Jimmy saw a one-story building of corrugated iron. At the rear and farther up the hill was a smaller building, which he surmised to be a stable.

Riding up to the house, he found that it appeared to contain about four rooms. Over the front door there was nailed a board, upon which, badly painted, was the word "Saloon." Not a soul was about, and the door was shut.

"Funny-looking outfit!" Jimmy remarked as he slipped from the saddle. Passing up two steps, he crossed the veranda and announced his presence by merely kicking the door. It was flung open. The most disreputable-looking individual Jimmy had seen for many a day faced him.

"What d'yer want?" he snarled, showing two yellow fangs.

"Well, I reckon I want a drink and my horse could do with a feed – that is, if you've got anything. It's going to blow some in a couple of acts, and a good solid roof would come in handy." Jimmy saw hostility in the man's face. "Any objection?" he drawled.

"Carn't do much for yer horse, and the stock's pretty low. Still, I suppose you had better come in. Find the stables at the back – some feed in the corner," he growled.

Jimmy led his horse round the corner of the house, and pulled up before the stable door. With his hand upon the key he listened. Low and far distant there came to his ears a dull roar – persistent and angry. It was the wind.

He turned the key and opened the door. Through the dark aperture there rushed a feminine figure, which slipped past him and fled to the house. He hadn't time to see her face in the dusk, but he turned and looked after her in astonishment.

"Well, strike me! What sort of place have I landed at this time?" he said, leading the mare inside. After removing the saddle and slipping the bridle from her head he watered her from a bucket and untied a bale of fodder he found in one corner. Ravenously she ate, and Jimmy, affectionately patting her neck, said:

"I reckon you'll do, old thing! If the place blows away tonight, then I'll bet you'll come back for me in the morning, eh?"

He left her then. Securely fastening the door, he ran to the house, for the roar of the wind was growing louder, and it would be upon them in a few minutes. It would blow, perhaps, for days, and the heavens would open and flood a thirsty, dying country.

The pleasant-looking individual whom he had seen at first was waiting in the passage, and, after barring the door, led him into the small bar, where he lit an oil lamp hanging by a chain from the ceiling. The room was halved by the counter, behind which was the usual assortment of poisons ranged upon shelves.

Jimmy leaned against the beer-stained counter and drawled:

"Got any whisky?"

"It's a shilling a nip – want any water?"

"No, thanks," replied Jimmy as he gulped down the fire-water. "What about a bit of tucker?"

"All right; come into the back room." Jimmy found himself in a small room lit by a lamp similar to that in the bar. A table, covered by a piece of oil-cloth, stood in the centre of the floor, and a few chairs were ranged about the walls, which were quite bare of pictures. At one end was an open fireplace, at the other a door leading into the kitchen. There was a third door which opened upon another room, but it was shut.

It was while Jimmy was sitting down in an old arm-chair with a broken spring that the storm rushed upon the house with a howling scream. Silence was succeeded by a pandemonium of sound. The whole building rocked upon its foundations, while flints played a tattoo upon its iron walls and the flying sand hissed against the window-panes. Through the cracks in the doors and windows filtered the dust and filled the air about the lamp with a brown haze.

A thud which shook the ground told of one giant tree laid low, and a flying branch crashed upon the roof, threatening to come through. Jimmy expected that at any moment the house would be torn from its foundations, and its sheets of iron whirled away by the wind and battered out of shape against the trees. He thought of his horse, and hoped the stables were strongly built.

Both men were obliged to shout to make themselves heard above the din of the raging elements.

"Will yer wait a bit till it's over?" the publican yelled.

"Just as well have it now – this is going to last for days," Jimmy yelled back.

The man grunted and withdrew to the kitchen, to return in a few minutes with half a loaf of bread and the remains of a leg of mutton. This he placed upon the table, adding a broken pot of mustard, some salt in a paper bag, and a bottle of whisky.

Jimmy sat down to his rough dinner, and was in the act of cutting the joint when, for the second time, he heard the dreadful, wailing scream which began in bubbling and ended in sobs.

White as paper, he rose to his feet, and, listening, heard what he knew would come – the answering wail which defied the storm to soften it. Against the opposite side of the table leaned the repulsive owner of the saloon. He leered into Jimmy's face, his black eyes shining evilly and his yellow fangs showing like those of a wolf.

"The Death Heralds are calling!" he cried.

Two hours later Jimmy was lounging in the old chair with the broken spring. He sat with his back to a corner of the room near the fireplace, and his feet rested upon the table. Near his boots stood a bottle, three parts full of whisky, as well as a glass which was empty. Jimmy never allowed any liquor to remain in a glass very long.

Outside, the wind still tried to wreck the building, but it withstood all the buffeting it received, although through every crack flowed a continuous stream of fine dust. Occasionally the ground trembled when a giant tree crashed to earth. The night, as seen through the window, was as black as pitch. If the lightning played with the clouds high up in the heavens, then it was unable to penetrate the flying sand which swept over the country.

Jimmy had decided not to try to sleep, for the reason that he was suspicious of his host; the latter had retired an hour ago, expressing the wish that Jimmy would be able to sleep soundly. Jimmy had wandered about the continent since he was ten years old; had entered, good-naturedly and with great enthusiasm, into many a brawl in the pearling stations of the north and in the saloons that sold vast quantities of poison along the great stock routes; but never had he experienced such a devilishly uncanny place as this. There were two other absorbing subjects to think about – the awesome screams, which the old swagman had named the Death Heralds, and the mysterious woman who, very evidently, had been locked in the stable, and had escaped when he opened the door. With regard to the first, he was determined to find out on the morrow what sort of things made such dreadful sounds, that is, if they could be seen, which be doubted. As for the woman, he had not seen her since she had disappeared around the corner of the house, but he felt certain that she and the man and the things were all mixed up in one peculiar scheme which would give his adventurous spirit full play.

Jimmy removed his feet from the table and poured himself out another glass of whisky. He swallowed it without the aid of water, and then slowly refilled and lit his pipe. Replacing his feet in their former position, he lounged down into his chair and quietly smoked away the minutes, while he pondered over the strange happenings of the evening. His thoughts were of the old man he had met that noon, and he wondered how he was faring out in such awful weather. Suddenly those thoughts broke off and his body stiffened. For the door at the further end of the room was slowly opening.

Jimmy did not move – merely lowered his eyelids and watched intently the dark slit between the door and the frame growing tantalisingly slow yet ever wider. At last the door, which opened outward from the room he was in, was wide. A white blotch appeared in the centre of the black oblong. As it approached the frame it proved to be a human face. With a swift, noiseless movement it came into the room, and Jimmy saw that it was a woman.

From the moment she came under the rays of the lamp and he took in the details of her strong and intelligent, albeit sweet and womanly features, Jimmy decided she was upon no errand of mischief to himself. He opened his eyes, and, removing his feet from the table, stood up and faced her – slim, dare-devil, handsome Jimmy. She put a finger upon her lips, while her eyes implored silence. Then, coming round a table, she placed a cool, brown hand upon his arm, and, leaning towards him, whispered softly:

"Take care and watch. Don't sleep, whatever you do. You are the fly, and he is the spider. Go in the morning, even if the storm is still raging. I shall be watching too."

Then, turning abruptly, she left the room swiftly, closing the door noiselessly behind her. Jimmy stood as still as marble for nearly a minute before he resumed his seat and tried to think.

"Ye Gods!" he murmured. "What a beauty – and here with that beast! Doesn't like him much, it's evident. Oh, no, I'm not going to sleep!"

He drank the whisky and smoked his pipe; it was the worst thing he could do, for the night was hot, and the dust made his eyes water. The bottle was half empty. At the end of an hour his pipe was out and he was dozing – just an unwary fly in a spider's silken web.

The events which woke him with startling suddenness followed one upon the other rapidly.

A woman screamed, and he leaped to his feet in a bound.

Coming round the table was his repulsive host. In his hand was a long butcher's knife.

In the doorway stood the woman, her eyes staring with horror, her mouth still open after her scream of warning. The man crouched, and, as he was about to spring with the knife raised above his head, the whole room was filled with an intense, lurid blue light. It played about the deep, long blade of the knife, and in a single instant Jimmy saw the man who held it shrivel into a cinder.

The light passed, and was followed by a pitchy darkness. The lamp, by some inexplicable chance, although twisted into a shapeless mass, still hung upon its chain, extinguished, and in those few seconds, while Jimmy pressed his hands over his eyes, he heard the oil drip upon the cloth on the table. Then came the thunder – a terrific, deafening crash. It was as if all the artillery in the world was fired in one single second; as if the very earth was being rendered into small pieces by a power undreamed of.

The wind had suddenly ceased to blow, and was succeeded by a dead calm. Upon the iron roof fell drops of rain. Then the heavens opened, and the water fell in floods. It roared down upon the house – steady, persistent, tremendous – and above it all Jimmy heard the woman cry, a wail of intense mental anguish.

"Oh, God – oh, God! Let me out – let me out!"

It was to the man's credit that during those moments of horror he kept cool and collected. He slid round the table – on the opposite side to that on which the thing lay, and, reaching out his hands in the darkness, he called:

"Where are you, little woman? Catch hold of my arm and we'll go together. Strike me, if this isn't the very devil."

They groped their way to the door leading to the kitchen. A little delay and Jimmy found the back door, and, passing through it, they left that dreadful house and were out into the downpour. The lightning flared incessantly, but the rain was as thick as a London fog, and it was only after great difficulty that the man found the stable door.

The mare welcomed them with a whinny of delight, and snorted while she nosed them affectionately. Jimmy locked the door with his disengaged hand. He "shooed" the horse to one end of the stable, and, with his feet, poked the remainder of the bale of lucerne into a corner. Then gently he commanded the woman, who had all the time remained silent, to sit down upon it.

"Sit down there for a while. You'll be quite all right now, and I'll see the mare doesn't tread on you. That was a nasty flash of lightning – I couldn't see for quite a time."

She obeyed him, and sank down upon the dry, sweet-smelling fodder. And then she sighed – a deep intake of breath, and began to cry softly.

In the darkness Jimmy found a bucket, and, turning it upside down, he sat upon it and leaned back against the closed door. The lightning had ceased, but the rain still came down in torrents and roared upon the iron roof. Quietly he smoked his pipe, while the mare tried to nibble playfully at his hair. After a while the sobbing died away, and the deep breathing which followed told Jimmy that the girl was sleeping – the sleep of exhaustion.

He still smoked on, listening to the rain and patting his horse, keeping her always away from the corner where the woman was sleeping. And he was glad he was there.

Upon the western bank of the River Darling Jimmy and the woman stood looking down silently upon the brown flood, ever rising and surging southwards. Three days had passed since that night of terror when they had met in circumstances so grim and dreadful.

Those three days had been very happy days for Jimmy. The woman had been his constant companion, and he had learned most things regarding her life; also the cause of the screams known by him as the Death Heralds.

Some four years ago, when her aged another had died and the home in the township of Wilcannia had been broken up, she had come to reside with her uncle, who kept the saloon at Bundip Creek.

It was not long before she realised the sort of man he was, and freely she told Jimmy that he had killed many roaming bushmen for the money they possessed. Once she had run away, but he had caught her and had locked her up for days in the stable, and ever after kept her in fear of her life. As the time passed his influence over her increased, and her spirit became subdued and resigned.

The Death Heralds were heard when the river ceased to run,

and, in a drunken, confidential mood, the old man told his niece that a subterranean river ran at two points directly below the Darling River. At these two points natural shafts joined the upper and lower rivers, and when the upper river was dry the two shafts were empty of water.

But occasionally the lower river forced water up into these shafts; this acted like air in the pipes of an organ, the varying diameter and shape causing the weird noises. It was a natural freak, of which the owner of the saloon took full advantage, openly attributing the disappearance of some of his visitors to supernatural causes.

"I was thinking that Wilcannia is not a bad place to live in. You have friends there, haven't you?" said Jimmy, still watching the river.

"Yes."

"I don't know him, but I've been told that there is not a bad old parson living close beside his church."

"He must have come there since I left," she asserted. "I've never met him."

"Wouldn't you like to – with me?"

Jimmy looked up and encountered her eyes – large and grey – eyes which reflected the light of the sun a thousand times over. Her lips parted in a dawning smile.

"What do you mean?" she whispered.

"Only that I worship the very ground you tread on and reckon a parson would come in very handy just now."

Then she smiled, wonderfully, and in her smile the man saw paradise.

The Head of the Revolution

It was a wonderful meeting. Fully three thousand people were in the hall, and for fully two hours a pin might have been heard to drop at any time. They hardly breathed, and their white, pinched faces scarcely moved, whilst they drank in Victor Manssen's fiery message.

The message was of freedom. Manssen, his eyes now blazing, now dreamy – a man of terrific energy, unbounded passion and gifted with poetic vision – spoke to them of a Promised Land wherein they could really *live*, each woman in her own house, each man cultivating his own garden – where the children would play in the sun, and whence the White Plague would be banished for ever – a world reconstructed on ideal lines, and which, had they but courage, might be theirs almost for the taking.

The enthusiasm at the close of this address left no doubt that the orator had reached the hearts of his audience.

Amidst a delirium of clapping, stamping, cheering and handshaking, Manssen left the meeting to the care of his committee – quiet, determined-looking men, wearing red armlets – and went to the telephone in an adjoining room.

"Yes," responded the person he rang up; "I'm Miss Fairthorn. Yes? . . . Oh yes! Mr. Manssen, I should be glad. Certainly you may come. No, I shall not be going out to-night."

Miss Fairthorn was one of those women, both intellectual and beautiful, who have successfully invaded man's professional preserves, live a life wherein Mrs. Grundy has little part, adore beautiful dresses and elegant furniture, and worship at the Shrine of Women's Emancipation.

She rented a flat above shop premises a few yards from Trafalgar Square, in which she received her friends with quiet simplicity, and spent a great deal of her leisure in editing a political monthly for women.

Half an hour after the telephone conversation, a bell tinkled in the small hall, and, when Victor Manssen was announced by a neat maid, his hostess was standing on the hearthrug with a cigarette between her lips.

"My dear Miss Fairthorn," he said, advancing with outstretched hands, "it is indeed good of you to see me at this late hour. Why, it must be after ten."

"As the old lady with the umbrella doesn't live here, there is nothing to worry over," she answered with a smile. Motioning the tall, somewhat thin, and plainly dressed man of some thirty-five years to a chair opposite her own, she went on: "Sit down, do, and have a cigarette. I'm glad you have come, for I was getting dreadfully bored. You've been addressing a meeting, have you not?"

Manssen leaned forward in the act of lighting a cigarette, his eyes blazing with excitement. Instantly she felt dominated by the force of his personality. He was soon describing his New Heaven and New Earth in almost the same words and with equal fervour as when he had held his vast audience for two hours spellbound.

But his present auditor was not so easily carried away.

"You told them how they could get there quickly, I suppose?" she asked with a slight smile. "You have such visions, dear man, that I think you do more harm than good. By your pictures of the millennium you make these poor people discontented, whereas, if they knew not of an existence other than that they are now leading, they would be happier."

"You don't really think that ignorance is bliss, do you?"

She was lying back in her chair still smiling. She said: "I repeat, they would be happier if they were ignorant. Knowledge brings discontent."

"Happy! Happy! Can man and women find happiness in the filth of the slums? Should they be allowed to try? No, Miss Fairthorn! It isn't right. It's – it's devilish."

The tricks of the orator were absent; the tone of his voice was terribly earnest. The abnormally broad face was lit up with a certain radiance, the pure light of a great enthusiasm shining from his pale blue eyes. The woman, watching him, was fascinated.

"But I haven't come to bore you with my meeting," he went on suddenly changing his intonation. "I've come to tell you what you know already. I'm going to tell you now because no longer can I remain silent. I am afraid I do not make a romantic lover but, Gladys, I love you and want you to marry me."

It was said calmly enough, if abruptly, but Manssen's soul was behind his eyes. The woman he addressed flushed slightly and gazed into the fire, wordless now that the crisis of years of friendship had come, seeking a way out which would leave them as firm friends as ever. She looked up at him suddenly, her eyes bright with tears.

"I cannot marry you, Mr. Manssen, for the simple reason that I do not love you enough," she said with a faint catch in her voice. "I shall give up my independence only to the man I would absolutely adore. Please say no more about it. Let us continue to be good friends."

"Ah!" Victor Manssen drew in his breath sharply, and, rising to his feet, lit his cigarette with trembling fingers. She played nervously with a gold pendant at her throat, and regarded him a little timidly.

"I was afraid your answer would be a refusal," he said, with a tremendous effort to remain calm. "Yet one day I shall be your husband. Your independence, Miss Fairthorn, will stand you in good stead shortly. You will want it, believe me, in the days to come, and then you may realise the value of a man's love and protection. It will –"

He paused and glanced toward the curtained windows. The roar of the traffic had inexplicably stopped. Over London had fallen a sinister silence.

Half a minute passed. Neither moved, the man standing facing the window, the woman gazing upward at his profile with terror dawning in her eyes.

Then a low babel of voices came up from the street, like the terrified moan of some pre-historic monster. A single shot was fired almost beneath their window. A pause. Then arose the cackle of a machine-gun somewhere in the Square.

Gladys Fairthorn clutched Manssen's arm. Her face was white, and she made no effort to conceal the terror in her heart. What did the stoppage of the traffic mean? – the shooting? – the machine-gun?

"Mr. Manssen, what is it?" she asked, with wide eyes. "You know. You said I should need my independence soon. *You* know what this means. Tell me."

He looked down upon her from his tall height. His face was a little white, his breathing came fast, and in his eyes there was a look she was never to forget.

"It is the Revolution," he answered tensely. "Or rather the evolution of the workers to a better existence. Don't leave your rooms to-night on any account. I will get a man to guard you. I must go now and look after my children. Their efforts towards liberty must be directed."

Manssen left her in the middle of her apartment, alone in the flat, since her maid lived out and had gone hone. Above the shouting in the street revolver and rifle shots rang out occasionally, and some distance away, in the direction of the Thames, the firing was more persistent.

Revolution! Revolution! The word kept ringing through her brain. What did it all mean? Surely London would not become like Petrograd and Moscow? She crossed to the window, drew aside the curtains and gazed down upon the street.

People were running into the Square, urged forward by men wearing red armlets. The traffic was pulled up on both sides of the road. Here and there a man was hurriedly putting up his shop shutters, and a little way along towards Trafalgar Square a dozen men or more were forming taxi-cabs, carts and omnibuses into a rough barricade. They had three machine-guns with them which they used with the skill of artillerymen.

She opened the window and looked out. At the other end of the street another barricade was in course of erection, and among the builders were women.

A burst of firing broke out in the Square itself, and the machine-guns at that end of the street cackled sharply. The men crouched behind paving-stones hastily dug up from the side-walks, and used their weapons in bursts of fire. Some of the barricade builders were carrying furniture out of a house, and with them the owner argued violently. Gladys Fairthorn saw him shot down, and the work of the barricade continued without pause. Shortly afterwards another man reeled, shot through the chest. She knew it was in the chest he received his wound, because he pressed his hand over his heart before falling inertly in the middle of the road.

Then suddenly the electric light failed and plunged her flat and the street into a darkness relieved only here and there by the gas-lamps. She caught her breath with terror and turned back into the darkened room. She must have light, she told herself, or she would go mad. It was so like a nightmare, so unreal, that she felt certain she would wake and find it was morning.

She groped her way past the furniture to the door. Candles she knew were to be obtained in the small kitchen at the rear of the flat. They must be used to make light, for the darkness was unbearable. She found the door and her fingers fumbled with the handle.

It was locked! Some one had made her a prisoner.

Feeling helpless and afraid to call out, lest she should attract unwelcome attention, she made her way back to the window, irresistibly drawn by the drama being enacted below.

In the black void of the street occasional flashes showed her the positions of the guns. The rattle of the machine-guns down by the Thames still kept at their devil's tattoo, and sometimes the field-gun shook the windows with its deep bark.

A deal of fighting seemed to be going on in and beyond Trafalgar Square, and from that direction came the sound of many motors rapidly approaching. It was very dark, but where one gas-lamp lit the road she saw four omnibuses abreast charging the barricade.

The machine-guns blazed furiously. Half a dozen yards from the pile of vehicles and furniture, the 'bus on the right flank suddenly swerved and dashed into a tobacconist's shop, where it fell on its side and immediately burst into flames.

The other three came on, and, as giant beetles, crawled over the barricade before toppling over or coming to a stop amid the wreckage.

Figures dashed toward the blazing shop. Others fired shot after shot from revolvers in the fight which ensued between the 'busmen and the barricade defenders. Who they were, and what each side represented, Gladys had not the faintest notion.

People ran into the street adjoining the tobacconist's shop, some shouting wildly and others screaming with terror. The party with the omnibuses appeared to have won the fight, for they dragged the dead and dying defenders to the side of the road, and hurled the wreckage aside to make a clear passage. No sooner was this done than a huge open touring-car, full of men, rushed through toward Westminster. One of them held a red flag. Another, looking up in passing and seeing Gladys, fired at her. They disappeared in the darkness, leaving an indescribable scene of debris and dead men to be shown to the heavens by the light of the rapidly spreading fire.

Hand pressed to breast, as though striving to stay her heart's fierce throbbing, she leaned against the window-frame and tried to think clearly. It had all come so suddenly. Why, it could have been but an hour since that Manssen had proposed to her in the quiet comfort of the room which now was dark and cold.

Where was he, then, and what was he doing? He had said he was going to lead his children, but she was quite sure no man could lead those maniacs in the streets. Dimly she thought of her maid. Had she reached her home? What would her employer and his colleagues, cabinet ministers, be doing that dreadful night?

How long she stood at the window she never could tell; indeed, her thoughts were a chaos. At last her attention became slowly centred upon the door, faintly to be seen by the light of the conflagration on the further side of the street. People were talking in the hall, their voices raised in altercation. A fierce oath was followed by a thud. Came then a momentary silence, and the crash of a heavy body on the stairs. She trembled violently when some one knocked loudly on the door.

"What do you want?" Her voice was little above a whisper.

"Is that Miss Fairthorn?" came a man's deep tones. "If so, let me in, please. It's Jack Craig."

With a glad cry, the girl moved swiftly across the room. Craig was a very old friend. She tried to open the door, forgetting she was locked in.

"Some one has fastened the door. I am a prisoner," she said. "Can't you break it down?"

"All right; I'll try," he answered. "I must not make too much row, though, or those devils will be up here instantly. Wait a minute."

Miss Fairthorn heard him stumble along the short passage to the kitchen. Something fell, and she was fearful the crash would penetrate to the street. At last he came back and applied force. The wood splintered, the door shook and flew inward.

Lighted by the red glare without, Jack Craig looked like a

71

pirate. His clothes were ripped in several places, a white scarf was tied about his neck, and he was hatless. Lurching into the room he swayed upon his feet. The girl caught him by the lapel of his coat and stared into his ghastly face.

"What is wrong with you?" she cried, a little wildly. "Jack – Mr. Craig – you are not wounded, are you?"

He tried to laugh and failed. If he noticed her use of his Christian name he gave no sign.

"It's nothing much, Miss Fairthorn," he said weakly. "Bullet grazed my leg a bit, that's all. Lost blood. No bones broken, I fancy."

"Just where? show me," she urged, glad to be able to do something practical. She made him sit down, and brought the brandy decanter and a glass. Whilst he was drinking she tore up serviettes for a bandage.

"This sort of thing was bound to occur sooner or later," he explained grimly, his clean-shaven, handsome face set in hard lines. "Sort of reaction after the excitement and strain of the war, which, added to unemployment and agitation, has set the murder lust going."

"But how is it all going to end?" She was quickly tacking the pieces of linen into a long strip.

"I don't know," Craig answered wearily, "it has only just begun. The revolutionary party seems to have stored plenty of munitions, and to have laid their plans deeply. Yes, it was a clever man who arranged it all. By the way, who was the gentleman I threw downstairs?"

"I never saw him. It must have been he who locked me in."

"Strange!" he said, frowning. "Seemed to be on guard."

Mentioning neither Manssen's visit nor his promise, she examined his wound fearlessly. As he had said, it was by no means serious, but the loss of blood had weakened him greatly. It appeared he was leaving a theatre when the shooting started, and had been an hour and a half trying to reach her flat, thinking it likely she would be at home and in need of assistance. He received his wound in the fight she had witnessed between the omnibus party and the barricaders.

Afterwards she helped him to the window, an act scarcely necessary, for he was quite able to walk, and at her nearness he felt his heart beating faster than was its wont.

Looking out cautiously, they observed the street to be practically deserted, and that a great concourse of people was gathering in the Square, shouting and singing something about "a flag of deepest red".

The firing by the river had died down into spasmodic bursts, and the big gun had ceased booming. Occasional shots were fired in the Square and in the direction of the barracks housing the Horse Guards.

Presently part of the crowd surged into their street, where the fire was now forcing people out of their houses to escape death. These people excited the animosity of the advancing crowd. Shots were fired at them whilst running to sheltering doorways. The air was filled with yells and oaths, and something like the reiteration of a name.

"What are they saying?" Gladys Fairthorn asked her companion. "It sounds like somebody's name."

"They are shouting for the leader of the revolution," he replied somewhat harshly. "Wish I had him here!"

Nearer came the crowd.   "– Sen! – En! Man –! Manssen!" it yelled.

Craig turned to his companion. Her face was white and full of horror.

"They want their leader, Victor Manssen," he said.

For an hour they watched undisciplined mobs surging backward and forward through the street, and parties of men breaking into shops and looting them; the owners being shot out of hand, or ill-used for protesting.

Craig then relit the fire, and rummaged in the kitchen for a kettle in which he boiled water and made tea. They drew the curtains, and partook of a light supper, picnic fashion, by the glowing fire. The atmosphere was hot, for the conflagration was nearing the shop on the opposite side of the street. No effort was being made to put it out.

"We shall have to get out of this," said Craig, after a silent interval. "Even if this house doesn't catch fire, London is now no place for a woman like you, Miss Fairthorn."

Twelve hours before she would have scoffed at any such idea, but now, in the midst of rapine and murder, she felt a deep sense of helplessness which she had not known for years. This big man's presence was comforting in the extreme: he was so self-reliant, so powerful.

"I have formed a plan of escape," he went on, "dangerous enough, but much less so than remaining here. I know where I have a good chance of getting a car, so it would be as well to put on your warmest wraps, say in half an hour, and take up a position just behind your street door, which I will leave closed when I go out. As the opportunity occurs, I shall drive up to it and sound the hooter three times. You must then rush out across the pavement, and climb in. You must be quick, for there will probably be people who will try to stop us."

"And where will you take me, Mr. Craig?"

"Down to an aerodrome in Kent where we shall obtain a 'plane to take us over to France. I don't expect the revolutionary movement will have reached the aerodrome yet."

She waited just the half-hour before donning her wraps and descending the dark stairs to the front door, where she waited in inky blackness. The minutes dragged vary slowly. Sometimes the street was full of shrieking men, whose tramping could be heard through the thick oak door. Once her heart beat wildly when a man stopped and struck a match on a panel of the door, and again when a fellow lurched against it with a drunken curse. With unspeakable relief she heard in the distance the "honk" of a motor-horn, the third time sounding very near.

With trembling fingers she flung the door open, and, seeing a low-bodied, powerful car at the curbstone, darted across the pavement, sprang into the car, and was whirled away toward Westminster. Attached to the side was a huge piece of red cloth serving as a flag. Craig in the driving-seat sounded the horn in one continual blast, steered with amazing dexterity through people marching and standing about, and once, when a crowd threatened a block, he turned down a side street to the river.

Shots were fired at them whilst crossing the bridge, but the shooting was bad, and they gained the southern side without mishap. At one time, whilst rushing at terrific speed through the narrow streets parallel with Westminster Road, a machine-gun was used in an endeavour to stay their progress, and later their way lay between two rows of buildings wrapped in flames, when the paintwork of the car was scorched by the heat, and they were in great danger from falling masonry.

Gladys Fairthorn was obliged to clutch the side of the rocking car when it turned corners literally on two wheels, and Craig with his goggles covering his eyes, bent over the steering-wheel and drove constantly within an inch of death.

Further south the yelling, screaming mobs of maddened men were met with less often, but the car kept up its sickening speed. Once in open country, Craig turned on the brilliant headlights and drove with maniacal fury. Suddenly it dawned upon the girl, when she glanced back and saw a dark blotch on the road, that they were being followed by another car, and it was for that reason only the pace was so great. Later they seemed to have lost the following car, for the speed slackened appreciably when they passed through a small village and entered a large aerodrome.

Here several machines were ready for immediate use, and about them stood mechanics in groups, talking. Their questions as to London happenings were many, but at last Craig, who held an important position there, got them to help him start one of the larger aeroplanes.

The twin engines roared, and the machine vibrated with the enormous unreleased power whilst one of the mechanics clambered in after them. The 'plane ran forward over the smooth ground before rising into the darkness.

At that moment a powerful motor-car with huge headlights ran into the aerodrome.

In the dim dawn of day the great man-made bird soared higher and ever higher toward the light, leaving below in the blackness a country suddenly gone mad, and in the grip of foreign murderers, bands of looters and incendiaries.

An hour later they were nearing the French coast in a clear atmosphere. The first Paris-London aerobus of the day had passed them at a lower altitude and was but a speck in the north, while a fast "bullet" machine had overtaken them fifteen minutes before, and was rapidly forging ahead. A third 'plane, which looked like a West European Company's mail-carrier, was fast overhauling them.

Craig sat easily at the controls with Miss Fairthorn immediately behind him. The mechanic, who occupied a position still further astern, appeared intensely interested in the machine overtaking them, which was something like a thousand feet higher up.

Gladys saw him adjust his speaking apparatus, but, of course could not hear a word of what he said to her companion. Craig, turning in his seat, studied the mail-carrier, and spoke to his mechanic. Immediately afterwards the machine rose in a long slant. At once the mail-carrier copied the manoeuver, which made it evident that its pilot had some interest in them. The girl adjusted her telephone.

"What is the matter?" asked she.

"I can't make out the fellow's game in the fast 'plane. Our mechanic says it is a new mail-carrier which has recently been built and tested at our aerodrome, and I can't help thinking he is the mysterious chap who followed us down from London. We don't like the way he is flying."

Who was the motorist who followed them from London with so much persistence that even an air flight could not shake him off? Manssen? Gladys Fairthorn thought it unlikely, since his leadership would be so necessary to the revolutionists. But, if not he, then who?

Do what he would, Craig could not get above the pursuing 'plane. It seemed a perfect machine to handle and possessed enormous speed and climbing ability. When they passed over Calais, it was immediately overhead.

Of a sudden the mail-carrier dived at them. Craig never moved his gaze from it for a fraction of a second. What be expected took place. The small machine swooped to within fifty feet and released a bomb. The shining, egg-shaped object would have done its intended work, but at that moment the sea and earth changed places with the sky, or so it seemed to Gladys, for Craig nose-dived and looped.

The mechanic got off three shots from the automatic rifle which had been stored in the fuselage, but failed to score a bull, and his chance did not recur until later.

Five hundred feet they dropped, and at them came the mail-carrier as hawk after sparrow. An upward rush followed, which caused the attacker narrowly to miss crashing into their rudders. The girl, looking down, saw a spurt of flame and a blotch of black smoke burst outwards in a circle in an open place at the back of the town. Her face whitened at thought of the lives which might have been lost through the mail-carrier's bomb.

Things happened, however, with so much rapidity that she was left no time to dwell on possibilities of that kind. The fast machine was at them again, this time soaring up astern of them as if the pilot was determined to charge and take them with him to certain death.

Again the mechanic fired, again, and yet again. Then he raised an arm and yelled. The words were rushed straight away into silence by the force of the wind, but Gladys understood.

He had hit the pilot of the attacking machine. Him she saw clap his hand to his left side, sink back and down into the fuselage of his 'plane, which immediately stalled and slid earthward tail first for a thousand feet, when the automatic balancers enabled it to right itself. The pilot was dying or dead, but the perfection of the machine would allow it to land in safety provided it did so in an open space.

After it the twin-engined 'plane followed in wide circles. They saw the mail-carrier skim across a field, narrowly miss a fence, land perfectly in the next field, only to crash into a second fence. Craig brought his machine safely to ground in the same field.

On their coming to a standstill he turned to the girl, his face hard and stern, his nerves cool and steady. She was trembling a little with the excitement.

"Do you know who is in that crashed 'plane?" he asked abruptly.

"Yes, Manssen. I saw him when he was hit."

"So you know him, then?"

Miss Fairthorn nodded. "Yes, I have known him for years. He proposed to me only last evening."

Craig frowned and would have said something, but his jaws shut as a trap, and he climbed to the ground without a word. It was the mechanic who helped her down.

"It will be as well if you stay here, Miss Fairthorn, until we see if he is armed," Craig said later; and he set off across the field accompanied by the mechanic.

She saw them approach with caution the wrecked machine which with one wing smashed, was lying upon its side. The two men met with no hostility from Manssen, whom they lifted out and laid upon the grass. When Craig returned to her she was standing with her back to the tragic scene.

"Gladys – Miss Fairthorn," he stumbled, "Manssen is only just alive, but conscious. He wishes to speak to you."

They found Manssen lying with his head on the mechanic's coat. She knelt beside him. His face was as white as chalk, and his voice failed repeatedly before he could utter a word.

"I – I want your – forgiveness – before – I go," he whispered. "I saw you – get into Craig's car – and – I went raving mad. I've sinned against – you – and against – my children. They will never – forgive – my desertion – but – you – you – may find it – in your heart –" His voice died away.

With shining eyes she bent over him. "I love a clever visionary," was all she replied. She stooped and swiftly kissed him on the lips. A wonderful smile came to his face, and the smile became fixed in death. Slowly the girl rose to her feet and confronted Craig.

"I had to do it," she said softly. "His ideals made him a saint, though his methods were wrong. He attempted murder, yet loved me. What a man!"

"He has served the people better by dying than he would have done by living," Craig answered in his grim manner. He ordered the mechanic to go back to his machine, for people were running towards them along the road near by. Continuing, he said: "He was the Head of the Revolution, and now that the head is dead the body will die also. But the people will have a better chance in the future, for the Government will never forget last night. By the way, I noticed you didn't say you returned Manssen's love."

"Silly! how could I?"

The answer to her question Craig read in her large grey eyes.

The Murderers' Home

"**I** met her in one of those cafés in Sydney, softly illuminated, thickly carpeted, wholly luxurious, where one could lounge away time in comfortable chairs and smoke cigarettes over coffee or cocktails," Daniel Hogarth was saying. "It was called the Orange Blossom. Within were to be found clerics in mufti, artist people, singers and boxers, and ladies of the camellias."

Cass Bennett was gazing through narrowed lids at his slight, handsome companion who sat on the opposite side of a leaping campfire. The bushman's face was expressionless, his magnificent physique relaxed in repose.

"Her beauty and charm are indescribable: Veronica Storr was simply my ideal," Hogarth went on, his rather pleasant voice low and rapid. "I loved her at the end of the first five seconds of acquaintanceship, and – eventually she loved me. Yet, well as I got to know her, I penetrated only the outer fringe of her personality: never, you understand, entered even the ante-chamber of her soul.

"And then one dreadful morning she was arrested for murder. The manager of her hotel was passing her door when the shot was fired in her sitting-room. The door was locked, but in less than a minute he and a porter burst it in and found her standing near the body of a man, her own revolver in her hand, one cartridge spent, the barrel still warm from the explosion.

"At that time I was attached to the political section of the C.I.D. and my position enabled me to glean the facts without trouble. Her origin and history were obscure, but the dead man was well-known to the police as an unscrupulous private inquiry agent suspected of blackmail.

"When I visited the prison she flew to my arms proclaiming her innocence, almost hysterical with passionate desire to clear herself in my eyes. And, God forgive me! I allowed her to see that I did not believe her.

"I couldn't. The evidence was so damning, the case so clear, even to the motive, for it was discovered that the man was blackmailing her, that the softest-hearted jury in the world would have condemned her. I did everything humanly possible for her comfort and defence, but my unavoidable belief in her guilt killed her love for me. Watching it die, I felt as did Judas – when it was too late.

"You may remember that that took place in November, 1919. For three years I have lived on the bread-line to advertise an appeal in every Australian paper, and several of the most important papers in England and America; for Veronica Starr escaped from prison before her trial. Yet the keenest brains in the Force failed to trace her for justice's sake, and all my advertising failed to bring me a word for love's sake.

"That was the position until a month ago, when I received a postcard bearing the Manly postmark and the words in Veronica's hand: 'Centre D F, No. 4, Myers's Atlas.'"

"A bit of a puzzle," Bennett remarked.

"Yes, yet a simple one," agreed Hogarth. "Obtaining a Myers's Atlas, I found that each map was numbered and that the longitudes and latitudes were lettered. No. 4 map was that of South Australia, whilst the centre of the square formed by D longitude and F latitude is a point about eighty miles west of the South Australian border fence and on the same degree of latitude as White Cliffs."

The big man's eyes opened widely for a moment.

"That will be about the north end of Lake Frome," he drawled. "Surely you don't expect to find Miss Storr there, do you?"

"I hardly know what to expect," quietly replied the other. "That Veronica wrote that postcard is certain."

"Yes, that may be so," Bennett as quietly agreed; "yet Miss Storr being at the north end of Lake Frome is as improbable as Miss Storr being at the South Pole. Lake Frome is merely a vast mud-flat surrounded by sixth-class cattle country and very little water. To my knowledge there is only an old hut on the west shore. What-in-hell would a woman be doing there – and a city woman, too? That postcard was a joke."

"I have tried to think so," Hogarth said, looking sombrely into the fire. "Yet she is not the sort of woman to joke. It may be that some form of revenge lies behind the implied command that I've to go there."

"The books say that hell let loose is a Sunday-school outing compared with a woman scorned," murmured the big man. "Better go east than west."

"Impossible! I am but a needle attracted by the magnet of Lake Frome," expostulated Hogarth with sudden passion; then, after a long pause, he continued more quietly:

"You see, Cass, at Broken Hill I heard two men talking about Bennett of the Corner. At Nilparinka I again heard of Cass Bennett of the Corner. Every one appeared to be bosom friends of Cass Bennett, who seemed to be the virtual king of the north-west corner of New South Wales. And when I persuaded a half-drunken stockman on a spree to describe Cass Bennett, I knew it was the same Bennett who fought with me in France."

"You flatter me," ejaculated the bushman drily, but Hogarth, not noticing the interjection, went on:

"They told me that what you did not know about Central Australia was forgotten by most. That fact, and because I am an utter new-chum in the bush, brought me to you. If you have nothing on hand, Cass, take me to that place. If you cannot, I must go alone, and probably stay there."

The big man rolled and lit a cigarette before replying, avoiding Hogarth's anxious eyes, hesitating not because he was reluctant to comply with such an appeal, but because he knew that no rain had fallen for eleven months and that the state of the water-holes was problematical. Yet somehow he felt incapable of refusing. To Cass Bennett the lure of adventure ever was irresistible.

"We'll start in the morning," he said abruptly. "But I think we shall be a couple of fools."

If the heat, the flies and the wind-blown sand make Central Australia more than unpleasant during the spring, summer and autumn months, the keen, clear atmosphere of the winter days are a joy beyond description.

As promised to Hogarth, the big man broke his camp on the Yandama Creek in the far north-west of New South Wales, and five days later the pair arrived at a point some fifteen miles east of Lake Frome in South Australia.

They had eaten their midday meal on the sixth day and were sitting in the lee of a sandhill – for a cold south wind was blowing – enjoying an after-dinner smoke, when with a sound like a wet bag struck by a stick one of the pack-camels fell on its side and died.

The two travellers, having fought in France, knew instinctively what had happened two seconds before the far-off report of a rifle reached their ears.

"Somebody shooting!" yelled the big man. "Get the mokes over to the other side of the hill, quick!"

Without panic they rushed to the camels, kicked them to their feet – at which moment Hogarth's riding-beast dropped with a smashed leg – and dragged them up the steep, sandy slope to the summit. A bullet whined past Bennett's hip and another struck the loading of the last pack animal before it slid down beyond the summit into safety.

"Now, what-in-hell's that for?" demanded Bennett angrily. "There ain't no fighting blacks here."

"It is a riddle."

"Yep! And a riddle we've got to find an answer for mighty quick," snapped the bushman, "hooshing" the riding-beast down on its knees. With quick fingers he unstrapped his beloved 25/30 calibre Savage rifle, a weapon of long range firing a deadly high-powered bullet.

With it he reclimbed the sandhill with cat-like stealth, finally crouching behind a yellow-flowering cotton-bush growing on the summit, from which he commanded a clear view across a three-hundred-yard flat to the next sandhill. Not a thing moved: yet that opposite sandhill could well cover a battalion. Hogarth, who had climbed up beside him, said caustically:

"Didn't know you had any bad men in these parts."

"Well, this bush country ain't exactly renowned for killings," Bennett admitted. "Still, if it comes to shooting, we can knock spots off them romantic cowboys 'way down Texas."

"Seen anything of the polite gentleman?"

"No, or now he would be a corpse," replied Bennett grimly. "And if he isn't a corpse mighty quick we stand a chance of being stiffened ourselves, for he may well double across yonder flat higher up, where we shouldn't see him, and plug us in the back from that near sandhill."

"M'yes," mused Hogarth. "It's not a pleasant situation. What about digging in?"

"No use. We couldn't stop dug in, 'cos we're short of water."

Being in country where the attacker has all the advantage, their position was serious, as Bennett fully realised. For miles northward and southward the moving red sandhills ran in parallel lines east and west. The lack of water compelled them to push on to Lake Frome, where Bennett was sure water-holes existed.

The old trick of pushing a hat up on the end of a stick failed to draw the enemy's fire, which would have revealed his whereabouts.

"I'll dash down to the dead beast," suggested Hogarth. "That ought to tempt him."

"You'll get holed for a cent," snapped Bennett.

"He has missed us if he has hit the camels. To draw his fire quick is our only chance. If we don't, he'll pot us from a different angle. I'm going. Look out!"

The city man, without further word, dashed over the summit and down the further slope in full view of the sniper, who was tempted and fell. Bennett's steady eyes, as keen and unwinking as those of an eagle-hawk, saw a dull thin haze made by an exploded cartridge just beside a dead buckbush growing on the opposite ridge a little to his left. His rifle cracked a fraction of a second before the enemy's bullet, grazing Hogarth's chest, put a merciful end to the wounded camel.

The bushman rose and walked casually down the slope, to the astonishment of his companion, who had taken cover behind the dead beast.

"Did you get him?" asked Hogarth.

"You bet."

"He showed himself, then?"

"Hope, but I planked a bullet an inch above his rifle-sights."

"But you might have 'missed him, man. Take care!"

"Missed him! You can't miss with this kind of rifle, old feller-me-lad," Bennett assured him. "He's busted all right. Let's go over and screw him off."

Dubiously Hogarth accompanied the casual bushman across the intervening flat, and up the slope to the buckbush, and found beyond it the body of a man dressed as a stockman. The light-blue eyes were glazing; the open mouth revealed the acutely-receding chin.

"By heaven! that's Marshall," Hogarth ejaculated.

"What's he supposed to be when he's home?"

"He was the murderer of Elsie Wentworth."

"The little Melbourne kid?"

"The same. I've seen his photograph at police headquarters."

"What do they generally get for hanging murderers?" asked Bennett softly.

"Why?"

"'Cos I'm going to claim the union wages,"

"Let us hope you will succeed in obtaining them," remarked a bland voice just behind them.

Bennett swung round, his rifle leaping to his right hip, his finger finding the trigger. Only an unusual hesitation saved from sudden death a tall, white-haired man who stood leaning on a gold-handled walking-stick and beaming at them benevolently.

"It is possible I'll draw overtime wages, too," snapped the big man with deadly coldness. "Who are you?"

"My name is Sylvester Crystal."

"Snakes' lips!" exclaimed the amazed Hogarth. "The 'Frisco millionaire who poisoned three wives and got away with it?"

"I was obliged, certainly, to put three women to slight inconvenience," came the bland reply. "You, I presume, are Mr. Daniel Hogarth. We expected you, but" – turning to Bennett – "I have not the pleasure of –"

"My name's Bennett – Cass Bennett."

"Indeed! Assuredly I am honoured," Crystal went on, with a smile of childish pleasure lighting up his brilliant blue eyes. "I am sure that that miserable slayer of little children would not have fired off his pop-gun had he known you were in the vicinity. He was asked to come and look out for Mr. Hogarth, you see, and, I suppose, seeing you with him, considered it advisable to – ah! – meet only Mr. Hogarth."

For the first time in his life Bennett was speechless.

"Let us not, however, tarry here," Crystal went on, "but gather up your camels, which I saw you hurry over the hill when Marshall became rude, and allow me the pleasure of escorting you to the Murderers' Home, which is but four miles further on."

"Say! have you ever been in a mental hospital?" Bennett demanded.

Sylvester Crystal smiled again.

"I am afraid that a jury could never be convinced that I had."

"Let me advise you, then, to play no tricks," the big man told him grimly. "When I start shooting, people don't roll over like they do in your moving pictures. They just drops."

Although Cass Bennett was outwardly as calm and deadly as a tiger-snake, yet, he admitted to himself, he was astounded. In the first place, there was the surprise of being shot at deliberately in country which he thought quite uninhabited. Came then Hogarth's identification of a particularly noxious murderer, followed closely by the encounter with the infamous American millionaire whose killings were the talk of the world just prior to the German offensive in 1918.

To meet such a man, dressed faultlessly in a navy blue lounge suit, wearing a panama hat and spats over brilliantly-polished boots, and negligently carrying a gold-mounted black malacca cane there in Australia's "back of beyond" where even the blacks cannot find sustenance, would give any man just cause for inquiry as to his own sanity.

Twenty minutes later, whilst they walked on each side of the amiable Crystal, Bennett said:

"A while ago you mentioned a Murderers' Home. Just what do you mean by that?"

"Precisely what the plain words convey," came the smooth voice. "It has always been a happy custom of wealthy citizens of my country to endow homes for all sorts of people; and, when I found it inconveniently necessary to retire from open social life, I at once discovered the need of a kind of home, not only for myself, but also for others similarly situated."

"Hell's hell!" muttered Bennett.

"On the contrary, my Murderers' Home is built and run on lavish lines. I have been told that it approximates to Paradise. But to resume.

"Of necessity, such a home must be assured of perfect seclusion. I found, unfortunately, that the Southern States of America are now too crowded to afford that seclusion. Another factor that decided me against the States was my inherent dislike of home-made whisky. South America did not suit my health, whilst the Pacific islands, I am told, are not a little relaxing.

"An experienced friend recommended Central Australia; and here we are. It required considerable organisation and expenditure to arrange matters, as you may guess – but I need not go into details. Of course, the Home built, it was necessary to fill it with inmates who required monastic seclusion. I found my Home only needed to be made known to be appreciated. It is represented in every Australian city, and when a citizen becomes socially embarrassed means are taken to advise him of my Home and its facilities, and, should he be interested, to organise his safe arrival here. Yet," and he sighed deeply, "some of my inmates unfortunately leave when they consider they are sufficiently forgotten; but all affirm emphatically that they would rather be in my Home than dead.

"I observe, Mr. Bennett, that you are a little sceptical," remarked the millionaire, intercepting a ponderous wink from the giant bushman.

"Not at all," drawled Bennett smiling.

"Mr. Hogarth, being a member of the Secret Service and in constant touch with police headquarters, will certainly recognise some of my guests," Crystal proceeded. "You will meet O'Halloran, who shot dead the Adelaide bank manager, and Cornell the Bathurst grocer, who, being interested in chemistry, experimented on his mistress with arsenic. Then there is Blackburn, who strangled the miser at Mt. Gambier with great artistry, and Horwood, who killed the mine paymaster at Cloncurry – really a most interesting man when he discourses on bibliology.

"You have already met Marshall and myself. Oh! I – forgot – my memory is not what it used to be – Mr. Hogarth will certainly recognize Miss Starr, who shot the blackmailer."

Hogarth was dumbfounded. If this bland individual was indeed Sylvester Crystal and he spoke the unvarnished truth, it would appear that they were walking into a spider's parlour. The mystery of the many unsolved murders of recent years was laid bare with a vengeance, and his doubts concerning their immediate future were expressed by his burly companion when he said:

"Don't you think, Mr. Crystal, that if you are speaking the simple darned truth you are very unwise? Neither Hogarth nor myself are qualified to become inmates of your Home. A word from us, and up goes a 'To Let' notice."

"Wisdom is deeper than the ocean and higher than the mountains," replied Crystal gently. "Wisdom is man's greatest asset, followed closely by tact. Allow me to think I have sufficient wisdom to discern tactfulness in you, Mr. Bennett. I feel positively certain you would never be so tactless as to make any suggestion to my guests of informing the authorities of their present – ah! – whereabouts."

"I wasn't thinking of making any suggestions to your guests, but rather to the john-hops," grimly persisted the big man.

"Do not, I pray you, discourse further upon so unpleasant a subject," admonished the millionaire; adding a moment later, with a wave of a gloved hand: "Behold! the Murderers' Home!"

The sandhills flanking the flat they were traversing ended abruptly and they emerged on the edge of a vast expanse of mud-covered country, stretching to the southern and western horizons. In a dim long-ago sun-kissed waves of liquid sapphire covered it before the waters fell to the level of a fetid swamp wherein wallowed gigantic reptiles. To-day remains but a mud-covered waste that supports only the prowling dingoes on their especially-chosen pads – a huge relentless death-trap for venturesome horses and cattle – Lake Frome.

Between the lake proper and the bluffs of the encircling sand-hills was a deep ribbon of firm, red, sandy flats, and on one of these, exposed to the full fury of the western storms, was built a spacious bungalow-house, surrounded by outbuildings and stockyards. A bore brought up an unfailing supply of water from two thousand feet below.

Outside the white-painted ornamental fence surrounding the house they "hooshed" down the camels and followed Crystal across the twenty-foot verandah, through a spacious hall and into one of the most luxurious rooms Bennett, at least, ever had seen.

A magnificent tapestry portraying the coronation of Louis XV completely covered one wall. On the opposite wall hung authentic paintings by Raphael, da Vinci and Correggio. From the other walls hung a superb collection of weapons. In one corner a priceless vase of ancient porphyry carved with figures of Roman divinities stood on a pedestal of rosy marble; on another an ebony table after Jean Gaujon supported half-a-dozen wonderfully carved shrines. Magnificent Persian carpets covered the floor, luxurious lounges and low-hung chairs invited repose, a great wood fire in the open hearth made a cheerful glow.

"This, gentlemen, is our reception-room," Crystal announced. "Take your ease here by the fire. If you will excuse me for half-a-minute, I will bring you some light refreshment. We stock an excellent brand of whisky, and, of course, the very best cigars. You understand we have no servants." With which he disappeared between a pair of green velvet curtains.

"I may be having a nightmare or I may not; but, when you see me rubbing my hands together like a Jew hawker, be prepared for a mix-up," Bennett whispered.

Hogarth had just time to nod comprehension before the millionaire returned and attended them with expertness and grace, the while extolling the beauties of his Home.

"Have no fear of poison," he remarked genially, "we never inconvenience our guests . . .

"I must leave you now," the remarkable man said half an hour later, after he had shown them a vacant shed wherein they could stow their gear and a paddock where water and scant feed were to be had by the camels. "When you have unearthed your personal belongings, come into the house and make it your own. I must see Murchison – the garrotter, you know. He is our cook and is really superb. Au revoir!"

"Dan! tell me if I have a wild look in my eyes," commanded Bennett, when Sylvester Crystal was out of hearing.

"They appear steady enough," Hogarth assured him with a sudden laugh. "But I shall soon begin to believe we are dead, or some-thing to that effect. He's got ten fortunes in that reception-room alone. What do you make of it all?"

"Don't ask me, or I shall fall down. I'm seeing it through. I am going to enjoy myself, I'm sure."

"I am going to see it through with you," Hogarth remarked later when, the camels having been hobbled out, they were sorting out their gear. "If the garrotting cook don't experiment on us with strychnine, I'll see Veronica or burn the place down."

The city man produced a vicious-looking automatic from a suitcase, and with a broad grin Bennett adjusted a Smith and

Wesson beneath his left armpit under his coat. After ramming a handful of shells into his trousers pocket, he and Hogarth made their way to the house. Crystal met them in the hall, and conducted them to a spacious bedroom containing two beds.

"I trust you will find everything you require,' he said with his affable smile. Parting some hanging curtains, he revealed a room fitted with a large alabaster-lined Grecian bath in the centre of the tiled floor. "Unfortunately, the days are now so short that it will not be possible to show you round my – er – hobby, as it were. To-morrow, perhaps. Miss Storr tells me she will be pleased to see you both in half an hour. If you will permit me, I will conduct you then to her apartment. Afterwards, dinner."

"Humph!" Bennett grunted. "You'll see that your lady-like cook don't mix strychnine with the soup? I hate having my innards disturbed."

"Tut, tut! My dear Mr. Bennett!" replied a horrified host. "Have I not assured you we never inconvenience our guests?"

Saying which, he withdrew somewhat ruffled.

"Well, I'm for that bath – I like to die clean," grinned the big man; whereon Hogarth advised sardonically:

"Put your finger in it first. It might be an unpleasant acid."

At the appointed time Sylvester Crystal led them down a marble stairway and along a passage, twenty feet below the ground floor, which gave entry to the summer rooms which, he assured them, were always below 70° Fah. Throwing open a door at the end of the passage, he announced them with his usual blandness.

The door closed softly behind them, leaving them gazing down an abnormally long room, furnished more luxuriously than even the reception-room. From the high ceiling a cluster of gold-tinted electric lamps shed soft radiance on silk-upholstered furniture, silken hangings, silk-covered divans and cushions – yellow silk. On the floor were jet-black carpets.

But their eyes sensed only the general magnificence and colour, for their gaze became rivetted on a deep alcove, or rather miniature stage, at the further end of the long room. Invisible electric lamps shone down on an orange-coloured silk-lined Chesterfield set on a golden Chinese carpet. And reclining on the couch was a woman.

"Will Mr. Hogarth and Mr. Bennett be pleased to come a little nearer?" called a mocking voice, low and vibrating.

Somehow it was Bennett who advanced first down the room, and, when they came before the foot-high stage or alcove it was Bennett who, towering above her, caught first her mocking eyes.

"Evidently, Mr. Bennett, you have the greater courage," she said, looking at him quizzically.

"It takes all I've got to look at you, marm," Bennett replied with disarming gentleness.

Before him reclined the loveliest woman he ever had seen, and, when he gazed into her eyes, the most terrible. Her hair was glinting bronze, her mouth a luscious fruit, her eyes green as emeralds held within their limpid depths all the winningness and wickedness of femininity since Mother Eve first tempted man. Wantonly she lay, her head resting against an orange-coloured cushion, her exquisite form arrayed in an orange-coloured wrapper which revealed the marble whiteness of her arms and breasts. One foot, stretched along the divan, was innocent of shoe and stocking; the other, hanging negligently over the side, was bare to the knee.

"So, Mr. Hogarth, you received the postcard written by a murderess?" she mocked. "The poodle-dog answered its mistress's whistle?"

"Veronica!" he said, pain in the timbre of his voice.

"Cur!"

Bennett glanced instinctively from her to his companion. Hogarth stood rigid and deathly pale. When he looked again at the woman he was shocked at the passion which marred the wondrous beauty of her face.

"Did you think that the woman who loved you, who would have bartered her soul to purchase you a pleasure, who would have died gladly by the rope had you but believed in her, would await you with open arms? Did you?"

"Veronica!" The name came sharply, agony in the tone of the man's voice.

"Look at me! Look at what was yours! See these limbs, this beauty which ravishes men, which you cast aside by your unbelief. My love would have swept you into the innermost recesses of Paradise; your love, sir, failed at the first gust of the storm."

She laughed, and her laughter turned Bennett cold.

"If you had loved me as I loved you, you would have disbelieved your eyes had you seen me actually commit the deed. Not as a rock before the tempest defying its fury, but as a thin dead reed were you. Bah!

"I sent for you, not for the pleasure of your company, but to give you these," and she tossed a bundle of letters contemptuously at his feet. "They are your letters, and with them is a confession, witnessed by reputable people, and signed by the man who shot the inquiry agent in my room and escaped out of the window, two seconds before the door was burst open. Not knowing what I did, I picked up my own revolver which he had flung down."

With visible effort Hogarth spoke low and rapidly.

"Will you not listen to my defence, Veronica?"

"What defence can you have?" she answered with blazing eyes. Nestling further down among the cushions, she yawned deliberately and insultingly.

"If you had seen the evidence as I saw it, you would understand that no man could have believed otherwise," Hogarth went on. "I will explain in detail if you will let me, and then I know you will not think me so vile. I assure you it made no difference whatever to my love."

"Please go!" The words came from her trembling lips as the hiss of a snake.

"Come, Dan, the lady is feeling unwell, I am sure," Bennett urged in a fatherly tone.

Her eyes but mere pin-points of emerald fire, she languidly pressed an electric button at the head of the couch, when instantly the door was thrown open and there entered six men, led by the millionaire himself.

"Remove these persons," commanded the woman coldly.

With the exception of Crystal the men were dressed as stockmen. Indeed it was evident that they occupied their time among cattle. The millionaire had changed into a dinner-jacket. His expression had its usual blandness, and, stepping towards Bennett, he said softly:

"If you care to accompany me, Mr. Bennett, I could interest you, I am sure, in my small but unique collection of miniatures."

But the giant's intention to withdraw was modified when the Cloncurry murderer, a good-looking, open-faced man of about thirty-five years, interjected bluntly:

"To the devil with your fine words, Crystal! Let us be honest with ourselves as well as these strangers. They have got to die, and the sooner the better. Even Miss Storr advises their removal."

At this announcement the others murmured approval, but the woman sat up suddenly, all colour drained from her face.

"Not here, I implore you," Crystal said in alarm. "Even a snail scarlet stain would ruin this priceless carpet. Please, gentlemen, let us withdraw."

Bennett was washing his hands with invisible water, an immense grin widening his rugged features. The woman shrieked out in fear and horror:

"No, no! I did not mean murder –"

Her words were drowned by Bennett's great laugh. Even in his laugh he sprang to the alcove. A bullet from his revolver crashed along the electrics, followed by a blue flash of fused wires. Then impenetrable darkness.

Things happened in split seconds. A flicker of flame preceded a second report, and Hogarth cried out. Then the sound of a body falling.

As if turned to stone, Veronica Storr crouched on the Chesterfield with bated breath. Mighty arms suddenly wound about her, and she was swept up and borne through the darkness. Some one crashed into her, then her body was jarred by contact with the wall. Another flicker of flame showed men crouching before the air rocked with the report. She heard the door wrenched open, had a vision of a long passage with dim daylight lighting marble steps at the further end. The next minute she found herself standing alone in the passage, with the slam of the door singing in her ears.

On the further side of the door a revolver shot rang out. A moment's deathly silence followed, and after that came a man's laugh, a loud laugh of supreme joy. Two further shots were fired in quick succession. A man screamed. Vivid curses came through the thick door. A bullet tore a hole in it, speeding past her along the passage till it smashed against the steps. Then silence. Again that enormous laugh. Another shot, then Bedlam itself let loose. Men shouted and screamed, screamed with terror, with insanity, with agony.

The door crashed open. Through the mist which swam before her eyes she saw the millionaire standing facing her on the threshold, abject fear shining in his wide blue eyes.

A revolver cracked. Crystal suddenly smiled, his old innocent smile, and died on the spot.

Silence again, a long silence this time, whilst Veronica Starr stared fascinated at the black aperture of the open door. A minute passed – two, three, five minutes.

Suddenly Cass Bennett appeared, walking swiftly towards her, his fine face covered with blood, which failed to conceal the happy grin.

"Glorious days, warm," he drawled. "Have you got a match about you? The light's busted."

Uncomprehendingly she whispered:

"Dan! what has happened to Dan?"

Slipping past his detaining hand, she ran to the door, fearlessly stepping over the dead body of the millionaire, and disappeared within the darkened room, where yet a conscious brain could direct a finger on a trigger.

When no shot followed her disappearance, the big man searched several rooms cautiously, on the look out for any possible enemies who had not been with Crystal. Meeting none, he returned at last carrying an oil-lamp.

And amid the shambles in that magnificent boudoir he found Veronica Starr cradling Hogarth's head in her arms, and kissing the blood-tinged lips. Her love had triumphed, and the light of it had guided her to him.

"Dear God!" she moaned with strange reverence, "let him live!"

Six weeks later she and Hogarth stood on the broad verandah, dressed for departure. Beyond the garden fence lay a string of loaded camels. Near them stood the garrotter, his hands in roughly-made handcuffs, his feet weighted by bullock-chains. Beside him was the man who killed the bank manager, with both arms in splints.

Bennett was erecting a board at the fence, a board on which was painted in huge, blood-red characters the announcement:

TO LET

A Desert Flower

It was like finding a nugget of gold, by chance kicked up from the dust of a dry track. It was like seeing the green freshness of Gippsland after long sojourn in drought-gripped Western Queensland. The large, oval-shaped lake was stained the colour of port wine by the scarlet sky above the westering sun, a lake surrounded by a narrow snow-white sand beach barring back the vivid green of gum trees.

While six camels were each taking in sixteen gallons of pure fresh water, Silent Mark and his companion stared over this bush jewel to the brilliant tapestry before which it lay, a towering breakaway, or land step, fully a hundred and fifty feet high.

"Looks good to me, Joe," Mark called loudly as four of the camels interposed between him and the aborigine who had been his friend and partner for several years.

"Good-o Mark-boss, orl right. Funny, though."

"What's funny?"

"Plenty of water, plenty of ducks and swans, plenty of 'roos and turkeys, but no blackfeller. Funny, no blackfeller," replied Joe, with a trace of anxiety in his liquid voice, anxiety strangely at odds in the setting of this bush picture.

The rugged, grey-eyed bushman made no further comment. The camels continued steadily to drink. Below the uproar of screeching cockatoos could be heard the more musical cries of the water birds. This was the smiling bush at its very best; on the surface it was peaceful and secure and friendly, but beneath the surface . . .

The sun-painted face of the breakaway was as brilliant as the scenery of an Eastern play. The westering sun, filtering its light through the smoky heat haze, illuminated the breakaway with soft golden radiance, revealing every protuberance and cavity and crevice, banishing all shadow. Along its flat summit sprouted a fringe of low scrub, dark at foot, grey-green on top. The upper strata of red ironstone, shot with white quartz, rested on a deeper strata of dove-grey granite. Here and there masses of rubble lay

95

against the cliff, and from this rubble, as well as from veins in the ironstone, countless mica particles reflected the sunlight with sparks of crimson, blue, white and amber.

The camels having drunk their fill, the two men led them back from the water across the white sand beach and in among the wide-spaced gums which, on account of the pigweed and the wild spinach, looked much like oaks in an English deer park. The beasts were hungry and anxious to feed, and they voiced impatience when the pack loads and the saddles were being removed.

"No bells," Silent Mark decided. Then, when the six beasts had been hobbled: "I'll make camp, Joe. You scout around and have a look-see. Leave one dog; take the other."

Joe laughed for no apparent reason, unless to hide the degree of nervousness created by this too peaceful scene, swiftly rolled a cigarette, chained one of the two intelligent cattle dogs to a sapling, and, with the other running ahead of him, set off to read what might be written on the news sheets of the bush. Knowing that the chained dog instantly would detect stalking wild blacks, Mark proceeded to arrange the heavy pack-saddles and long iron riding saddles into a rough barricade topped with the loading. Within its shelter he presently lit a fire from the store of tinder-dry, smokeless wood he had gathered with great care.

Never before had he seen the alleged desert in such excellent condition. Never during his long association with the dry lands which lie west of Central Australia had he found travelling so free from anxiety regarding the state of water holes and feed for his camels. The much-maligned interior of Australia, never a real desert at any time, was now a garden of bush and grass and herbage. The flies would have annoyed the newchum, and the dry heat would have tried him to the point of tempting him to rush back to the city, but these slight distractions had no effect on such as Silent Mark.

Mark was a prospector with a hobby. Away westward, in Laverton, he was known as "Silent" Mark because he never divulged information concerning his trips into the dry lands between that outpost of civilisation and the South Australian border. For all the information that Joe gave they might have called him "Silent" Joe, too.

Yes, Mark had a hobby. His vocation was prospecting for gold and tin; and his hobby was nothing less than the discovery of Leichhardt's box. The beginning of the hobby dated back to 1922 when first he had heard of it from a dying blackfellow in the Miller breakaway country. Between that year and this he had made repeated attempts to get farther east, but always had the quickly emptying water holes sent him back. Now abnormal winter and spring rains had permitted him to come within one hundred miles of the South Australian border in January when there was no prospect of being forced back for several months.

That Dr. Ludwig Leichhardt had set off to explore the interior from Western Queensland to the Swan River, Western Australia, in 1848, and that after leaving Cecil Plains nothing further was ever heard of him and his companions, are merely historical facts. What has provided ground for speculation is the exact locality where that ill-fated expedition came to a final halt. The question has ever been asked: How far across Australia did Leichhardt get before he suffered defeat and death?

Somewhere had the expedition finally halted, the members of it to struggle on a little way and die. Somewhere in northern South Australia or eastern Western Australia must still remain evidence of that expedition – if a moving sandhill has not rolled forward to obliterate it.

Then, in 1922, Silent Mark heard, from the lips of an old man left peacefully to die beside an emptied rock-hole, "of four big rings and a heavy iron box lying close to the edge of a deep hole far beyond the Miller Breakaway." Seven years later he heard the same story from a lubra he had found shockingly burned through having rolled into the camp fire in her sleep.

Experience had long since shown that kindness to the wild people always pays, because kindness and gifts of food is rewarded by little news items of the demi-desert – information sometimes of great value. With the years Silent Mark's hobby became a passion, heated by the constant victories of the dry lands which drove him always back. Until now, when abnormal rains opened wide the gates to the dry lands to such as he.

Beside a deep hole in the ground, which now and then held

water, lay rusting four iron waggon wheel tyres and a black iron box so heavy that the blacks had been unable to open it or to carry it away. There is no record of any expedition having to abandon a bullock or horse waggon in the dry lands between Western and Central Australia, and it could be naturally inferred that the tyres and box reported by the blacks represented all that was left of the great German scientist's expedition.

The bounteous rains had filled the rock-holes to overflowing. They had filled land depressions which had not held water for a century. They had brought up with amazing abundance the grass and herbage, and had given a fresh spurt to bush and tree. This had attracted game from great distances, and it had, too, allowed the scattered families of blacks to congregate into their tribes.

Thus was Silent Mark hopeful of discovering Leichhardt's box, and thus the reason for his unease at the absence of blacks where they should have been found in the vicinity of a magnificent lake of water in January. Not that he wanted them to be massed about this lake, but rather that it is as well to know what disguise the devil is wearing and to know just where he is.

He had washed at the lake's edge and had set out the eating utensils and the food on a sheet of waterproof beside the tucker box when Joe returned. Then the surface of the lake was rapidly being drained of its wine colouring, was being paved with silver. The edge of shadow lay half way up the breakaway, cast there by the sun setting beyond the great western salt-and-blue-bush plains which extend to Miller's Breakaway.

"All jake," Joe said succinctly, and, because Mark merely nodded, he untied the towel fastened to his swag and with it followed the dogs to the water. His hobby was to put on a clean shirt every morning, but as he rarely possessed more than one shirt, not an easy one to follow. Mark smiled when he saw this admirable station black remove his shirt and start washing it before he thought of eating. Then he joined the dogs swimming in the silvered water, and he came back all smiles. The dogs came, too, to rest their heads on forepaws, waiting for tit-bits to be tossed them.

"No blackfeller round here, I reckon," he announced as he poured tea from billy to tin pannikin. "Plenty tracks two, t'ree weeks old."

White man and black man ate quickly and silently. Both were a little uneasy, because puzzled. Mark never remembered visiting any large sheet of water where blacks were not numerous about it, and here was a magnificent water supply which had been in existence for months and which would last for three or four years.

"I climbed a dead tree and took a look-see," Joe said at last. Pointing southward, he went on: "Along there lake go for p'haps a mile." Then to westward: "Back there long rise to salt-bush plain we come over." When he pointed to the north, he added: "Plenty big sandhills come in from the plain to meet the breakaway. Maybe that Leichhardt feller come to top of breakaway to see the plain and this here lake full of water. Maybe he found a way down the breakaway for the waggon, and then, come along over them sandhills to camp near the lake. P'haps then not too much water in the lake, and the wild blacks fight him for it. 'Member that old feller left to die beside the water hole said that waggon tyres and box lay near sandhills at north end of big hole in the ground?"

"Maybe," Silent Joe echoed. "Somehow I think this is the hole in the ground. It would be a hole if there wasn't any water in it. How far are those sandhills away?"

"'Bout a mile."

"Then the lake is two miles long and, I should say, three quarters of a mile at its widest part. Well, it looks as though we are going to get peace searching for that box old Leichhardt left me to find. That box is going to make us famous, Joe, my lad. And it's going to make us rich, too, because the authorities will pay well for the old German's journals – if they can still be read."

"Too right," Joe agreed, although he did not properly understand just how "lost whitefeller papers" would enrich them. "What about catchin' some of them ducks bime by?"

An hour later the moon rose above the breakaway lip to paint the lake with silver and to tip the gum leaves with diamonds. Mark considered it safe to leave the camp in charge of the dogs that would sound the alarm, and they were looking forward to the sport of swimming towards the ducks, then diving beneath them and stalking them under water to catch them by the legs.

The dogs had been chained each to a tree, one north and the other south of the camp, and the men began to strip. Then, first one and then both the dogs began to bark. Neither animal would Mark have sold for less than a fortune, for they had been especially trained to scout ahead when he and Joe were travelling, and to bark only if a black-fellow approached a camp. Now they were barking.

In ten seconds both men were half-dressed again and crouching behind the barricade of gear, each with a Savage high-power rifle in hands, and an automatic in its holster strapped to Mark's waist. Nothing happened. There came no flight of spears to be followed by a rush of yelling blacks. The dogs ceased to bark and gave vent to uneasy yaps.

"What are you doing?" Mark demanded without turning round when behind him Joe began to shuffle.

"Puttin' on me shirt, Mark-boss," Joe replied, actually chuckling. "I ain't 'spectable.'"

"Well, keep your eyes in use. Those dogs wouldn't bark for pleasure."

A moment later, Joe snapped out: "Hey! Look at breakaway!"

A flame, a tongue of scarlet, shot up from the crest of the breakaway. It leaped higher and yet higher and broadened until it illuminated the bordering scrub and lay a dancing finger of crimson across the lake to point accusingly at them.

"Fire signal!" Joe exclaimed. "Now whaffor they signal with fire?"

"Search me!" Mark said wonderingly. "Be ready for a rush, and aim low. These rifles are inclined to shoot high over the first hundred yards."

Another flame shot skyward. A second fire sent its smoke pluming to kiss the moon.

"Fire signal all right. Two fires mean: Come quick," Joe pointed out. "That's blacks over there calling to blacks way out somewheres on the plain."

Still the night continued tranquil, its hush disturbed only by the feeding water birds.

"Mark-boss, you hear that?" Joe whispered.

"No. What?"

"Singing. Some lubra's singing." Mark listened intently. Ah

yes! He could hear it now. Someone on the far side of the lake, beneath the spreading fires on the breakaway, was singing.

Now Silent Mark had often heard lubras singing, but he knew that he had never heard them singing like this. Presently he realised that but one woman was singing, and that the song she sang was familiar, hauntingly familiar. Then the singing voice died away. The dogs began again their half-hearted yaps.

"This act is all wrong, Joe," he said impatiently. "No spears, no yells, no blacks. Only a couple of bonfires and an artist doing her stuff. Don't seem right to me. Now –"

From across the water it came, the most amazing thing in all Mark's long experience of the dry lands. Down along the scarlet path of the reflected fires came drifting the woman's voice, clear and strong. Mark stood up and actually gaped.

"Yon Brown's donkey's got a wooden leg, Yon Brown's donkey's got a wooden leg –"

"Stiffen the crows!" hissed between Mark's lips.

"– Yon Brown's donkey's got a wooden leg, As 'e goes marchin' on."

It was a beautiful voice, although the expert would have detected that it was untrained. Then from the slowly moving dark blobs which represented ducks on the water, they distinguished one which came steadily onward towards them. Thirty seconds later they saw that it was the head of a swimming woman who sang:

"Yon Brown's donkey's got a wooden leg –"

Joe raised his rifle, but Mark was in time to push down the barrel. Amazement was giving place to curiosity, and curiosity to chagrin. It seems that after all he was not in country thought to be virgin to such as he was. After all he had been forestalled by a party of prospectors among whom was this woman. That she was white he no longer doubted.

They saw presently a figure rise Venus-like from the shallows and come wading to the lake's edge. The moon's rays proved her to be white, for she wore only a short knee-high skirt. Her singing stopped and she called out loudly:

"Where are you, white men?"

The moonlight fell upon her from behind shadowing her face but glinting on the great mound of hair. Save for the skirt of plaited grass her body was naked and shown to be youthful. She was white and the dogs had known it. It was the uncanny knowledge of the dogs which was uppermost in Mark's mind at this instant.

"Where are you, white men?" she called again.

With Joe behind him, Silent Mark went forward to meet her and, when she saw them, her hands swiftly rose to her head. A gold-tinged cloud of hair fell about her to cover her almost to her knees. Mark said with effort:

"Good evening!"

Across a space of five feet they regarded each other, steadily and without speaking. She saw a man in his early thirties, a lithe man, clean shaven, stern and, to her, radiating a strange personal force. He saw a girl not yet twenty. She was not markedly good looking, but her eyes were big and their splendour matched her hair.

"Good evening!" he repeated.

"Oh! Oh, yes! I remember! Good evening!" she replied, and smiled. "We saw you this morning. We watched you come down the slope from the plain, and then we watched you standing beside the strange animals. When I saw them, I knew it was white men with them. My mother told me all about them, but I forget the name. My father had them."

"Camels!" Mark said gravely, wondering how far this apparent joke would be carried.

"Yes. Camels. I remember the name now. My mother told me to go to the first camels I saw, because with them would be white men. She told me that white men would take me away from the blacks to where there are many white people who live in big – There, I've forgotten. Live in big – big whirlies – yes – oh – houses. That's it. Houses!"

Mark waited, the conviction that she was playing a joke beginning to evaporate.

"I sang *Yon Brown's Donkey* so that you would not kill me. My mother told me to do that if I went to white people in the dark."

"Your mother was a wise woman," Mark said dryly. "Come back to the camp and tell me all about it."

Two wide shafts of moonlight illuminated the barricade of saddles and gear, and across one saddle was Joe's green and red striped towel. With a little cry, the girl stepped swiftly forward and snatched it up to hold it before her eyes, a soft cry of delight escaping her lips. Then, with the towel still in her hands, she stepped to Silent Mark, and first regarded his khaki drill trousers, and then hesitatingly put forth a hand and fingered his white shirt. From this examination her eyes rose to meet his, and in them he saw the unmistakable wonder controlling her mind.

"Well, who are you?" he asked. "Who lit those signal fires up there?"

"The lubras. They stayed behind with me because Wall-Eyed Geezer said I was not to go on a walkabout with the tribe. When I came away to swim here, they tried to stop me, but I fight them with a waddy. Then they run up to light the signal fires to tell Wall-Eyed Geezer to come back with the tribe. One of the lubras ran off to come round here to stop me reaching you. But you will kill them all, won't you? You will let me stay with you? You will take me away from the blacks, won't you? My mother said if I told all about her and my father that you would be kind to me. You will be kind to me, won't you?"

Silent Mark smiled at her for the first time, and the result was rather astonishing. She threw her arms round him, hugged him, and reaching up, clutched his hair in her fingers and forced his face down that she might kiss him on the lips. When he then tried to put her from him, she sprang back, exclaiming:

"You're like old Wall-Eyed Geezer. When he is very nice to me I kiss him."

To cover his confusion, he said gruffly:

"What's your name? Who are you?"

"Oh! My mother said that because my father was called Yon Brown my name is Alice Brown," she said, the words tumbling from between her lips. "A long time ago my father and my mother were looking for gold – I know where there is plenty – and they were captured by the blacks. My father they killed, but my mother they were kind to. Then I came, and for a long time I was happy with my mother. She told me all about the white peoples and the clothes they wear and the whirlies they live in. When I got to be a big girl, when the young men began to pester me, she – she – she died. The young men wanted me and I hate them. The lubras hate me because the young men wanted me. Only old Wall-Eyed Geezer was always kind to me. Oh, you will love me and be kind to me and take me away, won't you?"

Silent Mark abruptly reached the opinion that she was not acting, that she was speaking the incredible truth. Her suppliant attitude touched him. There was no need for hard thinking about a situation so clear, and about the only possible course open to any decent man to adopt.

He sighed. He would have to abandon the objective of the trip, the objective which had been as a beacon to him for years. The signal fires would bring the blacks, and because they were lit it proved them to be not so far distant. Questioning discovered to him their number as being about two hundred. Well, there are some things a man cannot refuse to do, and making the attempt to take this flower of the desert to civilisation was one of them. Leichhardt's box would have to wait.

"You will be kind to me?" he heard her say again.

She, watching his face, saw his eyes narrow, saw the rock-like outlines of his face disintegrate, soften.

"Yes, I will always be kind to you, Alice," he said, smiling. "We'll start being good right now. Joe, bring in the camels. This is no place for a war."

All night they travelled westward, the dogs running ahead, silent and invisible in the moonlight. Sometimes the girl rode one of the riding beasts, at others she tramped beside Mark and related oddments of her history, which he wove into an amazing pattern.

John Brown, prospector, had foolishly taken his wife with him into the dry lands and, never having been a good mixer, their disappearance passed unnoted. In the attack on his camp he had lost his life, but his wife had been preserved. According to their lights, the blacks were kind to the woman who, being accustomed to the hardships of a prospector's life, was able to survive for sixteen years. The girl grew up to young womanhood, able to speak and think in English, but she had become the desired of several young men, and it was only through the power and the affection of the chief, named Wall-Eyed Geezer by Mrs. Brown, that she had been able to resist them.

Even so, the chief's affection for the white girl would not hold his people in check, whilst it almost certainly would spur him on to take her back. Then there was the white man's treasure of sugar and tea and tobacco of which he would have heard from neighbouring tribes, even had he not sampled John Brown's treasure.

Of a certainty the blacks would swarm after Mark and his companions like a swarm of hornets. He was experienced enough to know that there was no escaping them, and that their chance of survival lay in the choice of ground for the coming battle.

When day broke they were crossing a large area of undulating country supporting buck-bush and offering plenty of brush for a fire. Further west lay a great tract of spinifex wherein danger was certain as offering material for a drive by fire which the blacks would carry out. He ordered a halt on the summit of a low, treeless hill, situated, he estimated, some twenty miles from the lake. They could see the great breakaway lying beneath the sun, and appearing no higher than a house step. From it, and from the north, columns of smoke told of their flight.

"We'll camp here, Joe," Mark said. 'We've got to settle the argument some time somewhere. We'll eat, and after that two of us can sleep while the third shepherds the camels and keeps guard."

Alice busied herself making a smokeless fire while the beasts were unloaded and hobbled out to feed. She cried loudly when the water in the billy boiled, and she gurgled when her mouth was full of sugar. When, later, Mark initiated her in the art of cooking a damper, her nose became powdered with flour. Her surprise and pleasure delighted him. She was so naive and yet so sophisticated in bush lore.

The camels had been brought in and were lying down contentedly chewing their cud, and the three were eating dinner with the two dogs waiting for tit bits, when at a little after five o'clock a column of black figures trailed over a northern rise.

"Well, it's a pity we couldn't leave most of the gear and do some Sheik stuff on the riding camels," Mark said regretfully. "I'd feel real romantic with you, Alice, on the front of my riding saddle galloping across the bushlands."

"Gallop! Them!" ejaculated Joe. "Why, them humpies would gallop all right for a mile, and then they would flop down and stay flopped for a week."

"Just so. Which is why we have to do the Horatio at the Gate act instead. Come on! Get busy."

With loading ropes they lashed the camels' fore-legs so that they would be unable to rise. The packs and gear were built into the usual barricade, and the dogs were chained to it. When the preparations were completed, the blacks were within a quarter of a mile and were beginning to open fanwise to surround the camp. They were all in fighting rig – Mark estimated their force to number one hundred and fifty – and they looked fearsome enough with their bodies lined with copi clay, with spears in their hands and the great murrawirries slipped through belts made with human hair.

It quickly became evident that they knew nothing of long range rifles and softnose, nickel-plated bullets, for they did not delay the attack until after it was dark, and they scorned the slight cover the bare hill afforded. Mark and Joe began to fire steadily and with deadly accuracy. The girl screamed at the rifle reports, and she stopped her ears with her fingers. Her face was flushed, and her eyes shone like twin stars. Bewildered by the reports, she yet was unafraid, and she began to scream defiance when the first flight of spears slipped, silently up the hillside to fall lengthwise on the defenders.

But as the attackers closed in and mounted up the hill, their spears became more deadly. A camel began roaring when mortally hit. The girl snatched up spent spears and threw them back, becoming a very Boadicea and revealing an astonishing expertness with such heavy weapons. The rifles kept up a continuous fire and black after black sagged and fell. Their fellows took not the slightest notice of them, apparently not understanding what had happened to them, and this ignorance of fire-arms, added to their numbers, was a weapon much more powerful than rifles.

They were no miserable, starved desert blacks. These were men of fine physique, made strong and filled out with good living. Over the past six months human laths had become veritable Apollos imbued with the courage of Ulysses. Undaunted by the rifle fire, because thinking that their wounded and killed comrades were merely stunned – if they thought at all – they rushed inward and upward to the centre of their circle with yells of triumph.

A machine gun might have stopped them, but the two rifles which had to be constantly reloaded were unable to cope with the assault. Excitement mastered Joe, causing him to fire high with ever-diminishing effect. Up rushed the painted savages, some to pause an instant to launch spears from the throwing sticks, others whirling about them the big curved murrawirries so like swords.

Cacophony ruled the world: roaring camels and savage shouts, the girl's frenzied screams as she hurled back the spears after which she scrambled, Joe's yells of defiance, and the rifle reports. Mark dropped a huge brute who stood to heave his last spear with his throwing stick. He sensed rather than saw poor Joe go down beneath naked black bodies. He was using his automatic because there now was no time to reload the rifle. And then a whirling shape sprang at him and sent him down into a black pit.

That he was not butchered was due wholly to the girl. With her body she shielded him as she shrieked insults and defiance at those who would have torn her away and whetted their blood-lust. A ferocious black aimed a blow at her head with his murrawirrie, and it would have dashed out her brains had not a man of extraordinary stature driven a spear through his vitals and stood above the girl and the white man she protected.

Not at once, but gradually did the din subside, and, when Silent Mark recovered consciousness, he found himself propped against a pack-saddle and the girl sponging his head with a wetted towel. The blacks were looting his stores with childish glee, their frenzy replaced with avarice which not yet had produced serious quarrels. Standing near, calmly watching the looters, his arms crossed before his cauterised chest, stood the man who had saved the girl's life, the most powerful aborigine Mark ever had beheld.

"Better?" whispered the girl, the excitement still smouldering in her eyes.

Mark groaned. "What about Joe?" he asked.

"They killed him."

A powerful savage hugging a seventy-pound sack of sugar, the contents of which was being carelessly wasted through a hole ripped in the jute fibre, strode to the black giant and began to speak whilst nodding towards the girl. She sprang to the side of the giant and began a tirade which effectively silenced him in possession of the sugar.

The giant stood unmoved, as though he were fashioned of granite, and his passiveness appeared to dare the other, for the lesser man dropped the sugar and sprang forward.

The attacker was but half the age of the giant and was of no mean stature, and when he met the older man the giant's arms opened wide as though they were springs, and as springs the right arm clapped the attacker's body against the cauterised chest as the left hand smacked against the attacker's face, the palm below his chin, the tip of a finger gouging into each of his eyes. The younger man screamed when for him the light went out. He would have screamed again but his neck was snapped like a thong. The body was raised high above the giant's head and flung across a roaring camel into the cold ashes of the camp fire. Then the big man resumed his pose of calm and stern watchfulness. It was as though he had dealt with an annoying ant.

So this was Wall-Eyed Geezer! Without doubt a king among men! Silent Mark lurched to his feet to stand clinging to the pack saddle whilst the scene spun round and round.

The blacks ceased their mad scramble for loot to gather in a bunch and to scowl at their leader. The girl returned to Mark's side. When she spoke she was trembling with indignation.

"That dog demanded me of Wall-Eyed Geezer," she cried passionately. "You see him – Wall-Eyed Geezer? Look at him! He's my father and my mother. Oh! He is strong and brave, and I love him. He take that dog in his arms and break his neck, snip, crack."

When Wall-Eyed Geezer spoke it was seen that he had his followers well whipped. When he pointed at the ground, they obediently squatted, clutching their loot to them like children holding dolls. The passive-seeming chief continued to look at them until, with a quick movement of his feathered head, he turned to regard the girl and Mark. With the facial expression and the vocal tones of a judge summing up at a criminal trial, he spoke. There was not a sound to compete with his voice, for the camels had ceased to complain and the beaten dogs to whimper.

Mark alternately watched him and the girl. He saw her frown, saw protest blaze from her eyes. Then she ran to the chief's side and began passionately to plead. Her pleading gave place to commands, her commands to pleading. He made not the slightest sign when she slipped an arm about him and pressed herself close to him.

When he spoke again, his words appeared to make the squatted men restless. The girl turned to Mark whilst yet clinging to the ebony statue.

"We can go!" she cried. "Wall-Eyed Geezer says that we can go."

The chief again spoke, and the girl said, less joyously:

"We can go, but we are to take nothing with us – no tea, no sugar."

Four hundred miles to Laverton and no transport, no food, not a rifle. It would mean certain death, a cruel lingering death. Mark stepped to the chief's side. To the girl, he said:

"Tell him that we must take two camels, and food, and a stick which makes a noise."

"He says you can take a stick that makes a noise," she translated.

Mark saw the Savage rifles in the possession of two of the squatting blacks. The chief spoke to them and they stood up. Mark crossed to one of them, his head aching atrociously, the wound above his right eye gaping wide and attracting the flies. The black made no attempt to proffer the weapon, of the use of which he had no understanding.

"You've got to take it from him," the girl cried out. "You've got to kill him to get it."

So that was it! He was being played with by a man who could break another's neck with the cold indifference of treading on an insect. Both men in possession of the rifles were big-boned and muscular. He whom Mark faced regarded him with a wide grin of anticipatory triumph. From the chief at his back did Mark gain inspiration.

He beckoned the black forward as he stepped several paces back. Clutching the rifle with one hand, the savage obeyed the summons, suspecting nothing, and confident, so that he and Mark came to stand with chest almost touching chest.

"Tell him to give me the rifle," he said.

The girl spoke and the black laughed.

Mark stepped back one pace. Then his left fist shot towards the black's stomach, and the black head ducked towards Mark's streaking right fist, which sent him to the ground with a thud which made the dogs bark. The black lay still, beautiful timing having produced a beautiful knock-out. With the assurance he did not feel, Silent Mark picked up the rifle and faced towards the chief.

"Tell him I want two camels," he said.

"He say you take the two camels you want," interpreted the girl.

Mark turned aside and began to saddle the two riding beasts. He snatched up the billy-can and a canvas waterbag and tied these articles to the saddles. The blacks began to murmur, but Wall-Eyed Geezer remained coldly passive – and watchful.

It was all or nothing now. Mark took up from the smashed ammunition box several cartons of cartridges and dropped them into the billy. He retrieved his hat which had lain unnoticed, and he hastily re-rolled a swag and lashed it to the front of one of the long iron saddles. Again the blacks murmured. The felled gentleman was beginning to stir. There was a faint mockery in the eyes of the chief – but Mark had slung from a shoulder the comforting rifle, which he began to load and clean. More than a hundred eyes watched him, and one word from Wall-Eyed Geezer would have meant his end. When the chief did speak, the girl translated.

"He says we are to go now. We must take nothing more."

"I want the dogs," Mark stated coolly.

"You cannot take them," the chief said through the girl.

It was not an important point, for Mark felt sure they would overtake him when once freed.

"I want that other stick which makes a noise," he said.

"You will go with what you have got," said the chief. "I have spoken."

That appeared to be final, for the girl crossed to Mark. He accepted the situation, not daring to force a rupture, and removed the ropes from the camels' forelegs and urged them up. As he and the girl turned their faces to the setting sun, Wall-Eyed Geezer strode to stand close to them and to address himself to Mark.

"You are free to go," he said. "I have loved the white girl more than my lubras, and because of it I have a pain in my chest. It is well that she goes with you. Her presence among my people is beginning to cause trouble. I look and see things which are to come if she stays with me. I would give you food would it not be unwise to arouse my people. Go. I will keep them from following."

The girl sprang to him and clung to his massive frame, and for the first time Silent Mark saw love in the face of a primitive man – paternal love, which is akin to all races. For the first time the chief's face held expression. He smiled down at Alice Brown, and she smiled up at him with misty eyes.

Then he pushed her towards Mark, and Mark swung her up into the saddle on the nearest beast. Wall-Eyed Geezer regarded him with perfectly normal eyes but with a face which again was expressionless.

Thus did Silent Mark receive from an aboriginal chief a flower of the dry lands, a gift of what is erroneously called the desert. He and the "gift" rode towards the sunset where, a week later, the two dogs caught up to them, and where, a week after that, they fell in with a Government survey party from whom they obtained rations enough to take them to Laverton.

And at Laverton all Mark's anxiety concerning Miss Alice Brown was resolved by Miss Alice Brown herself – with the necessary assistance of a minister.

Love and the Leopard

A Radio Play

Characters

Mrs. Vingie-Weston, a war widow.

Charles, her son.

Dr. Francis Whiteman, an English surgeon visiting Australia to attend a congress in Melbourne.

Mrs. Monks, Mrs. Vingie-Weston's cook.

Fred Monks, her youngest son.

Dr. Sayers, the family doctor.

Captain Talbot, Soldiers, Women, Orderly.

Story of the Play

Charles Vingie-Weston, when a baby, fell down verandah steps and so injured his spine that he is a helpless invalid when the play begins, in the year, 1925.

He is 10 years old when Dr. Whiteman visits Australia and is made interested in Charles by the family doctor. The surgeon operates before returning to England. One year later Charles is able to walk without crutches, and on this day Dr. Whiteman calls when on his second visit to Australia, proposes marriage and is accepted by Mrs. Vingie-Weston. Together, they work to build the boy into a fine young man.

In the present year, when Charles is 19 and is attending at the university, war is declared. Both the boy and his step-father volunteer for service overseas, the former in the infantry, the latter in the medical corps.

During an engagement, Charles is severely wounded and in due course is received at the Casualty Clearing Station commanded by the surgeon. The surgeon thus views the wreckage of what he has made, for Charles – even if he lives – will never again walk.

The underlying question is: what is the use of expending money, brains, and love in the health and happiness of the race if war is permitted to nullify such expenditure?

Scene 1

The action begins in the garden behind Mrs. Vingie-Weston's house in South Yarra, Melbourne. The day is warm and brilliant. In the dancing shadows cast by a wattle tree, the boy, Charles, is lying in an invalid chair. Beside him sits his mother. Charles is attempting to play God Save The King on a tin whistle.

Mrs. Vingie-Weston: That's splendid, Charles. You are progressing fast. Now I hope, dear, you will like Dr. Whiteman. He is such a famous surgeon, you know. He will be here at any moment. How wonderful it would be were he able to make you strong again and you could walk and run and play games.

Charles: I'm sick of doctors, mother. They say: do this and do that, and you will soon get strong. They say: just one more operation, and then you will soon be running about. But they can't do me any good. Only Freddy Monks can make me feel happy.

Mrs. Vingie-Weston: But Freddy Monks will never make you well and strong, dear. He amuses you, and for that I am very grateful, but he cannot cure you by making you laugh.

Charles: The doctors can't cure me, either, and they can't even make me laugh. Oh, I'm sick of doctors!

Mrs. Vingie-Weston: We must be brave and persevere and never lose hope, Charles. This Dr. Whiteman is a very great doctor in London. He has come all the way to Melbourne to attend the doctors' congress, and it is wonderful of him to consent to come and see you, and fine of Dr. Sayers to interest him in you. They say that he is a wonderful doctor with little boys. Here comes Mrs. Monks! Now, I wonder –

Charles: (*petulantly*) I wish Freddy would come. He promised to show me a new trick with cards. We are going to –

Mrs. Monks: Oh, mam! Dr. Whiteman has called. I showed 'im into the drawing-room. Such a nice man, mam. Oh, such a –

Charles: (*still petulantly*) Has Freddy come, Mrs. Monks?

Mrs. Monks: Yes, my angel. He's in the kitchen. He'll come and play with you when the doctor's gone, your mother permittin'.

Charles: I want Freddy now. I've been waiting all day for Freddy.

Mrs. Vingie-Weston: Very well, dear. Freddy shall come to you at once. But remember, now, you must be nice to Dr. Whiteman. Promise me you will be nice to him.

Charles: (*without enthusiasm*) All right, mother I'll try.

Mrs. Vingie-Weston: I thought you would. Now I will go into the house to see the famous specialist.

Charles plays the opening bars of the National Anthem with extreme dissonance. Notes fade.

Scene 2

Mrs. Vingie-Weston's drawing-room.

Mrs. Vingie-Weston: Good afternoon, Dr. Whiteman! It is good of you to spare some of your valuable time on us. Did Dr. Sayers –?

Dr. Whiteman: Sayers did ask me if I would call to look at your son, Mrs. Vingie-Weston. I accept it as a compliment that he should seek my opinion when, he confesses, several experts and he have failed to achieve success. May I be candid, by the way? Was your husband at the war with the A.I.F.?

Mrs. Vingie-Weston: Yes. He was killed on Gallipoli. Did – did you know him?

Dr. Whiteman: Not well. I met Major Vingie-Weston more than once in Cairo. When Dr. Sayers mentioned the name, I recalled a rather tall, handsome man about thirty years old.

Mrs. Vingie-Weston: That would be my poor husband.

Dr. Whiteman: And your boy – is he the major's son?

Mrs. Vingie-Weston: Yes, doctor. I – I never married again.

Dr. Whiteman: Again to he candid, Mrs. Vingie-Weston, may I say I am more interested in Major Vingie-Weston's son than in Dr. Sayers's patient? Please give me the little chap's history.

Mrs. Vingie-Weston: Charles was born September the first, nineteen-fifteen. That was after the Major had gone overseas. Poor Peter never lived to see the baby. When – when he was killed, I could not bear to live in the home he and I had received such pleasure in making, and the house I took had a rather high south verandah. There were eight steps leading up to it from the garden, and the top of the steps I had guarded with a light lattice gate. You see, that south verandah was beautifully cool in the summer. It provided Charles with a splendid playground. Then, when he was five years old, one morning he managed to open the gate. He fell down the steps. The fall injured his spine, and from that day he has been unable to walk, even to crawl. Dr. Marlow refused to operate, and he could give me no hope. Dr. Loftus advised an operation, and the operation was performed by Mr. Whaling. It was not successful a tiny bit. Dr. Sayers said that there is only one man who might operate successfully, and he is Dr. Francis Whiteman.

Dr. Whiteman: Humph! Mr. Whaling has a magnificent reputation. I fear, Mrs. Vingie-Weston, that I can offer you no encouragement to hope.

Mrs. Vingie-Weston: Not hope! Why, if I cannot hope, there is nothing left in life. Oh, I must hope! I must go on and on hoping. Dr. Whiteman – will you – will you at least examine Charles? Think – please think of him living all his life, perhaps for years and years, just lying helpless. I sometimes visualize him, a grown man, needing to be shaved every day, needing –

Dr. Whiteman: Now, now, Mrs. Vingie-Weston. You must continue to be brave. I will just chat with Charles this afternoon. To-morrow, I shall be exceptionally busy, but the day following I will examine the X-ray photographs of the case kept by Dr. Sayers. And then –

Mrs. Vingie-Weston: (*softly*) Yes, and then –

Dr. Whiteman: I will pronounce the verdict. If I think that an operation might be successful, I will operate do you wish.

Mrs. Vingie-Weston: (*breaking down*) Oh, doctor, doctor, thank you! Shall we go to Charles? He is in the garden.

Music.

Scene 3

The garden again. The National Anthem is being badly played on a tin whistle.

Freddy Monks: No, that ain't the way to play it, Charlie. Gimme the thing. Now look! You draws in yer breaf, see. Then you lets 'er go full speed ahead on the first bar, God. The Save comes out quiet like. So does the The. And then the Gracious comes out full blast, and the King come out with extra full blast. Like this.

Example played with energy and not badly.

Charles: Oh, I see! Let me try again. And, please, don't make that face. I cannot blow on this whistle if you make me laugh.

Freddy Monks: I got a new one this morning.

Charles: A new what?

Freddy Monks: A new face. That Bartlett kid, he lives up the street from our 'ouse, I catches 'im 'owling like any-think, and the face 'e made was lovely. I'll show you. Eyes turned in and down a bit. Left eyebrow right down and the right one well up. Mouth like a concertina after a fight at a football match. Som'm't like this.

Charles: (*shouting with laughter*) Oh, please stop, Freddy! Did he look like that?

Dr. Whiteman: He could not possibly have looked like that.

Freddy Monks: 'Deed 'e did, sir. I was a'watchin' of 'im, interested like.

Mrs. Vingie-Weston: This, doctor, is my cook's youngest boy. He comes in to amuse Charles.

Dr. Whiteman: He seems to be doing it remarkably well. How old are you, Master Monks?

Freddy Monks: Twelve, sir. Twelve last March, sir.

Dr. Whiteman: Well, well! And so, Master Charles, you are one of the fortunate people. You actually have a jester, a court jester. And this beautiful garden is your court, or audience chamber. I thought only kings had jesters.

Charles: Freddy is not a jester. He's my friend.

Dr. Whiteman: Jesters were always the friend of the king they served, were they not?

Charles: I know. Like Cinquo? Mother read the book to me twice.

Dr. Whiteman: Yes, like Cinquo. But Cinquo was not all he seemed to be, and I am sure that your court jester is true-blue.

Charles: Oh yes, yes! Freddy's true-blue, all right, doctor. Are – you going to prod me about?

Mrs. Vingie-Weston: Charles! Please!

Charles: Well, old Dr. Loftus did, and so did Dr. Sayers. And I was so sick after Mr. Whaling's doctor put me to sleep.

Dr. Whiteman: Charles, old man, I promise never to hurt you. We want to see you ever so happy, and running about and playing games.

Charles: I would like that. I want to run and to play games. I want to be like Freddy. But I don't want to be prodded about.

Freddy Monks: Wot's a little prodding, Charles, if it goin' to let you leave that chair thing and come along-er-me to see that Bartlett kid howl? He a bloomin' corker when he howls.

Charles: But – but – there was Dr. Loftus and Dr. Sayers –

Freddy Monks: Well, wot o' that? One swaller don't make a summer, as mother says.

Dr. Whiteman: (*delighted*) You are quite right, Master Freddy. We will not talk any more about it to-day. What shall we talk about, Master Charles?

Charles: The War! Were you at the war, doctor? Father was there, you know. He was on Gallipoli. He died fighting for the King and Australia. We are very proud of him, aren't we mother?

Mrs. Vingie-Weston: Yes, dear. We – we – we – are very proud of him.

Dr. Whiteman: Of course, you are. Now, I must be off. I say, Charles! I like your Australia. It's a fine country, isn't it?

Charles: It is the best country in the world. Isn't it, Freddy?

Freddy Monks: Too right, it is!

Dr. Whiteman: Well, good bye! I'll come and see you again, Master Charles. You are a lucky fellow to have such a jester. Good bye, Freddy the Jester! Good bye –! I will come and see you all again on Thursday.

Music.

Scene 4

A musical fantasia to be played softly as a background. The actors speak in the order given, a space of several seconds permitted between each. [Author's note: The technique of this scene may be unusual. Its objective is to cover two places concurrently – a hospital, and a home. The idea of presenting these unconnected speeches with a distinct pause between each is to give the listener scope for his own imagination to play upon scenes continuing over a period of many hours.]

Dr. Whiteman: I will operate to-morrow at ten.

Dr. Sayers: I will have the boy prepared. If you wish it, I will be your anesthetist.

Mrs. Vingie-Weston: Yes, of course, doctor. I will do my part. Very well! Yes, I will be brave. I will stay at home.

Dr. Sayers: I will come for him this evening. He must have a good night's rest at the hospital before the operation.

Charles: Oh, mother! I hope the doctor won't make me sick.

Mrs. Vingie-Weston: Dr. Whiteman is going to be good to you. He is going to make you able to walk, to run and to play games darling. Dr. Sayers will take you to the hospital. He will be with you all the time. I know you will try to be brave like your father was.

Charles: Well – Dr. Whiteman didn't prod me about. I like Dr. Whiteman. Was my father like Dr. Whiteman?

Noise of arriving ambulance.

Freddy Monks: Look up cheerful, Charlie. You'll be able to walk after. I'll take you along to see the Bartlett kid. He's a treat when he 'owls. He looks like this.

Charles: Don't make me laugh, Freddy. Not now.

Dr. Sayers: Ah – here we are! Ready, Charles?

Charles: Mother! Mother! I don't want to go! They will make me sick. I don't want to go!

Mrs. Vingie-Weston: You will be quite all right, darling. I'll come early to see you to-morrow.

Freddy Monks: (*as ambulance departs*) You've forgot the tin whistle Charlie. I'll bring it in the morning.

Soft music.

Dr. Whiteman: All soldiers' sons are brave, Charles. There is nothing of which to be afraid. You are not afraid of me, surely? Tired, eh! Well, bye-bye! Sleep, little man! I will sit beside you. Be not afraid! Be not afraid!

Mrs. Vingie-Weston: Oh, God! Dear God! Watch over Charles this night. Oh, Jesus! Oh, Jesus Who loved little children, stand beside the doctors to-morrow. Direct them, give them spiritual strength and alert, calm minds. Make Charles well and strong, Oh God, Thou Who knowest my heart, Who knowest how I love him, Who knowest how these ten years I have lived only for him, have given him everything I had to give!

Music swells, then dies away.

Hospital Sister: Hullo, sleepy head! Awake at last?

Charles: Yes. Oh, it's a sister! Oh, it's a hospital! To-day! Not to-day, sister, please!

Dr. Sayers: Everything ready here, sister?

Dr. Whiteman: All ready, Sayers? We'll have the light moved a fraction that way. I'll go out and accompany the boy in.

Mrs. Monks: You've eaten no breakfast, mam. The coffee is cold. You mustn't fret, mam. It'll be all right, 'deed it will. Now, now, don't take on so.

Mrs. Vingie-Weston: Dear God! Oh, God, stand close beside Dr. Whiteman now.

Mrs. Monks: I've made fresh coffee, mam. You must eat some breakfast or you'll be all to rags.

Dr. Whiteman: Just lie still, Charles. It won't be long.

Dr. Sayers: All right! He's under.

Dr. Whiteman: Ready, sister?

Freddy Monks: I couldn't stop at school, mum. I couldn't. They'll be carving into old Charlie now. Charlie's me cobber, and I couldn't stop at school. Poor old Charlie.

Mrs. Vingie-Weston: Ten minutes! Have they done? Ten minutes!

Dr. Whiteman: Number five, sister. How's the heart, Sayers?

Freddy Monks: Cripes: It's twenty past ten, mum!

Mrs. Vingie-Weston: Thirty minutes! Half past ten! I can't stand it! Oh, I can't stand it!

Mrs. Monks: Now, now, dearie! Don't take on so. It'll soon be all over. The telephone will go orf any minute now.

Dr. Whiteman: Phew! That'll do, Sayers! I'm almost finished. I've managed it.

Telephone bell rings.

Mrs. Vingie-Weston: Yes, yes! All over! Suc – you believe the operation has been successful! Oh, thank God! Oh, Dr. Whiteman! Oh, Dr. Whiteman!

Freddy Monks: All O.K., mum? Three cheers. Good old Charlie! All right, I'll go back to school now.

Mrs. Vingie-Weston: He will walk again! He will run! Oh, he is going to grow up a whole man.

Burst of swelling music.

Scene 5

In the garden.

Mrs. Vingie-Weston: Charles! Your crutches! Oh, you will fall! Where are your crutches?

Charles: (*laughing*) I put them out of sight behind the wattle tree. See, mother, I can walk without them.

Mrs. Vingie-Weston: Why, it's wonderful, dear! Will not Dr. Whiteman be pleased? He said you would not be able to walk without crutches for at least eighteen months, and now you have done it in twelve months to the day.

Charles: Yes, a full year. It was a year ago to-day that Dr. Whiteman operated. I thought – I thought that as the Orsova got in this morning, Dr. Whiteman may visit us this afternoon, and so I attempted to walk without the crutches. And I have done it. Mother! Hold me! Thanks, mother! I must not be too venturesome at first, must I? Perhaps, should Dr. Whiteman come, I can throw the beastly things away once more.

Mrs. Vingie-Weston: It's just wonderful, darling. Only a year ago you were lying perfectly helpless, and now you are able to walk.

Charles: (*sighing*) Yes, I can walk at last. But, oh, the weary exercises and the massaging. I was getting so sick of it all.

Mrs. Vingie-Weston: You have been heroically patient, darling.

Charles: It was Freddy. You pleaded with me. Dr. Whiteman wrote wonderful letters urging me to persevere. But it was Freddy who really made me go on.

Mrs. Vingie-Weston: Freddy has been splendid, hasn't he? And dear, kind Dr. Whiteman, too. You know, he refused to accept a penny for the operation. He said he would not think of accepting any money for trying to cure the son of Major Vingie-Weston.

Charles: He is great, isn't he, mother? I wish we could do something in return.

Mrs. Vingie-Weston: So do I, dear.

Dr. Whiteman: Ah – there you are! I persuaded Mrs. Monks to permit me to announce myself. I am delighted to find you looking so well, Mrs. Vingie-Weston. And you, Charles. Why, you have grown! (*crutches clatter to ground*) By Jove, you can stand without the crutches! Why, you can walk without them!

Charles: I did it for the first time only a minute ago, Dr. Whiteman.

Dr. Whiteman: There, you see, is the result of obeying orders like a soldier's son. Well, well, well! I am astonished. And delighted!

Mrs. Vingie-Weston: It is splendid, isn't it? We are both so pleased to see you, Dr. Whiteman. Did you have a good voyage?

Dr. Whiteman: Excellent! I am glad to be back again in Australia. This time I am staying. I've taken a positive dislike to London's fogs. Anyway, I am going to practice here. Hullo! Here comes Freddy the Jester.

Freddy Monks: Good afternoon, sir! Why, Charlie, you're standing without your crutches!

Mrs. Vingie-Weston: Yes. Isn't it splendid, Freddy?

Freddy Monks: Too right, Mrs. Vingie-Weston. We said he

would some day if he kept up the exercises, didn't we? I say, Charlie, I brought the stamps. There is some snifter ones among 'em.

Charles: Are there? Oh – oh, Dr. Whiteman! Would you excuse us for a few minutes? I would like to take Freddy to my room to examine the stamps.

Dr. Whiteman: Of course, young man. Could you cross the lawn without the crutches, do you think?

Charles: I am going to try. Freddy will be beside me if I feel like falling.

Dr. Whiteman: Good! But, Freddy, take the crutches along. We must not at first allow Charles to walk too far without them.

Charles: All right, doctor! We'll be back presently.

Dr. Whiteman: Well, that's great! He is more forward than I dared to hope.

Mrs. Vingie-Weston: We owe, Charles and I, a heavy debt to Freddy Monks. The lad is unfailingly cheerful. When Charles despaired and wanted to give up, it was Freddy Monks who coaxed him to persevere.

Dr. Whiteman: His mother seems a staunch servant.

Mrs. Vingie-Weston: She is a fine woman all through. When her husband was sent to gaol for seven years, she was left with five growing boys. Three of them had just left school and were working but not earning much. The youngest two were still at school. Her sister provided them all with a home, and the mother came here to cook and housemaid. She was my maid before my marriage to the major.

Dr. Whiteman: Are the other boys like Freddy?

Mrs. Vingie-Weston: The eldest is rather wild like his father, but the next three are steady and seem to stay easily at their work. Freddy, the youngest, still goes to school. Yes, they are all strong and healthy. Mrs. Monks often says they would grow to fine men if His Majesty would continue to be the host of her husband.

Dr. Whiteman: He is, then, still in gaol?

Mrs. Vingie-Weston: Yes.

Dr. Whiteman: A young country like Australia needs all the strong and healthy men it possibly can obtain. The day might well come when Australia will have to stand alone with her back to the wall. But tell me – are you pleased to see me?

Mrs. Vingie-Weston: Of course. I am more pleased than I can say, and more grateful than I can say, too.

Dr. Whiteman: I delighted in writing. Often I wanted to write more than I did. I could not return quickly enough, and now I can no longer delay telling you what is in my heart. Mary – will you marry me? I have loved you now for one year and two days.

Mrs. Vingie-Weston: Dear, kind, splendid man! I will marry you whenever you wish it. I want love and, almost as much, I want security in the years to come, security in love and marriage.

Music.

Scene 6

Dr. Whiteman: A little momento of our wedding day, dearest.

Mrs. Whiteman: Oh, Francis! You never forget. Thank you! What a necklace! How beautiful! Just fancy, now, a mere man remembering to give his wife a present on the ninth anniversary of her wedding. Nine years, dear! Charles at the University and Francis the Second at school. Freddy getting on so well as a wireless engineer and Mrs. Monks still with us and, and –

Dr. Whiteman: And Mr. Monks once again a guest of his Majesty. Ah, good morning, Mrs. Monks!

Mrs. Monks: Good morning, doctor. Many 'appy returns, sir, of this good mornin'. I've brought some fresh-made coffee, and the eggs and bacon is just off the pan, sir.

Dr. Whiteman: You are a good sort, Mrs. Monks. Thank you. I am sorry to hear about your husband. The judge was too harsh with him.

Mrs. Monks: Nary a bit, sir. Gaol is the place for Monks. Monks ain't never 'appy out of gaol, sir. And no one else ain't 'appy, neither. Now he'll be 'appy, and we'll all be 'appy. My Ted, he says only last week, he says: it's about time the ole man went back to gaol. He don't know what to do with 'isself out of gaol. I'm gonna write the judge a word of thanks on be'alf of father if he gives the old man five years.

Dr. Whiteman: And did he?

Mrs. Monks: I believe 'e did, sir. He's a rare one with a pen is my Ted. Ted's the second one, sir. Motor mechanic, 'e is and doin' well. Alf, that's the eldest, 'e's mad on 'orses, sir. If 'e ain't careful, 'e'll foller 'is ole man. But Freddy! I can't never forget wot you 'ave done fer Freddy, payin' fer 'is courses an' all.

Mrs. Whiteman: We cannot forget what Freddy did for Charles, Mrs. Monks.

Mrs. Monks: Bless 'is 'eart, mam! What a tall, fine young man Master Charles 'as growed to to be sure.

Door closes.

Dr. Whiteman: Anything in the paper this morning?

Mrs. Whiteman: Only the threat of war. Do you think Belgravia will deliberately plunge the whole world into war just for the sake of conquering the Labanians?

Dr. Whiteman: I fear it is almost certain. Ah – man and his confounded spots! Will he never change them, or is he a leopard, indeed? What is the sense of my work? What is the sense of me? What on earth is the sense of working, with thousands of other surgeons and doctors, to make strong the human race if we are to have ever re-current wars to slaughter the best of the human race and cripple the remainder?

Mrs. Whiteman: You, and all your kind, dear, bring health and happiness to thousands.

Dr. Whiteman: For people like the Belgravians to make unhappy and miserable. There's that dictator fellow howling to his people to have bigger families so's he can eventually have more cannon fodder, and there's our own Bishop Slater and others jawing us about our small families and race suicide and such. Only yesterday, I told Sayers that, in my opinon, families should be regulated according to the earnings of the breadwinner. Half the efforts of the nation is devoted to the maintenance of social services directed to the betterment of the national health, and then one dictator in a foreign country can make those efforts null and void through upsetting the world in order to satiate his vanity. Something will have to be done to change man's spots, for he is utterly incapable of doing so himself.

Mrs. Whiteman: Of course, dear. Are you inviting me to lunch out to-day?

Dr. Whiteman: Certainly. Is it not the anniversary of our wedding? Let me see! Yes! At one o'clock, I'll meet you outside Huntley's. Will Charles be along?

Mrs. Whiteman: I will ring him at the University. Will you be very busy this morning?

Dr. Whiteman: Fairly so. I have two gland cases, one amputation, and one cancer. I must be off. See you at one, dear. I'll send the car out for you.

Music.

Scene 7

Street noises. Clock striking the hour of one.

Dr. Whiteman: Ah, here you are!

Charles: Hullo, dad! On time as usual.

Dr. Whiteman: Of course. I suppose your mother is not on time as usual.

Charles: Oh, the mater will be here any second. I say, it looks like war, doesn't it? Britain will be pulled in, too. She can't keep out if she's to keep the Empire together.

Dr. Whiteman: Yes, it looks as though we are all headed for a tough spot, Charles. It's a good job you'll be too young to get mixed up in it.

Charles: You forget, dad, I'm nineteen.

Dr. Whiteman: I don't forget. Neither does your sweet mother. Don't let us talk about war at lunch.

Charles: All right! There's the car coming.

Mrs. Whiteman: I hope I have not kept you waiting long.

Dr. Whiteman: (*mockingly*) We didn't notice it, dear. You are here, and that's the chief thing.

Cry of Newsboy: War! War! Belgravia declares war on Britain.

Mrs. Whiteman: War! Oh! Oh, Charles!

Martial music.

Scene 8

The dining-room of Dr. Whiteman's house. The tinkle of glass precedes the opening of the door. Mrs. Monks is sniffing distressfully.

Mrs. Whiteman: Oh, here you are Mrs. Monks. I'm a little late. Is the lunch table all set? Why, Mrs. Monks, what is the matter?

Mrs. Monks: I'm sorry, mam. I'm all to pieces. They bin calling for volunteers, as you know, mam, and now my John and my Alf 'ave gone and joined up and left for camp this morning, so me sister's sent word to tell me. Didn't we 'ave enough pain and sorrer over the last war to go and 'ave another? Ain't one war in a life-time enough? Me sister lorst 'er 'usband and we lorst three brothers, and now I'm gonna lose my Alf and my John.

Mrs. Whiteman: It appears likely that the war will be over long before our men could reach the front. You mustn't fret, really. You should be most proud that your two boys have been brave enough to volunteer.

Mrs. Monks: And it's in me bones that my Ted and my Frank will be volunteering, too. Only last night when I went to see me sister, I seen a flash young hussy 'anding out white feathers to young men wot was passing 'er. White feathers already, mind you, mam. 'Anded out by a chit of a girl who wasn't born when the last war was on.

Mrs. Whiteman: There are always people acting like that on these terrible occasions. The young men will do their duty just like they did the last time; but it is hateful, horrible, that they should be called to such a duty.

Mrs. Monks: Yes, 'an mothers like me wot 'as slaved almost orl their lives rearin' children to be decent citizens, now 'as to sit down and think and think wot's 'appenin' to 'em. An' the parsons screamin' against birth control – which I don't 'old with, any'ow – an' the doctors telling us that if we don't 'ave larger fambleys we will be doomed to extinction. Do your dooty to the race, they says, and now what about us mothers wot's done it? We're nothing better than the partridge 'ens at 'ome laying eggs for the gamekeepers to rear the young birds for the gentry to shoot.

Dr. Sayers: (*from beyond the open door*) No doubt, Mrs. Monks, you are quite right from your standpoint.

Mrs. Whiteman: Dr. Sayers! Forgive me, please. Come along in.

Dr. Sayers: (*entering*) The outer door was open. I claim the liberty, you know, permitted old friends. Yes, Mrs. Monks, your point of view is soundly logical, but, in this world where the peoples of many nations are unceasingly rearing large families, it is our duty to have large families, too. Not only is it a duty: it is a God-given privilege.

Mrs. Whiteman: You should have married, Dr. Sayers.

Dr. Sayers: I might have done so had Dr. Whiteman never come to Australia.

Mrs. Whiteman: Thank you for a nice, if roundabout, compliment. There is my husband's car. Inform the doctor, Mrs. Monks, that Dr. Sayers is here, and then serve lunch.

Mrs. Monks: Yes, mam.

Door closes. Again opens.

Dr. Whiteman: Hullo! Sorry I am late. What has upset our good Mrs. Monks?

Mrs. Whiteman: Two of her sons have volunteered for service overseas, dear. She is fearful about them.

Dr. Sayers: She compares herself with a partridge hen who produces unlimited young birds for gentlemen to shoot.

Dr. Whiteman: An excellent simile and a true one. In a perfect society families will be regulated, as I have so often said. Our objective should be quality, not quantity.

Dr. Sayers: I agree – provided that the regulation you speak of is adhered to by every nation in the world. As it is not, it is dangerous for the white race to think of regulating families according to the capacity of the father to earn money. It would be truly suicidal for Australia.

Dr. Whiteman: There is a great deal in what you contend, Sayers, but even were the economic conditions what they should be, the inevitable result of large families is overcrowding. Where that occurs the general health is poor. Of course, for the purpose of producing cannon – Forgive me, dear. In the present circumstances of war, the nation requires every fit man. Without plenty of them, we would long since have been a conquered people.

Dr. Sayers: This war will, I think, really end war. The League has survived, and, by acting as it is doing, it will be a long time before another nation breaks loose.

Mrs. Whiteman: War to end war! That is what they said last time.

Dr. Whiteman: It is what has been said about dozens of wars. We are not going to stop war through Leagues of Nations, Conferences, and Government regulations. When a man contracts small pox we do not paint him with iodine to cure the plague. Man's spots cannot be obliterated by material aids any more than a leopard's habits can be conquered by dying out his spots. Fear of consequences will not deter man from fighting, because he fears neither his own laws nor natural laws. The change in him for the better must come about through spiritual forces.

Dr. Sayers: Then it will never come.

Dr. Whiteman: It will come in time and gradually. You see these spiritual forces at work among the Anglo Saxon nations. They form but a fraction of the world's population, but others will eventually follow them. Through terrible sufferings only can man be brought to see that war is as senseless as a street riot. Material forces can never control the rulers, and the League of Nations is a material force.

Dr. Sayers: May I differ? If the League possessed sufficient material force to command all the agencies of propaganda: the press; wireless broadcasting; the cinema –

Dr. Whiteman: But it does not and never will.

Dr. Sayers: Eventually it will.

From without Mrs. Monks shrieks and wails. The door opens.

Mrs. Monks: Oh, mam! My Freddy! My Freddy's bin an' joined up!

Mrs. Whiteman: Dear, dear!

Freddy Monks: A fellow couldn't do anything else but join up. Everyone's joining up.

Mrs. Monks: Freddy's goin' inter camp to-morrer. And 'im me blessed baby, too.

Further wails and sniffing.

Dr. Whiteman: Well, Freddy, I hope you have acted wisely. I suppose you have. In any case, you have acted rightly.

Dr. Sayers: Of course, he's done right. Hullo! Here is Charles! My dear boy, you are becoming a Hercules.

Charles: (*quietly*) Yes, I had to come along with Freddy.

Mrs. Whiteman: Charles! (*louder*) Charles! (*louder still*) Charles!

Charles: Please don't be upset, mother. Freddy and I joined up together. We have simply got to do our bit, you know.

Silence, broken by an anguished wail from Mrs. Whiteman.

Dr. Sayers (slowly): Well – that is that.

Dr. Whiteman. And now I may as well tell you that yesterday I applied for an appointment in the army for service overseas.

Dr. Sayers: Ah! All right, I've got her! Charles, bring a glass of water! Your mother has fainted.

Soft music, against which moans –

Mrs. Whiteman: Love and the leopard – ah, the leopard.

Music swells and fades.

Scene 9

Scene opens on a wharf when a troopship is about to leave. Against a background of martial music and crowd-murmur, the actors speak in order given and with a distinct pause between each speech as in Scene 4. A ship's siren booms, drowning out human chatter. Then:

Man's voice: (*at distance*) Come along, major! All aboard!

Dr. Whiteman: Coming! I must go, dearest. See, they are unmooring the ship.

Woman: (*at distance*) There's daddy, darling! Wave to daddy!

Mrs. Whiteman: Au revoir, Francis! It must – it must not be good bye.

Man: (*at distance*) Who says we're downhearted?

Mrs. Whiteman: You will keep in touch with Charles?

Dr. Whiteman: Naturally. I will yet persuade him to apply for a transfer to the Medical Corps, and when he does that I'll see that he gets it. He's got sand, that boy, which accounts for his present determination to remain in the infantry.

Mrs. Monks: Freddy! Good bye, Freddy!

Ship's siren booms.

Dr. Whiteman: Au revoir, darling. Only au revoir! I must go. Be brave! Dear – you must be brave! There is Charles waving to you. There, on the top deck just below the second funnel. Good bye! No – no – only au revoir!

Mrs. Whiteman: (*softly*) Au revoir!

Man: (*at distance*) Good bye, young feller! Keep your end up.

Woman: (*near*) I'm not crying, silly.

Mrs. Monks: Gawd! It's going! The ship's going! Oh, Freddy, Freddy, my baby! Alf and Ted and Frank 'as gorn. There goes my Freddy. And John goes next. Oh, it's going! It's moving out! (*screams*) The ship's moving away. The water's widening!

Mrs. Whiteman: (*softly*) Au revoir to love. I – I must be brave. Francis and Charles can see me yet. They must not see me cry. Oh, I can't see them! I can't see them for my silly tears!

Woman: (*near*) Any'ow, she got the separation allowance all fixed up. To my way of thinkin', she'll be drawin' two separation allowances. I knoo a woman who draw'd three the last war. Married'em all dinkum, too.

Mrs. Monks: Freddy! My boys! My boys!

Mrs. Whiteman: Farewell to love! The leopard wins. It always wins.

Dr. Sayers: It will not always win, Mrs. Whiteman. Not even the leopard can conquer love. Come, let me take you home. We are going, Mrs. Monks.

Ship's siren in far distance.

Mrs. Monks: Well, they got me boys. Why don't they take me ole man outer gaol and send 'im? Why don't they send us ole partridge 'ens, too?

Mrs. Whiteman: He made a Hercules out of a helpless cripple, Dr. Sayers. Think of the terrible waste if Charles is killed. The waste of love that went to his creation, the waste of love that watched over him when he was helpless, the waste of love which made him a whole man. Think, think, of the waste of money and energy and love that all went into the making of my husband – if he is killed. Think of the waste of all the love here on this wharf, the love that has been and is still being poured out like a river after that fading ship.

Dr. Sayers: Don't think just now.

Mrs. Whiteman: We have surrendered love to the leopard because we must. The leopard! I can almost hear the guns. I am so tired, and yet I can hear the guns, the awful guns. The guns – the guns!

Music crashes abruptly into storm, continues in fury, finally dies to silence, and as it dies so swells the thunder of distant guns and the whine and explosion of shells.

Charles: One minute to go. Pass the word along, sergeant.

Freddy: We're ready, sir.

Voice: (*at distance*) Pretty near as bad as a league game when the scores are equal and there's only one minute to go.

Freddy: Never you mind me, Charlie. I'll be minding you.

Voice: (*at distance*) Blast! Whiteman's ticker musta stopped.

Charles: Steady, boys. Be ready to get away.

Whistle comes shrilly.

Charles: (*shouting*) Come on, you fellows!

A man sobs. Another cries out.

Voice: Keep going, Tim! The sooner we gets across the better.

Charles: Sergeant, get a couple of men to bomb out those rabbit holes. Quickly – o – oh!

Freddy: Charlie! Charlie! Where you got it?

Charles: Stomach! I'm done for! Go on! Don't stop here! The counter barrage will drop at any second.

Freddy: It will be quicker to carry you back into that rat-hole what was once a shell-hole than to take you on, Charlie.

Charles: Never mind me, Freddy. You go on. Don't stop here.

Freddy: I'm minding you, Charlie. (*grunts*) Cripes! You're thunderin' heavy.

Charles: Sergeant, put me down and go on with the platoon.

Freddy: Very well, sir – after I've got you outer this.

Crescendo of guns drowns out voice. Then guns die down.

Freddy: Hi – stretcher bear – ers!

Voice: Wot's up with you. You ain't scratched.

Freddy: It is not me. It's the officer here in this shell-hole.

Voice: Look out! Gas! Put 'is mask on.

Freddy: Good bye, Charlie! You'll be all right now.

Charles: (*faintly*) Sergeant – go on.

Freddy: Very good, sir!

Voice: Cripes! Hi sarg! You can't get through that counter barrage. Hi, don't be a fool! This officer bloke's delirious. He didn't mean that.

Another voice: Dippy! Come on, or we'll get it in the neck.

Soft music.

Doctor: Humph! Poor devil! A spot of morphia. I can't do anything more for him here. Run him out to the ambulance.

Voice 1st: All set?

Voice 2nd: Right! Number Seven C.C.S.

Noise of ambulance departing.

Music swells, dies.

Orderly: Captain Talbot's compliments, sir. Cases comin' in fast from that push, sir. Could you come and give a hand, sir?

Dr. Whiteman: Yes, all right. (*pause*) Ye gods! Twenty-three hours of it and now another spell after only an hour's sleep.

Noises of arriving and departing ambulances.

Dr. Whiteman: Plenty of work, Talbot?

Captain Talbot: Bad! Sorry to call on you. Beastly unfair. Will you take that lad over there? Stomach, I think.

Dr. Whiteman: Hum! Gently, orderly, gently! What – Ah –

Captain Talbot: What's wrong, sir?

Dr. Whiteman: (*after terrific effort to speak*) This – this stomach case – is – my stepson. Charles – my triumph! My man whom I made whole. Look, Talbot! Look at my triumph! I can't – Sorry, Talbot. Would you take him? I'll be better presently.

Captain Talbot: Your stepson! How damnable!

Dr. Whiteman: He was a helpless cripple child, Talbot. With my fingers and his mother's love was he made a whole man. Now look at him. Look at him, Talbot! Money, brains and love made a splendid man, and a single bullet has wiped it all out. Love – what the hell is the use of love, Talbot? Tell me that. Ha! Ha! Love be damned! Waste energy! Waste thought! Only the leopard matters. The leopard, Talbot! Ha! Ha! The leopard is stronger than love, for the leopard is Death.

Captain Talbot: Here, sir! Take a stiffener of this.

If possible – the laughter of kookaburras.

Scene 10

Church bells are heard peeling joyously at distance. An electric door bell rings and heavy steps move to the front door of Dr. Whiteman's house. On the door being opened, the sound of the bells swell.

Dr. Sayers: (*cheerfully*) Good morning, Mrs. Monks! How are we all to-day?

Mrs. Monks: (*severely*) As well as can be expected, Dr. Sayers. The master's in the study. Mrs. Whiteman and Mr. Charles are out in the gardin.

The door is closed, shutting out the sound of the bells.

Dr. Sayers: Well, well! I will announce myself, Mrs. Monks.

How is John?

Mrs. Monks: He's gettin' on, doctor, thank you. Wot 'e's gonna do with only one leg beats me, but 'e's that cheerful about it.

Dr. Sayers: He will be found a niche in life. A man having but one leg is more fortunate than another having none at all.

Mrs. Monks: Too right, doctor. (*lowers voice*) John's terrible fortunate compared against Mr. Charles, Poor Mr. Charles, a'lying out there in the same old invalid pram. It does seem as 'ow 'e only left that pram to get strong enough to go to the war and be brought 'ome again worse'n 'e was before. Thank Gawd He took my Alf and my Ted and didn't let 'em come back like that.

Dr Sayers: Yes, you have a deal for which to be thankful. Now I will go along and see the doctor.

Door opens and shuts.

Dr. Sayers: Hullo – hard at work?

Papers are moved.

Dr. Whiteman: Oh! Hullo, Sayers! I have nearly finished my war book. Should anyone, having read it, desire war, then he, or she, is destined for a mental hospital. Why are they ringing the bells?

Dr. Sayers: Don't you know? The Armaments Pact has been signed by all the nations at Geneva. Under it no nation is permitted to manufacture armaments, and henceforth the League of Nations only will possess an Air Force.

Dr. Whiteman: Ah! So that has been agreed to! No nation to be allowed to possess a navy or an army or an air force! The world is to be policed by the League! Humph! That will not stop wars. Men can still make bows and arrows and swords and knifes and spears. And when it comes to the point –

Dr. Sayers: There will be the League's Air Force to drop bombs and even gas on them.

Dr. Whiteman: Bah! Can the foul leopard change its spots?

Dr. Sayers: Perhaps not the animal, Whiteman. But man can change his, and he has got to be made to change them. By the way, I have the X-ray photographs of Charles' back.

Dr. Whiteman: What do they reveal?

Dr. Sayers: What we knew. That never again will the poor lad walk.

Dr. Whiteman: (fiercely) I'll make him walk if it takes me twenty years.

Dr. Sayers: I fear you never will. The injury is too vital ever to be made good.

Dr. Whiteman: We have then to resign ourselves?

Dr. Sayers: My dear old friend, yes.

Dr. Whiteman: Cigarette? (*a match is struck*) Well, there is Francis the Second. Let me see, now. In 1946, he will be twenty-two. Just the age – just the right age.

Dr. Sayers: The right age for what?

Dr. Whiteman: The right age for the next war. We labour and deny ourselves for our children. We plan their careers and watch over them – so that they will be intelligent and fit to fight in the next war to end war.

Dr. Sayers: But the bells are ringing our hopes for perpetual peace. (*pause*) Come here to the window. Come and see the salvation of the human race.

A pause, then:

Dr. Whiteman: Well?

Dr. Sayers: Watch the play of expression on your wife's face as she bends over her firstborn. Then study the face of Freddy Monks, standing on the lad's other side. In that picture, what is paramount? Can't you see, old friend. It is love, devotion.

Dr. Whiteman: I see despair and pain.

Dr. Sayers: But, man, love reigns over all despair and pain. In the world today a yeast is working in the dough of mankind. Once you said that a spiritual force was working for peace among the Anglo Saxons. At that time I did not agree that it would be ever strong enough to wipe away the possibility of war. I do now. At long last, after the many centuries, Love and Reason are going to rule the world, and the nation who attempts to manufacture armaments is to be treated exactly as the man who trades in drugs.

Dr. Whiteman: It is at least a hope to which we may cling. You do me good, Sayers. I am a bitter man, but out there in the dancing shadows cast by the wattle tree is that which might well cure me of my bitterness – love with a capital L. Let us go out to them. Let our faces be smiling and our hearts be full of courage.

French windows are opened and the music of the bells swell and swell.

The Bewildered Castaways

Australian history is crammed with contradictions, with repetitions and with acts difficult to reconcile with commonsense. It is, too, filled with errors. For instance, who discovered the Brisbane River? Cook found Moreton Bay, but did not discover the river emptying into it. Flinders visited the bay without seeing the river. History says that Oxley found the Brisbane River when, in fact, he did not.

Oxley was a surveyor-general, a man of some importance, and therefore the historians hasten to credit him with a discovery which should have been placed to the credit of four unfortunate castaways who thought themselves to be somewhere on the coast of Van Dieman's Land. It was one of these four men who revealed to Oxley the presence of the fine Brisbane River, and had it not been for him it is doubtful if Oxley would ever have seen it, for to Oxley as well as to Flinders and Cook, the river was hidden by two small islands situated off its mouth.

Early in the year 1822 four men sailed from Sydney to obtain a cargo of cedarwood at Illawarra, at that time more widely known as The Five Islands. They were Thomas Pamphlet, Richard Parsons, John Finnigan and John Thompson. Their craft was an open boat fitted with a mainsail and a jib, certainly no fit craft in which to undertake a prolonged ocean voyage against their will. Nor was the boat provisioned and its crew suitably prepared for a long journey.

Men more weather-wise would not have ventured beyond the Heads that morning, for there was a fitful wind blowing from the north-east and the sun was almost masked by a high level haze which thickened every hour. And so, with the abruptness and fury of storms along the coast of New South Wales, a gale of wind and rain rushed upon the open boat and its occupants.

Instantly the land was blotted from their sight by the rain. Swiftly the sea rose and showed its ugly teeth. There was no possibility of returning to Sydney, even if they could have seen the Heads, and with only the jib set they could but run before the wind. All night through, the wind whined in the scant rigging, and endless mountains of water sent leaping white crests to charge after and overtake the boat.

Pamphlet appears to have been the organiser in the search for cedarwood. He was as tough as the best produced by that age – a man without craven fear, but without remarkable intelligence. Of the four he and Parsons had a little knowledge of the deep sea.

The dawning was sinister and the day to follow presented a picture of wild water and wild sky painted a uniform grey. The rain had stopped, but the wind began to increase in power. The sea was empty of ships, and of the land there was no indication.

"The wind'll go down towards sunset likely enough," predicted Pamphlet. "All the same, I'd like to know where we are."

Short and sturdy, he clawed his way up the waving mast so that he came to stand on the thwart through which it was stepped. And now every time the frail craft was lifted high on a wave summit he peered between screwed eyelids to all points of the compass.

"There's no sight of land," he shouted down to his companions. "I can't see further than five miles, if that far." Sliding down to the thwart and then scrambling back to the tiller, which he took from Parsons, he faced his companions with quiet confidence portrayed on his homely face. "We'll have to ride it out and then, when the wind has gone down, head westward to the land. More'n likely when the weather clears we'll see the shore."

"An' if we don't?" asked Thompson, a young man who had not been obliged to shave for more than a year or two.

"Steer by the sun, lad," cheerfully replied Pamphlet. "Let's get out some grub. We've got plenty of that, anyway, and we've enough water to last a day or so."

The store of food was broached, and silently the four men ate and took their water from a cask.

"Supposin' this wind be blowin' from the west, Pamphlet?" demanded the Irishman.

Pamphlet's brows rose a fraction and his mild blue eyes regarded Finnigan.

"What of it?" he inquired.

"Wot ave it? You're askin' me wot ave it! Ain't we sailin'

afore the wind? If 'tis so the wind be blowin' from the west, then 'tis further from land we be ivery minute ave it."

"That's so," agreed Thompson. Parsons said nothing. An imaginative man, he saw more clearly into the future than the others, especially a future resulting from a prolonged gale of wind. He knew, of course, that the Irishman was merely arguing. Finnigan seemed happy only when in a dispute.

"We can do nought else but run before the wind," averred Pamphlet. "We've nothing aboard we could use as a sea anchor and so ride the rollers in safety. We can't tack against this sea, for we'd be capsized in a jiffy. The first comber that crashed against us would turn us over. And, Finnigan, we don't know that the wind is coming from the west. It might be coming from the north or the south. We only know for certain, that it's not coming from the east."

"That's right, Finnigan," shouted Thompson. "If the wind was blowing from the east we'd have been wrecked on the coast long ago."

"Shut yer gab!" bellowed Finnigan, to add fiercely: "Don't I be knowin' ave that?"

After this flare of anger the four men subsided into a long silence, Finnigan glowered at the foaming sea, Thompson's eyes were like those of a frightened steer, and he looked eagerly across the racing white horses with tremendous hope of seeing land. When Pamphlet's gaze met that of Parsons' these two each knew that the others realised the hazards and appreciated them. Without a compass it could not be ascertained from which quarter the wind was blowing and to which quarter the wind was taking them. They knew, too, that if the wind did drop and the sky cleared within an hour that the odds were against a sight of land.

All day the wind maintained its fury. It lessened in strength only a degree or two when night fell again to encompass them with terrors made greater because unseen. With no timepiece between them, and with the stars banished from the sky, they had no means of keeping time. Pamphlet and Parsons awoke each other in turn to take the tiller for a spell and continue to keep the boat's stern to the savage white wave-crests leaping after them out of the dark.

With the dawning of the next day, hope vanished of observing a clear or clearing sky. The racing cloud-drift almost touched the sea, whilst visibility in broad daylight could barely be more than two miles.

"We'd better go easy on the water," advised Pamphlet.

"And fer why?" demanded Finnigan.

"Because when it's done there is only the sea water to drink," quietly replied Pamphlet.

"We needn't be afeared, Pamphlet. This wind'll die afore sunset."

"It might not."

"I be sayin' as it will," bellowed Finnigan.

"I reckon it will, too," interject Thompson, whose nerve already was threatening to break beneath the strain of the terrible conditions, and who had arrived at the stage when to argue and to complain was to gain temporary relief.

"Pamphlet's right. The wind mightn't go down till to-morrow," Parsons said in support of their captain. "When it does drop it might fall to a calm, when we'd be no better off than if we had no sails."

"Look at the sky. Why don't it rain?" wailed Thompson.

"Shut yer gab, I tell yer!" growled Finnigan roughly. "How the blazes do we know why it don't rain? S'posin' it did, we'd be a mighty sight colder with drenched clothes and all. As it is, 'tis none so bad durin' the daylight."

"You're right, Finnigan," Pamphlet agreed. "I'm remarking that you're right. That tells us something. This wind ain't cold enough to be blowing from the south. It can't be coming from east, so it must be coming from the west or the north. If this sky would only break and give us a glimpse of the sun!"

Yet the cloud-wrack did not break that day, or the next, or the next. The gale of wind raged for five days and nights without ceasing, and then when the wind did wane and finally fall to a flat calm the clouds refused them a sight of the sun or the stars for another day and a night. When the sun rose clearly on the morning of the seventh day the mariners had not the faintest idea of their position.

And added to this confusion of locality were the grim facts of an empty water cask and no indication of land.

That morning the sun broke clearly above the horizon, and it was seen that the wind was coming from the east – a light wind which, with jib and mainsail set, sent the boat lumbering westward with white water at her fore-foot.

Land! They must reach land and water. It mattered not now if the gale had blown them north or south of Sydney Town. All that mattered was to secure a fresh supply of water – water which was an increasing necessity with every hour beneath the hot rays of the sun. Already they had been without water for two days and nights. And towards sundown, when the wind dropped to a complete calm, there still was no sight or sign of the coast.

"If that gale blew from the west and took us away from land for five days and five nights, then it'll take us a bit more'n five days and five nights to reach land again," predicted Parsons.

"That's right, matey," rumbled Finnigan. "We're still four days and five nights o' favourable winds off land and a drink of cold water."

"What's that you say?" shouted Thompson. "Oh, my God! Four days and five nights more? I couldn't bear it. I'll die. I'm choking for a drop of water now."

"Ye'll be after chokin' for a drop o' air if you don't shut yer gab, you whinin' rat," roared Finnigan, and he smote Thompson so hard that the complainer rolled into the bottom of the boat and lay there moaning.

Pamphlet's blue eyes hardened, while his gnarled hand gripped harder the useless tiller-bar.

"If the wind came from the north – or the south, which I don't think it did – we would not be nearly so far from land than if the gale came from the west. Likely enough the wind'll come up again after sunset and we be seeing land at daybreak. Anyway, it's no use losing our tempers. That won't get us anywhere."

This utterly windless night was yet more terrible than had been those nights of raging storm. Thompson remained in the bottom of the boat, but after a period his moans of self-pity ceased and he slept. Towards midnight Finnigan and Parsons slept, too, and now and then Pamphlet dozed. Every time the boat rolled the mast creaked and thudded in its stepping, and alternately the rigging creaked and the main boom snapped at the ropes when reaching the ropes' extremity either side of the boat. But these sounds were not continuous. There were spaces of silence, during which the sea whispered and tapped at the boat with siren fingers.

Another day dawned, calm and hot. The swells now were unmarked by the wind's catspaws. They came down from the north-east – long, low hills of bronze-tinted glass which reflected the sunlight into semi-blinded, tortured eyes. The morning dragged away as though the world was slowing on its axis. Parsons and Pamphlet sat and stared at the bottom of the boat, for only there could partial relief be obtained from the glare. Finnigan slumped amidships and stared at Thompson, who in turn leaned over the side of the boat and with bent head stared into the translucent depths of the ocean.

Of the four men none had had a real experience of deep water, but Pamphlet had been long associated with sailors, and had absorbed some of their lore and knowledge. To himself he remarked the absence of sharks, knowing that this indicated that the boat was far from land. He remarked, too, the obvious fascination the clear water was exerting on John Thompson, who now, for several hours, stared downward like one gazing into a crystal, hoping to see paradise. Finnigan, too, apparently observed and understood the young man's fixed interest in the water. Pamphlet thought that the Irishman was holding himself ready to stop Thompson leaping into the sea.

The glaring sun began its slow journey to the horizon, above which no blue-tinted blur indicated the presence of land. The creaking mast and the complaining rigging offered the only sounds in an otherwise completely silent world – until Thompson screamed.

He was sitting well forward in the boat. Pamphlet and Parsons lounged right astern on either side of the tiller-bar. Between them and the youth slumped Finnigan. It might have been his prolonged and calculating stare which caused Thompson to raise his head.

He began to mutter. After a little time he again fell to staring into the water below the boat. The others did not know what he now saw – two graceful shapes circling about each other while they circled the boat. Perhaps those shapes invited Thompson to join them. Perhaps they showed him a doorway through which he could escape this world of heat and thirst into another world where it was cool and green. Perhaps he thought that where those things lived so he, too, could live and thus gain relief from the torture of cracking skin and aching body.

He was over the side of the boat so quickly that Finnigan was too late to stop him.

Finnigan bellowed, Pamphlet shouted, Parsons remained mute. They leaned over the side of the boat and stared downward into the water inside the outward, curving little wave created by Thompson's body. They could see Thompson twenty feet below. He was on his back. He was making hardly any movement with his arms and legs. His eyes were wide open and they thought he could see them, and thought, too, how peculiar it was that he made no sign to them for help.

So clear was the water that they could see his hair floating from his head like floating seaweed. And then they saw the two shadows. Lying on his side, Thompson was facing them. The men in the boat realised that he saw the converging sharks. They saw that he regained sanity and knew what they were and their purpose.

His limbs jerked in a flurry of desperate panic. One of the dark shapes turned and showed the putty white of its throat and belly. It reached Thompson, but did not stop, and the three men saw him lying along the shark's side as, with one of his legs in its jaw, it sped onward and downward, closely followed by the other.

"An' that's the ind of 'im!" growled, Finnigan.

White-faced, Pamphlet and Parsons regarded each other and the Irishman for a full minute without speaking. It was Pamphlet who broke the strained silence.

"I've heard that sharks are not often seen far off the coast. We can't be far from land."

"Maybe you're right," said Parsons hopefully. "But we can't move without wind."

"The wind will come at sundown," predicted the leader, whose spirit refused to be beaten down and crushed by adversity.

More in order to stretch his cramped body than for anything else, Parsons crawled to the mast and clawed his way up it to stand on the stepping thwart. For a minute he stood clinging to the swaying stick. And then he shouted:

"Here comes the wind! Look! From the south!"

The others also saw the sea darkened by the wind's touch. With terrible anxiety they watched the edge of the darkened sea running to the boat, and then took in deep lungfuls of cool air. At once the boat gained way, and within half a minute was lumbering westward with white water at her prow.

Near to the dawn of the following morning it rained, and, with the mainsail, the castaways caught enough water to quench their thirst and to half-fill the cask. After the rainfall they made but little progress, for long calms were interspersed with short periods of light wind. The days and the nights passed with weary succession, and still no land came into view above the horizon – until the twentieth day, when, shortly after noon, the faint slate-blue bar lying along the western horizon was deemed to be land. Not till the next day did they sail the boat into a huge bay and finally stagger ashore on one of two islands. Utterly exhausted, barely able to stand, the wrecks of three once-hardy men were suddenly confronted by a party of aborigines.

Now follows a remarkable illustration of historical contradiction. The past provides many instances of inhuman cruelty practised on white men cast away among the aborigines. To conform with all the other examples, those aborigines who confronted Pamphlet, Parsons and Finnigan should have taken them to their mainland camp and there forced them to labour until so weakened that, no longer useful, they would be put to death. But Pamphlet eventually related nothing could exceed the kindness shown to him and his companions by these Moreton Bay blacks.

There on the beach of one of the two islands masking the mouth of a fine river, afterwards to be named the Brisbane River, Pamphlet stepped towards the blacks with empty hands outstretched in supplication, a sign of such distress that none could mistake it. Parsons collapsed on the sand, while Finnigan, the wild Irishman, waited the signal to behave docilely or to fight to the death.

One of the aborigines stepped forward to Pamphlet and stood to stare into the bewhiskered and emaciated face. He did not smile his welcome, and poor Pamphlet accepted this lack of visual joy as evidence of hostility, not knowing that a warrior smiles only upon an enemy he intends to kill. Expecting the worst, he was on the point of falling when, caring not whether he lived or died, a naked black arm was slipped round his waist, and he was assisted to the shade of the low bush scrub.

The three white men were taken to the blacks' mainland camp and there were fed with the best to be had. Thereafter certain of the bucks were detailed to catch fish for the guests, and some of the lubras sent off to gather fern-root for food. Others stripped the castaways and smeared the healing juices of herbs on their sun-cracked bodies, and so tended them day after day till they were fully recovered.

But never again did they see their boat. The blacks took it to pieces to secure every scrap of copper and brass with which they ornamented themselves. They had no understanding of theft and reasoned that what the white men had brought was communal property, and that should they want another boat there were many canoes from which they could choose.

Pamphlet was wise in his generation, while Parsons was not slow to appreciate the side on which their bread was buttered. Astonished by the kindness they were receiving at the hand of alleged savages, both realised only too clearly that if in ignorance or carelessness they broke one of the many taboos, this kindness would change into brutal violence. They impressed this danger upon Finnigan, and they pointed out to him that the greatest taboo was interference with a black woman without black authority.

"To hell with the wimmin," snorted Finnigan. "What do I be wantin' with them black hussies? If I could only be gettin' ave these whiskers of'n me, I'd recite poetry for very joy."

"I'd feel better, too," Parsons asserted.

"Well, we can shave each other," Pamphlet said. "We should be able to break a conch shell to get a sharp cutting edge, and we could boil some water in the boat's drinking pot which one of the bucks is wearing round his neck. We've got no soap, but real hot water will soften the whiskers enough, I think."

"That's an idea," Parsons said with enthusiasm. "You get after a conch shell. Finnigan and I'll find out that nigger with the pot and persuade him to give it back."

Finnigan went away to the beach to secure a stout conch shell, and on his return to the camp he found the entire tribe gathered about one of the fires. There were no gesticulations, no evidence of excitement, only intense interest in something on or near the fire. Edging his way through the crowd, he came to see Pamphlet and Parsons kneeling before the fire and on the hot embers the drinking pot filled to the brim with water.

"What's to do?" he demanded.

Solemnly Parsons said he was sure that the blacks never had seen water boiled, and that their curiosity was based on the reason for the water being placed in the pot and the pot on the fire.

In this he was right. When the water in the pot began to stir gasps arose from the crowd. It being a hot day, very little steam was discernable. Then the water began to bubble, and the blacks uttered loud cries of wonder. Curious to see what would eventuate, Pamphlet permitted the water to boil, to leap about in the pot and overflow its side into the fire with a loud hiss and clouds of steam.

In accord, the entire tribe vented a long and loud yell of terror and bolted for the bush. No persuasion, no argument with signs, would induce then return to camp until with ceremony the magic pot was buried on the beach. After that the white men decided to put up with the irritating whiskers.

Despite their idyllic life of ease and interest, there was born in their hearts a kindling desire to attempt to get back to Sydney Town.

"That gale of wind wasn't cold enough to have come up from the south," Pamphlet reminded his companions. "It didn't come from the west, according to the sailing-times it took us to reach land. It must have come from the north or the north-west, and we can't be far off Van Dieman's Land, if we're not really there. It'll be a long way north to Sydney Town, but if we keep on we'll surely get there."

"That's the lay of it, matey," agreed Finnigan. "I ain't a-feared o' the blacks on the road, neither. Talk about blacks being savages is lies. Let's be after explainin' to these blacks what we're doin', and lay in a store of fish and dingowa root and so be off."

It occupied Pamphlet some considerable time to inform the chief by signs what they wished to do and what they wished to have done for them, but once the chief understood that they desired to go on walkabout he, thinking to understand the urge compelling them, offered no objections. He gave orders to the lubras to gather fern roots, and the bucks to set about obtaining a supply of fish to dry in the sun. Wisely Pamphlet forbade his companions to urge haste in these preparations.

A few days later all was ready for the expedition, and they set off northward, accompanied by the chief and his bucks as far as the tribal boundary, beyond which the blacks would not make one step. However, with due ritual, the chief despatched a messenger with tidings of the white men's coming to the next chief, and, after a show of genuine affection on both sides, the white men parted from their black friends and set out, as they imagined, for Sydney Town, but in reality walking north towards China, instead of southward to the settlement founded by Phillip.

A day or two later it became evident that the chief's messenger had carried a powerful passport, for they were received in a friendly spirit by all the natives with whom they came in contact. By following the coast, not daring to enter the bush in fear of becoming lost, they reached some fifty or sixty miles north of Moreton Bay, when Pamphlet decided he could proceed no further on account of the condition of his feet.

The journey was undertaken long after they had been deprived of clothes, when their bodies were painted with red and white ochre, when their bare feet were not nearly sufficiently covered with hard skin. Parson's feet were in but little better shape, but he decided to push on with Finnigan, who thought that Sydney Town could not be many miles further on. And so the Irishman and Parsons went on, leaving Pamphlet wearily to limp back by easy stages to the Moreton Ray blacks, who received him with warm welcome.

It is a fact not to be disputed by fair-minded people that to these alleged ignorant heroes of the early days of white settlement in Australia is due the major portion of our knowledge of the aborigines, their lore, laws and customs. Pamphlet and Bracefell and Derhamboi[13] were outstanding and have contributed more to our knowledge of the blacks than all the early scientific observers whose names are so lauded by the historians.

In this particular instance Pamphlet, who was a keen observer, eventually gave to Uniacke and Oxley a mine of information which they recorded and for which they have received all the publicity and credit. The art and practice of brain-sucking was as much alive then as it is to-day.

Pamphlet says that the Moreton Bay natives had the cartilage of their noses pierced and large pieces of bone or shell thrust into the hole. He reported that the women – and these Oxley and his crew were not permitted to see – like those in the vicinity of Sydney, had all had the first two joints of the little finger removed, and that, unlike the Sydney blacks, the Moreton Bay males did not have one of their front teeth knocked out.

In a sketch of this kind it is impossible to relate all that Pamphlet told Oxley. During his sojourn among the blacks the castaway did not once see a woman ill-treated. He touched on, but did not fully reveal, the laws governing the intricate totem system of marriage selection and relationships, a system which remained obscure to us until Professor Sir Baldwin Spencer came to Australia and threw the searchlight of his wonderful mind on this matter.

It must not be thought that Pamphlet's life among the blacks was not without human interest. By no means! At their main camp was a specially prepared arena sunk some three or four feet in the earth, about twenty-five feet in diameter, and surrounded by a low fence of brushwood to provide a barrier as well as to offer all a grandstand view of the events.

Sometimes, occasioned by one gentleman casting an eye on the wife of another gentleman, or the wandering of an unfortunate sleepwalker into a stranger's humpy, a challenge to a duel would be issued. The combatants would drop down into the sunken arena with all their spears, which they would stick into the ground behind them.

Encouraged by the yells and shouts of the spectators – anyone hearing the discussions on Australian barracking would think that we moderns originated the custom – the duelists would shout

---

[13] See "Wandi and the Bilker" and "Derhamboi the Makromme."

insults at each other in order to arouse their passions to fighting point. That point being reached, they would start. Sometimes both would fall mortally wounded. Occasionally an excitedly thrown spear would pass through the body of a spectator. It was all in the game. After it was all over one way or the other, the parties backing the contestants would become reconciled and would retire to the fires, there to indulge in a feast and afterwards to engage in wrestling bouts.

Parsons and Finnigan returned, defeated by the coast scrub north of Moreton Bay, but shortly afterwards Parsons persuaded the Irishman to make another attempt to reach Sydney. They still believed themselves to be south of Sydney Town, but now Pamphlet was experiencing grave doubts about it, owing to the semi-tropical vegetation and the various species of warm-water fish. He declined to go with the others on this second attempt, and it was some six weeks after their departure that a buck came racing into camp with the news that a strange canoe was out on the bay.

With the tribe, Pamphlet rushed down to the open beach, there to stand with his mouth agape. Slowly drawing nearer was a smart cutter which he recognised as the *Mermaid*, the Government cutter from Sydney.

After so many months spent with the blacks, he was overwhelmed by excitement and the prospect of rescue. Those on board the Mermaid witnessed a party of blacks appear at the edge of the scrub and run down to the water to stare, at them. Among them was one taller and bigger than the rest – one whose skin was lighter in colour than that of the others, despite the red and white ochre with which it was painted. This man raised aloft his arms and shouted:

"Ahoy, *Mermaid*! Come ashore! We are friends and I'm English."

And so it was that Oxley and Uniacke stepped ashore to receive a warm welcome. So excited was Pamphlet that they could not get much from him that day, but later he related all that had happened to himself and the others, and then proceeded to give to the world that mine of information concerning the blacks, which Uniacke jotted down in a book.

Shortly after, Finnigan returned to relate how Parsons and he had quarrelled and how they had parted, Parsons to continue to struggle forward towards his goal. A year later Parsons was found alive and well.

Upon hearing of the purpose of the expedition undertaken by Oxley, Pamphlet drew on the sand a rough map of the coast of Moreton Bay and of the river running into it. He piloted the cutter behind the twin islands and showed Oxley and Uniacke this magnificent river, and then took the cutter for many miles up along its course.

It should have been called the Pamphlet River, but Pamphlet was a common man, like you and I, and Brisbane was the Governor of New South Wales.

A Man Who Dreamed

History is crammed with the exploits of the great ones. Even so, the progress of a nation is dependent on the collective acts of the units composing it. The lives of very many humble folk, whom ordinary history has never mentioned, have had important bearing on the course of history. It is easy for us to recall the names of Phillip, MacArthur, Batman, and Bligh, but hidden deep within their shadows lived unknowns who were as courageous and whose careers were as colourful, whose lives contributed much to the beginnings of this Australian nation.

There was one such whose name history does not mention, but whose life was touched upon by the master of the schooner *Elizabeth*, John Hart, when he wrote a letter to His Excellency Governor La Trobe, under date, April 24, 1854. Captain Hart gives us the bones, as it were, and with these it is possible to build up the man, Silas Jenks.

About the year 1825 Silas Jenks, with a companion, effected a well-planned escape from the penal settlement in Van Dieman's Land. It is obvious that both prisoners had earned with good behaviour much amelioration from the lot of the general run of convicts, for they were able secretly to provision and water one of the official launches in which they stood out into Storm Bay early one December night.

The sea was moderate, the wind coming softly from the south, and such was the success of their escape that their absence was not noted till the following morning, and the launch was not missed till three days afterwards. By then the adventurers were sailing round the south coast of Tasmania, assisted on their voyage by continuously favourable winds.

Silas Jenks had been a sea-faring man before his transportation. At this time he was physically hard. Not a big man, he was gifted with imagination and extraordinary mental tenacity. He had realised that nowhere in the world among white people was there a place for him – save at the convict settlement – and he had conceived the plan of escaping to a lonely and uninhabited island where life could be lived in comfort and absolute freedom.

Boyne, his companion, was a carpenter by trade, a dull-witted man of great strength. He had implicit faith in Jenks to make the dream come true, and so it was that these two men sailed along the south coast of Tasmania in search of an island sufficiently removed from Hobart to assure safety from recapture. They were supplied with plenty of water, and among the food supplies stolen were potatoes, flour, seed wheat, peas and beans. They had hatchets, building tools, and even nails. Jenks had forgotten nothing, and all that now remained was the discovery of an island well watered, well timbered – and remote.

"Dang me if I like the look of this here coast," growled Boyne, staring at the rock-armoured land off which they stood some two miles. "This here's supposed to be mid-summer. It'll be rough and wild and cold down here in winter, I'm thinking. We should have sailed north when out of Storm Bay."

"An' likely enough be picked up by a ship bound from Sydney Town, or bound to Sydney Town," sneered Jenks. "I told you afore, as I've told you a hundred times, that our only chance of freedom is to get away to where no ships sail and where white men never get to. We'll find an island, never fear, where we'll be as snug as Barney's goat. This craft is sound and she's a good sailer. The weather looks like keepin' fine. We've water and grub, and nothing to do but sleep and eat and smoke. Stow your grumbling."

"I ain't grumbling, Silas," averred Boyne in his usual sullen manner.

Two hours later, when they rounded a great headland, subsequently named South-West Cape, Jenks shouted joyfully:

"Seems as though the coast runs north from here. And that looks like a tidy-sized island off the coast away over on our port bow. We'll look it over."

It was a small island, uninhabited, with plenty of water and game, but Jenks decided that it would not suit him, as there were no trees of sufficient size for building purposes. With the passage of the days, other islands were visited, but all lacked one or another of the requisites demanded by the fastidious Jenks. Boyne growled much, but Jenks' will was of iron. Slowly the little craft passed northward along Tasmania's western sea boundary until Hunter Island was reached, beyond which there was no land in sight.

To proceed further round the coast – to the east and south – would have brought them into the track of ships, and eventually back again to Hobart and to the chain gangs, and so Jenks decided to land on Hunter Island, despite the smoke signals sent up by the watchful blacks.

"We'll find out what them blacks is like," he told Boyne. "They might be peaceable: if so, we can live among 'em and perhaps marry a woman apiece."

Into a small land-locked bay Jenks steered the launch. On the half-moon sandy beach stood a group of naked savages silently regarding the strange canoe and evidently awed by the appearance of two men white of skin and dressed in strange garments. They made no menacing movements with their spears and clubs, nor did they offer any sign of friendship when the prow of the launch gently grounded on the beach. Jenks stood up, and, raising his empty hands above his head, he shouted cheerfully:

"What cheer, me hearties! Is it war or peace?"

The gesture of the empty hands, allied with the cheerful tone of the greeting, caused the blacks to lay down their weapons and approach the boat. Jenks stepped out to meet them, Boyne remaining with one hand gripping a primed musket hidden by the gunwale.

The blacks of Hunter Island, so named before these two visited it, had not previously seen white men, nor had they heard of the atrocities committed on the blacks of the east coast by the white men. Naturally peaceful, their unbounded curiosity formed the basis of their welcome to Jenks and Boyne. They accepted these adventurers into their evolved community – but they wanted, too, to take the white men's possessions into their community, where no individual possessed property save only the ownership of women.

It was not without misgivings and great difficulty that Jenks saved the major portion of the launch's cargo without open strife, and quickly he realised that to remain on Hunter Island with the blacks would mean the loss of everything and the rapid sinking of Boyne and himself to the level of the savages.

They had been but a week on Hunter Island when he decided to quit, despite the fact that he was sorely puzzled by the problem of the course to sail. The uninhabited islands he already had visited lacked at least one essential to making his dream come true. To proceed southward along the west coast of Van Dieman's Land was merely to re-trace their sea-steps; to sail south and east along Tasmania's northern coast would bring them into the track of ships. There appeared but one solution of the problem – the reversal of the old saying about the devil known and unknown. The known contained no suitable island: the unknown might.

The fresh north wind blowing off the little beach gave to Jenks his sailing orders. To his companion, he said:

"We'll have to get away from here, Boyne, before the blacks take everything we've got – even our shirts and pants."

Boyne was scowling at the group of men, women and children, even then pawing the launch and staring at the gear.

"P'haps if we bashed one or two, they'd keep away," he suggested.

"We want to live at peace, not at war," snapped Jenks. "We've got to find an island with water and timber and game, and no inhabitants, black or white. Now's the time to get away from here, the wind being just right. This is what we'll do. We'll push off the craft so's only her bow is touching the beach. You keep her like that. I'll get some sugar in a basin and lure the blacks a bit up the beach. Then, when I'm handing out the sugar, you come along, too. We'll each grab a lass when I shout the word and run with her to the boat, toss her on board, and push off. Then you swing the craft round with the oar while I run up the mains'il. Before I've got the sail up to the truck it'll fill, and we'll be away before the blacks knows what's what. By that time they can't hope to catch us in their canoes."

Boyne's small eyes glittered.

"I'm your man," he assented.

"Good! Now you stay aboard and don't come ashore till all is ready. And don't make a move to grab a wench till I shout the word go."

Obtaining a bowl, Jenks filled it with the treasured coarse brown sugar – watched by three dozen pairs of bright eyes – the while Boyne pushed the stern of the launch seawards and then maintained its position by thrusting an oar-tip deep into the sandy bottom of the bay. Upon Jenks stepping ashore with the sugar-filled bowl, the blacks shouted with the joy of anticipation, and, surrounded by them, Jenks walked up the beach to the edge of the scrub.

There, with slow deliberation, he proceeded to dip from the bowl a spoonful of sugar into the eagerly outstretched hands. Boyne came craftily to watch his companion and a young girl who had taken his brutish fancy.

The arranged signal being given, both men snatched up a native girl and ran with them to the launch. The girls screamed and struggled, and were clouted into insensibility before being tossed into the boat. With the impetus given it by the two men prior to their clambering aboard, the launch slid away from the shore. Whereupon Jenks hauled up the mainsail, and Boyne shoved the bow round to the open sea. The wind immediately filled the sail, and when the astonished blacks broke into frenzied action the little craft was leaving the bay and meeting the swell of the open sea.

It was indeed fortunate for the adventurers and kidnappers that the wind did not fall away into a complete calm when the launch was at the entrance of the bay, as it did some three hours after they left Hunter Island. Somewhere north of Robin Island the launch lay becalmed all night and all the following day.

Due to Jenks' mastery of Boyne, the native girls were treated with consideration, and they were overcoming their fear of the white men – assisted probably, by the white men's tucker – when, with startling swiftness, a southerly buster broke upon the craft off the mainland, almost capsizing the boat. Capsised it would have been had not the mast snapped cleanly from its stepping.

The sea rose with magical fury after the calm, and with hatchets the mast was cut away – a difficult task, as Jenks insisted that not only the broken mast be salvaged, but, too, every inch of the stay ropes and the torn sails. Dawn broke ugly with racing clouds, beneath which the lead-coloured, crested water-mountains sprang upon them from the south-east in never-ending succession.

Drenched with sea-spray, the native girls crouched beneath what covering the men had aboard. Under Jenks' direction, a stunted jury-mast was rigged and a yard or two of sail hoisted. It gave the launch only steering way, and did not permit Jenks to tack either way against the wind.

The land had vanished altogether, and the gale drove the launch steadily away from Van Dieman's Land, past King Island, two days later, and thence onward towards the coast of South Australia. Day after day did the wind blow hard from the southeast. It was a week before the wind abated and then veered to the north. The clouds passed away to the east, permitting the sun to shine and to warm the castaways. But there still was no land in sight, and, despite all Jenks' ingenuity, the launch could not be sailed save before the wind.

Throughout this period of storm and stress Boyne behaved well, obeying orders with alacrity, his energy taken up by tasks necessary to preserve his life. But when the dangers were past, his mind was occupied with other matters, chief of which was that concerning the bare gallon of fresh water remaining in the water-cask.

"I could drink what's left of the water in one swig," he said to Jenks.

The other man's brows drew together. He said, with dangerous quiet:

"*You could*, Boyne – but you *won't!*"

The weather now was warm, and the sun hot. The launch was making about four knots. Jenks sat holding the tiller; Boyne, amidships. For'ard the two girls sat, laughing and talking, seemingly now quite happy and oblivious to the desperate needs immediately ahead. One of them saw a fin close astern, and with an excited cry pointed to it. Both Boyne and Jenks looked back, to see the ugly fin of a shark zigzagging after the launch. For a moment or two both men stared at the sinister triangle cutting the water, and then their gaze converged and met.

"With less'n a gallon of water in the cask, Jenks," growled Boyne, "we ain't got no right to carry passengers."

"There being no land handy, we can't put 'em ashore," pointed out Jenks.

"There's that 'ere shark," said Boyne. "He'd make things quicker than drownin'."

Jenks said nothing, but his masked eyes were hard as agates as they bored their gaze into Boyne; and Boyne scowled and looked swiftly away to hide his thoughts.

Jenks' perceptions were sharp, and Boyne's face plainly indicated the workings of his mind at all times. There was much of the dreamer in the practical Jenks. He now was a man governed by one idea – that of finding an island on which he could enjoy the comforts of a dwelling, a wife, a garden, and freedom. The fact that at this moment he was adrift on an unknown ocean in a craft that could not be sailed other than before the vagrous winds, did not dim the brightness of the dream or the determination to realise it whilst life continued – nor did the fact that less than one gallon of water remained in the cask to serve four people. What threatened to cast a shadow over it was the intention, plainly portrayed on his companion's face, to murder him and the two girls in order that Boyne might prolong his life.

For several hours following this understanding of Boyne's intention, Jenks pondered on his course of action. Like all dreamers, he was ruthless in circumstances proving dangerous to the realisation of the dream. Moodily, he, with the others, watched the shark that continued to follow the boat with dreadful expectancy. The sun went down into the sea, and nowhere was the horizon broken by land, and it was just after the sun had set that the chance was given Jenks to relieve himself of the threatened shadow, choosing a hatchet with which to kill the fellow in order to avoid the expenditure of powder and shot. The shark was rewarded for its patience.

It was a quite passionless killing, arousing in Jenks no more mental excitement than that felt by anyone when swatting a blow-fly. The native girls were stricken dumb with reawakened terror – terror aroused less, perhaps, by the deed itself than by the dreadful calm on the killer's face and the equally dreadful calm of his subsequent actions. Fearfully did they stare at him in the gloaming. All night long they huddled together, watching the bulk of the white man as he sat like a stone in the stern, tiller in hand.

The sun rose on another cloudless day, the wind blowing at breeze strength from the south-east. It was now almost a fortnight since Jenks and Boyne had left Hunter Island, and almost ten weeks since they had escaped from the penal settlement. Twice this day did Jenks give the girls a little of the water. He served himself but once.

The next clay was one of enduring torment. The day following, the women were listless, their fears and terror submerged, hunger and thirst predominant. They rose at times to stare at the man who held the tiller under one arm, and the water-cask between his feet. All the flour was gone, but two precious bags of whole wheat still remained – Jenks' seed wheat. There were bags of peas and beans – Jenks' seed beans and peas. There were a few potatoes – Jenks' seed potatoes. These commodities were not for consumption: they belonged to the dream, and were untouchable.

As Boyne had suggested should be done, a coarse-grained man would have disposed of the native women in order to conserve the water for himself, but not this one-idea-man Jenks. He still dreamed a dream in which seed and women had definite places – a dream which would not be coherent were there lacking one or the other. From the lolling, listless blacks, the gaze of the man's salt-encrusted eyes went out over the sea in search of the dream island. And towards the sunset he saw it.

On the north-west arc of the horizon reared blue-black hills of rock. The wind was driving the launch directly to this land mass, and when the day waned and the stars appeared Jenks noted them, and throughout the night tried to steer the craft on a straight course. At his side seated hope.

Towards dawn often he stood up to cling to the mast and to strain his hearing for the sound of breakers, but when day broke once again, and the sea was coloured crimson and black, Jenks tried to shout his joy, for the island was less than a mile distant. That it was a large island he now was confident – but what island, or where situated, he was utterly at a loss to determine.

The two girls lay asleep or unconscious. They had been given the last of the water the previous evening. Weary and exhausted as he was, the golden promise of his dream gave to the man strength and mental clarity, so that he was able to choose a passage between semi-sunken rocks, through which he managed to sail the launch into the mouth of a small creek.

The air was laden with the scent of heath and broom and the moist earth beneath the bordering trees. The wind blew directly up the creek, and, because its first reach looked so inviting, Jenks put aside the desire to run the boat on to the sandy shore of either bank. Round the bend the width of the creek abruptly narrowed. The trees shut off the wind and the launch lay becalmed. And there on the left bank Jenks saw a party of wallabies drinking, and he thrust overboard a basin and drew up fresh water.

He was reviving the women when he saw at least a hundred wallabies emerge from the trees and join those at the creek edge. They drank, or sat up, regarding the launch without trace of fear, thus informing Jenks that the island was uninhabited, and that never before had these animals encountered man. He shot one without difficulty, and thereafter pushed the launch ashore and made fast. Then he made a fire and set meat grilling, afterwards lifting the women to the cool, sweet grass beside the fire and feeding them and himself.

He had reached his dream island at last.

As Jenks had seen while at sea, this proved to be quite a large island, blessed with plenty of fresh streams, big timber, countless wallabies on the hills and in the gullies, and countless seals that basked on the rocks around the coast. Shoals of fish came to the mouth of the creek. At every sheltered inlet wild fowl abounded. And there were no inhabitants other than Jenks and the two native girls.

They built a house of logs, with a grass roof. They sowed the peas and the beans and the potatoes, wisely keeping back the seed wheat until the winter had passed, in a clearing they fenced with brushwood. Jenks explored his island, fished, or trapped wallabies for meat. The first wheat harvest was excellent. Beside seed for the following year, it provided a plentiful stock of grain for bread.

Life was good – very good – to Jenks and his two wives for four years. In the fifth year a ship came to the island.

Jenks first saw it when it was standing off some three miles, and we can imagine his feelings whilst he watched it draw near and nearer, and then when a boat put off and was rowed into the south of the creek. That part of his early life, which had been good, cried for contact with these white men, and that which culminated in the dreadful penal settlement shrank from such contact. There were three men at the oars and a young officer at the tiller, the hacked water-casks telling of their mission to the island. And while the men filled the casks the officer and Jenks met on the creek bank above the house.

At this meeting Jenks imparted nothing of his history, and the ship's officer evinced no curiosity about it. They entered into a contract whereby, in return for clothes, tobacco, powder and shot, to be at once issued from the ship, Jenks would collect seal and wallaby skins for sale when the ship returned a year hence. He learned that his island was situated in Spencer's Gulf, and that on very many of the islands off the Victorian and South Australian coasts were men who lived by collecting skins for sale to visiting ships.

So the ship sailed away, and Jenks and his two women set to work snaring wallabies and shooting seals. But the ship did not return the following year, nor, indeed, ever. No ship called at the island for three years, by which time the women and Jenks were back again in skin clothes. But towards the end of the third year there arrived the schooner *Elizabeth*, in command of Captain John Hart, who, many years later, in his letter to Governor La Trobe, included this enlightening passage:

> Early in December, 1831, we landed on the Lawrence Rocks, Portland Bay, where we were joined by a boat's crew left there the year before, they having procured nearly 400 skins (seal). Proceeding towards Kangaroo Island, anchored on the 16th in Guichen Bay; landing on Baudin's Rocks and killed 30 seals, leaving one man with a supply of water and provisions until our return.
>
> These islanders were principally men who had left various sealing vessels when on their homeward voyage, the masters readily agreeing to an arrangement by which they secured for the next season all the skins obtained during their absence. At Kangaroo Island there were some sixteen or eighteen of these men. There was another class of men, also, who probably had escaped from Van Dieman's Land; these lived generally on islands apart from the others: some on Thistle Island, near Port Lincoln, and other islands in Spencer's Gulf. One I visited had two wives, whose woolly heads clearly showed their Van Dieman's Land origin.

Jenks and these other fur-getters, to all intents and purposes, were servants of the shipowners. They lived by trading skins for food, tobacco, and clothes. But where Jenks was outstanding was in the fact of his establishing himself without the aid of ship or owners. The intelligent Captain Hart found a well-built, roomy house, a fenced garden, fenced paddocks, in one of which was ripening a fine crop of wheat; tamed wallabies and many hens from the original birds obtained from the first ship to call. He saw two robust and happy aboriginal women, and numerous children. And in a store-house Jenks showed him seven thousand well-preserved wallaby skins, which were finally sold in China.

"You appear to be very comfortable," Hart remarked when about to step into his boat to be rowed to his ship.

Silas Jenks waved his hand to his home and farm, saying:

"We have made all that out of practically nothing. It all belongs to us – me and the women and the children – and we all belong to that, Cap'n."

And so they parted: Captain Hart to sail away and make two further voyages before proceeding to London, where he assisted the new board of South Australian Commissioners, and was able to furnish them with sailing directions for Colonel Light, who was to plan and found the city of Adelaide – Silas Jenks to live out his life with his wives and his children, and to leave behind him a monument to his courage, tenacity, and wonderful pioneering ability.

Wandi and the Bilker

The *Stirling Castle*, a full-rigged ship, passed northward along the east coast of Australia from Sydney, bound for Singapore. The weather was clear and calm. It was the afternoon of May 23, 1836, the eighth day of the voyage, and, as was usual, Captain Fraser's wife sat in a chair on the poop deck in order that she might keep a bright eye on Mr. Baxter, the second mate, whose watch on deck it was.

"Yes, Mr. Baxter," repeated Mrs. Fraser. "As I've often told you, if you aim to command a ship, you've got to learn to stand no tricks from the crew. You've got to keep 'em always on the jump, else they'll loaf on you like that useless Martin Conway is doing now. Look at him, standing there by the mainmast gawking at the sea."

Baxter was young, good looking and well-built. A humorous mouth belied the cold gleam now deep in his blue eyes. Silently he thanked Neptune he was not married. Aloud he said:

"Conway's a good and willin' seaman, marm."

"Fiddlesticks!" snapped Mrs. Fraser. "None of them are good and none of them are ever willing."

The woman's mouth was already a straight line. Still young and pretty, she would have been really attractive if she had not revealed evidence of soon becoming the complete shrew. Swiftly she smiled at the broad and straight back of the officer standing with his big hands gripping the poop rail. The seaman at the wheel glanced sharply at her and as quickly looked down at the compass. Seeing the woman's smile, a leer had leaped to his mouth. Mrs. Fraser reminded him of a certain harpy away back in Sydney Town.

"Yes, Mr. Baxter," she said tormentingly. "You've got to be rough with the crew to get on on the sea. You've got to be –"

The second mate sighed with relief at the moment Captain Fraser emerged from the companionway to interrupt his wife's philosophy of success for a ship's officer. Captain Fraser was burly and stern of countenance, but, as ship masters went in those days, he was considerate to his officers and crew.

"What's your course, mister?" he asked gruffly.

"Nor'-west by north, sir," replied Baxter promptly.

"Correct," checked the captain, who had looked over the helmsman's shoulder at the compass. "Ah, there's eight bells. You can go below, mister. I'll take her till Mr. Brown comes on deck."

Joseph, a West African who rated as steward, arrived with a pot of tea, at that time a great luxury. Mrs. Fraser gave her husband a cup of it and a couple of wholemeal biscuits from a small barrel she had brought from Sydney. The helmsman, who was being relieved, whispered to his relief something about the captain's wife being a mixture of vinegar and honey.

An hour later, when Captain Fraser, for the tenth time, turned to look uneasily to the southward, he gave the order to shorten sail. The order astonished his wife as well as the boatswain who received it, for the sea was calm and the wind came easily from the north-east. Without the reliable instruments and wireless of the twentieth century, Captain Fraser was yet too good a seaman not to note the long rolling line of cloud sweeping northward after the ship.

"Wind's a-coming, wife, and plenty of it," he explained while he watched the crew reefing the drawing canvas. "Although we're a hundred miles north of Moreton Bay, we're still in the path of the sudden gales which spring up along this coast."

At six-twenty the southerly buster overtook the ship. The course was still nor'-west by north, and it was maintained. At nine o'clock, when visibility was almost nil, the Stirling Castle struck a reef.

The impact was terrific. The masts snapped like carrots. The two seamen grasping the wheel were so flung against it that both were killed. The poop cabins and the store-rooms and their contents were all flung forward into the after-hold. The darkest of nights was made the more terrible by the shrieks of the injured, the screams of Mrs. Fraser, and the roar of the sea breaking about and over the ship and upon the reef, which held her fast.

By morning, however, the wind had dropped to a light breeze and the sea had moderated. Daylight revealed indescribable confusion on the main and poop decks, and after the killed had been cast overside, and the injured attended, efforts were made to re-float the vessel. Despite all the crew could do, the ship remained a wreck, and, after several days of effort, the captain ordered that the two remaining boats be launched and provisioned as well as possible from the chaos of stores in the after-hold, now filled with water.

"We must keep together, lads," he shouted as many of the crew piled into the pinnace. "We're more'n a hundred miles north of Moreton Bay, and between us and the settlement there, there's only them."

He pointed to the distant land from which a dozen or more aboriginal signal smokes were already rising.

A strange point in this tragedy is that not one of the officers entered the pinnace, which was commanded by the boatswain. The captain and Mrs. Fraser, the two mates, two boys and the rest of the crew boarded the longboat. Provisions were short, and the only fresh water they had was added to a partly filled keg of beer.

There now began a long, hard row to the south against the wind and strong currents. When day broke on the third day, the pinnace was missing, and was never again seen. The sixth day found the castaways in serious plight. The scanty provisions had given out, while the mixture of water and beer in the keg was almost vanished. Constant bailing was necessary to keep down the level of the sea water which splashed over-side and entered the longboat through sun-stretched planks. Half the time everyone, including Mrs. Fraser, sat waist deep.

The woman wailed that she was cold, hungry and thirsty.

"Let us get to land. The savages could not be more cruel than this ocean."

In their rough way, the men did all they could for her, bearing patiently her incessant complaints. At length, on the seventh day, Captain Fraser steered the longboat into the shelter of a small and barren island situated only a few miles from the reef on which the ship was wrecked. There the boat and its occupants were made dry by the sun, and all hands went ashore to gather shellfish. They obtained but a small supply, and one of the two boys slipped off a rock and was drowned.

The mates and the men now began to add their urgings to those of the captain's wife that they accept the mercy of the blacks rather than prolong the struggle against the elements and the tides.

And so, more on his wife's account than on theirs, and dead against his own judgment and inclination, Captain Fraser consented to steer for the land.

The wreck of the *Stirling Castle* had aroused tremendous excitement among the blacks. Those natives who saw it the following morning announced the wonderful news by smoke signalling, and on the day that Captain Fraser and his companions landed, four distinct tribes had gathered on that part of the beach waiting for flotsam and keenly watching the occupants of the longboat.

The reception of the longboat and its occupants was truly remarkable. Many of the wildly excited blacks entered the sea to meet it, and before the boat could be beached they seized upon it, lifted it bodily from the water, with its occupants still in it, and ran with their load up the beach and into the scrub. There then followed a kind of rugby scrum, in which, collectively, the white people were the ball. The jubilant blacks, shouting and yelling, milled about them, tearing at their clothing with eager hands. The captain's chronometer and sextant they smashed to pieces and distributed to wear in their head decorations. From the blacks' point of view it was quite a joyful party.

Mrs. Fraser huddled on the ground, in torment of mind and body. She was beginning to realise that the ocean would have been kinder. By signs the white men begged for food and water, and there was contemptuously tossed to them the head and entrails of a shark.

"Don't spurn it, be friendly," urged Captain Fraser. Glaring at a fine-looking young seaman named Major, he added grimly: "You start fighting, my lad, and the day'll come when a chief will walk up to you and smile. That will be the signal for his warriors to kill you and stick your head on the prow of his canoe."

Sullenly the furious seaman subsided.

The castaways had devoured the horrible food, when the blacks again surrounded them, and with fire-pointed sticks prodded them away to drag wood to the camp fires. Of Mrs. Fraser they took no notice, but she was a horrified spectator of the murder of two seamen who rebelled against this form of labour conscription.

A day or two afterwards the several tribes divided the prisoners, and those tribes that were merely visitors to the district departed for their country. Captain Fraser was able to whisper to his wife before being taken away:

"Remain here as long as you can. I'll find means of getting back to you."

Throughout the subsequent night Mrs. Fraser lay in a cleft of rock, shivering beneath the light blanket of seaweed she had managed to gather, her mind stunned by the horrors she had witnessed. In the morning she found her self entirely alone, and, the new-risen sun having warmed her, she fled along the beach until she was stopped by a party of black women who stepped out of the bush to intercept her.

These women belonged to the tribe who had taken the captain, and, whereas the men of all the tribes had not molested her or forced her to work, the lubras did both. They set her to work dragging wood to the new camp fires. Later they rubbed her body with gum and the sticky juices of shrubs. Not being quite satisfied with this, they pulled out all her hair and covered her scalp with gum, into which they stuck birds' feathers. Then, one of the lubras having two babies, Mrs. Fraser was given one to nurse. Should the imp cry, the nurse was soundly thrashed for being the cause of its crossness.

A terrible week passed for the poor woman. Then she saw her husband dragging a huge log of wood through the bush. He was so weary that he often fell, and Mrs. Fraser ran to him and cried:

"Where have you been all this time?"

"Hush!" he warned her. "Take care! They told me by signs to never dare to speak to you or any woman. I haven't had a chance to join you."

Abruptly they were surrounded by a contingent of yelling warriors. One killed the captain with a thrust of his spear. Another roughly pulled out the spear, shouting angrily at the killer. At last, at the end of endurance, Mrs. Fraser fell senseless on the body.

Beneath the load of hardships, starvation and ceaseless labour, the white captives began to fail, thus depreciating in value to their captors. Brown, the chief mate, on hearing of the murder of Captain Fraser, went berserk, and was subdued only after a severe fight. At the time, Mrs. Fraser had just kindled a new fire, and beside it Brown was laid down and his feet thrust into the flames. He was fed into the fire by inches until he died. Major, the fine-looking seaman whom the captain had warned, was at work when one of the chiefs walked to him and smiled. Remembering what the captain had said, Major turned to run and escape his doom, but a waddy crashed against the back of his neck. Sometime afterwards, Mrs. Fraser saw his head decorating the prow of a canoe. Two seamen, Doyle and Big Ben, did manage to steal a canoe and escape in it, but both were drowned while crossing a wide creek. The remaining ship's boy was clubbed to death when he fell desperately ill.

And so the dreadful tale continues to the point presented by the arrival of Wandi the Talker.

We have been too easily led by the by romanticists into believing that the men transported from Great Britain to the penal colonies in Australia were entirely innocent or guilty only of such minor crimes as snaring a rabbit on the squire's preserves. In actual fact, the transported men were, in most cases, the very worst of British criminals, for the authorities had other uses for lesser criminals, who were press-ganged into the navy and sent to fight in the army in France.

One of the toughest men ever transported to Australia and sent to the new penal settlement at Moreton Bay was a man named Bracefell. There is some excuse to-day for thinking that there was nothing good to be said of the penal settlements, but there was at least one good point in favour of the "system." It either killed its victims or it so toughened their bodies as to make them men of iron.

Bracefell survived the initial tortures in the chain gangs, and grew so in strength that he was able to break his shackles and escape into the bush, where the hardships he suffered were as heaven to the hell of the "system."

By comparison with this man, the aboriginals were as mild as Mary's little lamb. When he saw the smoke of the first camp fire Bracefell did not veer away from it. No, he was too hungry, and the fire spelled food. He ran to it, burst into a clearing in which half a dozen bucks were being fed by their women. Bracefell calmly took what he wanted. The outraged bucks sprang at him to argue this matter of etiquette. Bracefell, laughing, smote one so hard that he dropped dead. Still laughing, he picked up one to use as a flail against the others, and because of his strength and his laughter they submitted themselves and everything they had to him.

Had Bracefell been living to-day he might well have become a League of Nations interpreter. With astonishing rapidity he mastered the language of this tribe he had so quickly subdued, and when eventually he met Eumundy, the chief of the strongest of the several tribes back of Sandy Cape, he possessed many distinct advantages over the aborigines.

Eumundy was no kitten, but Bracefell began early on him, punching him severely in the stomach, then upper-cutting him to the jaw, and finally dumping him half a dozen times in true wrestler's fashion. On Eumundy recovering, Bracefell explained his intention not to usurp the throne, and his desire to live in comfort and in peace and be a real pal and supporter of royalty.

Like all Australian blacks, Eumundy was gifted with a sense of humour. He had Bracefell initiated into the tribe and fixed up with countless blood relationships and marriage connections. In addition, he re-named the escaped convict Wandi – meaning the Great Talker.

Now the strength of the toughest of he-men is limited, and this Bracefell recognised. Again, no matter how strong a man be, he must sleep sometimes, and he cannot always have his back to a tree trunk as a shield against a spear. Wisely, therefore, he determinedly remained in royalty's shadow and studiously avoided taking to himself any of its glory.

Thus it was that for many years Wandi continued to live and actually to enjoy life. He was the power behind a throne governing four or five tribes, and he was able to speak fluently all their many dialects. Not being in the vicinity of the coast when the *Stirling Castle* was wrecked, it was not till after the deaths of Captain Fraser and the others that he appeared one day at the entrance of the rough humpy the blacks had permitted Mrs. Fraser to build for herself.

For a long minute she stared at Wandi, who at the moment was voiceless. She saw a huge man partly covered with skins and carrying an outsize in waddies. He saw a tattooed, painted, caricature of a white woman whose eyes were terrible to look into, whose appearance was the acme of degradation. Toughened and hardened as he was by his own terrible experiences, his rough sympathy was instantly extended to her.

"So ye're from a ship, eh! What ship?"

"You – you are –"

"What ship, I asked ye, marm?"

"The *Stirling Castle*," she replied breathlessly. "But – you're white. You are not one of our men. They have all been killed but me. Who are you?"

"Me!" The big man tossed his shaggy head and laughed. "I'm Wandi, the white blackfeller. I'm Bracefell, the convict. And ye – ye're a white woman, by the Lord Harry. But never mind that now. Tell me about the ship – and keep yer distance."

He had not moved from the position he had taken before the door of the humpy, but she was about to approach nearer to him when halted by the sharp command:

"We're not gonna parade together afore the blacks," he said. "They'd think I was takin' you from 'em, and they'd come down on me like a ton of bricks. Now get on telling me about the ship and its company."

And then, when the fearful tale was told:

"So the pinnace lot disappeared, eh? Hum! Might have bin swamped. Might have got down to Meginchin,[14] where they'd have told the officers about you. The officers might send sojers here lookin' for you and – marm – snare me if I don't look out."

"But, Bracefell – Wandi – you'll get me away from here? You'll do something for me, surely?" implored Mrs. Fraser.

"Why should I, marm? Why should I get in trouble with the blacks for helping you? And why should I take you to Meginchin, where I'd likely enough be snared and put into the chain-gang again. No, marm, I'm a free man, and I'm remaining free."

"But – but –"

"Shut yer trap! I'll tell yer what I'll do for you. I'll raise you a bit in the social life hereabouts. I'll ask old Eumundy for you."

Mrs. Fraser continued her plea for aid, but Bracefell turned and strode away, and the watching bucks saw his facial expression

---

[14] Afterwards Brisbane.

and heard his laughter and were content that their "possession" was safe from the white black-fellow.

Bracefell halted about fifty yards from Eumundy's humpy and there thrust the handle end of his waddy deep into the sand and sat down beside it as any black visitor would have done. He knew how to approach a chief, when to talk and keep on talking, when to hit and keep on hitting. He waited there a full hour before Eumundy appeared and came slowly to greet him.

"Ah, Wandi, my brother!" exclaimed the elderly but still powerful aborigine. "My heart is made light by your return."

"I have learned many things, brother – great things," Bracefell said fluently in the aboriginal tongue. "You have enemies who desire to smile on you. I know them, and because I know them I shall smile on each of them long before they dare to smile on you."

"Their names, oh my brother?"

Replied the cunning Bracefell:

"If I tell you the names of your enemies, brother, you will get to work on them and other enemies will take their place. You leave it to me. Being king, you've got other things to think about beside killing your enemies. That's my job, brother."

Eumundy concurred. He had a real affection for Wandi, who, from the beginning, had made life so much easier for him.

"My brother," he said, "you do many things for me which makes me glad. What now can I do for you?"

Bracefell pretended to ponder on this offer before he indifferently said:

"We are brothers, Eumundy. Your enemies are mine. Yet I am of the white skin. You have given me wives – many wives – and you have learned me the way to manage wives than which surely there is no better way. Here I have seen the white castaway. Give her to me to wife and to manage and –"

Eumundy grasped Bracefell's arm.

"Take her," he said without hesitation. "She has ever been a thorn in my flesh. My young men quarrel and kill each other because of her. The lubras scream at their men because of her, and then their men beat them too severely and kill them and want other wives. So take her, and when you tire of her quietly choke her to death that we might have peace among us. But, my brother, do not let her take you away from us to Meginchin, for then the young men will blame me and many will become my enemies and some will attempt to smile on me."

"That's a bargain, my brother," Bracefell agreed heartily. "But the woman can wait. Listen! I've found waterholes where there are waterlily bulbs, and away beyond Black Hill there is a mob of kangaroos that will delight the young men and bring much food to the fires."

For a week Bracefell dared not approach Mrs. Fraser, wishing not to over-value the gift bestowed on him by Eumundy.

Even when he claimed her, her life was no easier. She still had to forage for food and take greater care in its cooking. She still had to labour at the camp chores. But, however, she quickly realised that she had more power over this white man than she had over the blacks.

"I can't understand you liking this horrible life," she said with a flash of that biting tone she had used with the second mate of the *Stirling Castle*.

"There's a life more horrible than this," Bracefell growled, and she flinched in expectation of a clout, "and that's down at Meginchin with the chain-gangs."

"They wouldn't put you back in the gangs if you rescued me and took me there," Mrs. Fraser said firmly. "They'd reward you for rescuing a white woman from the blacks. They'd grant you a free pardon."

"Perhaps!"

"I know they would. I'm still Mrs. Fraser, the wife of a ship's captain. I would appeal to the Commandant. I'd go to Sydney and appeal to the governor. I knew his wife."

This gave the man much food for thought, and for a long time he mentally masticated it.

"And supposin' I did get a pardon? What then? Why, I'd have to go to work for another man to earn tucker and a roof. Work! Do I have to work here?"

The woman sighed. Bracefell spoke the truth, as she had learned to her bitter cost. Where they were, only the women worked. And how they worked!

"Listen," she urged, Eve in her voice. "I'm not penniless. I've got property in England beside what my husband swore he'd leave me. Now you take me down to Moreton Bay. They will grant you a pardon for sure. Then we can be married and go back to England, and with my property we can buy a roadside hostelry and live in comfort for or the rest of our days. Wouldn't that be better than this?"

"It would!" roared Bracefell. "And you'd marry me? You'd keep your word?"

Instantly came the assurance, and again Bracefell pondered long and deeply.

"All right, I'll do it," he consented. "You're right. Life back in England, and in an inn, would be good. Anyway, I'll think it over."

Mrs. Fraser allowed almost a week to pass, waiting and hoping for Bracefell to revert to the subject of escape.

"Wandi, what are you going to do about me?" she asked.

Bracefell looked up from his task of pointing a spear by alternately charring it with fire and scraping it with an oyster shell. For ten seconds he stared at her, his brows almost met above his fierce eyes. And into the fierce eyes crept a wistful expression.

"If we're caught by the blacks, we'll be finished, both of us."

"But you wouldn't let them catch us, Wandi," cooed Mrs. Fraser, knowing now that the victory would be to her.

"Well, promise again what you did."

Mrs. Fraser reiterated her promise to marry him and give up to him her little bit of property, and her heart leaped when he said:

"We'll get away to-night."

A master of bushcraft as expert as any of the blacks, Bracefell stole away out of camp with Mrs. Fraser about two hours before midnight. They had only a fighting chance. The man recognised it and did not under-estimate the blacks, who were certain to pursue. He and Mrs. Fraser walked in streams and along the shores of lagoons. He swam creeks, with her on his back. Never once was he at fault when he led the woman across a vast and treacherous swamp. Day broke and found them still travelling swiftly southward. Not till noon did they halt for a few minutes to eat, and when the sun was setting Wandi the Talker was still travelling fast – with Mrs. Fraser in his arms.

That they eluded the pursuing blacks was due to Bracefell's bushcraft and super-strength. When Mrs. Fraser could not walk he carried her. He slept only twice, and then merely for a few hours. And then, one afternoon, he halted, put her down and pointed to wheel and boot tracks on a road they came upon. Mrs. Fraser cried at sight of these signs of her near deliverance, and Bracefell led her along the road to the summit of a low hill from which they could look down upon the new settlement of Brisbane.

"Meginchin!" he shouted triumphantly. "The chains or freedom? Slavery with iron or England and ease? Promise me again what you have so often promised before we go down to Meginchin."

In the woman's eyes was born a blaze of hate, and upon her face grew an expression of scorn.

"Marry you!" she shrilled. "I a ship-captain's wife, marry a gallows bird? Marry a white savage? I'll tell you what I'll do. I will say how you forced me to your will. I'll complain of you to high heaven! Look! There's a party of soldiers coming up the hill. I'll complain to them, you brute, you beast, you cannibal!"

From his superior height Bracefell looked down into the passionate face of the woman he had brought out of a cruel bondage. All his dreams were shattered with a callousness unknown among the savages. He stretched his magnificent body. He raised his clenched fists. He came within an ace of striking the woman dead at his feet. The soldiers were yet half a mile away.

And then he laughed as his arms fell to his sides. He laughed again when Mrs. Fraser ran from him down the hill to the soldiers, calling loudly to them. Wandi the Talker watched her until she met the soldiers, and then he turned and ran – ran back to the natives, with whom he stayed another seven years.

Derhamboi the Makromme

The chief of the Ginginbarah stood on the lip of the headland forming the southern extremity of Wide Bay and gazed upon the sun rising from the welling waters of the Pacific. Behind him, sheltered among a grove of trees, cowered his subjects, the men silent and stern, the lubras wailing and crying aloud and beating their own heads with sticks to indicate the pain in their hearts. As that dawn had approached, so had the soul of the chief's only son departed for the mansions of Beegie, the brightness of which lit the earth by day and now sent slanting golden rays upon the grief-stricken father.

Pamby-Pamby groaned aloud, but his back remained straight and his eyes retained their habitual sternness. His son had but reached youth's estate, and had been soon due to undergo the rites of initiation that would seal him into the great tribal family. And he had fallen from a bunnia tree, doubtless cast from it by a bunyip at the instigation of an enemy, and so, before the dawn, had passed on to the bright mansions of Beegie, the sun-god.

With resolution, Pamby-Pamby conquered the grief which threatened to weaken him. He was of ferocious aspect. Protruding and lowering brows met low above a great and flattened nose which separated restless black eyes. Necklaces of sharks' teeth encircled his bull neck. Armlets banded his mighty biceps. A strong man was Pamby-Pamby, the chief of the Ginginbarah tribe, whose ground lay behind Wide Bay, on the Queensland coast. Turning, he strode back to the camp.

Tota and Meenee, close relatives, came to meet the chief, and for a space Pamby-Pamby stood and glared at them, knowing what was in their minds.

"We are sickened by the sweetness of the bunnia-bunnia fruit, O Chief," Meenee said.

"The sweetness has soured our stomachs," added Tota. "Of fish we have had enough. As Opi has departed for Beegie he no longer requires his body. It would be his wish that that which he has left here with us should fill the bellies of his relatives."

Pamby-Pamby spoke no word, but nodded and strode forward.

The two men parted to let him pass and then gazed upon him as he entered the camp. They saw him snatch up his spears and waddy and then vanish among the timber beyond the camp. The chief of the Ginginbarah had departed on a lone walkabout.

The nearest male relatives of the departed Opi gathered about the body. Maintaining strict silence, they turned it upon its face. Their women then proceeded to make a wide and long fire. When the fire had subsided into a bed of red coals the men then set to work dressing the corpse. Expertly the body of the *makromme*[15] was opened like a modern herring and then impaled on emu spears and set above the live coals to grill.

All those who feasted gained portion Opi's virtues. His vices were not recognised. From the bright mansions of Beegie Opi looked down, and was glad he was able thus to serve his relations.

Up the hill ran John Davis, the convict. Sobs tore at his throat. Sweat streamed down his face, filled his eyes and blurred sight. With each thudding footfall sounded the clank of iron. Far down the hill a musket rapped at the brazen sky, and the metallic sound of it caused Davis to laugh exultantly. He knew he was too far distant from the weapon to be hit. Not until he reached the summit of the low hill did he stop running, then to dash the sweat from his eyes with a dirty forearm and stand fighting to regain normal breathing.

Far down the narrow and winding track a group of red-coated soldiers had come to a halt, having recognised the success of the fugitive in escaping them and bondage. Beyond them lay the penal settlement of Moreton Bay, with, here and there, silver glimpses of the river between uncleared timber. The youth turned his back upon the river, the new Brisbane, the soldiers, and again ran on – ran northward, ran to meet strange adventures and Pamby-Pamby.

A remarkable youth was John Davis, born in Glasgow only thirteen years before he broke and ran from Moreton Bay. At the age of eleven he had been presented at the Sussex assizes – history does not name the charge – where he had been sentenced to transportation for life. To obtain a world tour at the expense of

---

[15] Dead man.

His Majesty's Government at so early an age proves him to be a precocious child, and to have arrived safely at Sydney among a cargo of desperadoes proves that he possessed an agile mind and a body as tough as an alligator. Such wearing influences as those exerted on him by his fellows in crime, and grandfathers in age, most certainly would have been fatal to a weakling.

His youth commended him to his gaolers at Sydney, but soon it was made manifest that, notwithstanding his tender years, this juvenile was as learned in the arts of crime as those ruffians in whose company he had crossed the world.

At this time the powers favoured Moreton Bay as a settlement for those requiring secondary treatment. The establishment at Sydney was becoming "respectable," and, too, it was too close to Government House. Consequently the worst characters were transported to Moreton Bay, where they were beyond sight and hearing. So at the ripe age of thirteen John Davis was sent there.

Although history has nothing to say about Davis' crimes, it does have something to say of Captain Logan, the commandant of Moreton Bay Penal Establishment. In fact, it has a great deal to say about the commandant's exploration trips up the Brisbane River, and little about the methods he evolved and adopted to remind the unfortunates under his charge how lucky they were to breathe the air.

Had he lived to-day Logan would probably have been an honoured member of the Royal Geographical Society and a welcome visitor at Government House. He would have secretly exercised his sadistic instincts on dogs, cats and horses. As it was, he was permitted to do just what he liked with his prisoners bar hang them, and, as hanging was the acme of kindness compared with the lightest of his measures of reformation, he was in no wise disturbed by this curtailment of his power. Prisoners to be hanged had to be sent back to Sydney.

So unspeakable were the conditions at Moreton Bay under Captain Logan that many prisoners committed murder in order that they might be returned to Sydney and duly hanged, it being recognised that swift hanging was preferable to incessant labour, the lash and the sear of iron against bone. The age which produced the John Davises also produced the Captain Logans, and from a modern standpoint there was not a tittle of difference between them.

Young Davis became a member of a gang pent-housed at night and chained together by day. Another member of this same gang was a beetle-browed blackguard known as Bill the Biter, whilst another was called Smiling Harry. There was little talking done during the labour hours, but at night, in the pent-house, the prisoners discussed the pros and cons of escaping to the bush and the blacks, or killing one of their fellows that they might be sent to Sydney and hanged.

"I ain't goin' to stand this much longer," Smiling Harry repeated a dozen times. "I'm goin' to make a break fer the bush and become a cannibal king. I knoo a sailor who was wrecked once in the West Indies, and him and a mate killed two others and et them. He told me human pork was good to eat."

"You'll be human pork if you gets among the blacks," snarled Bill the Biter. "You don't stand no chance with them, I can tell you. There's only one way of escapin' this 'ere hell of Cap Logan's."

"Wot's that?" demanded young Davis, eager ever to learn.

Bill the Biter leered at him:

"I'm thinkin' hard, me lad, of brainin' you with a mattock one day afore witnesses so's I can get sent back to Sydney where I'd be hanged fer murderin' of you. That's the only escape we got."

Davis already knew this to be true, but after the discussion that night he found Bill the Biter constantly regarding him with his terrible thoughts expressed in his eyes. And then the day came when Davis was at the end of the line of men clearing tree roots with mattocks, with Bill the Biter next him. What happened was done in an instant. The ruffian had raised his implement to bring the cutting edge down into the youth's skull, but Davis had dodged the blow and the blade had fallen to shear the chain about his leg.

Seized with terror and yet recognising his chance of freedom, if only for a few days, John Davis had bolted, taking the little-used track up the hill, with the guards' bullets whistling about him. Better the unknown blacks than the known blackguards who sought release from bondage through murder. Better the chance of continuing to live than the certainty of death at any moment.

The exhilaration of assured escape gave place slowly to fear and then to hunger. As strange to the bush as he would have been to another planet, Davis knew not where to obtain food or how. Yet the desire for food was quite secondary to the haunting fear of being captured and returned to Captain Logan's hell on earth, in which dwelt the Bill the Biters and the Smiling Harrys. For many days he hurried onward, maintaining a fairly straight course to the north, seeing never a blackfellow, glimpsing rarely a kangaroo or an emu, eating leaves and herbage which made him sick, and drinking much of the water in the gullies.

For how long he ran and walked, walked and staggered, Davis was unable to measure, but he must have travelled a hundred miles or more from the settlement before his strength gave out and he was discovered in a state of unconsciousness by a party of Ginginbarah blacks.

To them this white youth was a phenomenon, a living makromme, a dead man come back to life. It must be stated, to explain the subsequent status reached in the tribe by Davis, that the skin of a dead relative was removed before the body is grilled, when all the blood had been drained from it and the flesh was a dirty white. These blacks thought Davis to be the re-incarnation of a dead blackfellow, minus his hide. They ran and told the chief of their discovery.

Pamby-Pamby, disbelieving their tale and yet impelled by curiosity, went with them to the place where Davis had reached the end of his road of escape. The boy still breathed. He appeared to be sleeping, for, when poked by the butt end of a spear, he opened his eyes, sat up, and then sank again into the torpor produced by starvation.

Pamby-Pamby uttered a great shout. He then bent over the semi-naked figure and stared at the dirt-grimed, beardless face. He saw in the relaxed features of John Davis some resemblance to his dead son, Opi, and he shouted again with joy, for, indeed, Opi had returned from the mansions of Beegie.

With his own hands the chief gave Davis water and carried him to his own wurlie, where he nursed him back to consciousness and then to normal strength. What if this white incarnation of Opi was clothed with the tatters of a strange garment! What if he could not speak his father's tongue! He spoke, of course, as the spirits did in the mansions of Beegie, and he still wore the raiment of the spirits. This was Opi, his own son, returned to him and the tribe. Oh, the tales he would tell when he had forgotten a little of the strange spirit language and had remembered a little of his own!

So the usual sentence passed on white escapees by the blacks farther south – let him be knocked on the head and provide us with a feast – was not passed on John Davis. He came to be called, strangely enough, not Opi, but Derhamboi, meaning kangaroo rat, which is emblematic of cunning and speed.

Pamby-Pamby doted on this son who had returned from Beegie, and he found much delight in the rapid manner that Derhamboi remembered more and more of his own language, although at times he did speak much in the spirit language. While a boy of good upbringing and normal instincts would have shrank from the ferocious savage, Davis found much of merit in his father by adoption. Deeds of savagery and depravity committed by the "father" always found approbation in the "son."

Derhamboi learned much and quickly of the crafts and customs of the people. He became adept in "walking" up trees with the aid of a fibre rope. He gained fame in the chase, and when his time arrived to be taken away into the bush by the old men and there sealed into the tribal family with painful rites, he comported himself as the son of a chief should do. With the years he grew in strength and gained in power. And then he fell in love.

Unlike those tribes farther inland, the girls of the Ginginbarah were not given in marriage when babies, but had a certain amount of free choice. Into Derhamboi's life entered a bewitcher named Camiqui, who was the desired of a villain named Nitgee, a bird of bright feathers, a dour fighter and of enormous strength, and powerfully connected. To tell him to remove himself elsewhere would have met with no success, whilst the idea of challenging him in combat was considered to be unwise both by Pamby-Pamby and his "son." Still, Derhamboi wanted the wench, and Pamby-Pamby wanted that Derhamboi should have everything his "son" desired. After much thought the chief said:

"O Derhamboi, be not impatient. Wait, watch, and then strike hard and sure. Be cunning, O Derhamboi, for I fear the fellow's family almost as much as I fear his great strength against you."

And so Derhamboi waited and watched, until one bright day he saw Nitgee standing up to his waist in the bay water observing the shoal fish being driven shoreward by the porpoises. Nitgee's spear was stuck into the ground on dry land, and he was, therefore, weaponless.

What Derhamboi lacked in brute strength – and he was no weakling – he made up for in courage, determination and brains. Observing his rival to be unconscious of everything but the shoal fish lashing the surface of the water into foam, Derhamboi crawled to the water's edge and thence, on his stomach, entered the sea and, by clinging to the rocky bottom, crawled under the surface of the water until he saw Nitgee's ankles. Grasping these, he shot to his own feet. Up went Nitgee's ankles and down went Nitgee's head – under the water.

When he was almost drowned Derhamboi dragged him ashore and there killed him with his own spear. Assuring himself that the job was done with neatness and finality, he stirred the ground about the scene and then ran to tell the tribe that he and Nitgee had fought over Camiqui, and he was the victor. The tribe did not believe him, but the spear sticking into Nitgee's great body proved Derhamboi's words, and convinced them.

Thereafter Pamby-Pamby went into conference with Camiqui's people, and the totems of the parties being in order, he conferred with the elders and smoothed over the exit of Nitgee.

At once Derhamboi began the construction of a honeymoon wurlie, selecting a site for it in a grove of slender tea-tree. He was watched and advised, and sometimes assisted, by Pamby-Pamby, and when one day he explained privately how he had vanquished Nitgee, old Pamby-Pamby slapped his thighs and almost wept with loving pride. The maiden, meanwhile, demurely waited, overjoyed by the prospect of social elevation and distinction of rank.

On the completion of the honeymoon wurlie it was necessary to wait four days for the full moon. The day preceding it the lubras built a great fire in a small clearing among a grove of tall gums, and as the silvery moonlight gave place to twilight, around the fire sat Pamby-Pamby and his bucks, whilst behind them squatted the excited women, much as white women excitedly hang about a church door when a wedding is proceeding.

The full moon having reached midway to the zenith, Derhamboi appeared with his climbing rope, and with it round his middle and the tree trunk he swiftly "walked" up the trunk of a tree to gain position among its topmost branches.

"O Camiqui!" he shouted. "Come up to the moon with me."

Whereupon Camiqui ran to a neighbouring tree with her climbing rope and ran up it to rest on its topmost branch.

"Ah, Camiqui, I see you!" shouted Derhamboi exultantly. "I see you, Queen of my heart."

"What of it, O Derhamboi?" inquired the bewitcher. "I don't believe I am Queen of your heart. You love me tonight, but in the morning you will beat me with a waddy – if I let you. Go away, O Derhamboi. Your nose is too thin for my liking, and your eyes are set too closely together. Be quiet, O Derhamboi. You are keeping my people awake with your foolish squawkings."

At this, Pamby-Pamby and the bucks laughed, and the women shrieked their mirth.

"O Camiqui," advised Derhamboi, "if you keep me waiting too long, I'll give you such a beating that you won't walk for a month." More yells and much thigh-slapping and shrieks from below. "And I'll get Pamby-Pamby, my father, to carve me an extra big waddy and then hold you down while I set to with it."

So this strange courtship ran its course, punctuated by much thigh-slapping and laughter of those seated around the fire. Then, at length, up rose Pamby-Pamby to make a speech to the tribe, when he extolled his son's virtues and refrained from mentioning his vices. Tilting his face upward, he shouted:

"Hi, there, Derhamboi! Don't you be fooled too long by that cheeky wench." A noisy clamour of thigh-slapping. "Come down and go after Camiqui with a waddy slung across your back."

A thunderous roar of thigh-slapping applauded this advice.

Down came Derhamboi, and down, too, came Camiqui. They were met by Pamby-Pamby, who conducted them along a specially prepared path to the honeymoon wurlie. There the chief left the newlyweds and returned to the fire, his heart full and his mind full, too, with plans for the future of his "son."

Derhamboi proved to be a worthy son of Pamby-Pamby. For him the years passed not too unpleasantly, and with the passing of the years he learned many things and grew in cunning. Which was as well for news drifted north of many white men in the south, and all but Pamby-Pamby lost faith in the re-incarnation idea. Then, too, there sometimes came to the camp Wandi, the great talker, known to the British authorities as Convict Bracefell, since escaped to become the Grand Vizier to Eumundy, the neighbouring powerful chief.[16]

So we pass to the fourteenth year of Davis' sojourn among the blacks; to that day a messenger from a southern tribe arrived, to halt a hundred yards from the camp and there, having thrust his spears into the ground, sit to await the command to enter.

The messenger, sent by his chief, came to tell of lonely white shepherds living in isolated huts in which was much strange and delightful food. It was proposed that the tribes mass and attack several of these shepherd outposts, to take the strange food and to kill and eat the strange baa-ing animals, to kill the white men for daring to intrude on tribal grounds. Pamby-Pamby and his followers rose instantly to the idea.

Derhamboi, however, clearly saw two inevitable results of such a foray. The blacks subsequently would be wiped out, and he himself might be captured and taken back to Brisbane, and it would be a matter of time only when his relatively peaceful life of power and ease would end. But none listened to him, and with reluctance he accompanied the expedition. On the journey south to the head waters of the Brisbane River, which was fast being taken up by the squatters, he said to Pamby-Pamby:

"Let us not wait at the white men's worlies to eat the food, but return quickly to our own country. Then, when the other white men come with their sticks which made a killing with a noise, we shall be far away. And let us not kill the white shepherds, who are but the servants of other white men, for then the warriors might think it easy to kill me."

"O cunning Derhamboi, what you say is good. That we will do," assented Pamby-Pamby.

The shepherds on the newly created runs had become alarmed by the constant visits of blacks who menaced them with demands

[16] See "Wandi and the Bilker."

for food, and at sight of Pamby-Pamby's crowd two of them bolted from their hut, leaving a prepared bait. Despite the urgings of the chief and Derhamboi, the warriors fell upon the rations of sugar and flour and tea and at once consumed them. The one reason why Pamby-Pamby did not eat was that Derhamboi had interested him in the taste of plug tobacco, and, finding it good, the chief ate it in chunks and quickly became very ill. But his warriors had not eaten any of the tobacco, yet they, one after another, groaned and fell writhing to the ground.

There ensued a dreadful scene. Knowing what had happened to them, they screamed their rage and horror of approaching death. They had been poisoned by the arsenic placed in the rations by the departed shepherds. Derhamboi alone remained well and on his feet. Between terrible fits of vomiting, the warriors crawled a few yards towards the water lying in the nearby creek. Some reached it – to die the more quickly.

Tough as he was, the scene horrified Derhamboi. He picked up old Pamby-Pamby, who was too weak to walk because of the tobacco sickness, and ran with him into the surrounding bush. Believing that of all his warriors poisoned by the white men his life only had been saved by the ministrations of his "son," the chief's affection grew stronger yet. He recognised the cunning and the wisdom of Derhamboi and assented not to make a raid of vengeance but, instead, to remain quietly on his own tribal grounds behind Wide Bay.

For the tribe and for Derhamboi life went on peacefully and undisturbed until one day Derhamboi and a buck were skinning a kangaroo they had brought into camp. It was a warm day, and Pamby-Pamby snored in the shade with many of his subjects. Even the women were silent, while the children and the dogs were less vociferous than usual. And then, with the strident sound of a bugle, a white man strode into the camp shouting:

"I am Wandi!"

With amazing swiftness the tribe came to its feet and, yelling, rushed to their spears, stuck into the ground, like stacked muskets. Derhamboi saw Wandi advancing, but he saw, too, beyond his fellow-convict, two white men semi-hidden in the scrub and dressed in civilised clothing.

Derhamboi and Wandi had not seen each other for several years, and each had thought that the other had gone aloft to dwell in the mansions of Beegie. To the former, Wandi's presence in Pamby-Pamby's camp was of much less significance than that of the two clothed white men standing in the bush. Derhamboi rushed past Wandi and came to confront the white strangers. It was then that he discovered that he was unable to articulate his own language. Utterly astonished, he glared at them, and they, equally astonished, shrank back from him. Calming himself, Derhamboi by signs asked whence they had come – by land or by sea – and they replied that they had come by boat over the sea from Brisbane.

"Derhamboi, my friend," interrupted Wandi. "Our deliverance is here. These are servants of a party of squatters seeking new runs. They and their masters are good men – not police come to take us. These two have come with me from the boat, down the river. Their masters await us in the bush."

"They are police," shouted Derhamboi. "They have trapped you, and you want to sell me into their hands to gain a pardon for yourself. I tell you, I'll never go back alive to Captain Logan's hell."

"We are free men," persisted Bracefell, who had been found and convinced by the white land seekers a week or two before. "Captain Logan is dead. The manacles and the lash are no more. The prison house at Meginchin has long been thrown open, and only free men come up the River Brisbane now." Then, as he spoke in the native dialect, he added softly: "Come with me, Derhamboi, back to Meginchin. Let us go together with our white brothers. Now is your chance of real life among our own kind. Take it, Derhamboi, take it."

"Ah – no – no!" shouted Derhamboi. "You shall not take me from my father, Pamby-Pamby. This is my home. These are my people, my relations. You are a traitor to us."

He then proceeded to tongue-lash Wandi in screaming voice, believing that behind the two white men, still standing in the bush, was a great force come to take both himself and Wandi after the raid on the shepherds' huts. Accusations were followed by searing invective until Wandi made a step to his rear to snatch a spear from the ground, and Derhamboi rushed to snatch a similar weapon from a friend. Now these two outcasts, these two who had made themselves kings of 'savages, glared each at the other and hurled defiance, the one suffering from a sense of injustice, the other aroused to a frenzy of hatred at the prospect of betrayal. Both were naked, save for coverings of fibre. Derhamboi's chest was tattooed and scarred with the initiation signs, and both bore dreadful welts on their backs and the backs their legs – prison scars.

Before the affair came to the exchange of spears Derhamboi saw advancing upon them the party of white men, of whom four or five were dressed as gentlemen of the period. One called sternly upon him to throw down his weapon and to advance to meet them, and even after the lapse of fourteen years of freedom the ghost of Captain Logan commanded Derhamboi to obey. He retained his spear, however, when he strode forward and so came to glare into the eyes regarding him with not a little pity.

"Me name's Jem Davis," he managed say in English, and could say no more.

Wandi interpreted. The white men confirmed Wandi's assertions that the settlement, as a place for convicts, had been abolished long since upon the demands of free and decent people. They offered – nay urged Derhamboi to return with them to that place where he would again be among his own kind, and where they would find him employment and see that he got a free pardon. And only yet thirty years old, Derhamboi hadn't forgotten the flesh pots of his youth.

He said he would make his decision in the morning, and meanwhile he warned them to look out for themselves, because, after the poisoning of the blacks by the shepherds, the tribe still lusted for revenge.

That night the whites retired into their boat which they anchored in the middle of the river's mouth, now known as the Mary River. Ashore in the camp, Derhamboi called the tribe together, when he addressed the blacks at some length to prepare them for his departure on the morrow. He said repeatedly that after three moons he would return to them, as he could not bear to remain absent from his loved "father" and all his many relations. The women began to wail; the men to look downcast. Pamby-Pamby ran to him and clasped him about the knees while he implored his "son" not to depart from them. Others came to hang about Derhamboi's neck and arms and to add their pleadings to those of their chief. For that night Derhamboi was a king, indeed.

Early the next morning he and they rose from about the camp fires. He faced Pamby-Pamby – he, a wild, bearded, shock-headed white savage no less savage than they.

"My Father, I must go," he said brokenly. "Wandi says it. The white men in the boat swear they will be as brothers to me, and will be kind. I must obey their call, but, O my Father, I swear I will return before the full of the third moon from now."

When Opi had died Pamby-Pamby had shed not a tear. Now that old villain shed many tears.

"O, my son!" he wailed. "Leave us not. Remain by us – remain by us!"

"I shall return," reiterated Derhamboi, and then strode to the river bank where awaited the boat containing the white men and Wandi. The quiet morning was disturbed by the wailing cries of half a thousand grief-ridden blacks. That they allowed Derhamboi to go, that they made no attack on the boat's party, revealed the complete mastery John Davis had gained over their hearts and their heads.

When off the shore, Derhamboi stood up and cast from his body his necklaces and armlets. He was actually weeping, and his great hands beat his forehead. As the boat was pulled down to the sea the natives followed it along the river bank, wailing their sorrow and grief, striking their heads with sticks so that the blood streamed from them, producing in their bodies the pain that racked their hearts.

"Come back! Come back, O Derhamboi!" they implored.

And Derhamboi, still standing in the boat, beat himself and shouted: "I will return. Oh, I will return before the third full moon. O Pamby-Pamby, my Father! O Pamby-Pamby, Pamby-Pamby!"

Now the boat was pulled away from the river's mouth to meet the gentle surge of the sea, and as slowly, slowly it drew away from the shore, so the pleading voices became soft, softer. Long after the voices could no longer be heard Derhamboi stood up and cried to Pamby-Pamby. He moaned and wept as Pamby-Pamby and his tribe wept and moaned on the receding beach.

But Derhamboi never returned. Both Davis and Bracefell received pardons and lived the remainder of their lives among their own kind.

The Black Squatter

At the beginning of Victorian history – when Batman prospected the land about Port Phillip Bay after the Hentys were established on the south coast – there was growing to maturity a young aboriginal named Koram, whose tribal grounds extended along the foot of the Pyrenees. He was about thirty years old when the shadow of the white race, speeding northward from the coast, first reached his people – a shadow which was to blot them out with all the tribes of Victoria in a very few years.

Throughout the short period which witnessed the decline and disappearance of the Victorian aborigines, several of them stood high above their fellows and earned for themselves a niche in the hall of historical fame. Of these, Koram was not the least. He was intelligent as well as fearless; a thinker as well as a fighter; an organiser as well as a strategist. Had fate been kinder to him he might have become a power in the land.

To appreciate this story of Koram, the Black Squatter, one should visualise the background before which he lived. Little less than a hundred years ago the white man was not much less savage than the black man he was displacing. Away back in those years the white man was not thoroughly accustomed to the new liberty which swept across the world like a tidal wave from the new States of America under Washington; through France under the first Napoleon; and in England, where Wilberforce and Salisbury led the way. A hundred years and less ago the white man was used to hangings and floggings, and, still alive, his grandfather told tales of the torture chambers and the dungeons.

The black man did not torture unless governed by the frenzy of anger which soon passed. The black man's morals were excellent and his tribal laws rigidly maintained and obeyed. Before being soiled by the white man he was a decent citizen, but he was drawn into the white man's shadow in an age when the white man was a lusty brute, and in a locality where the white man – convict and settler and prison official and soldier – were all tarred with the brush of brutality. Visualising all this we can all the better appreciate how remarkable was this Koram.

Inter-tribal messages reached old chief Winya-Warwar and his son Koram, describing the landing of the white men, from canoes having huge white wings, at the mouth of the Yarra and where Geelong now stands, and, too, of the landing of strange baa-ing animals and other creatures that moo-ed loudly, and had horns like the dreaded Mindye, who resided on the mountain named Bee-ker Bun-nel.

Now one day Koram hunted alone along the north bank of a creek in the bed of which lay a chain of waterholes. He carried a long fighting spear called a *tare*, two *tirrer* spears used in hunting, and a fearsome hand weapon – a club fashioned like a bird's beak and head, and called a *leonile*.

It was mid-afternoon, and Koram had seen no game since early morning, when he had failed to bring down a kangaroo with one of his *tirrer* spears. Keeping along the north bank of the gum-lined, twisting creek, he now and then went down to a waterhole to examine it for fish or yabbies, when he was careful always to keep to the north side of each and every waterhole. For along the exact centre of the creek bed ran the imaginary line separating Koram's tribal ground from that of the neighbouring tribe, and, although for many years these two tribes had lived at peace, the members of both scrupulously observed that boundary and never crossed it.

Koram came presently to a long, straight reach wherein were no water-holes, and, knowing that half a mile lower down the creek took a hairpin bend, he crossed a quarter-mile of grass land to arrive again upon its bank. And there, down at the far edge of a beautiful waterhole, he saw another black man thirstily drinking.

At Koram's shout the neighbouring tribesman leaped to his feet, snatching up his spears and club, then to stand on springing legs ready to dodge a fighting spear.

"Ho, ho, there, Beergaru! It is I – Koram! Put down your weapons, as I do, and let us *wongie*."

"Ha, Koram!" shouted Beergaru. "I was as a bird asleep and was caught by an old lubra. How are you?"

"I am well, Beergaru, and I am glad to see you. See, I lay aside my weapons. Do you likewise, and let us draw together and talk."

Down went the weapons, and two naked but splendid

specimens of *homo sapiens* walked to the upper end of the waterhole, where they were careful to meet on the boundary line, and clasped each other's hands.

"It is many days since we last met," said Beergaru.

"That is so," agreed Koram. "It was long before the great rain. I remember it, as I should, for then you threw me in the wrestle. Can you do it this time?"

Beergaru laughed. They sprang apart and stood with hands pressed to thighs. Then, with a bound, Beergaru heaved himself at Koram, and Koram, quick as light, stooped and seized Beergaru by the knees. Whereupon Beergaru went limp, and instead of throwing over his shoulder a man stiff like a log, Koram held a man as limp and as awkward to handle as a half-filled bag of oats. Beergaru's right arm snaked down along Koram's back, flashed round to the side, and Beergaru gripped one of Koram's wrists and pulled it behind and up Koram's back in a kind of full nelson.

Down upon his knees fell Koram, and with a heave Beergaru gained position behind him without relaxing the painful hold. Now slowly Koram was being forced upon his back, but his feet were free, and they gave him purchase to throw himself nimbly in a somersault over Beergaru and thus apply a stranglehold, with one leg about his opponent's neck.

Now Beergaru became excited, and punched Koram in the stomach, but Koram maintained the neck scissors, which was a good stranglehold, and he tore at Beergaru's hair in a manner which should have no place in modern wrestling rules, but very often does. With his breathing stopped, Beergaru's punches lost their sting, but he did not give in by making signal with a double hand-slap to his opponent's body. Abruptly he went limp, and Koram, thinking his opponent was strangled into unconsciousness, removed the hold. It was then that the foxy Beergaru whirled himself out and away, and before the astonished Koram could do anything he was picked up, spun like a top, and heaved into the water-hole, where he created a mighty splash.

On coming up to the surface, he beheld Beergaru treading water a yard or two from him and laughing without malice or mockery.

"I thought I had you, Beergaru," gasped Koram, and then himself laughing.

"You would have won had I not tricked you, Koram. A strangled man is safe only when he is properly down. That was a good hold you got on me, but you should have loosened it; not taken it off till you were certain I was vanquished. Yes, you nearly beat Beergaru, the champion of the mountain tribe.[17] You are stronger, too, than you were the last time we met. If I am not most careful, the next time we wrestle you will win."

Still laughing, but now much cooled, they waded out of the water and sat themselves down on the boundary line to be warmed by the sun – two normal human beings, good sportsmen, and friends.

"In my dilly-bag, there beside my weapons, is brown sand good to eat," presently said Beergaru. "Would you like some to eat?"

"Surely," assented Koram, "brown sand good to eat! I have not seen such a thing."

"Taste of it first: then I will tell of it."

So Beergaru rose and fetched his dilly-bag, and from it he took a smaller skin bag containing about a quarter-pound of coarse, brown sugar. Helping himself to a pinch of this sugar, he dropped it into the palm of his other hand and then licked it off with the extreme point of his tongue.

Koram was permitted to do likewise, and, on tasting it, his eyes grew round and big, and his jaws worked in ecstatic appreciation. Without speaking, he took a second pinch of sugar, and, also without speaking, Beergaru helped himself again. Thus they sat, silent and enraptured, like connoisseurs of wine tasting an eighty-years-old vintage.

Presently:

"Where you find it?" asked Koram wistfully.

Beergaru grinned, answering:

"I did not find it. I got it from a white man who cares for many of the baa-ing animals."

"A white man! Ah – I have heard of them and of the baa-ing animals. And the white men possess this brown sand?"

"Yes. They always have it in their *mia-mias*. A white chief has come to our tribal ground and built his big *mia-mia* beside our best waterhole. And there are many of his servants who

[17] Mount Macedon.

walkabout with the baa-ing animals and put them into *mia-mias* at night. My!" Beergaru smiled expansively and rubbed his stomach, adding: "The baa-ing animals are good to eat, too. I and others killed and ate three. And then the white chief and many of his servants came upon us with their spears which kill with a noise. Some of us became dead. I and others fled."

"Fled!" echoed Koram, staring at his friend.

"There are times when it is better to run than to lie dead – killed by a noise," sagely remarked Beergaru, and for the next hour he related to Koram the coming of the white men into his country; the arrival and establishment of the first squatter with the first of the sheep and the bullocks and horses; and the first of the overseers and assigned servants.

For Koram and his tribe, two years passed in their idyllic manner – years that gave much to Koram of gifts and authority. A succession of accidents raised him to the chieftainship of his tribe, and because he was wise as well as cunning he maintained friendship with the medicine men and was reasonably merciful to all.

And then, early one brilliant afternoon in November, one of the bucks came running pantingly to camp with the news that a party of white men, mounted on strange beasts, together with several other white men driving countless baa-ing animals, had crossed the creek, and was travelling through the tribal land. On receiving this news, Koram sat before his fire, absently pushing together the glowing ends of the burning sticks, his mind occupied by the invasion he long had expected.

He had never seen a white man or a horse or a sheep, but he had learned much of all three from his friend, Beergaru. He was aware that sheep were good to eat, as was the brown "sand" he had tasted; and he was aware, too, of the power of the "spears which kill with a noise." Based on the tales told him by Beergaru was a clear understanding that, although the whites were few and the blacks were many, the whites were not successfully to be resisted. And so, remembering Beergaru's sugar and descriptions of the mutton feasts, Koram gave little thought to the foolish idea of resisting the white men. Getting upon his feet, he uttered a shout which brought all the bucks about him.

"Listen to me!" he cried authoritatively. "Although at last the white men have come with their baa-ing animals which will eat the grass our kangaroos eat and thus make them scarce and hard to slay, if we are cunning, if we tread softly, we may take away many of the baa-ing animals and hide them to kill and eat when we want food, thereby saving ourselves the labour of hunting. The white men carry spears which kill with a noise at a great distance. With our spears we may kill several of them, but afterwards the white men will kill many of us. It has been so with Beergaru's tribe, and with those tribes beyond Beergaru's land. So we will take a look-see at these white men and their baa-ing animals, and ourselves be hidden and unseen by them."

There followed probing argument, and moments when anger threatened to burst with explosive violence, but in the end Koram's words were taken as good words by the medicine men. He and the bucks marched out of camp armed and painted for war, although it was to be no more than a scouting expedition, and by devious ways they arrived in the van of the travellers and their sheep. Clouded by the dust of early summer, the loaded bullock drays, the men on horses, the widespread flock of sheep, presented a spectacle to the astonished blacks, who knew less by far than their astute chief. Hour after hour they followed this pastoral cavalcade, and as the sun set they watched curiously the white men rapidly build makeshift brush yards, into which the sheep were put for the night.

Thereafter, Koram watched for very many days a gentleman named William Clarke,[18] with his overseers and his shepherds, establish a station of 180,000 acres, with several thousands of sheep. When his bucks wished to attack those of Mr. Clarke's shepherds who were posted at lonely places, Koram pleaded and threatened until he persuaded them to caution and delay. Slowly in his mind was growing a great scheme which would recoup the tribe for the theft of their land and the loss of their food supplies. Weeks passed, and Mr. Clarke was congratulating himself about the peaceful intentions of the never-to-be-seen blacks – weeks during which Koram studied the ways of the white men and the ways of the baa-ing animals.

Mr. William Clarke had many and diverse difficulties to

[18] The father of Sir William Clarke, Bart.

surmount. The land he had taken from the blacks was poor, but healthy sheep country fairly well watered. For the first two years of his occupancy his sheep suffered badly from scab and want of attention due to the great lack of adequate labour. Even in modern times it would be difficult to persuade men to shepherd sheep alone, and always menaced by a ferocious attack by the hidden blacks. One fancies that men to-day would demand more than the basic wage for taking such risks, but those old time shepherds worked for a few shillings a week, and were liable to be returned to the chain gangs for neglect of duties.

North of Mr. Clarke's station still remained land open to Koram and his tribe. It was mountainous country, with pockets of good grass, and the astute Koram determined to carve among these mountains a sheep station for himself. He induced his "subjects" to see what he saw – the method of procuring the wherewithal of replacing their vanishing food supplies, minus the necessity of constantly hunting for it.

By now he and his followers were familiar with the habits and the crude management of sheep; the position of every shepherd's hut and sheepyards; and before he was ready to stock his own station members of the tribe had systematically "lifted" from several yards sheep for immediate consumption, and carrying the mutton back to the mountain camp. Like children, they were not satisfied with stealing just so many sheep to keep themselves fed; needlessly, they hamstrung sheep and left them for the shepherds to discover in the morning.

This wanton destruction met with Koram's disapproval, but for some time he was unable to make headway in impressing upon his followers that hamstrung sheep were useless for his purpose and of no benefit to themselves. But in time water will wear down a stone, and eventually, with the assistance of half a dozen bucks, he lifted thirty or forty sheep from a fold and drove them away into the mountains, where already had been built brush yards to receive them, and where the lubras waited to shepherd them by day.

This loss being reported to Mr. Clarke, he, with Mr. Francis, the station's head overseer, and several employees, set out to track the stolen sheep. Either they were poor bushmen, or Koram had cleverly wiped out the sheeps' tracks, for their tracks were not followed far when the white party were compelled to give up the search.

Success emboldened Koram and caused rashness and daring among his followers. Francis seems to have been a fearless and active man, for he, one night, concealed himself among the sheep in a yard, and during his second night's vigil surprised the marauders and opened fire with a charge of duck shot. Perhaps it was the fact that one unfortunate black received the shot in that place which prevented natural resting, instead of cleanly in his head, that so annoyed Koram and his tribe, for a few nights afterwards they assaulted in full force another yard, and took away all the sheep after the shepherd rashly had expostulated, and even more rashly stood with the hut light behind him, thus presenting in his person a clearly defined target for a spear.

Knowing what to look for in the shepherd's hut, The Black Squatter managed secretly to secure for himself the late shepherd's supply of brown sugar. None knew that he had it, and subsequently he would steal away into the forest and indulge himself in a solitary sugar orgy – a sort of saccharine "Jimmy Woods."

Koram prospered, but yet not without fighting. A rival to his throne was a powerful buck called Woolah, who could not be made to understand that a thousand sheep in hand were worth more than ten thousand sheep in Mr. Clarke's yards. Woolah voiced objection to droving sheep to The Black Squatter's yards when he and others could go to Mr. Clarke's yards and take away what was required for transitory needs.

"Listen to me!" shouted Koram. "Soon we will not be able to take any more of the sheep, for the white man Clarke will put more men in charge of them and give them the spears which kill with a noise. If we have plenty near our camp, we need not go down to the station yards for them."

"You are clever," sneered Woolah. "We work all night driving the sheep up here, and all the day the lubras watch them while they feed, and so they are too tired to do the camp work. If you want more sheep brought up here, then you must take the lubras down to fetch 'em. We are warriors, not shepherds."

Like all great men, Koram knew when to smash rebellion, and he recognised this as being the psychological moment to crush this one. Snatching up his *leonile* club, so fearsomely shaped like a bird's head and beak, he rushed upon the rebel. Woolah jumped for his weapons and managed to grab a spear and a *kudgerin* club. With weapons upraised above him, he made to turn and fight, but was a split second too late. The "bird's beak" pecked into his brain and he died instantly.

Now, indeed, was The Black Squatter top dog. He warmed to the opportunity of consolidating his position, and challenged all Woolah's relatives to step out if they felt annoyed, but they loudly protested that far from feeling annoyance at the death of their kinsman they really were delighted by it, as all along they agreed with Koram's ideas of providing for the future and keeping the wolf from the door with a plentiful supply of stolen sheep. Nevertheless, violence begets violence, as shall later be proved.

So Koram continued to prosper.

By now he possessed a fine station property which was subsequently to be called by the white men, Billy Billy's Waterholes. He "owned" some two thousand sheep, while the tribe continued to draw its ration sheep from Mr. Clarke's yards.

This continuous loss angered Mr. Clarke, who reprimanded Mr. Francis, who in turn taxed the unfortunate shepherds with negligence. The shepherds finally went on strike and refused to take the flocks out grazing, because during their absence the blacks raided the huts. Whereupon Mr. Francis thrashed one shepherd. This violence, too, was to beget violence in due time.

Burned by Mr. Clarke's anger, Mr. Francis gathered into an armed band a dozen of the more courageous station hands and set out to track the thieving blacks. Koram was quickly notified of the party's departure from the head station, but not for some time did he become aware of the party's objective. When he did, he had it watched night and day.

Either by chance or through design, the party moved direct towards the mountainous country, and so by leaving Mr. Clarke's run began to examine that belonging to The Black Squatter. Steadily it progressed in an almost straight line towards Koram's secret camp, and Koram's anxiety increased daily. Eventually he saw that if Francis and his companions were permitted to continue, they most certainly would cross the tracks of the stolen flock and thus discover it.

Koram's camp and sheep were then situated in a fertile and hidden valley having access only through a narrow gully between tall mountains, and, when Francis and his men reached the outlet of the valley and saw the tracks of both sheep and natives, Koram knew that the moment for action had arrived. He planned an ambush, having for its objective the driving back of the party to Mr. Clarke's station.

At the narrowest part of the gully a flight of spears fell upon the white men and their horses, but the damage was slight, because Francis expected the attack, and within ten minutes a considerable number of Koram's bucks lay dead or wounded. His heart leaden with despair, Koram saw the party, not in retreat, but pressing forward with haste into the hidden valley.

He and the survivors ran forward ahead of the white men to warn his old men and the lubras, and they had not time to dispose of the flock before Francis, with keen satisfaction, was gazing with amazement on more than two thousand of his employer's sheep. From a mountain slope The Black Squatter saw his tribe's *mia mias* consumed by fire and all his sheep driven down the valley, through the neck in the mountains, and so back to Mr. Clarke's station.

A dream had come true, only to be shattered with lead and gunpowder, but the remnants of Koram's tribe were glad that now they could go back to the delightful hand-to-mouth existence they had enjoyed before the coming of the sheep and the birth of their chief's extraordinary ambition to be a squatter.

They had not Koram's imagination, and as food supplies now were cut off many made peace with the shepherds and thankfully accepted what was thrown to them in return for gathering wattle bark and assisting in the shepherding.

But Koram made no peace with men who had robbed him of his land and depleted its natural food resources. With half a dozen bucks and their families, he maintained a kind of desultory warfare, taking what sheep they required, often being shot at and sometimes leaving one or more of their number dead on the battlefield.

Early one evening Koram had gained position at the edge of thick timber not a hundred yards from a shepherd's hut, with the sheepyards close beyond it. The evening was far advanced and the yards were filled with sheep for the night. The two shepherds were cooking a meal at the outside fire before the hut door when, followed by a cloud of dust, Mr. Francis arrived on a sweating horse. Before reaching the hut he stopped to look at the yarded sheep. Their condition plainly indicated that they had been kept in the yards all that day.

Koram could see as well as hear that the overseer was in a great rage. Mr. Francis shouted down at the two shepherds while still mounted on his horse, and the two men sullenly looked up at him. Presently all three went across to the sheepyards. This gave Koram a golden opportunity, which instantly he seized. Running to the hut, he dashed inside and gathered everything at hand: damper, cooked meat, and many tins, some of which he hoped contained brown sugar. He was back again among the trees when Francis and the shepherds returned to the hut, and from this vantage point he witnessed Francis dismount and one of the shepherds take the horse across to the horseyards. Francis continued to bully the remaining shepherd, and then Koram saw the dull gleam of light in the fellow's hand and saw the flash of the shears blade as it swept downward into the overseer's neck. He did not know that the murderer was he whom Francis once had severely thrashed, and he waited only to see the second shepherd, who had witnessed the crime, run off into the gloom in the direction of the head station.

On turning to run back to the remnants of his tribe, Koram came face to face with none other than his old friend Beergaru. His arms, laden with spears and the *leonile* and the stolen rations, Koram stood stock still, with quick anger in his breast that Beergaru should thus trespass on his tribal land.

"Koram, my friend," Beergaru said softly, "I am far into your tribal land, but I have now no tribal land to call mine; no hunting ground, no family, no tribe. All is gone – taken and killed by the white men."

Laws and taboos rose before them like iron bars, but in the falling darkness Koram rose to the greatest height he had ever reached, and so found strength to break the bars of tradition. Of what use now were taboos and laws when his own people were quickly treading that path taken by the people of poor Beergaru?

"Come with me, Beergaru," he said, and silently Beergaru

followed Koram through the sleeping forest for many miles, and so to a glade where burned a fire, about which the squatting aborigines rose to receive them.

Koram explained Beergaru's presence, whereupon the brother of Woolah – he who had rebelled against Koram and had been killed by the terrible *leonile* club — made objection to Beergaru's presence and trespass. Wordy argument ensued which lasted for a long time, but in the end Koram's determination to give Beergaru sanctuary prevailed.

That night Koram and Beergaru slept side by side at the same fire.

Day was breaking when the brother of Woolah crept from his fire to the sleeping friends. Silently he reached Koram's *leonile* club, and with one blow he killed Koram in his sleep. He killed Beergaru, too.

And so passed The Black Squatter, named by the white men Billy Billy, he whose English name will live in history forever.

A Storm in a Quart Pot

Most certainly Mark Flemming's mind was not concentrated upon Mr. Henry Wittacker's business, which at the moment was the weighing and bagging of rations for the shepherds and others working on Bunnia Bunnia Station, Darling Downs. He was making quite stupid mistakes – mistakes which caused that gentleman's temper to become excessively violent. Yet how could a young man be expected to concentrate on the job in hand when, outside the store-room, the spring sun was bright, the bush birds were vociferous, and Isabella Wittacker waited impatiently in the stoutly walled garden? When a young man is in love what does it matter if the ration of tea has been reduced from four to two ounces per week per man?

"Mr. Flemming!" roared the irate squatter as he held a hessian bag, judging its weight. "Weigh this again, sir, and announce to me the figures."

Reddening with vexation, Mr. Henry Wittacker's overseer caught the tossed bag and re-weighed it on the scales.

"Ha, ha!" shouted Mr. Wittacker. "What is the weight, sir?"

"Three pounds, sir," faltered Flemming. "I – er –"

"It is to go to Sandy Creek hut, is it not?"

"Yes, Mr. Wittacker. I'm sorry that –"

"There are three men stationed at Sandy Creek hut, are there not?"

"Yes, sir. I – er –"

"And tell me, Mr. Flemming. The ration is for four weeks, I understand?"

"Yes, sir. I regret –" again attempted Mark Flemming.

"Then why the devil do you issue three pounds of tea to three men for four weeks when you know dam' well that the ration has been cut down to a pound and a half – otherwise from four to two ounces per week per man – because of this cursed tea famine caused by the Chinese war? Kindly inform me on that point, Mr. Flemming."

As Mr. Wittacker did not press for an answer, young Mark Flemming turned back to his task of weighing and bagging the rations which were to be delivered to the seven shepherds' huts on Bunnia Bunnia.

The squatter's reference was to the Chinese war which broke out in 1838 and which in this year, 1840, was drawing to a close and producing in the vast Colony of New South Wales a serious tea shortage. In those days China was the only tea-exporting country, and by 1840 the stocks held by Sydney merchants had become almost cleared. The difficulty of obtaining supplies for station houses and huts had become so serious that Mr. Wittacker and his fellow pastoralists were compelled to reduce the never-generous ration.

While in England tea was a luxury and ale the national beverage, here along the outposts of the Colony of New South Wales tea and tobacco were the only comforts of men whose weekly food ration, other than abundant meat, was the famous scale of ten, two, and a quarter, otherwise ten pounds of flour, two pounds of sugar, and one-quarter pound of tea. Even in this writer's experience the ten, two, and a quarter ration prevailed on many stations, with the addition of tomato sauce and, at long intervals, dried potatoes.

The tea famine of 1840 added to the squatters' many worries, chief of which was the difficulty of obtaining sufficient labour. There was never a sufficiency of labour, and any cause which might interfere with the meagre supply had to be strongly combated. But what was to done when the Chinamen would fight and would not export tea?

We, can, therefore, understand Mr. Wittacker's choler when his overseer made up the full instead of the half-ration of tea; and, of course, knowing that Mark Flemming was in love with Isbella Wittacker, we can understand how that young man's mind could not be directed to the inter-related questions of tea, Chinamen and shepherds, for Mark and Isabella were secretly in love. They feared Mr. Wittacker's temper less – much less – than they feared the dynamic Mrs. Wittacker, who, had she known of the love affair, would instantly have banished the girl to relatives in Sydney.

Mr. Wittacker's early struggles for success had been hard and long, but in 1840 he was, figuratively speaking, well balanced upon his sturdy legs. His flocks were rapidly increasing. Wool was gaining in prices owing to the ever-increasing demands of the English mills. The ferocious blacks were being reduced in number. In consequence of all this, Mrs. Wittacker was dreaming dreams of Isabella's future, in which a mere overseer, no matter if gently born, had no possible place.

When all the mistakes had been rectified – Mr. Wittacker made quite sure about that – the filled ration bags were dumped outside the store door and the squatter strode across to the comfortable house to drink his mid-morning cup of tea with his wife. Nearby the stockyards one of the men was harnessing a horse to a cumbersome dray, and, estimating that he had at least five minutes to spare, Flemming hurried over to the barracks to obtain his valise and blankets and to take them to the dray.

"The rations are all waiting by the store door, William," he said to the man with the horse. "Get on with loading them into the dray. I'll be ready when you are. Don't forget your musket and the powder and shot."

"That I'll not, Mr. Flemming," the dour William assured the now thoroughly anxious overseer. "I'm not forgetting the last time I took out the rations. Them black varmints nearly corpsed me, that they did."

Now when love is shy it must be wise: otherwise it is found out and punished if not entirely crushed. Mark Flemming walked back to his room in the barracks. Had either Mr. or Mrs. Wittacker chanced to look through the open window of the morning room, in which they were drinking tea – the green tea of China, for there was none other in those days – young Flemming would have been seen legitimately hurrying to his quarters to fetch things necessary for his duty of escorting the ration dray. The worthy couple were not permitted by the barrack building to see the overseer climb across the sill of his window, and dart across a narrow space to the high garden wall.

Without doubt, Mr. Wittacker would have been staggered had he seen how easily young Mark Flemming scaled the garden wall which he considered impregnable even to the wild blacks against whom it had been built. And had Mrs. Wittacker seen the overseer jump lightly down into the garden and dart into the summer house wherein a fragrant rose of a girl slipped into his hungry arms, she, poor soul, would assuredly have had a terrible fit of the vapours.

"Darling!" breathed the shameless Isabella.

"My love!" whispered Mark.

"Tell me, how long will you be away from my side?" Isabella asked.

"At the longest, ten days, my sweet. You will think of me? You will remain true to me?"

"Always – day and night. But you will be careful, Mark! You will be sure to keep constant guard against the awful savages? You have not forgotten your pistols and a supply of powder and ball?"

"I have forgotten nothing, my sweet," Mark said confidently. "Have no fear concerning me. I can shoot straight, and William is a great fighter. O Heart of Mine! I must be away, for the dray is waiting."

So Isabella kissed and cried, and Mark kissed her and patted her dimpled shoulder. And then she was alone in the summer house, and, like a bird, Mark passed over the garden wall. A minute later he was saddling a horse. Ten minutes after that he was jogging along beside the dray down the gentle slope from the homestead, and so on across the downs. Beneath the dray trotted the overseer's two well-trained dogs.

Shaded from the sun by his cabbage-tree hat, William sat well forward on the dray, a loaded musket by his side, a clay pipe in full blast between his teeth. Once a sailor, once a convict, now he was a free man, but he was as tough as ever. At the beginning of every month he, with an escort, drove the ration dray to each of the seven huts on Bunnia Bunnia, occupied by shepherds. On eight or nine trips he and the escort had been attacked by the blacks. On one memorable trip the escort had been killed. However, it was thought that the times were improving because the numbers of the blacks, subsequent to the murder of the escort, had been "satisfactorily" reduced.

For an hour neither man spoke a word. William was content to smoke his pipe and keep a weather eye on every clump of scrub timber which the track forced them to pass. As for Mark

Flemming – well, youth is ever optimistic, and at the close of the hour's thoughts on suicide, because of love's uneven road, he regained his usual cheerfulness and succumbed to the craving for a cigar. Quick to see the change of mood, thus spoke William:

"These 'ere tea bags seem a bit lightish again, Mr. Flemming, sir, for a month's rations."

"Yes, William, they are light," admitted the overseer. "Mr. Wittacker has had word from the merchants that because of the Chinese war their stocks are getting perilously low, and when they will be able to fulfill the last order from the stations they are unable to state."

William clawed a fly from his greying beard.

"'Twouldn't surprise me if the shepherds raised ructions," he predicted. "They didn't like the reduction last month, and they weren't afeared of saying so. Great fellers for their tea are the shepherds, but I can't says as 'ow I blames 'em seein' as 'ow there ain't no rum to be got on the stations nowadays."

"I fear that the shepherds will have to put up with the reduced ration of tea, William. It is not Mr. Wittacker's fault. He has had the tea on order and he is able and willing and anxious to pay for it. What cannot be helped must be endured."

William pondered on this new angle of the situation.

"That's as may be, Mr. Flemming, sir," he said dryly. "It's sensible enough fer us coves 'oo 'as brains. But the shepherds ain't got no brains. If they 'ad, they wouldn't be minding sheep in danger of getting a black's spear through 'em. They groused last month fit to make your 'air stand on end. I wouldn't be surprised if some of 'em don't clear out 'cos of this tea shortage."

"They can't break their agreements with Mr. Wittacker," Mark said sharply.

"Some of 'em 'ud prefer gaol to going without their tea," countered William. "Blast the yellow devils, says I. Be all accounts they're a' torturin' the poor whites 'oo fall inter their 'ands. Them two coves wot passed through last week told us that the Chinese out here are planning to poison all our wells and our food supplies. Down near Sydney Town the coves are wantin' to know why the Governor don't go and order all the Chinese here to be put away. Better shoot 'em all, says I, afore they poison us."

"I hardly think that the Chinese here in the Colony would go as far as that," objected the overseer.

"Wouldn't they, Mr. Flemming, sir, just wouldn't they! Why, they wind holler tubes round their victim's arms and legs – tubes fashioned like serpents with open mouths uppermost. And inter the mouths of the holler serpents they pour boilin' water and then stand back and grin when the poor victim begins to yell. Why, them yeller devils gives their enemies a poison wot eats away a man's innards terrible slow like. Now the war is nigh over we can depend on it that the Chinese out here will take a try to have revenge some way or t'other."

The conversation drifted into a prolonged silence. Now and then, when a particularly dense or large clump of scrub was approached, Mark Flemming rode forward with drawn pistols and sent his two dogs into it to smell out possible savages lying in ambush.

In late afternoon they reached the first of the seven huts, to be met by the shepherd whose turn it was that day to guard it. The sun was westering in a clear sky, and away to the north-east rising dust indicated the flock being brought to the yards close by the hut by the second shepherd. Leaving William to unharness the horse and generally to make himself useful in preparing the evening meal, Flemming cantered away to render assistance to the returning shepherd.

"You are over-late, Mick," he said on riding up to the man who was afoot. "The sun is nearly down, and the sheep should now be much nearer the yards."

The man's garments were ragged. His beard was matted. A half-hour soaking in a hot bath would have much improved him. He was a historical nobody, but he was a member of a race of men which was lost to Australia until rediscovered at Anzac. Gazing with his clear grey eyes up at the mounted overseer, he grinned humorously:

"The sheep 'ud be nearer the yards, Mr. Flemming, hadn't two savages tried to 'ave murdered me. 'Twas about noon, whin I was eating me grub and the sheep were a-lying down. There's me sittin' with me back to a tree when I seen a bird behavin' foolish-like over beyant another tree. I watched. Then I seen a black varmint agen it. How many of 'em, says I? It was by Milder's

Crick it happened. Then I takes a look-see – I don't know why –
behint the tree I'm sittin' agen, and I see another black varmint a-
walkin' towards me with a spear held in his foot. When he seen I
seen him he makes a sign he's friendly-like, but that spear gripped
by his toes don't appear none too friendly to me, and I let him
'ave a charge of buck-shot. He felled down and then he cleared
off in a mighty 'urry, but I don't know how many more of 'em is
close by, so I lay low for a longish bit, and when I got the sheep
moving agen into open country I 'ad to act cautious-like. Any'ow,
Mr. Flemming, sir, there was only them two as far as I could
make out."

Here spoke a man, unknown to Australian history, whose
courage was of finer grain than that of the gaily bedecked officers
and uniformed soldiers who lived in comfortable and comparative
security in the newly formed settlements. He, and hundreds like
him, lived hourly in grave danger of being murdered by the
blacks. Countless shepherds were killed, and countless others
were wounded in the prolonged battle to place our pastoral
industry on its feet.

Mark Flemming helped this shepherd to yard the flock. Then
the shepherd's mongrel dog was tied to the yards to give warning
of prowling blacks, and Mark's two dogs were tied to the
verandah posts of the rough hut. Then came forth the second
shepherd, carrying the tea ration, demanding in a loud voice how
it was that for the second time the tea ration was reduced to half.

"It's most unfortunate, Fred, but it cannot be helped,"
Flemming told him propitiatingly. "The tea merchants tell us that
because no tea ships are now coming from China they are forced
to cut Mr. Wittacker's ordered supplies down to half. We are all
on reduced rations. It's better to be that way than to have no tea at
all."

"Well, I'm not shepherdin' without me tea," big Fred returned
roughly. "No tea, no shepherdin'. That's me."

"Mr. Wittacker says that he will make up the price of the
reduction in tobacco or money, whichever you like."

"That suits me," Mick put in. "I'll be 'avin' extra terbacco."

"But it don't suit me, 'cos I don't smoke," roared big Fred.
"'Ere we been without tea for six days, and now the supply is
gonna peter out agen a week afore the next supply is due. I ain't

no sheep wot can live on water."

Big Fred was still angry and mutinous the following morning when William, in his dray, and Mark Flemming, astride his horse, left for the next hut. Thus was hut after hut visited and the shepherds given their month's supply of rations. All of them bitterly complained and threatened to walk off the station, and only the overseer's patience with them and their own sense of fairness to their employer kept them at work minding the flocks.

When the now-empty dray and its escort rumbled and clattered up the gentle slope to the Bunnia Bunnia homestead Mark Flemming's feelings were decidedly mixed. He clearly realised the possibility of the shepherds walking off the place despite the legal agreements binding them to their employer, and he as clearly understood what would be the inevitable result of such action. His news for Mr. Henry Wittacker was certainly depressing, and the squatter's reaction to depressing news was the antithesis of calm resignation. However, there was the silver lining in the person of the fair Isabella, who would be sure to meet him in the summer house late that evening when papa would be in his study, and mama would be writing letters in readiness for the outward mail on the morrow.

Dray and escort came to a halt nearby the homestead stockyards. Mr. Wittacker, plump and pompous, emerged from the office adjoining the store-room, but young Flemming barely noticed him, as his attention was held by a square of white fabric being cautiously waved from that end of the homestead verandah which was semi-masked by grape vines.

"Well, Mark, how did the trip go this time?" asked Mr. Wittacker with unusual cheerfulness. Almost always he stressed the "mister" and the "sir!"

"Fairly well, Mr. Wittacker," replied the overseer cautiously, wondering at his employer's cheerful greeting. "We saw no blacks, but Mick was troubled by two the day we arrived at his hut, and Tom Spalding was slightly wounded on the eighteenth of the month in an encounter with a party of blacks who came to his hut and demanded food. There was, however, much grumbling by the shepherds at the continued reduction of the tea ration. I fear –"

"You need fear nothing," Mr. Wittacker said, smiling. "We

have had news that a ship called the Orwell has come into Port Jackson with her holds crammed with tea. Bates and Company have promised to despatch to us a dozen chests of tea immediately." The squatter laughed like a man who has won a lottery. "Well, now, my boy, attend to your horse and then come over to the house verandah for tea. The ladies are waiting to have particulars of your trip."

It was an invitation which the bearer of unpleasant news had not expected, although on the completion of former expeditions to the outback of the run he had been invited to recount his experiences to two news-hungry women. So for an hour he drank tea and ate cakes, and then smoked a cigar with the squatter while he told of everything which had happened on his travels. His employer sometimes grunted and sometimes ha-ha-ed, and Mrs. Wittacker often softly ejaculated "dear-dears." Isabella sat quite still, her slim hands passively in her lap, her eyes demurely shaded by the dark lashes. Butter would not melt in her mouth, seemingly.

Unconscious of the brewing storm in the quart-pot, life at the homestead went on in its energetic manner. The wool teams arrived and had to be loaded and got away, and their presence at the homestead always produced uproar, what with the shouts of the teamsters and the lowing of the bullocks. Then, towards sunset one day, there came into sight over the crest of the distant land swell to the east the long line of animals drawing the great waggon bringing the half-yearly supplies, among which was the precious tea straight from the capacious holds of the Orwell.

Throughout the next day Flemming and Mr. Wittacker laboured in checking the goods off the waggon with the invoices, and overseeing their disposal within the store-room – bags of flour; chests of tea; bags of sugar; sides of bacon, to go down presently into the underground cellar; drums of tar; nails and rope and axes, and other commodities so necessary to the station.

The tea-chests were not opened till the afternoon prior to the day when, once again, William was due to leave with the ration dray on the round of shepherds' huts. Mr. Wittacker stood by while the overseer prised up the lid of a chest and threw it back to reveal the tea without any kind of packing material protecting it.

The squatter's nose wrinkled. The inside of the chest had been smeared with a kind of paint before being filled, and the odour of the paint quite obliterated the pleasing scent of the tea leaves.

"What the –!" spluttered Mr. Wittacker, blood mounting swiftly into his choleric face.

"Whoever packed the tea overlooked the fact that painting the inside of the chest would taint it," Mark said in a small voice, and waited for the squall to break.

"Faugh!" roared Mr. Wittacker. "The damned tea is ruined! We can't drink stuff which stinks like that. Open another chest."

Alas! Every chest had been treated with the evil-smelling concoction called paint. Mr. Wittacker danced with impotent rage as Mark emptied chest after chest on to a sheet of canvas spread on the floor. It was a period of picturesque oaths, and Mr. Wittacker used them all many times. Then he strode to the door and yelled for William. William came, and was ordered to remove the offending chests to a place alleged to be governed by very high temperatures.

"This foul paint has got into the tea," moaned the squatter. "Those cursed Chinamen did that on purpose, and now they'll be laughing at us. Even the shepherds won't drink stuff made from that."

Mark offered a helpful suggestion.

"If, sir, the tea was well spread all over the canvas, so that the air could get among it, it might lose its smell after a time."

"Do it, sir," commanded Mr. Wittacker. "Here, give me a handful. I'll get cook to make a brew of it, and then we'll ascertain if it tastes as evilly as it smells."

Out he charged, with a podgy fist enclosed about a handful of tea. Ten minutes later in he rushed, carrying a quart-pot, his face red and his eyes blazing.

"By Gad, Flemming! Smell it! Smell the damned stuff!" he shouted.

The steam from the quart-pot sent forth an odour much stronger than that sent up by the heaped tea on the canvas.

"Why don't you smell it?" howled Mr. Wittacker. "Can't you smell it?"

"Have you tasted it, sir?"

"Tasted it! Isn't smelling it enough, sir?"

"It may be less offensive to-morrow, sir," Mark suggested soothingly. "We can only hope that air and time will remove the smell of this vile paint."

Shortly after eight the following morning the anxious squatter entered the store-room to find Mark Flemming weighing and bagging the rations for the shepherds.

"That cursed tea –" he began.

"I think it has much improved, sir," interjected the overseer.

Mr. Wittacker bent forward over the tea and sniffed loudly.

"Humph! Yes, Flemming, I believe you are right. Still, the smell is in the tea yet. Time and air might reduce it still further. Couldn't expect even shepherds to drink that. Double the ration this time to make up for the reduction last time. By the time it is being used all the odour may have gone from it."

And so once again Mark bade farewell to Isabella in the summer house, the while Mr. Wittacker drank tea – not of the last consignment – with Mrs. Wittacker in the morning room, and once again, mounted and well armed, Mark escorted the ration dray on its long round of the huts. At each hut the tea was received with vociferous welcome: at the departure of the ration dray from each hut the men's language was lurid and their threats ominous.

The ration-dray party was approaching the last of seven huts when the storm burst over Bunnia Bunnia. The first of the shepherds arrived at the homestead to demand their wages.

"Don't ee think we'll be drinkin' yer ruddy tea," they yelled at the squatter, silent perforce and aghast at the calamity at which these first arrivals hinted. The flocks! What of the sheep?

"We loosed 'em from the yards, and they must take their chance with the dingoes and the black varmints," returned the men. "We're not workin' without our tea, and the muck you sent out can't be stomached. Give us our money and let's be gone."

"But your employment agreement! You can't break that."

"Can't we? But we ain't broke it, mister. You broke it when you sent us that muck you call tea."

Mr. Wittacker was helpless. He paid off the men and called for his horse to ride furiously to neighbouring squatters and implore them for aid. But his fellow squatters were in the same plight.

They, too, had received consignments of the Orwell's tea, and their men were leaving as fast as they could quit the runs. On Mr. Wittacker returning home, he found the remainder of his shepherds waiting to demand their wages.

We can gain some idea of the chaos into which this pastoral world was plunged if we concede the possibility of an enemy exploding with a ray all our petrol supplies. There were no fenced paddocks as to-day. The station boundaries then were only beginning to be defined with roughly constructed brush fences. In utter despair, Mr. Wittacker returned home after visiting a distant neighbour to find his overseer and William returned with the ration dray.

What was to be done to save the flocks – especially from the blacks? It was a crisis in which Mark Flemming was proved to be a better man than his employer. Never in his life had Mr. Wittacker done a day's real sheep-work, but young Flemming had done little else since his school days. It was he who suggested calling together the homestead men and asking for volunteers to assist rounding up the scattered sheep. The appeal was made. Double wages were offered. Only a lad of sixteen volunteered, and William, the driver of the ration dray.

That same evening Mark Flemming and his two helpers rode away on fresh horses. The overseer selected the middle of the run to open his operations. To the centre he and William, each working alone, drove the scattered sheep, where the lad held them about the yards near well and hut. The lad was frightened, but full of grit. He was well armed, but fortunately was not attacked. William was twice held up by blacks, who only too well understood their temporary advantage. Mark had to engage in a two-day running fight with a body of blacks that tried to split up the sheep he had collected. They killed his horse and wounded him in the thigh, yet he got the sheep to the now-growing mob in charge of the lad.

Meanwhile Mr. Henry Wittacker was dashing about like John Gilpin, seeking here, seeking there, for fresh shepherds. Men he met on the tracks jeered at him and told him bluntly to drink his own tea.

The storm in the quart-pot might have reached a state of violence had not the rumour spread that the tainted tea was actually poisoned by the vengeful Chinamen in China. The men found that they could not do without tea, and they had drunk the tainted tea despite its odour and taste. Anger gave place to fear, and fear to dreadful expectancy. Man looked into the face of man, dreading to see the first onslaught of slow poisoning. But no man died. Summer was upon them, and the heat brought thirst. The tainted tea was better than water.

Out on Bunnia Bunnia three men guarded the boxed flocks. At first Mark Flemming's wound appeared to be healing. He kept to his post for nine days, when the wound broke out afresh. William, assisted by the lad, roped the overseer and bound him to a fallen sapling, and then did William do things with a knife and a red hot iron that would have sickened a modern surgeon.

They were still guarding the sheep, William and the lad, and the overseer who lay in the shade of a hastily built bough shed, when Mr. Wittacker, himself conducting his shepherds back to their huts after the strike was over, arrived on the scene.

Now Mr. Wittacker, although a pompous man and an autocrat, must have possessed many admirable traits of character, for he insisted that the dangerously ill young man be put to bed in the spare room at the homestead while he himself rushed off to fetch the nearest doctor. During his absence Isabella astounded her mother by proving that she was a chip of the old original block in her determination to nurse the wounded overseer.

After all is said about those early-Victorian maids, that they were demure and obedient and subject to hysterics and the vapours, they had a way with them when thoroughly aroused. Isabella, when she did break loose, mastered papa and mama to such an extent that they offered no objection to the subsequent marriage.

So passed the storm in a quart-pot. It was, however, followed by a breeze when William and the escort took to the shepherds' huts the first of the next consignment of tea, which was normal in scent and taste. The shepherds grumbled loudly, and even threatened to strike again, because the normal green tea wasn't as strong as the tainted tea. Which is simple proof that taste in many things has to be acquired.

Charlie the Cook

Towards sundown a visitor joined our camp. He was welcome, for the Australian bush is loneliness itself, and my only camp-fellow was a dog.

The visitor stood a good six-feet-two in his elastic-sided boots. He wore moleskin trousers, a black cotton shirt and a wide felt hat. Between perfect teeth was a large briar pipe. Across his back was swung a swag, and he carried in his hands a billy-can and a canvas water-bag.

We talked of the drought and other local politics over supper, and, whilst the shadows lengthened, the visitor told us that he was known as Charlie the Cook, one time of Bradford. Later, when the darkness hedged us in and the Great Silence fell, he told a yarn in his quiet, drawling voice which, as a masterpiece in Australian camp-fire yarning, I set down exactly as told.

"The last job I had was on Wanaaring Station, which, as you may know, is these days suffering from the Chidmain Blight," Charlie the Cook stated in preface. "Ever been to Wanaaring Township?"

We nodded and said we knew it before the war.

"Well, if you went to Wanaaring now you'd see what Chidmain is doing to this country. I knew the town and the station fifteen years ago, a stretch of time that ought to have turned Wanaaring and most of those back-country towns into cities, had there been a man in government who loved his country better than his pocket. In those days the town and the district was booming. Wanaaring Station, close by, was not a big run as runs go, but it employed more'n twenty men and shore thirty or forty thousand sheep. But the station, like a lot of others up in the Corner, fell into the hands of Chidmain. And, when Chidmain buys a station, he sacks all hands, sells the sheep and runs cattle. That is Chidmain's long suit. Cattle don't want boundary-riders to look after 'em, nor shearers to rip off the wool. You bet, when a district gets Chidmain Blight, the towns get it bad, too. Wanaaring, like Wilcannia, is as dead as that billy.

"As I said, me last job was on Wanaaring Station, and I was

getting Chidmain Blight meself. All I had to do was to keep me eye on the homestead and buildings, and watch 'em fall down. Not a hard job, you'll agree, but a one-man job, and a damned lonely one. I might see a stray swaggie during a week, but more often than not I seen no one for weeks at a stretch.

"I'd been there about seven months, and was nearing the state when a man puts his hat on a post and argues with it, when a 'Ghan, packing a dozen camels, pulled in. He was a stranger to me, just the ordinary kind of clothes-hawker, but not a bad sort of a cuss, taking him all in. Although I never met him I'd heard of him, and knew that he generally packed small quantities of opium and cocaine, and other sorts of dope.

"Still, for all that, I wasn't a buyer of his excitement-producers, although I bought other things from him. He stayed a couple of days and livened up things a bit, so much so that I wanted him to stay longer for company's sake. But he wouldn't. He said he was due at Cobar in three weeks, and away he went one morning before sun-up, leaving me to my job of watching the place rot. And a week after he left the thing happened which made me get me cheque and hit the track. It was like this.

"I used to live in the men's kitchen, occupying me time in reading ancient newspapers and playing solitaire. It was solitaire I was playing one afternoon, feeling anything but good, when I sort of stiffened in me seat. I never heard nothing, but I knew somebody was standing close behind me.

"And there was, too. A little white-whiskered old bloke with a red face, and greenish sort of eyes which glared. Eyes!

"'Good day-ee!' says I.

"'Good day-ee!' said he.

"'Have a drink of tea?' says I, and points to the billy 'side the stove.

"I seen his eyes blink and his tongue sort of slide about the roof of his mouth. But the way he fixed me with them eyes of his sort of made me cold down the back. He got a pannikin from a nail in the wall and filled it, looking over his shoulder at me while he did so.

"'Sugar?' says I. 'Over there on the dresser.'

"Then he jumps nearly up to the roof. He bangs the pannikin on the table, spilling half of it, and yells loud:

"'Sugar! I don't want no blank sugar in my tea. Give me strychnine.'

"I looked at him hard, and tumbles. 'He's as mad as a hatter,' I says to meself.

"'Come on! give us that strick,' he roared.

"Now, I ain't the chap to take orders in that tone – no, not even from old Chidmain himself – so I heaved to me feet to teach him his manners, madman or otherwise. But lor! he was too quick for me. He snatched up a butcher's knife from the end of the table, and held it back from his head.

"'See here!' he yelped, 'give me that strick: quick, or I'll heave this knife into your gizzard.'

"What was I to do? I didn't fancy six inches of steel slitherin' through my innards. So I dug out a full bottle, and told him to help himself to as much as he wanted. I even bet him a bob he wouldn't drink the lot. He just smiled at me in a nasty sort of way, digs out the cork with the point of the knife, and pours enough into the pannikin to poison a million dingoes. Then at one tilt he drained the pannikin.

"Did I try to stop him? No fear! I'd been on Wanaaring seven damned months, and reckoned I was due for some excitement. I sat down and waited to see the first spasm shoot across his nasty mug, and hear the first yell.

"But somehow there was nothing doing. He was a sure dud in the entertainment stakes. Instead of throwing a seven on the floor and doing the human frog act like I seen in London one leave, he just gasps with bliss like a gentleman drinking half a bottle of good whisky. My luck was out. I never backed a winner but once, and that was at Louth when there was only one horse in the race. He eyes me fierce-like.

"'You're Charlie the Cook, ain't you?'

"I says I am. I felt all limp. I was that disappointed with the poison having no effects that I could have cried tears of blood and gnashed me teeth till they all fell out.

"'Then,' says he, 'git up on yer feet. Charlie the Cook, I want you.' And he waves the knife about.

"Now, ever since a Jerry tried to bayonet me, and would have done it if I hadn't stuck him, I've a perfect horror of any sort of knife playing around me scum-jack. Whether it was the fact that

that Jerry didn't look at all pleasant, or I'm a bit womanish on the matter, I don't know. But there it is. And I was so sure that he would throw the knife before the poison got properly to work that I got to me feet as quick as if I had been stung by a bulldog ant. By the way, there's no bulldogs around this camp, is there?"

We told him that we had investigated most thoroughly before making camp. There were only meat ants and a few sugar ants.

"I've bin bit twice by bulldog ants," Charlie went on, "and I reckon I don't like 'em." From the fire he picked up a red-hot coal between finger and thumb, and lit his pipe by expertly balancing the ember on the bowl. "Let me see now. Oh yes I remember –

"'Now,' says the little man, 'I'll tell you what you are, Charlie the Cook. I'll recite your history. You deserted your wife and ten children two years ago. You murdered your father eight years ago. You smoke opium worse'n any Chinaman; you robbed Cleary at Hungerford; and you scabbed at Momba Station in '08. What have you to say in answer to these charges?'

"Cripes! I did wish I had a gun – one of them automatic things that shoots quick. Of course I've never been married. I got no kids, good luck! Me father busted when I was in long clothes. I never heard of a bloke name Cleary in Hungerford, and I was away in Queensland in nineteen seven, eight and nine. As I said before, I bar dope. Anyway, the knife sort of hypnotised me, and I wouldn't have denied his fool charges for all the tea in China.

"'What of it?' says I.

"'What of it?' he yelled, something terrible. 'What of it? Only that your time has come to face justice. Your accusers are here. Witnesses are here to testify against you. You are damned, thrice damned: wife-deserter, murderer, robber, scab and drug-fiend! You will march out of that door right now. You will do exactly as you're told. I shall be just behind you, and this knife will be just one inch off your kidneys. Don't argue. Git!'

"What could I do but march? There was nothing else but to pacify the little beast, and the way he slipped behind me was just wonderful for a man of his age. Quick as a cat he was, and as spiteful. Away I went out the door with him just behind me, and me spine all shivering like jelly. But I forgot the state of me spine when I got outside. I received the knock of me life. There, over by the office, was about thirty men lined up in a semi-circle facing us.

"How in hell they got there, I don't know. I didn't think there was thirty blokes in a bunch within five hundred miles. Why! the whole population of Wanaaring must have been stuck up agin that office.

"'Walk straight ahead!' snarls the little man behind me. He give me a nasty jab to hurry me on. I felt sure he had twisted me left kidney wrong side out, but I didn't dare swing round and boot him. It was only fifty yards odd to the office, and away we goes till me sergeant-major brought me to a halt within that semi-circle of roughs.

"I stood there and glared at 'em savage. By that time I was getting fair narked. Here was I, supposed to be earning me wages, and allowing meself to be held up like a parson by a pet parishioner.

"'Hey!' I says, 'don't yous blokes think this has gone far enough? What's the joke, anyway?'

"No one spoke, so I yelled me question again as loud as I could. I reckon I roared to some order. Still they didn't answer. Just stood around, mind you, and glared at me back.

"'You lot of sun-raysed crow-eaters!' I howled. 'What's your damned little game?'

"With that, one of 'em steps up to me and eyes me up as if he was buying a horse. I got another knock then, for I seen it was a woman dressed in man's clothes.

"'Charlie the Cook,' she says like a spitting snake, 'I am your wife whom you deserted in Sydney.'

"'Go hon!' I says, sort of sarcastic.

"But she never said no more, but went back to her place in the half-circle. Another one comes up to me. A man all right, this time, but a man with a hare-lip and a bad squint.

"'Charlie the Cook,' he says, 'I am your first-born, whom you deserted in Sydney.'

"'So, so!' says I, 'you take after your father, sure.'

"Another one took his place An albino, this bloke: white eyebrows, pink eyes and all. Says he:

"'Charlie the Cook, I am your second-born, whom you deserted in Sydney.' Back he went, and eight more come out and swore blue hell they was my kids. And such kids they were, too!

They must have been beauts as babies a day old.

"Then who should come up to me but that blessed 'Ghan who camped there a week before?

"'Charlie the Cook,' he says, 'I've sold you dozens of tins of opium.'

"'You're a blank liar, Ah Khan!' I yelled. 'I've never bought none of your dirty opium, you pork-eating nigger.'

"But he just smiled sort of solemnly and went back; and the next one was wall-eyed, crooked-nosed, the kind of face that's been rolled along a gravel path the day before. Says he:

"'Charlie the Cook, I'm your father, whom you cruelly murdered with an axe.'

"'Hindeed! says I, 'I wouldn't have thought it.'

"Another said he was Cleary, and I robbed him of his roll, and another that I scabbed at Momba shearing shed in 1908. I tell you, by that time I was getting full to the neck. I could have swiped the whole crowd if that accursed knife hadn't been jabbing into my back. Entertainment! I was getting too much entertainment. It was the sort of excitement I leaves to lion-tamers.

"I just said I could have jolted up the lot of 'em, but it turned out that I couldn't. They rushed me suddenly, all of 'em. I managed to kick my father in the stum-jack, knock out one of my sons, and give my wife a backhander before they had me down and bound hand and foot. They had me as stiff as Tutankhamen afore they dug him out of the desert. They then picked me up like I was a board, and carried me to the nearest box-tree, where they stood me on me feet, two of 'em holding me in case I should fall straight back or forwards. One of 'em says:

"'Charlie the Cook, prepare to meet your just doom. Our sentence is that you be hanged immediately, that you be drawn and quartered, and that your remains be dispatched to numerous hospitals in spirits.'

"'Very nice!' says I, but I wished immediately that I had kept me mouth shut, because they produced an uncomfortably thin rope and heaved it over a branch above me head. They brought a case and lifted me on to it, made a running noose at my end of the rope and slipped it round me neck.

"You can bet I was getting windy. You see, I couldn't make out what it was all about, but I did feel that damned tie-wire of a rope under me chin. Of course they must have all been loony. A madhouse must have burnt down, and that 'Ghan must have brought 'em back to avenge a fancied wrong. I up and addressed 'em. I hollered at 'em like a parson. I whispered to 'em alluring-like, like a vamp in Piccadilly. I told 'em they had got the wrong bloke, that I was a single man, and that me father kicked off when I was too young to heave a feeding-bottle, let alone an axe. I denied knowing Cleary. I swore Ah Khan was a liar. I went on to threaten 'em with the police and the wrath of Chidmain. Such goings on were not natural at Wanaaring. Believe me, I spoke with tears in me eyes, like Billy Hughes at a conscription meeting.

"Me burning, heart-rending words had some effect. The two beasts holding the other end of the rope, waiting to jerk me up into the blue, time being when they kicked the case from under me, went over to the rest and held a special whispering meeting. They argued for quite a time, the while I was getting stiffer and stiffer.

"It must have been a full hour afore they made up their minds, and I was suffering torment, when they came over and took off all the ropes except that which bound me wrists. One of 'em said:

"'It has been decided to reprieve you from death. You will, however, be taken to that currant-bush, around which, quite naked, you will walk without stopping for five years.'

"And, believe me or not, they hustled me to that currant-bush, stripped me of everything, even me socks. One of 'em ran a ring round the bush with a stick, and I was put on the line and ordered to start me five years' walk. How I did start, I don't know. I was that stiff and sore that I fell down lots of times, but they heaved me to me feet and started me afresh.

"The blanky sun soon peeled off all the skin I ever had, and I never knew before I had so much. Burn! I burned like blazes all over. Thirst! I could have drunk the Atlantic dry and got half-way through the Pacific. Them blighters hauled off when I got fairly going and lay about in the tree-shadows, watching me with their pig-eyes. I daren't stop walking while they was there. I thought they'd git for a drink or some grub soon. But no! they didn't move. Round and round that blanky bush I walked all that night and all the next day.

"It was just hell, let me tell you. A little before the second sunset, a swaggie came along. I tried to warn him off, but me tongue was that big I couldn't speak. He seen me and come up close. I shook me head and pointed to the watching devils. I made sure they'd grab him and set him, too, walking round the currant-bush. He looked where I pointed, and away he went, like Satan being chased by an angel. Dust hid him from view in no time.

"And on I went, doing me term, and I would have been doing it still if the police hadn't come out from Wanaaring and rescued me. They took me into the hospital, and it was a hell of a time afore I came out – of the horrors.

"You see, when a man drinks two cases of crook whisky in eight days, he's guaranteed a full issue of the jim-jams. Heaven help Ah Khan when next I meet him! I'll give him permanent jim-jams!"

Bringing in the Outlaws

When Hereford the Wake left to rush to the magnet at Wilcannia, I was set to do his work until another groom could be hired.

For the station groom the day began by riding out after the horses at half past six in the morning, in order to have them in the yards by seven-thirty. The horse paddock was four by four miles in area; the mornings were solid with frost; and the horse boss was a vicious, man-killing outlaw called Tiger.

Long before the sun rose above a distant line of box trees marking the course of a winding creek, I would be stalking the groom's horse in the small night paddock. For half his life Toby had been a groom's horse, and for the other half he had been a stock horse with cattle on the track of Western Queensland, He knew his job from the top down. His legs were short, his dark-brown body was like a barrel, and his shoulders were so massive as almost to present a deformity.

In the dawning of a winter's day it was unwise to slap a saddle on him and then immediately slap oneself into the saddle.

Such haste was productive of circus stunts at a time when legs and hands were numbed with cold. No, sir! One placed the saddle on him gently, and one tightened the girth-strap against his expanded chest gently, too. Then one walked him across to the yards to make sure that the gate was efficiently propped open.

If it were exceptionally cold, one walked him past Government House, and then, before he had time to expand his chest, one took up the girth-strap another two holes.

The homestead and stockyards were situated in a corner of the horse paddock. Outward from the corner lay a mile-wide stretch of open clanpan country, as flat as a table and as hard as iron. At the far side of this open stretch, a line of box trees marked the edge of a vast land depression which held water for a year or two about every 30 years.

Now it was covered with herbal rubbish among which at this time of the year grew wild spinach. The lake's surface was composed of hard clay rubble, and, too, it was starred with wide and deep leg-breaking cracks Here and there the stock had tramped narrow winding pads, all of which appeared to lead from the shore to an island about the middle of the lake, which also was edged with timber.

Sheltered among these island trees would be the forty-odd horses from which the day's workers were selected. They were always found there, replete with spinach, and a few yards out from the island would be standing Tiger, a chestnut beauty with white hocks and a white star on his forehead. His heavy mane and long tail were as yellow gold against the gleaming color of him.

The horse pads were so winding that it was impossible for any horse to gallop.

Off the pads, they nosed every step before they took it. Near the island, the ground offered none of the leg-breaking cracks, and Toby would make to one side or the other of the island, watched by Tiger and his following, and by the two greys used for buckboard work that always tried to hide themselves behind trees.

It was necessary to ride close to them before they realised that cunning failed, and then Tiger would squeal, fling up his heels, trumpet with contemptuous defiance, and lead the way across the lake towards the homestead and the yards.

This procedure never varied during the five weeks I was station groom. I came to understand that it was an equine game played every morning by Tiger and his mates, the two greys and Toby. The rules were explained by Toby, who offered violent objection were one broken.

Thus was the game played:

Off stream the horses, winding like a monstrous snake as they trot in single file along one of the pads. They are hidden from us by the fine grey dust rising to hang motionless in the brittle air. No amount of cajolery will induce Toby to hurry. That would not be in the game.

Presently we reach the harder surface near the lake's shore, where we find the horses waiting for us, with Tiger standing few yards beyond them. He is like a bronze statue while we are treading the dangerous ground, but, on reaching the harder ground, he is off, running beneath the border of trees to gain the open claypan country, beyond which the risen sun is varnishing the red roofs of the homestead. After him go the others.

There begins a cavalry charge, a thundering assault upon the yards. Leading the regiment runs the magnificent Tiger, head well up, mane and tail all smoking yellow. No longer has Toby a mouth. Terrific rein pressure has but little effect on his iron jaw. He draws close to the heels of Nugget, the light dray horse, who is the finest charger of the lot, and who does his bit with enthusiasm.

With stockwhip cracking, and the icy air slip-streaming by face and ears which no longer register feeling; with the thunder of hooves exciting to madness a passing flock of galahs; the regiment of horse sweeps past Government House, which is saluted by Tiger with a squeal of hate. There lives those whom he his fought and vanquished.

There is no pulling back Toby before the yards are reached. In we go with the mob, I to fall off him and rush to shut the gate before Tiger can fight his way out of the press and lead his followers back to the lake.

There was never anything so glorious as that whirlwind rush across the claypans to the stockyards on a crystal-clear, frosty morning. Tiger loved it no less. Even Nugget was rejuvenated. As for Toby, well he appreciated the permission to show off.

And then the boss had visitors. They were a banker and his wife and their two daughters. Such daughters! The day after their arrival the boss said:

"Tomorrow morning I want you to bring in the horses smartly. My guests are American, and I want to show them how we begin the day. I'll have them out on the verandah to watch".

I was young, the girls were lovely, and Toby was ever willing. So we had not been bringing the hones in smartly! We set off the next morning with a new silk cracker on the stockwhip, and in our hearts was the determination to show how things are done in Australia. In due course, Tiger and his followers were waiting for us at the lake's shore.

When all was set I uttered a yell. Tiger glared his surprise before answering me with a scream of defiance, and we got off the mark in very promising fashion. The whip cracked and Tiger lifted his heels to the sky. The mob laid well down to it, and Toby travelled well. He sensed the importance of this day, and forty-odd bush-fed real gallopers streaked for the homestead yards.

And then I committed the unpardonable sin of touching Toby with the whip, an act of sheer carelessness. Clamping his jaws on the bit, he determined to prove just what he could do.

We passed Nugget as though he were harnessed to his dray. Then we passed the greys – and they were not loafing. Then we were in among the mob and edging up behind Tiger. With Tiger we raced neck to neck, and Tiger's vile temper flared up at the impertinence. His ears dropped flat, the pupils of his eyes became mere pin-points of fire on a white background. His teeth were bared, and he swooped to crunch my near-side leg.

Toby moved with him, and then Tiger was falling behind. Tiger shrieked with temper. With undignified effort I tried hard to haul Toby beck, but a winch could not here hauled him back to his rightful place.

Tiger continued to squeal, but lost no toe. We were winning, and he was a mere placed horse when we passed the homestead and the dressing-gowned figures on the verandah. We were easily the first in the yards and, because I could not reach the gate for the mob, Tiger got out and led them back to the lake.

It took us all the morning to get the horses back again to the yards, and the boss had to explain to his guests that in this country where water runs uphill and the trees shed their bark, not their leaves, the station groom always leads the working horses to the yards early in the morning.

The Colonel's Horse

Why was I in the Ninth Batt.? Lemme tell you. Back in 1914 I'm working on a joint well west of Charlieville, and, havin' plenty of spark in them days, I enlists in the Second Light Horse at Enoggera Camp, what's not far out of Brisbin.

I been riding horses since I was four, being shoved up on brumbies what was supposed to be broke in and let fall off till I learned how to fall off without being stunned, and naturally when the last show started it was me for Brisbin and the Second Light Horse.

One morning, the sergeant-major nominates me and five other blokes to go with a corporal to Nundah railway station to collect half a dozen horses sent down specially for the officers by a squatter.

The N.C.O. in charge is a character we call Georgie Porgy, after seeing tarts kiss him one evening and him blush to the roots of his 'air. Mind you, there's nothing nice and innocent about this Georgie Porgy. He's a nasty piece of work, and he never knoo how lucky he was I did get transferred to the Ninth Batt.

At the railway yards we're marched to a truck where the half-dozen mokes are waiting, and I'm stonkered by seeing that these mokes are down from the last outback joint I worked on. I recognises all of 'em. I knows they is a good lot to look at, but other than being looked at they're all pretty crook, the worst of 'em being a cunnin' devil called Artful Arthur.

Without wasting any time over it I makes up me mind that the bloke what's to ride Artful Arthur ain't gonna be me.

He's a big, upstanding black gelding without a white mark on 'im. He's got just a shade of a Roman nose and sheepy eyes what are generally half shut. He looks docile, easy enough for a lady to ride; in fact, he is docile, and any lady can ride 'im, but the times he comes home without his rider is remarkable.

He'll wait his chance, wait for hours watching his rider, and the first time the bloke's attention is on something else the next moment he's on the ground and wondering how he got there.

Seeing Artful Arthur in this truck, I hugs myself with joy

227

because, as he looks the best of the bunch, he's sure to be taken by the Colonel, and so is sure to be ridden back to camp by Georgie Porgy.

I take great care not to take Artful Arthur out of the truck, and I'm delighted when Georgie Porgy tells one of the other blokes to leave Artful Arthur for him to ride.

While we're getting the saddles on 'em they're all a bit lively, bar Artful Arthur, what stands with his eyes half shut and don't seem to be taking any notice of the scenery. Georgie Porgy walks him out in front of us while we're tightening the girth straps, me being careful about this, as the prad I've got is a mare called Susan, what's sure to give a pigroot or two. Any'ow, she ain't gonna do anything to me like what Artful Arthur is gonna do to Georgie Porgy.

"Hey, Henery!" he sings out to me. "Don't you know better than to ride with long stirrup leathers? Shorten 'em, d'you hear! Try and be a soldier. Oh, damn! Come and take this black gelding and gimme that one."

This flattens me, and I says:

"I ain't afraid of her, Corp. I can ride anything."

"Not real livin' horses," he says, sarcastic. "You take over this one and you ride 'im carefully, 'cos he's the best of the bunch, and is sure to be selected by the Colonel."

And before I knows what's what he's taken my Susan and I'm holding on to Artful Arthur.

"Now then," he shouts, "mount and follow me!"

Instantly four of the prads begins to play up something shockin'. But Artful Arthur, he looks like he's astonished, and then he looks back at me to see what I'm thinking about, and then over to Georgie Porgy, what's up on Susan, who is bending down in the middle like she's got a stomach ache.

Then up she goes and whirls around like a top, as I knew she would, and was expecting it. Georgie Porgy is slewed off like he was a arrer, and when he lobs he continues to go along on 'is chest.

Now me, I'm so interested in this performance that I clean forgets Artful Arthur for just one second. However, he ain't forgot that I'm on 'im; no, not a split second, and he gives a mighty lurch forward, takes the bit hard in his teeth, and gets going for home and glory.

It happens that he's headed towards the camp, and so sort of reduces the time we're due to arrive. After the first surprise at him getting away like this, for it ain't his usual method. I tries to settle down to ride him. But, you understand, I'm not sitting in a comfortable bush saddle having knee-pads to grip to take anything what might come. I'm in a military saddle what's high fore and aft, and what ain't got no more give than a rounded sheet of iron well oiled and slippery like a banana skin.

I knows quite well that when Artful Arthur decides to dump me I'm gonna be dumped without argument and loss of time. The point that concerns me is just when and where.

I see we're coming to a motor car what's keeping to the centre of the road like us, and I'm wondering if the car or Artful Arthur will get off dead centre and give way to avoid a collision, when the bloke in the car makes up his mind in such a hurry that he drives into a culvert, and I can hear his language as we go by.

Then we're passing through a bit of a township, and I'm wishing I could fall off outside the pub before it's too late, and I'm calling meself a yellow skunk when I knows I'm afraid to fall off.

Artful Arthur is going all out, and it occurs to me that, after all is said and done, he's been frightened to death ever since he left the bush, and that he's still so frightened that he's forgot all his old tricks of waiting an hour or so before going to market.

We've come a mile that fast that I'm thinking of asking the Colonel to enter Artful Arthur for the Melbun Cup and then I sees ahead a long line of mounted troops coming my way. As we approach these troops Artful Arthur increases speed, getting well down to it, holding his Roman nose well out in front and looking straight ahead.

I finds that Georgie Porgy hasn't tightened the saddle girth too well, and by the time we arrives at the head of the troops I'm not feeling too safe.

I see an officer rein his prad off the road, and a sergeant-major he stands up in his stirrups and shouts: "Halt, that man!"

I'm wishing like hell that I could halt, but it can't be done, and Artful Arthur he keeps right on in the middle of the road, and the mounted men are passing on either side like they was travellin' at

100 miles an hour.

After they'd passed the air gets sort of peaceful and respectful. I can now see the camp entrance and the lines of bell tents beyond, and believe me, I'm highly delighted when we leaves the hard road and does a prance over the soft grass.

To the left of the tents is open country, and me, I'm for the open country to quieten Artful Arthur if it can be done, and to fall off if it can't be done. By this time I'm not liking the way the saddle is slipping around, and it's this saddle what prevents me from hauling Artful Arthur away from the tents what's coming towards us with remarkable speed.

The first of these tents is the officers' tents, and there's hardly any room between the pegs keeping them up, but Artful Arthur chooses one opening in the line and heads straight for it. And then at the last moment, he wants to change his mind, sees that it's too late, and so stops dead.

Things sort of happen. What with the loose saddle girth and this unmilitary fashion of arriving at a military camp, I has forgot Artful Arthur's favourite method of getting rid of his rider. I see him sort of drift back and down from under me.

For a long time there's me and the saddle sort of flying through the air, and after this long time we sort of gets separated, the saddle kind of dragging in the rear with the irons swinging wide like they was spider's legs.

While I'm trying to understand all this I see that I'm headed straight for one of the tents, and I no sooner see this than I'm passing through the canvas like it was paper, and I comes to a nice and soft rest on a stretcher bed.

This bed seems sort of weak or something, because it sinks under me, and I can feel the ground hard under me back. This situation, however, is less interesting than the Colonel, what appears to be in the act of changing his trousers and who is now describing me father and grandfather and aunts and uncles.

Still, I think everything would have been all right after a little explanation if it hadn't been for the saddle, what came through the 'ole in the tent after me and what sort of wrapped itself around the Colonel's neck and sent him sprawling over the washstand.

I'm now hearing him at his best, and I gets to admiring his efforts so much that I'd have risen to doff me lid if I 'ad one on me 'ead and if I could have got out of the stretcher what was sort of clamping itself around me.

What with the Colonel and the Sergeant-Major and the Captain I never got a say about anything, and the next day I'm in the Ninth Batt. among the foot sloggers. Still, they're a good lot of blokes, and I get quite happy being with 'em – especially as Artful Arthur come to dump the Colonel in front of the entire Second Light Horse.

Night of the Tin Cans

A h – them were the days!
  When me and Snodger was doing our training, marching round and round the Pyramids, in 1914-1915, we didn't give two hoots for nobuddy. We felt like men should, all the time and continuous, sort of satisfied that we'd done the right thing at the right time by joining up.

Me and Stodger was good mates 'cos we had found out that I could fire the bullets he could make.

He only had one failin', a sort of passion for getting into trouble – and me with him. He's a character what's always getting ideas, and one of these ideas is to visit a cobber of his what's in the Light Horse.

Now we're camped at Mena what's well west of Cairo, at the Pyramids, and the Light Horse is camped at Heliopolis what's well east of Cairo, and to go through Cairo we has to pass the St. James Hotel where they sells Pilsner beer what's made of proper hops and things and no strychnine.

Consequently, when we gets off the electric train at Heliopolis it's close on midnight.

"We'll have to prospect carefully 'cos there's a strong military picket somewheres around," says Snodger, and because we ain't got no leave passes this picket has some importance to us.

We takes a bird's-eye-view about the township of Heliopolis and falls in with a New Zealand bloke who draws us a plan of the country on the roadway and marks where the military picket is always waiting at night for drunks and late-homers.

It seems that we has to go straight east through the township, then across a big open space with a Greek church in the middle of it, and so arrive at the end of the main street going through the native town beyond which, on the desert, is the camp.

"What about you coming to show us the way?" says Snodger.

"Can't," says the New Zealander. "I gotta date to see a bloke about a canary."

"Bit late, ain't it?" I puts in.

"It's never too late to see any bloke about any canary," he

says, like there can't be no argument about it.

When he has departed, me and Snodger gets up and searches around for gharry, and it's like this that we meets Abdul, what's driving two upstanding nags in a gharry with the hood down.

"You take us to the Light Horse camp?" says Snodger.

"Yes, sah," says Abdul. "You pay twenty piasters."

"All right," agrees Snodger, having no more idea of paying this blackmail than I have of climbing a pole this time of night. "You take us well wide of the picket, eh? You take us out wide round the native town, to miss the picket? Know what a picket is?"

"Yes, sar," says Abdul, and he describes the picket in such a way that we knows he's heard blokes tell of pickets in general. "You get in sar. All up to hick, bonzer."

In due course me and Snodger and Abdul arrives at the end of the street passing through the European township. Now we can see the big open space looking as dark as the Ace of Spades excepting for the Greek church in the middle of it sort of lit up by the road lamps.

Having arrived at the church, Abdul should have turned north along a road to reach the dark and narrer streets and so miss the picket what's guarding the end of the lighted street ahead of us.

We tells Abdul he can't go right ahead, but must turn round and go back to the branch road, but what does he do but whip up his prads and keep going straight along the road towards the waiting picket, fully a hundred strong by the look of 'em in the distant lamp-light.

Now there is this Egyptian character standing up on his driver's box and yelling blue murder. And there is me and Snodger sort of stonkered for a second or two.

All this is very annoying, and we comes to understand that Abdul's aim is to get in well with the military by handing us over to pickets – especially as he has already collected his fare.

Snodger, he rubs his 'ands together and rolls up the sleeves of his tunic. I could never understand why he does this because I never trouble to roll up my tunic sleeves when there's plonking to done.

I grabs Abdul off the box and hauls him down into the gharry.

The horses are going all out and distance to the picket don't give us much room. I soon has Abdul held in the right position, and Snodger, he lets him have a good 'un on the chin.

Naturally, this causes Abdul's yells and scream to stop sudden. We can now hear the yells of delight coming from the picket blokes who can imagine frog-marching us off to a guard-room.

This don't concern us so much as the speed at which we are approaching them, because we don't seem able to reduce this speed as the reins has fallen down between the prads, and there's no time to do a moving picture act and stop what has become a proper bolt.

As we're now less'n fifty yards from the picket, what has opened out to receive us, we hops over the back hood and slides off to the road.

"Come on!" says Snodger. "Foller me!"

It stands to reason that me and Snodger don't pause any to admire the scenery.

As I told you, we ain't got no leave passes, and the recent run of extra fatigues we has done because of being unlucky don't make us want to do no more for a week or two. Snodger is now all out, heading for the north across the open space.

Once away from the road lights we're travellin' in darkness, and I only knows we're passing over desert by the soft sand under-foot.

We can see the dim outline of the house-roofs against the sky bordering that side of the open space we're making for, while away to the left is the Greek church lit up by the lamps near it bordering the passing road.

It is so dark that I can only just get a bird's-eye-view of Snodger who's ahead of me by a coupler yards.

Behind me is the picket, and a N.C.O. what's yellin' to 'em to open out in extended order.

Back beyond them is Abdul what's woke up and is yelling "Picket! Picket!" like it's the only word he knows.

Running over this open, sandy space don't produce no noise. I can see Snodger but I can't hear him.

The picket can't hear us, neether, and they ain't got that close that they can see us – which is why they're told to open out in extended order. Taking things big and large, me and Snodger has a good chance of getting off the open space and among the houses because we has had plenty of practice at getting away from pickets and things.

I'm thinking all this when all of a sudden there comes a terrific uproar from where Snodger is. It is a crashing sound what gets worse and worse, a sort of sound what reminds me of a good old tin-kettlin' away back in Australia.

Now me, I don't understand this sound, but I knows it is caused by Snodger what seems to be booting a hundred petrol tins around, like he was playing football, and as I'm nearer the picket blokes than he is, I thinks this is inconsiderate of him.

Especially as the pickets hears this sound, too, and someone yells out:

"There they go, boys! Sool 'em!"

The noise Snodger is making is getting real bad, when quite abrupt like I finds meself floundering among millions of four-gallon petrol tins all empty.

I can now just see these tins stretching out for miles either side and looming up ahead like a mountain. There don't seem anything to do but to charge up and over this mountain of tins what must be the gatherin' of twenty years or more.

To me and Snodger silence just now is the essence of the contract. But silence ain't to be. Toilin' up and over all these tins ain't like an afternoon stroll beside the ole Darling. There's nothing peaceful or nerve-soothin' about our progress.

As me and Snodger goes on up and up, thousands of tins come rolling and rattling downwards.

Sometimes I am finding meself balancing on the edge of a tin and has to make a dinny-aiser leap forward to stop crashing.

At other times I finds meself waist deep in tins, and think I'm goin' to sink down deep and drown among them. This is a feeling I don't like, especially in the dark.

Then things change for the worse. The row me and Snodger is making is like a tart whispering words of love before a thunderstorm breaks, the thunderstorm being the row made by the picket blokes when they arrive at the heap of tins and things. No longer can I hear them yelling to each other to sool us up.

Well, time goes on, and presently me and Snodger arrives at the summit. Here we ain't got no time to pause and admire the scenery because the pickets is coming up the mountain behind us tolerably fast.

What surprises me is that I can see them, when I couldn't see 'em before as it is so dark, and now I gets the idea that it's getting sort of lighter, and I observes that this growing light is caused by all the houses ahead of us being lit up as though for a party, or like it was a shoppin' night.

"Come on," says Snodger. "What you delaying for?"

He gets going with additional speed, him being the kind of character what likes plenty of energy and movement. I makes a spurt after him down the mountain-side of tins and then trips and takes a header.

As I goes I takes a few millions of tins with me, like a boulder heading a land-slide. Me and the tins sort of catch up with Snodger, and he comes to be another boulder, like me, so that we both arrive at the bottom at the same time.

Then the noise we has been making sort of gets quieter, meaning there is no longer any tins crashing around us. But from the other side of the mountain the uproar continues something terrible, this being made by the picket blokes what's only just arriving at the summit.

And there's another sound, too, a sound me and Snodger ain't heard before, and this sound is a roar of yells and screams between us and the houses bordering the edge of the open space.

When me and Snodger stands up we finds all the population round the open space has arrived to view us coming down the mountain, and it would appear that they don't like their mountain of tins to be so disturbed.

Some of 'em are waving sticks and things. Some are laughing like they are in agony. It don't occur to me at this time, but what has brought the population to this place at this time of night is the noise we has been making.

Any'ow, while me and Snodger is getting our wind for the second act, we hears more yelling and screaming backed by somebuddy bashing a gong with an iron bar.

The crowd opens out and there appears a fire engine connected to four white horses and manned by at least a hundred firemen.

Mind you, there's no fire as I can see, but this don't matter to this fire brigade. No, sir! Having arrived, the firemen, all dressed up in night-shirts and brass 'elmets, get down and run out the hoses in all directions.

In two ticks there was water spurting out of the hose nozzles what is held by a dozen firemen to each nozzle.

There being no fire to aim at, they squirts anythink they sees, includin' me and Snodger and the vast crowd. What they don't squirt, much to me and Snodger's annoyance, is the picket blokes what's coming hard down the mountain-side.

Every time me and Snodger stands up we are pushed back by five thousand tons of water to the square inch of face and chest, and after about an hour of this the novelty wears off somewhat and me and Snodger decides not to stand up no more but to advance to the attack on 'ands and knees and heads kept low.

Once we have each taken command of a hose, conditions ain't so bad. Me and Snodger begins to take a real live interest in life once more when we lifts the picket blokes off the side of the tin mountain and sort of hurls 'em back over the summit – takin' a sweep round at the crowd now and then.

How long this by-play would have continued I never paused to consider, and I might have been continuing to enjoy meself to this day if it 'adn't been for the arrival of a squadron of Egyptian Lancers from the barracks.

We seen the light of the road lamps shining on their harness and spears, and we seen, too, that they're travellin' fast in our direction.

Then the crowd sees 'em, and the mob begins a rush for the shore, what is the houses, leaving me and Snodger in command of the hoses, and all the fire brigade on their hands and knees waiting to take back their fire engine. They look sort of dejected from the spraying they're getting.

"We'd better push off," says Snodger. "Foller me!" We downs tools and makes a dinny-aiser rush for the engine. When the fire brigade see us do this, they all jump up and makes a similar rush for the same engine, they anticipatin' that me and Snodger is goin' to pinch it.

Which, of course, is what we does. Being in much better trainin', we arrives at the engine first, and in two ticks we're well aboard with Snodger on the box and the reins in 'is 'ands. He whistles up the horses, they gets well into their collars, and we're off like a Cobb & Co.'s coach.

I looks back to see how the Lancers is coming along, and I'm highly delighted to see the fire brigade being a shade too late to reach their engine, but just in time to reach one or two of the long hoses what's streaming out behind.

Most of 'em gets a holt of a hose, and there they all trying to stop the engine from leaving 'em by pulling back like they was engaged in a tug-o'-war. After a bit they looks like bits of paper tied every so often to the tail of a kid's kite.

I'm astonished by the manner Snodger is driving the four white horses, like he was a coach driver making up for lost time. I see we're well on the way to the camp we set out earlier to visit, because directly ahead of us is the road leading to the main streets passing through the native town.

When I looked back again I finds that the fire brigade has all let go of the hoses. I can see a sort of movement in the darkness of the open space we're leaving at high speed, and blokes going all out across the road by church where the lamps are.

They all seems to be very excited about something and I remarks to Snodger that it must be the Lancers what's causing the excitement. But Snodger ain't taking any interest in nothink but steering the horses.

Now we're in the main street with people rushing out of shops and house to see us arrive, and then all rushing in again before we do arrive. The yells, screams, roars of wheels, Snodger's shouts, etcetera, I finds very exhilerating. And then we're at the far end of the street and on the road crossing the open desert to the Light Horse camp at the old aerodrome.

We've come far enough. Snodger-pulls up the horses and we stop.

Then me and Snodger takes the animals out of the engine, whips off their harness, and slaps 'em into a gallop back towards the town.

We parts from the fire engine with regret, and after bit of trouble we locate Snodger's friends who wake up to welcome us with joyful cries because me and Snodger still has the bottle of Pilsner we've brought from the St. James' Hotel.

And to-day they tells me I'm too old to go to this ruddy war. How do the cows expect to stoush 'Itler and Co. if me and Snodger ain't on the war-path?

The Cairo Spy

I'm reminded of 1914 when me and Jones is in the A.I.F. and doing our trainin' by marching round and round till we gets dizzy.

The only cure we find for this complaint is to lean against the bar at the St. James Hotel for a coupler hours of an evening, this pub being a most respectable joint and about the only one in Cairo having a bar to lean against. Our trainin' them days being a bit severe, me and Snodger finds it necessary to visit the St James pretty near every evening, and in due course we becomes friendly with a civilian calling himself Paddy, what had a good job on Egyptian Railways, an elderly gent suffering from the same complaint as us and who had found the same cure.

One night when me and Snodger is feeling exceptionally dizzy we finds the bar the St. James Hotel holding only this Irish character and a skinny, white-faced, Dago-looking bloke with a black mo decorating his dial. The argument between these two not being violent, me and Snodger casually gives Paddy a good night as we passes along to the far end of the bar where we calls for our usual Pilsner.

After a bit our attention is removed from Pilsners to the two characters at the door end of the bar. There's Paddy, big and boozy, and getting on for sixty, and there's the slim dark bloke what reminds me of somebody I knows and has forgotten. The argument is getting warm and we can hear it's about the record time a train has travelled between Cairo and Alexandria. Presently the character with the black mo' says quite distinctly that he don't believe no train ever travelled that fast and that no ruddy Irishman ever spoke the truth about anythink.

We seen Paddy go redder in the dial than usual and his big moustache stand out like snow-covered scrub. Then Snodger puts down his glass very slowly, and it is this sign what makes me nervous because the St. James Hotel is much too good a pub to be wrecked.

The thought causes me to restrain Snodger, and then Paddy starts shoutin' and the dark character says loudly:

"Yes, and all these Australian savages is liars, too."

Naturally Snodger's glass goes down on the bar counter with a thud. Me, I can now smell the brimstone in the storm what's certain to break. The situation doesn't please me because, as I said, there's no pub in Cairo to equal the St. James Hotel for curing giddiness.

What's to do! All of a sudden I has a brainwave. I've been trying hard to place the dark character and now I remembers having read about his dead image in a book dealing with a spy gang. If ever a bloke looked like a spy it is this, dark character arguing with Paddy and calling us savages and liars.

Grabbing Snodger by the arm, I runs him outside to the street before he can get his breath and go into action, and there I begins to tell him about my little scheme when I sees standing at the kerb and admiring the traffic the very bloke I'm hoping to see – an Egyptian policeman.

"Eh, sarge!" I sings out. "You spika da Engleezee?"

Hearing this, he turns to comes to where I'm still restraining Snodger, and he says, a bit polite and stiff:

"I have that pleasure. Can I be of service?"

This sort of stonkers me, but I says to him:

"Well, me and Snodger, 'ere, has been listening to a bloke in that bar boasting to another civvie that he knows all about the dockyard at Portsmouth, and that he once earned a thousand quid for information he sold. In fact, he's that drunk he's boasting he's a spy. I reckon you ought to run him in, sarge. He's a skinny dark-moustached character."

"Ah!" says the policeman, standing at attention. "I'll take him along for being drunk."

He steps to the kerb again and holds up a hand for a gharry driver to pull his bone-shaker to a halt at the pavement, and then he marches into the St. James Hotel leaving me and Snodger astonished at the way he speaks English and beginning to chuckle at the coming comedy. Presently out he comes with the dark character shouting at the top of his voice and a pair of handcuffs unitin' them. Snodger, he helps the policeman get the dark character into the gharry, and then the policeman says to me:

"What is your name, please, and unit?" And like a fool I tells him.

Havin' waved him good-bye, me and Snodger goes back to tell the joke to Paddy and the beer-slinger, and we all enjoy the joke so much that me and Snodger misses the last tram back to camp and has to pay a gharry-driver fifty piastres to do the trick.

The follerin' morning the Orderly Sergeant tells me I'm on the mat, and in due course I'm paraded before the Company Commander.

"Private Joseph Henry," he says, without batting an eyelid. "Were you in Cairo last night?"

I admits I was, thinkin' it's a bit crook that Snodger ain't with me now as he was with me last night.

"Were you at the St. James Hotel?" the O.C. asks me.

I tells 'im I was, and then he knocks me rotten by asking:

"Were you instrumental in having a civilian arrested on the charge of being a spy?"

I says I was – rememberin' the sucker I'd been in giving the policeman me name and unit.

"Very well," the O.C. says. "Take this chit and report at Battalion Orderly Room at once. And dust yer boots before you go in, too."

On me way I finds I'm not likin' the situation as well as I might. It seems to me that the dark character has objected to being run in for a spy, and if this is so then the Colonel is going to kick me fair in the neck. Any'ow, in I goes, and the old coot eyes me orf and says like a judge giving the death sentence:

"You in Cairo last night? You at the St. James Hotel? You instrumental in having a civilian arrested as a spy?"

I says yes to all this. What in 'ell else can I say? I'm that stonkered that I don't know what I'm doing. Then the Colonel says:

"Take this chit and report at once to Brigade Office."

I takes the chit and does a get. Once more out in the bright sunshine I tries me best to make the old konk work. It seems to me that having to report at Brigade Office is making this spy business a bit serious. A measly private don't have to report at Brigade Office for playing a joke on a tourist or somethink just to save the St. James Hotel from being wrecked by me mate, Snodger. If the dark character happens to be a English officer out on a bender in civvies, then it's me for a belt in the neck for sure.

So by the time I gets to Brigade Office I'm feeling mighty sorry I have arrived.

I has to wait half an hour before a staff captain appears and orders me to foller 'im into another room where I'm paraded before none other than the Brigadier himself.

"Ah, Ah!" he yelps, taking a double deck at me. "So you're Private Joseph Henry, eh? Were you in Cairo last night?"

"Yes, sir," I says, going on quick to save him asking the rest: "And I was in at the St. James Hotel and I was instrumental in having a ruddy civvie pinched for being a spy."

"Ah, Ah!" he yelps again, and, like the others, he shoves a chit at me across the table. Seeing that chit makes me feel bad, because if I has to report at Divisional Headquarters then, the dark character must be brother or somethink to the Sultan himself. But the old boy don't mention no Divisional Headquarters. Instead, he says:

"You will proceed at once to Cairo and report to Jarvey Pasha at the barracks. You will not call in at the St. James Hotel on your way. I am going to trust you to go along without an escort."

I takes up the chit and I sees it's a leave pass and I says to the general:

"Excuse me, sir, but it's a long way to walk."

"Yes, it would be. No money?" he asks.

"Not a raszoo," I tells 'im, and to this he says:

"Ah, Ah! Take this, and bring me back the change – if there is any."

Then he smiles at me in a way I don't like at all, and he tells me that if I ain't reported to Jarvey Pasha before 12 o'clock I'll be due for six months without the option. Again he smiles at me as though I'm about to die, and when I gets outside again and am making for the tram I'm feeling a damn sight more dizzy than ever I has done marching round the flamin' Pyramids.

In the first place this Jarvey Pasha is a white officer what's the head serang of the Egyptian Police, and I knows now that I'm for the tank and a stoushing on the soles of me feet with bamboo rods and things. The dark character is no tourist, and he's no British officer on a bender, neither. Naturally, having been cut off sudden like from a chain of Pilsners he's pretty narked at having been run in for a spy, and he'll be demanding his pound of flesh, blood and all.

Eventually I arrives and am paraded before Jarvey Pasha what's sitting at his desk and wearing the Egyptian fez on top of his uniform. At the door is standing a ten-foot Egyptian lancer.

"Sit down there, Private Joseph Henry," says Jarvey Pasha, pointing to a chair at the end of his desk. I sits down, and he leans back in his chair and screws me off, and he says: "You are the soldier who gave a civilian in charge as being a suspected spy?"

I admits this, and I begins to explain about the joke and Snodger wanting to spoil a good pub when he cuts in with:

"How did you know, or rather how did you come to suspect that that civilian was a spy?"

This gives me a sort of lead, and instead of telling about the joke I goes the whole hog and tells bits of the book I read and what reminds me of the dark character.

"Well, sir, it was like this," I says. "Me and me mate Snodger was sipping a glass of Pilsner when –"

"Sipping!" Jarvey Pasha cuts in. "Did you say 'sipping'?"

"Well, not exactly sipping, sir," I corrects meself. "Me and Snodger was lapping down a chain of Pilsners when I hears a dark-looking civilian say to a big fat civilian that he knew his way around Portsmouth Dockyards and had once got a copy of a report about a wax model of a new battleship what had been tried out on the experimental tank. I gets convinced he's a bit drunk and in a boasting mood, and so I thinks it best to get him shoved in for examination. Of course, sir –"

"Stout feller, Joseph Henry," he tells me. "Have a cigar?"

I'm knocked rotten, and in a sort of daze I accepts a cabbage out of a gold box.

"Have a Pilsner?" asks Jarvey Pasha.

A Pilsner! I can't speak. All I can see is his smilin' face above a long glass of Pilsner he's holding out to me.

"But – But –" I stutters.

"Good work, Henry," he says. "You've earned it and a bit more. Your spy will be shot one morning soon. The fool had sufficient evidence on him. Have another Pilsner? For heaven's sake don't sip it, man!"

And so that was that. What did I get out of it? I got fourteen days extra fatigues for being absent without leave that night.

Miss Oo-La-La

We had crook times in the old A.I.F., but, believe me, we had plenty of beer and skittles, too, and when you ask me if I ever got married I'm reminded about one particular bit of skittles what I've always called Miss Oo-La-La.

It don't seem more'n a week ago that me and Snodger is doing our trainin' by marching round and round the Pyramids all day and lappin' up real Pilsners at the St James Hotel, Cairo, by night. It don't seem that long ago that me and Snodger is making our way to our favorite pub when we come across a Gypo what's baling up a coupler tarts by trying to sell 'em some lace. It seems they don't want no lace, and that the sight of the lace-seller annoys 'em.

Now Snodger is one of them silent blokes what does things without a smile. He crashes a knee into the Gypo's stern, wrenches the lace-tray from around his neck and crowns him with the edge. It then appears that this is enough for the Gypo to go on with, because he does the disappearin' act without further argument.

The next thing is that Snodger's giving the glad eye to the two tarts, and this is most surprisin' because Snodger don't usually have a failin' for skirt. Not that I'm blaming him now, for these are young tarts what are dressed all in black, with black hoods over their heads and their faces half-hidden by yashmaks. The yashmaks are made of fine transparent stuff so's a bloke can see the white skin behind it. They are two Circassian women.

There's me and Snodger bowing and scrapin' to 'em, and there's them smilin' at us and sort of giggling, and Snodger, he says:

"Tarla hinna, ya bint!"

He thinks he's saying 'Good Evening!' when he's saying 'Come here, girl!' but these two they see the joke and sort of gurgle at us. Then a gharry pulls up short at the curb, and they take a little run and jump in and the driver he shouts to his horses and away they go, leavin' with me and Snodger a scent what we never smelled anywhere else.

"Cripes!" says Snodger. "Ain't they a pair of corkers!"

I don't say nothink. The one with the blue eyes has given me a wink just before they drove off, and I yells to the driver of an empty gharry and in two ticks we're follering the tarts. The St. James Hotel, the pilsners, everything is forgot.

"Which one d'you fancy?" says Snodger, looking like he's sick or something.

"The one with the blue eyes," I tells him. "She gave me the chase-me-kiss-me eye-full, and now no one's seeing me for me dust."

"Me too," says Snodger. "What a pair of corkers! Keep going, Abdul, you cow. Eggeree awam!"

After that we stands up in the gharry so's to see the gharry ahead. Now we can see first one and then the other of them tarts waving a hankerchief to us, inviting us to foller 'em, as though we wanted any more invitations. The setting sun makes the dust what's rising from behind their gharry look like a pink mist. The air is cool and sort of soft and silky. The minerets of a mosque we're passing looks like port wine does seen through a bottle. And somehow I gets the idea that this is the first time I'm looking at this Egypt properly, as though me and Snodger has only just arrived.

The dusk falls, calm and silent and swift. The pink dust turns to purple. Even now I gets mooshey when I think of that night. We make Abdul get a bit closer to the gharry ahead, and we can still see the hankerchiefs waving us on and on, until we all arrives at a wharf beside the Nile and opposite a big houseboat.

The two tarts run across a gangway to the deck of this houseboat, and they go in. Me and Snodger we pays Abdul a fifty-disaster note, and in we goes, too, sort of tip-toeing. We finds one of the tarts lighting a lamp, and then she runs into another room, leaving me and Snodger looking at the scenery.

It's a large room. There's sofas and big cushion-things on the floor, and little tables and wall-shelves full of ivory and black elephants and idols and things. We're standing on a plain white carpet having a black dragon on it, and Snodger he pulls out a packet of fags and then he puts 'em away quick like he thinks he's got no right to smoke in such a joint.

After a little time some curtains shiver and the two tarts come back. They're dressed in some white stuff what shimmers in the lamplight, and the bridge piece of their yashmaks sparkles with the diamonds set there. They bring in little trays of coffee and cakes, and they puts the trays on little low tables and set the tables before a big sofa. Then they sits down and pats the sofa beside 'em, and me and Snodger knows they wants us to sit with them.

Now I'm sitting beside the one with the blue eyes, and I'm hanged if I know what's shining the brightest, her eyes or the diamonds set in the nose-piece of her yashmak.

"Caffay, mon soldat?" she says to me.

I nods and smiles at her and takes the cup what's no larger than a hen's egg. Her hands are small and looks like – well, you know. I'm not seeing Snodger what's sitting beside me with his tart at the far end. I'm looking down at Miss Oo-La-La's red mouth what's all sort of quivering as she says I'm a brave soldat. Me, I'm feeling that sort of worked up that I want to kill someone just to prove what a damn fine feller I am.

"You lik la caffay, mon soldat?" she says.

"Not as much as I like you, Miss Oo-La-La," I tells her, and she claps her hands and repeats:

"Oh – Mees Oo-La-La! Mees Oo-La-La! Oh – mon brave Australee soldat! I love you – I love you!"

This sort of stonkers me. I can't do nothink because I've got a cup of caffay in one 'and and a cake in the other, and I reckons it would be a sin to spill the caffay over the white carpet with the black dragon on it. Any'ow, it isn't long before I've got me arm around Miss Oo-La-La, and she's lying half way across me and I'm kissing her hard and harder because she seems to like it best that way.

The funny thing is that I don't get tired of this kissing business. At the same time, at the back of my think-box is the idea that all this ain't real, that somethink must have happened to me, like I'd seen run over by somethink and was mutton and had arrived somewhere else. There am I kissing this tart and liking it, and there is this tart telling me she loves me as though she thinks it's hard for me to believe it. And then someone says, like a cat purring:

"And so the brave Australian soldiers would steal my jewels!"

I looks up and I'm stonkered at seeing standing just inside the doorway a paunchy bloke wearing a frock coat, red fez and red slippers. Standing either side of 'im is two of the biggest buck niggers I've ever seen in me life, and these niggers is wearing only black silk shorts and gold ear-rings.

The two tarts start screaming, and they get up and run and try to hide behind some palms in a corner, leaving me and Snodger still sitting on the sofa and waiting for the next act.

The next act begins with the paunchy character making a clicking noise with his tongue and advancing towards us, the niggers coming with him but keeping a little to his rear. The paunchy character is keeping one hand behind his back, and by the look in his eye he seems to be annoyed. He and his niggers come to a halt just the other side of the coffee tables and things, and there he says like he's whispering:

"My young friends, you are extremely fortunate that the two ladies with whom you have been conducting an amor are my daughters and not my wives. Had they been my wives I would have ordered my servants to take you outside and drown you by slow degrees. Therefore, I intend to administer corporeal punishment to impress upon you the gravity of the offence of entering without invitation an Egyptian gentleman's abode and besmirching the gentleman's women."

Now the paunchy character brings to light his right hand, and me and Snodger sees that he got in that hand a really nice pliable rhinoceros-hide whip. Snodger leans forward over the little table in front of him and takes a cigarette what he lights. One of the niggers takes a pace towards him, but the paunchy character tells him to keep back. The second nigger is standing opposite me, a gent of about sixteen stones in weight and four feet thick. He's looking at me as though he likes me – I don't think. Then Snodger says, calmly:

"Joe – begin."

The word 'begin' was like the crack of a starter's pistol at a race. Snodger was first off the mark, picking up the little table in front of him and crashing it against the shins of the nigger what is his opposite number. Although I'm not as quick off the mark, it is somewhat less'n a minute when I'm applying me number eight military boots to the shins and feet of my opposite number.

The special treatment don't seem to agree with my pet nigger.

What he don't like is a number eight stamping on his feet every time he's obliged to put one on the floor, while a knee now and then thudded into his stomach don't seem to improve his welfare. Now and then I has to pause in this treatment in order to dodge the paunchy character's whip. I takes this as very unsportsmanlike of Miss Oo-La-La's pa, and I am making up my mind to start on him when Snodger grabs a table by the leg, jumps a coupler feet to get proper height, and woodens his nig with it. Thereafter he attends to the paunchy character, adoptin' the methods he likes best, charging in under the whip, kicking the paunchy character under the jaw, and then flicking the whip round his neck and proceeding to strangle him.

My nigger is still full of steam. He comes at me with a roar of fire and blood, and, having done a bit of bull-teasing in me youth, I takes a header between his legs, heaves him up and over so that he comes down on his head and almost strikes sparks out of the carpet-dragon's mouth. Before I can jump more'n once with me boots on the back of his neck, he's up again and at me, informing me that he's a character as full of steam as Joe Louis.

Thus I has this black character all to meself, because Snodger don't seem able to unwind the whip from around the paunchy character's neck. It occurs to me that the paunchy character's face don't look particularly healthy at this time, but I can't give this much thought as my own particular job isn't what I'd like it to be.

Boots and bull-teasing having failed to subdue my pet nigger, I tries other methods. The sofa's a bit big to pick up in a hurry and throw it, so I dives across the room and takes up a large blue-and-white bowl. I thinks this vase is empty, but it is full of water and consequently I'm a bit slow in heavin' it up to sling at my pet nigger. He's on me all of a sudden, and once his hands are on me I knows I'm a gonner. In two ticks I'm performing flywheels and bouncers. Then I'm on me chest, and the nigger has one foot on me kidneys and is hauling me head up so's to break me back.

The situation is beginning to worry me when I hears a loud, sickening thud, following by a terrific yell from the nigger. He lets go of me and I'm on me feet in a flash, in time to see that nig doing sixty mile an hour out of the room with both his hands clasped to his stern what Snodger has touched with that rhinoceros hide whip.

I now has time to survey the scenery. The furniture and things seem all upset sort of. The other nigger is trying to be sick all over the carpet and is taking no interest in anything any more. The paunchy character is rolling around and gasping and clawing at his neck, and Snodger is laughing at him and starting to light a fag. And then there's Miss Oo-La-La at me side. She grabs my arm. Her eyes are shining like stars and she is a bit breathless, but manages to say:

"Come, mon soldat! We fly! That Nubian, he brings back others. Eggeree awam, mon hero, mon Australee! Come queek!"

So me and Snodger and the two tarts does a fast get. Out on the wharf we finds Abdul and his gharry, and into the gharry we all pile, me and Snodger going first, the tarts coming after to sit on our knees and take what was coming to them.

There's Miss Oo-La-La with her arms round me neck and telling me that she and her sister will be all right as Abdul will take them to their uncle's joint where they'll stay until the old man cools off. She ain't got no yashmac on now. It got in the way, any'ow, and didn't improve her looks. Her trouble's about her pa being almost strangled!

When we arrive at the city, me and Snodger gets down at the St. James Hotel. What a night! There's no doubts in our minds that we're due for a Pilsner or two, and there, outside the pub, we halts and stares at each other and Snodger says like he's got a lump of rock in his mouth:

"Blast me if we didn't forget to ask 'em where their uncle lives."

And before we could find out, we leaves for France.

Joining up with Rafferty

Y ou see, it was like this.

I'd been on "Tilcarra" Station seven years when the boss says he reckons I'm due for a holiday. I told him I didn't want no spell, but he kept on saying that I did, and in the end he won the argument.

Leaving me hut on "Tilcurra" after being there seven years was a bit of a wrench. A bloke does get used to a place and its inhabitants. There was Friday, the pet wether who would eat up all the spuds if I left the door unlatched, and there was Lucy, the pet kangaroo who slept at the foot of me bunk every night and wouldn't let none of the dogs come near. The two galahs, Dot and Dash, were tricks, and there were so many cats that I had to keep a tally of their names and markings on a board.

A man gets terrible fond of animals and birds, and I even offered to let the boss keep me cheque if he would only let me stay on. But no! He says I would have to go for a spell, and he takes me and me swag and me dogs in to the homestead, and there he writes me out a cheque for three hundred odd quid, and tells me he might give me back me job next year. That's wot I got for servin' 'im faithfully, so I tears up the cheque and throws the pieces at him, and I sets off up the river. I was always an independent bloke, mark you.

A month after I was sacked off "Tilcarra," I hit "Sunday" Station, above Bourke. The boss of "Sunday" is one of them wild Irishmen who can't talk without screaming. His hair is as red as the setting sun and it sticks up straight from his head. He's got a mouth like twenty-to-four o'clock, and he tells me his name is Paddy Muldoon come all the way from County Clare in such a manner as indicates he's hoping I'll call him a liar.

"It's a job av worrk ye be whantin' is it, ye –" he yells.

When I tells him he's a wonderful guesser, he says I can go out and join up with Rafferty, and that afternoon he takes me out fifteen miles to Rafferty's hut, dumps me there, and drives off back home before Rafferty gets back from one of the paddocks.

"Wot are you doin' 'ere?" he yells when he does get back.

"I'm going to boundary ride," I tells him.

"Well, you ain't gonna camp 'ere," he yells again. "I bin livin' 'ere for four years without a mate, and I don't want no mate now."

"If that's how you feel about it, ring up the boss and tell him so," I says, calm like. With that he wants to know how long I intends stopping, and when I tells him that I kept me last job for seven years, he rushes to the telephone. Then, instead of ringing up the boss, he turns round and snarls:

"Can you cook a damper proper?"

"Well, I oughter," I says. "I bin cookin' dampers nigh on forty years."

"All right," he says, toned down a bit. "Only remember, I want me dampers cooked round. I never bin used to any other sort. They got to be perfectly round."

You can see, then, that I didn't have no easy time when first I joined up with Rafferty. He would roar somethink terrible if a damper I turned out wasn't as round as the sun, and he'd roar if I dropped a used match on the earth floor of the hut, or chucked the dishwater out through the winder instead of down the drain he made. There was no more particular man in Noo South than Richard Rafferty.

Still, in time we sort of got used to each other and settled down. We didn't clash none at our work, for one thing, both having our two paddocks to ride and sighting each other only from sundown to sunrise excepting Sundays. The boss didn't come out much, so we wasn't annoyed by 'im. We had our arguments, as might be expected of two men long used to living alone, and it was a full two years before we 'ad a serious argument that brought matters to a head.

Rafferty comes out with a yarn that he was born at Castle Orleigh, near Waterford, and he says he's the eldest son of Sir Richard Orleigh wot died during the war. When I tells him I thought he told me he was born in Tassy, he flies off the handle. To humour him a bit, I tells him that me grandfather was Baron Hart of Tilverston Abbey, in Dorset, and that the bailiffs were put in when he died so that me father cut 'is throat when the inheritance was lost to 'im.

"Then you must be the present Baron Hart," says Rafferty, all his rage gone like rain in drought time. Suddenly he changes into another bloke, all bar 'is clothes. Up he jumps, draws 'isself up to the top of his four feet eleven inches, and says:

"I salute thee, me lord baron. Mine ancestors were ever friends with thy ancestors. At all times am I prepared to tip a lance or wield a sword on thy behalf."

That begins it. Seeing the joke, I says:

"I thank thee, Sir Richard. Methinks 'tis fine to meet with chivalry these parlous days when the jacks are better than their masters."

"Better, me lord baron, better?" he yells. "Skewer me! They art no better."

"Oh, all right," I says, getting a bit tired of 'is temper. "Don't you go and get your hair off so easily."

With that, Rafferty thumps 'is chest. His eyes are like blue stones. At the top of 'is voice, he yells:

"Recant, me lord baron, recant."

"Wot's that?" says I.

"Withdraw – withdraw thy assertion that the common herd is better than the descendants of the knights of ancient chivalry."

"Be hanged if I will," says I.

"Traitor!" he hisses. "Traitor to thy illustrious forebears."

He snatches up the dish-cloth, winds it round one hand, slips it off like it was a glove, and dashes it down on me left boot.

"A challenge!" he screams. "I challenge thee, me lord baron. I challenge thee to mortal combat in the tournament."

Seeing that he was properly worked up about it, I thinks it best to humour 'im a bit more, so I picks up the dish-cloth and says solemnly:

"Thy challenge, Sir Richard, I accept. I will don me me armour, and I will have the varlets bring me me charger. We will meet on the tournament ground down by the sheep yards to-morrer at noon. Prithee! I'll stick thee like a pig on a spit."

"I'll cleave thy pate asunder with mine axe, thou traitor to our nobility!" he threatens with roaring voice. "Hi! To me, John o' the Forge! To arms! Bring me mine armour. Saddle me mine horse. Polish me mine axe and sharpen its edge."

Out he rushes to the rubbish heap, and from the door I watches him picking up old bits of iron and kerosene tins which he takes to the harness shed. Then I hears him hammerin', and when I sneaks across to see what he is doing, there, sure enough, he is making a helmet out of a piece of corrugated iron.

Now this sets me off thinkin'. All the evidence goes to prove that this resurrected Sir Richard Orleigh is in dead earnest, and to keep up appearance like, I goes to the rubbish heap to get me some material with which to fashion some armour, too. Then I sees that he's took all there was, and that the only tin left 'andy is the cut down kerosene tin wot the cats drink out of.

Over in the shed Sir Richard is going strong, and I thinks of 'im arrayed in shinin' armour and bringing down a glittering wood axe on my unprotected head. By the hammering he's doing he seems to be gettin' on good-o, and when I take another bird's-eye-view at 'im, he's riveting iron into the shape of a stove pipe. I looks around, and the only iron I can see is on the hut roof. That reminds me that a corner sheet is loose, so I gets the ladder and takes it off because I can see that I'll have to meet Sir Richard in battle, which won't be fair if he's got on armour and I ain't.

I hammers out the corrugations, marks a pattern on it, cuts out the pattern, and with a couple of rivets makes a helmet wot fits down over me head on to me shoulders. Having cut out two eye-holes, and a hole through which to talk, the job wasn't too bad. And then, when Sir Richard sees how I'm gettin' on, he throws away all his bits of iron and drags a sheet of iron off the roof for 'isself.

The next morning when the boss rings up at half past seven as usual, me and Rafferty – Sir Richard, I should say – is too busy making front and back plates to bother with 'im. We works all day, and by sundown we each have made a full suit of armour. As it looks like rain, we shifts our bunks and the table closer to the fire-place as only half the roof is left. At seven that evening the boss rings up again. Sir Richard answers the 'phone, with me alongside 'im so's I can hear what the boss is saying out of the ear-piece wot Sir Richard holds a little way off his 'ead.

"Why didn't you answer me this morning?" yells the boss.

"'Cos me and Baron Hart was away in the green," says Sir

Richard sternly. "We went about our chivalrous duties early this morn."

"Oh, did you?" says the boss, sarcastic like. "How was the sheep in the green?"

"The gentle beasts were feeding with content, sire," says Sir Richard, without a smile on 'is face. "We saw nought of the outlaws wot accounted for them two last week, but me and Baron Hart will be trackin' 'em to their lair and smite them most heartily. We might sally forth at peep o' day. Fear not, sire. Our lances are ever at thy service."

"Fool!" shouts the boss. "Wot's wrong with you this morning?" From the clickin' noises goin' on in the 'phone, it is evident that the boss is banging his receiver down on the office desk. Then he roars: "You take a ride down to Mulga Corner in the morn and have a look at the water on that swamp hole. And you tell Baron Hart, or whatever he calls 'isself, to ride the back fence of Blackfellows in the morn."

"Sire, your commands shall be obeyed by one of us," says Sir Richard. "Ere noon tomorrow one of us will be dead, fallen in mortal combat. We are to meet on the tournament ground down by the sheep yards to settle an argument with lance and axe."

"I'll be comin' out to settle an argument with me boot if you don't get on with your work," yells the boss, and the telephone has statics or somethink when he tries to hang up his receiver.

Now there's me and Sir Richard dressed in full armour from helmets to leggings, we not being able to make iron boots, and when he falls to sharpening one of the wood-heap axes there ain't nothink I can do but to sharpen up the other. Things ain't lookin' as bright as the axes do by the time we goes to bed, still wearing our armour. Sir Richard is too dead in earnest for my liking. He don't talk any, that's the funny part about 'im. He's lying on his bunk, armour and all, the axe within reach. He's twirling his long moustache wot he's got to tie down under his chin when he put on his helmet so's it don't get pushed into his mouth. When I asks 'im why he don't talk, he mutters the word "Traitor" several times and glares at me. Tryin' to 'umour 'im don't make 'im any better, and I keeps awake hours studyin' a scheme to do away with them axes.

Consequently, when we are eating breakfast through the mouth-holes of our 'elmets, I says aloud:

"Sir Richard, a boon."

"Spill it, me lord baron," says he.

"My armourer reporteth that a varlet 'as pinched me charger's armour," says I. "Methinks another suit will have to be forged for the noble beast before I can meet thee in mortal combat."

"Thy boon is granted, me lord baron," he gabbles, because just then his fork got stuck in the mouth-hole of his 'elmet.

I leaves 'im lookin' for a tin opener to make the mouth-hole a bit bigger, and off I goes into the night paddock after the 'orses. When they sees me in all me armour they races to the hut yards in such a 'urry that when I gets back they're white with lather. Me and Sir Richard has a bit of trouble making 'em stand whiles we fit on their front lead pieces, and their shoulder and rump plates. When we 'ad got them fixed up properly, we lets the mokes go and then paints all the armour. I make up a gallon of blue paint with some raddle and linseed oil and paints me own and me charger's armour. Me shield I paints red with some of Sir Richard's paint. He paints all his armour red, and his charger's armour red, too. When I rivets a bunch of emu feathers to the top of me stove-pipe 'elmet, and Sir Richard rivets to 'is a bunch of canegrass, we calls it a day.

Next morning we go orf up along the crik to cut us a lance apiece. Sir Richard gets one about twenty-four feet long, and I gets one about a foot shorter. We times the fight for three o'clock this afternoon, and all the morning we're paring down the gum suckers wots our lances and nailing close to their points, wot we hardens in the fire, a square of blue shirt. When we dons our armour, we looks a fair treat.

The sun is shining brightly and all the birds is chirpin' when we slips our axes into our Sam Browne belts and mounts our chargers. If only King Arthur 'ad seen us he'd 'ave asked us to join him in a pot at 'is Round Table.

The chargers are a bit restive like, not being used to their armour. In spite of the lashin's of kangaroo hide the armour clatters a bit and that don't make 'em any better. Any'ow, we rides 'em down to the tournament ground, and without speaking a word we rides round the ground and passes the sheep-yards wot we imagines is the grandstand where sits the Lord President of the Tournament and all the beautiful wenches. There we raises our lances high and give a yell of defiance. Then Sir Richard says:

"To the death me lord baron. If I fail to spit thee with mine lance, I'll smite thee with mine axe."

"Do me, Sir Richard," I says, not letting on how nervous I am. "Anyway, no axes, mind, till we've 'ad a go with the lances."

"Well and good," he says. "It shall be as thou sayest. Me lord baron, I salute a man about to die."

"Same to you," says I.

When he sets spurs to 'is horse, the clatter of 'is armour sets my moke going, and he goes a full half mile afore I can pull 'im up, and when I rides back to the field of combat, there at the far end is waiting Sir Richard, a red knight on a red 'orse, the wind wavin' the canegrass of 'is plume, and the pennant on 'is lance. And there, to one side, looking at us is the boss, sitting up like Jacky in 'is buckboard drawn by the usual four mules.

The next second Sir Richard lets out a terrific yell and starts off at a gallop towards me. I spurs forward me charger into a gallop to meet 'im. The armour on the 'orse flaps a bit and it ain't really necessary to do any spurring. Me 'elmet gets shook round a bit so's I can see only out of one eye-hole, but down goes me lance point as we thunders towards each other yelling like fightin' womin.

The boss is yelling, too. Above the uproar I can hear the clatter and clash of Sir Richard's armour wot gets louder and louder every second. I can even hear me own yelling, but I can't see straight and there ain't no time to set me helmet properly. Then there is somethink the matter with me lance. It don't balance right, and here is Sir Richard right on top of me. Then I gets a terrible jolt, and Sir Richard and 'is charger sinks downward as I become a sort of flying knight. I sees 'is lance miss me 'orse by a fraction, and I knows that if I was on 'is back I'd have been skewered. Me horse keeps going straight on. He passes Sir Richard, and then I'm back again in the saddle. You see, the point of me lance sticks in the ground, and I take a pole-jump right over me opponent and just 'appens to land again on me 'orse. Me luck is well in, and I still 'as me lance.

The first round being a draw, we sets about to engage in the second one. Then the boss must needs drive across the field between us, and he goes up along to the hut. Me and Sir Richard both yells at 'im to keep orf, but he shakes 'is whip at us and hollers out that we're a pair of lunatics.

By this time I 'ad got me helmet straight so I can see properly all wot's going on. Then Sir Richard signals the start with a shout, and we into each other. Going this way the wind is against me. It's a bit powerful, and it catches me shield and whips it against me face, or rather me 'elmet, making me as blind as a bat. I can't see nothink, but I can hear the crash and clank of Sir Richard's armour above the clank and crash of me own. Then I gets a mighty jolt in the neck and goes on another aerial flight wot ends in a worse jolt when I hits the ground.

I sits up at last, screws round me helmet to see through the eye-holes, and then I gives a yell when I sees Sir Richard bearing down on me at the gallop and with 'is axe raised high. Me blood runs cold. I think I'm done for. I've lost holt of me lance, and it's broken to pieces, anyway. Fortunately me axe is still stuck through me Sam Browne belt. I staggers to me feet, and out comes that trusty weapon. Like a council cart, the red knight comes at me.

"Have at thee!" he roars, aiming a mighty swipe at me 'ead. The axe blade catches the, top of me 'elmet and knocks it right orf in spite of the hide strap keeping it down on to me breast plate. Somewhere handy the boss is shouting like mad. Up goes Sir Richard's axe for a second swipe. Back goes my axe for a cut at his middle, me being on me feet and unable to reach his 'ead. Then a gun goes orf twice, and I remembers that the boss always has a double barrelled gun with him. The pellets of them two charges pings against our armour, and several of 'em sting me scalp like hornets.

"A truce! A truce!" yells Sir Richard, evidently getting stung a bit, too. "Slay me this interfering varmint. To horse – to horse, me lord baron."

He gallops away after me charger and brings 'im back, wot time the boss is hollerin' and threatening to shoot us dead at closer quarters. Back comes Sir Richard, as I says, and on I gets. Then with battle axes a-swinging round our heads, we rushes on the boss who is reloading 'is gun.

It must have been the rattlin' an clanking of that hut roof done up into armour wot done it. The mule team bolts so suddenly that the boss topples over the back of the buckboard seat and flops into the body of the turnout. The mules head for home and glory, we after them. The harder they go the louder is the clatter of the hut roof, and the louder the clatter the harder they go. We chased the turnout for three miles, wot time the boss is standin' hanging on to the seat back and hollering at 'em to go faster. We give up at last, and when we get back to the field our chargers is too weary to do any more gallopin' that day.

The next evening when we are preparing to give the battle another go, the boss arrives in 'is car with three troopers. He's follered by the truck with all the station 'ands. Me and Sir Richard puts up a good show, but in the end they gets us, and eventually we gets brought 'ere.

Me and Sir Richard 'as been 'ere a long time now. 'Tain't too bad, mind you. The tucker's good, and there ain't much to do. Look! That's Sir Richard over there talking to that bloke under the tree. He's a character, 'e is.

Wot! You gotta go? Well, so long. Drop in again sometimes. Sorry I can't go out with you and 'ave one, but you know they won't let me out through the gates.

Breakaway House (Revised)

CHAPTER ONE

Invitation to a Walkabout

For many years the house had never been so quiet, and not in years had Marie Bonaparte found herself listening to the clock in the lounge and that on the kitchen mantelpiece. Not for years had she noticed a passing train, and now when one did pass on its way to the city the noise thundered about her.

It had been like this since her last boy had married and left with his bride for a honeymoon at Sydney. Little Ed, now six feet two and an electrician, was boisterous, untidy, lovable. He had hugged her, kissed her, and for the umpteenth time told her she would be all right. She wasn't all right. It was now five months since her Bony had been home between assignments, and no woman could be satisfied with making just the one bed, dusting the dustless rooms, sitting at the kitchen table doing the daily crossword and reading. Just sitting.

She would get horribly fat leading this kind of life. She was cubical as it was. Her face was large and wrinkled, and the only feature she still had pride in were her feet, strong and trim. With dark eyes she gazed moodily beyond the front fence, across the road to the railway on which thundered a train from Brisbane to Sandgate. Patting her permed black hair she sighed and thought she might run into town to get away from her own shadows.

It was then that a powerful car stopped outside the gate, a police car and she knew the man who left it and came to knock on her door.

"Hello, Marie! Enjoying the spell or getting sick of loafing?" enquired Sergeant Dovey.

Marie Bonaparte beamed and invited the policeman to come in for a cup of tea. "I was looking forward to a good long rest and I'm sick of it already. All I do now is to look out the window. As Bony says, I'm a sailor's wife, and no doubt of that. Heard from him?"

"After I get my tea and those scones I know you have in the cupboard. And plenty of butter. Know something?"

Marie turned from pouring water into the tea pot.

"What am I supposed to know? You heard from Bony?"

"Looks like." Sergeant Dovey lit a cigarette, gave her the smile he reserved for his wife and children, and waited for his tea.

"The sailor's in West Australia, Marie. Mucking about, we think. Just got a fresh assignment. We have his orders – orders, mind you, like give or else. We play ball or he's coming home."

Marie placed the tea before the visitor and provided scones, butter and jam. She sat facing the sergeant, knowing that to hurry him would be vain, and she picked up his cigarettes, lit one and blew smoke all over him and his scone.

"Now out with it, Mister Sergeant Dovey."

"Oh, yes, I forgot, Mrs. Napoleon Bonaparte. Ha, I thought I'd brought it. A telegram for you. Came this morning."

"He's coming home after all this time," Marie exclaimed, forgetting about the new assignment. Her fingers trembled as she opened the envelope and held the flimsy to read:

"Come awaltzing Matilda with me. Department will put you on plane for Kalgoorlie. Will have you met. Bring old fishing clothes and boots. All the real Australia is waiting for you to come home. If I don't say I love you you'll sulk, so I say it. Bony."

For almost a minute she sat with her head bowed, and Dovey saw a tear drop fall splash upon her forearm on the table. On looking up her eyes were full of sunshine after rain. She tried to speak and the sergeant relieved her of it.

"The wife and I know how you've lived in this house making a man of your Bony and men of your three boys, all the time eating out your heart for the bush where you came from. Well, here's the chance. You'll go? You can leave for Melbourne this afternoon, and catch a west bound plane early to-morrow."

Of course Marie had to find objections. There were the old clothes and boots to unearth and pack. There was the house to be looked after, and what would Little Ed and his wife say to an empty house? Besides what about the tradesmen, stopping the deliveries, and she'd have to pay a call at the bank for extra money. Oh no, she couldn't possibly go.

"Women!" exclaimed Sergeant Dovey. "You give 'em what they been crying for for years and then they argue the ruddy toss about taking it. You pack those clothes and I'll get to the telephone.

Sergeant Dovey took her to Brisbane, entertained her at lunch in a fashionable restaurant, put her on the Melbourne bound plane. There she was met by another policeman who drove her to a comfortable hotel for the night, and then called for her and took her to the airport. She could have done all this for herself, but she was a policeman's wife.

On leaving the plane at Kalgoorlie, some three thousand miles from her empty house, she was wearing a summery blue frock, a light plastic coat over an arm and a heavy suitcase. At the bottom of the disembarking steps she was accosted by a large young man having smiling grey eyes, and face and hands burned almost black by the sun.

"Mrs. Bonaparte?"

"Have been for thirty-five years. Who are you?"

He had taken the case from her and was conducting her to the gate, and he said softly:

"Constable Rockcliff, Mrs. Bonaparte. I've been instructed to convey you to a camp where, I know, your husband is waiting."

He flashed his credentials which she recognised, and a few minutes later they were by-passing the main town and driving north over a bush track. Marie was silent. The gimlet gums grew in clumps, and presently they were passing saltbush and bluebush and the much larger wait-a-bit shrubs. Marie breathed in deeply and held her breath as though the air was too precious to let escape. When it did, she sighed and her driver said:

"Tired, Mrs. Bonaparte? We could stop to boil the billy. Just say so. We've a long way to go."

"I'm not tired. Oh no, I'm not tired. Oh, it's lovely to belong, and I haven't belonged for years and years." The puzzled constable waited. "You see, Mr. Rockcliff, for thirty-five years I've been living on the outskirts of Brisbane. I've been from home all those years and now I'm back home again. Yes, I would like a cup of tea."

She was out of the utility before the driver, gazing about as a child in wonderland, breathing deeply, making no attempt to assist the policeman. He gathered a few leaves and then added dry sticks, and the smoke from his fire slanted gently away to the south and painted a bluebush purple. From the load on the utility he took down a tin of water and filled a blackened billycan, and looking up from it, he saw Marie Bonaparte standing in the smoke and enjoying it as though it were attar of roses.

Marie watched him bring from the vehicle a bushman's tucker box, and left the smoke on seeing he was observing her. Now she was smiling, a broad smile disclosing her teeth, and from her mouth issued a sound less like laughter than a gurgle of sheer happiness.

The constable tossed a handful of tea into the boiling water, left it for thirty odd seconds and lifted the billy off the fire with a stick. From the tucker box he took a cup and its saucer, but Marie demanded a bushman's tin pannikin and, now sitting on the ground, gurgled again like a small child. The policeman squatted on his heels, and opened the large packet of sandwiches he had bought in Kalgoorlie.

So this is Inspector Bonaparte's wife who reminded him of his mother. Minus affectation, minus the little bitternesses begotten by the years. Like his mother this woman would never grow old. Damn it, when she laughed she reminded him of his own child splashing about in her tub.

Two hours later they could see the sun-reflecting roofs of a small township, and Marie was asked to bend low when the policeman covered her with a light rug. Beyond the town, he explained.

"I've to get you to your husband without anyone seeing you on the road, Mrs. Bonaparte. Why, I don't know, but that was the order."

Beyond the township the flat land gave place to rolling dunes covered with dark scrub and revealing now and then a range of red sand. The track twisted to avoid steep grades, originally laid down by the old time bullock and camel waggons.

"I never ask him why he does anything," Marie said, and exclaimed delightedly when several kangaroos bounded across the track. "What he does outside the house is his business, but he tells me most of it. My business has been in the house where I raised three boys, and now that the last has flown the nest he and I are going on walkabout. The last walkabout was nine years ago, and that was only for a week."

"My wife wouldn't go walkabout for a million. We've two children: one three years and the other just a year," remarked the constable, and on being asked where he was stationed said it was at Kalgoorlie. "Don't get much bush work, and so I can enjoy a trip like this. We'll be coming to a wayside store in a couple of miles, and I'll ask you to get down again. We don't stop."

The bush store was a ramshackle conglomeration of slab buildings and, beneath the rug, Marie heard the barking of dogs and the shouted salutes of two men.

"They'll be wondering why we didn't stop," Rockcliff said. "Have to make up something when I go back tomorrow. Getting hungry yet? I thought we'd park at sundown."

"Go on and on and on for ever," Marie replied happily. "This is what I've ached for, this moving on, this going to some place or other. Strange, you know. At the end of this trip I'll meet my husband I haven't seen for eleven months, and I'm very happy, indeed. But it's the bush, this going on just to see what's round the next bend. It's tingling in my blood right now."

Eventually Rockcliff stopped the utility amid a grove of broad-leafed mulgas. The sun was setting, and all the shadows were tinted with red.

Then on again with the joy of coming home filling Marie's mind, and as the dusk passed abruptly the night made the headlight one great sword to pierce its black body. Presently she slept slightly, later recalling hearing voices on two occasions. The policeman woke her:

"Camp's just ahead," he told her, and there a short distance away were two flares of camp fires and people all about them. Then she could see a tent to leeward of one fire and two men standing close by. Finally at journey's end the utility stopped, the door was opened and the firelight revealed her husband's beaming face.

She was being hugged and hugged in response. She was being kissed and gave back the kisses. She said, breathlessly:

"Well, here I is."

"Same Marie. Same expression. Yes, here you is. Welcome to

the bush. Welcome to home. Come, dinner's ready."

He turned away to greet Constable Rockcliff. She noticed Bony's disgraceful clothes in which he appeared to have slept for a year. His straight black hair needed to be cut. The seat of his trousers was covered with patches, and his feet were bare.

The constable provided dinner and they ate and drank tea from pannikins in the light of the fire. Those about the second fire vanished into what she could see were wurlies, and there came one man to greet her. He was short and plump. He wore only a pair of dungaree trousers, and a snakeskin band to keep his hair tufted. The firelight gleamed in his coal black eyes. He could not be more than forty, and the cicatrices as well as the Mantle of the Devil proved him to be a Medicine Man.

He surprised Marie by his articulation of English saying:

"The Begonia Tribe welcomes the wife of Inspector Bonaparte. He became our friend when my father was the chief. We hope now to repay something of the debt we owe."

"This is Chief Merlee," Bony explained. "He has offered to assist us, as I well knew he would. Tomorrow we go into conference at which you will be given a grounding in the job of work we have to do. Off you go to bed soon, for you have come a long way since early this morning."

Marie made no objection to being bundled off to bed. She was very weary but her brain refused to give up the delights of coming "home", and before sleeping she looked outside the tent to see her husband and the constable with Merlee at the fire. They were squatting on their heels, and Merlee was drawing on the sand with a stick.

On waking it was broad daylight and, when realising where she was, felt vexed that she had missed the sunrise on this wonderful world instead of on house roofs which for too long had been her horizon. A breakfast of thick slices of bacon and eggs, together with yeast bread, awaited her at the fire as guest of Constable Rockcliff.

"Our mutual hero says that it will be some time before you'll sleep off the ground again," he told her, smilingly. "He's away inspecting camels with Merlee. Seems that he plans to go on a kangaroo shooting trip. Wish I were going, too."

"You cook fine, Mr. Rockcliff. Yes, it's a wonderful morning.

The smell of the cooking and the fire, the call of the birds, the aroma in the very air from all the trillions of trees, the scent exuded from all the pure sandhills. It's home for us."

"Could be home for me, too," conceded the constable. "What a hope! What with the town-loving wife and the kids, what a hope! I was born and reared on a coastal farm, but I can understand what you feel."

Marie saw that the camp was on the bank of a wide water-hole in a creek emptying into a great salt lake, when it ran, and that both banks were lined by magnificent gums. It was a flawless day in mid-March, and although on the same longitude as Brisbane lacked Brisbane's heat and humidity at this time of year.

"I was born in Queensland," she said. "For thirteen years I ran wild with other children. Then for three years I was in a mission. There came a man who looked at me with eyes like the sea on a bright cold day. He made me tremble inside, and after another year he came back to say he wanted to marry me. I trembled more than ever, and he pinched me till I said the words.

"Afterwards he carried me off to his camp close to a water-hole in a great area of tobacco bush taller than you. We stayed there for a month, just a wonderful month beginning and ending with the full moon. Afterwards he took me to a small house in the country outside Brisbane. He was away on duty when the first boy was born. He was with me when the second came, and away again when the third boy was born to us.

"He calls me his sailor's wife, and that's what it's been all these years. The countryside became a suburb of Brisbane. Deep down I grew to hate it. He promised and promised that one day we'd both go off on walkabout and stay together till death parted us, and now we are to go on walkabout, so he says, but not forever as he's still a policeman. D'you know what's it all about?"

Rockcliff shook his head. He said:

"I know only I've to collect the stretchers and other gear, and return to Kal to-day. I brought your husband here four days back. He had a pow-wow with the local chief, and I was then told to return to Kalgoorlie, load up with rations and second hand gear, meet you and bring you here." The constable grinned. "You're on walkabout all right, Mrs. Bonaparte. As I said before: lucky you."

"His eyes are still blue?"

"And how they can bore into a man's block."

Eventually he left her sitting on one of two rolled swags, a chipped iron camp oven, a rough tucker box, a sack she knew contained rations. There was an un-cared-for thirty-two calibre rifle, several boxes of cartridges, boxes of cake tobacco. There remained her own suitcase and another she recognised as belonging to her husband.

The flies, smaller than the common house fly, rose from her shoulders at the approach of a fly-killer which darted into the small cloud and captured one. She felt a stinging on her forearm and found there a silent flying March fly and smacked it. She saw a bull ant balefully watching her, and knew it was a scout from a distant nest. She knew that the aborigines, none of whom approached her, would be too lackadaisical to track the nest and destroy it as being too close to their camp.

Yet it was a beautiful day, a wonderful day. Later still she saw Bony and several aborigines emerge from the timber beyond the water-hole, bringing with them two adult camels.

CHAPTER TWO

Walkabout

The morning salutation expressed, Bony and Marie with Merlee drank tea and smoked. The men were silent, listening to Marie's chatter, and presently her husband observed that she was wearing her travelling clothes which she must wear out and match his own sartorial condition.

"You brought old clothes and boots?" he questioned. She nodded and he went on: "We have to pass through neutral countries to reach enemy territory where we must arrive as a wandering kangaroo shooter and horse breaker with his lubra and equipment. Let's go over it again, Merlee."

"Well, before you start kill that bull ant stalking me," Marie said. "I'm wearing a skirt although I did bring an old pair of your pants."

"Can't kill bull ants, sweetheart. Merlee's a bull ant totem people."

Merlee said: "I'll fix him," and picked up the ant and tossed it into the creek. "For sure we're bull ant totem. They don't sting us."

Bony squatted and smoothed an area of sand with a stick. With its point he indented dots. Having made the first, he said:

"Here is Breakaway House, owned by a man named Gosfer whose grandfather built it after having taken up a million acres of land. Here is Mount Magnet, a railway town. Three policemen were sent to investigate Breakaway House and its people. One was found dead eighty miles from Breakaway, the second was well nigh crippled in a row with the aborigines, and the third has disappeared. Our job now is to investigate this Breakaway House.

"The three men were reported as having left Mount Magnet. Gosfer must have known they were policemen because previously he hired cooks from a city agency and they left normally to return to Mount Magnet.

"How did Gosfer know they were policemen? Answer, because each of them conferred with the Mount Magnet Senior Constable prior to taking the track to a place called Narndee and so on to Breakaway House. How did Gosfer know of their coming? Because the aborigines of Mount Magnet either smoke signalled or King Billy sat over his little fire and telepathed it.

"That way, you see, is by the front entrance. We have to enter by the back door, through this desert country to the east of Breakaway House. The Medicine man or Chief of the tribe living at Breakaway House is one called Yarco. He is a violent man, and he and his tribe would be wholly supported by Gosfer."

Bony drew a circle around Breakaway House, and outside this a larger circle. He went on:

"This larger circle is an iron curtain, and here and there close to it are numerous tribes almost wild but in contact with Breakaway House aborigines, and thus with Gosfer. We have to get through the outer or neutral tribes, and here we have help from you, Merlee. We cannot move anywhere without notice because being strangers we are bound to be reported everywhere. In fact, not to be reported would make us very important news on approaching the iron curtain.

"Thus we proceed northward from this place, and Merlee will

report to the neighbouring tribe that a wandering half abo and his lubra are on the way, and add that our business is shooting for skins and breaking in horses. They in their turn will pass us to the next tribe. We travel by this circle from Breakaway, and finally approach the tribes on the fringe of Breakaway House from the north. We shall thus be received as a trapper and horsebreaker with his lubra, identities well established and having no possible connection with the police."

"And when we get there?" asked Marie who had removed her city shoes and was digging holes in the sandy loam with her toes.

"You will have lost a little weight, my sweetheart, and might be offered a job as house cook, and I shall work breaking in Mr. Gosfer's young horses."

"When do we start?"

"As soon as we harness the camels to a two-wheel dray."

The history of the dray would have been a remarkable document. Probably it had been built in the days long past for prosperous gold seekers based on Coolgardie. Its iron tyres were still sound and five inches wide. Its shafts were gone but in their place were bush cut poles. Of recent date someone had fashioned a bush frame to support a covering of bags. The wheels were in fair condition but there remained no paint and the wood was cracked and hungry for oil. How it came to be possessed by Merlee Bony didn't bother to ask, being grateful for something more than a windfall.

The aborigines assisted to harness a cow camel into the shafts and Bony shuddered at the harness of fencing wire and an old bag for a saddle pad to rest before the hump. He was however thankful that she was docile, but this could not be claimed for the male camel which was harnessed in front to form a tandem team.

"You'll have to watch him, Bony," Merlee advised, laughingly. "He'll make for home for sure if you don't. The cow will want to eat your rations and feed from your hands. They were spoiled as pets by the young 'uns."

The gear was loaded, and Merlee contributed two dingo traps and a quantity of ancient corn bags for the canopy. Bony presented him with two five-pound boxes of chewing tobacco, and with a last command to watch the brake and with the departing cheers of the entire tribe sending them forward, Bony called to the team and away they started.

At noon they had progressed five miles headed into the country far west of Wiluna. They neck-roped the lead camel to a sandalwood tree, ate the last of the bread and drank milkless tea, lunched from a leg of kangaroo baked in the ashes by the lubras, smoked a little, and then proceeded to sort and rearrange the loading.

Thus engaged they could see Merlee's smoke signals rising into the almost still air to announce their departure to the next tribe.

"There are our passports, Marie," Bony pointed out. "We're on our own as from now. Tired?"

"Well, it's different from tramping about a house. I'll toughen up, though. Perhaps I could ride a little."

"Certainly. You had better put on a pair of boots, or these sand shoes before your feet give out. We have nine miles to go to reach the night camp."

The lead camel they named Joe, and the cow was christened Marie. The human Marie rode on the load, and Bony drove with his hand on the rear brake in case of a bolt, and whistled and hummed tunes, and delighted listening to his lubra's enthusiasm over a sandhill, a tree or of something she saw. They passed an arm of the salt lake near which Merlee's tribe was encamped. They watched several bush turkeys skurrying away through a field of saltbush, and about a long ribbon of scum-covered water stood two ibis who made no more movement than clay birds in a garden setting.

The night camp was a dry one amid a group of cabbage trees, so called as they look from distance like cabbages. Bony accepted no chances with the camels: he roped each to a tree and lopped a meal which he dragged to them. After a meal of instant potatoes and a can of Irish stew, they gathered leaves on which they placed the blankets.

In the deepening dusk, with the camels fed and lying down to chew cud, they sat at the camp fire and Marie told of the marriage of their youngest son. The stars came out to dance through the high level haze and a mopoke in a nearby tree announced his presence.

"You'll have to take it easy for a few days," Bony told his

Marie. "We are still in Merlee's country. Eleven miles on there's a rock-hole and there we can draw water with a rope and bucket. Perhaps we'll stay there for a day, and make the canopy, and in general prepare ourselves for the role we have to adopt."

Marie rolled her city clothes to fashion a pillow, and she lay listening to the silence. The mopoke had flown away to seek what this arid desert could provide. Now there was a hole in the noise of a city. There was not a tiny sound to spoil the perfection of the silence. It was deep. It was as tall as the dancing stars. Its limits about them were non-existent. For so many years Marie had not listened to it, and she was becoming drowsy when it was broken by her husband's faint snoring. It seemed that the next moment day was breaking and she woke to see him adding wood to the hot ashes of the camp fire.

It was mid-afternoon when they first saw ahead the rock hill of granite rising from the desert floor for two hundred feet and found on arrival it was surrounded by clumps of acacias and spindly muglas amid a plentiful supply of camel feed in a profusion of wait-a-bit bush, the thorns no defeat of the animals. The rock-hole was indicated by the slabs and rocks gathered above it to thwart animals, and being uncovered disclosed an underground cavern containing cool and delicious water.

Bony tended the camels and Marie made camp. She lit a large fire which on the morrow would supply hot ash and coals with which to bake powder bread in the oven. And afterwards they went up to the summit of the rock hill where they could see Merlee's smoke signals still rising above the horizon to the south and other signals based beyond the horizon to the north.

"That'll be the next tribe we'll contact two days ahead," Bony said. "They're gossiping with Merlee."

"Can you read them?" Marie asked, and Bony explained that the signals by their number and disjointed columns were always vague and expressed a thought rather than white-fellers' sign language.

"I thought you knew that," he queried, and laughed. "I can't read them, but I do know that the main aim of smokes is to call attention to the man in the other camp that telepathy is called for. And so a man in each camp sits, as you must remember, over his little fire and sends his thoughts to the other fellow. The secondary aim of smoke signals is to give the young men practice in the art, for an art it is."

"Had you been out of the bush for forty odd years like me, and had you been dragged from the bush when merely a girl as you dragged me, you would have come to think white-feller fashion and forget the things you were never told about in the first place. So, clever, quit your kidding."

Bony grabbed her, and there on the summit of the rock hill they embraced and danced in full view of stunted trees and dusty shrubs. They managed to serve two thirsty camels who were not broken to long spells without water, and, still mistrusting them, Bony neck-roped them to trees and cut scrub for dinner, while Marie baked a damper of baking powder bread in the oven. Bony could have done better, and laughingly forgave his wife as she had had baker's bread delivered to her door during the years.

"The trouble with you is that you're dressed too flash for the country," he told her. "A city dress not yet stained. Silk stockings and I suspect undies as white as snow. You're supposed to be the lubra of an unwashed horsebreaker, not a school teacher. We shall have you being reported far and wide as too flash for the role. Dig out your old clothes, and lie around on the ground to make them older. As we go on we'll cut and mend the rents."

Marie giggled. "What I suffer!" she exclaimed. "First aching bones from sleeping on the ground, and now I've to wear old and tattered clothes. I can't go back to the bush after all the years in Brisbane where I had to keep up with the neighbours."

"And get that perm out of your hair. A horse breaker's wife with a perm is like a queen without her crown. Anyway, the time is ripe for a bath, so come ye my little maid to the tank."

They took the bucket and rope to the rock-hole and there drew water and sloshed each other as children on a beach. In the deepening dusk they went back to the fire and dried themselves with frayed towels which were at least clean, and this night Marie dropped off to sleep with the muttering of birds to lull her.

She woke at daybreak but not before Bony who was at the replenished fire from which rose acrid smoke. He was burning her city clothes and shoes, having left beside her leaf bed ancient garments which she should have put into the trash can months and years before.

"You'll have to learn how to get around. You have to be an actress, my sweetheart," he explained to his distressed wife. "Keep repeating to yourself: I'm a knock about horse breaker's lubra. I read somewhere where a woman called Marie was the wife of a great detective, but it was only in a book."

"Well, here I is, and I feel awful. Thank goodness you left me my pants and slip."

"You may keep those because they don't show. Walk short distances to-day in your boots, but don't overdo it."

They broke camp an hour after dawn and Bony reclosed the aborigines' rock-hole with the granite slabs, and about noon both were surprised when coming to a wide swathe of green grasses and pools of claypan water dropped by a wandering thunderstorm several weeks previously. All the kangaroos in the back desert were gathered here and Bony shot two, skinned them and wrapped the carcasses in bags from the flies. The skins this coming night he pegged on bone dry claypan, and they dined on kangaroo chops for the animals had been in fine condition. The rest of the meat Bony salted.

For Marie the thrill of being 'home' never waned. She was walking in the elastic-sided stockman's boots more easily, assisting Bony by being within reach of the brake and thus permitting him to keep beside the camels and guide them across the easier land to avoid trees and such like obstacles. For Bony this was the real holiday in years, for he, too, was 'home', and thus the day and the night passed and the next day when they came to another rock-hole at the foot of another rock hill.

It was the morning of the following day that they were met by Merlee's near neighbours.

CHAPTER THREE

Top Hat Rock

The camels were nervous and Bony attributed it to the iron-shod wheels on the long slope of gibbers down which they were heading for a line of trees marking a creek. He was walking beside them, and Marie was walking at the rear of the dray with a hand on the brake. There was nothing to be seen on the apparently stone-armoured slope when there materialised an aborigine to their left and another on their right.

Nowhere on this wide and long gentle slope grew a tree or a shrub. There were no water gutters this far down to give concealment, and now there abruptly stood two men armed with throwing spears and wearing nothing but the pubic tassel. Although both Bony and his Marie were pre-occupied they would have seen a sleeping kangaroo spring to attention, but not either of these aborigines. They had been invisible, and now they were standing like the stumps of burned out trees. They began to converge, and Bony called a halt and signed to Marie to brake hard.

One then pointed with a spear to the right of the original course, and comically walked in that direction with the loping gait of the camels. He then beckoned, and Bony signed again to Marie to loose the brake and called to the camels to proceed. He could not understand the reason for this action until they were nearing the very bottom of the slope when there were revealed deep sided channels which carried rain water from the slope to the creek. The escort had taken them to a crossing, and then proceeded to take them direct to the creek trees where they were stopped and the mimed order given to unharness the camels.

Marie assisted Bony, greatly to Bony's approval, taking one of the animals to neck-rope to a tree. She was then commanded by signs to stay with the dray, and Bony was motioned to follow the aborigines. He was conducted for a quarter-mile along the dry creek to where at the outer elbow were a rocky hole and the camp. It was a crude camp, and far more pleasant to behold than the littered and ragged iron and bag shanty camps outside many Australian towns.

On the outskirt of this camp Bony was told to wait in time honoured etiquette, whilst his escort went on to report. They did not return, but another did, and this one took Bony to the inevitable little fire well away from the main camp fires where hovered the lubras and children.

Two men squatted at this small fire, the one very old and carefully attendant in pushing together the burning ends of five sticks splayed like the dray's wheel spokes, the other not yet middle aged, and in fairly good physical condition. Bony sat on his heels and summed them up.

The younger man he deemed to be the chief as on the wrinkled dust-caked body of the older man he detected the ochre marks of the medicine man. Their unruly hair was bunched high by what appeared bands of human hair encircling their heads. With his hand the chief smoothed the ground between them, pointed to the south, drew a circle and then made another and pointed at his own camp. He then drew another and pointed to the north-east, presumably informing the stranger of the location of the next tribe.

Meanwhile, farther along the creek a gathering of aborigines were sending up smoke signals and so perfect were the conditions that each disjoined column on reaching cold air became a white cloud which drifted eastward and so make room for the next column, ultimately forming a line of small clouds adhered to the azure sky.

With miming and his map the chief made clear the way to the next tribe, and where water could be found and where it might be found. The conference over, Bony gravely presented him and his companion with several cakes of tobacco, which brought a broad smile from the chief. For ten or fifteen minutes they sat and smoked or chewed, saying nothing, and finally Bony rose to go and was given permission.

When at the end of day he and Marie took the camels to the water hole at the bend, the aborigines revealed no curiosity in them or the animals. They carried water back to camp, and whilst grilling kangaroo steaks and having an early evening pannikin of tea they spoke of their reception by Merlee's neighbours.

"You did well with the camels to-day, and especially lugging that bucket of water to camp," Bony commented. "You'll do better, and later on you must snap back when I growl at you and complain of being slow or something. We must not arrive at Breakaway House like a couple of very young lovers."

"Well, aren't we?" argued Marie.

"No, we're not."

"I tell you we are."

"I say we're not. Looking for a clump on the ear?"

"You hit me and see what happens."

"You'd fall down," shouted Bony.

"You try it and see," yelled Marie, and collapsed with laughter.

"That's the idea, sweetheart. That's it. We must practise but no laughter, or giggles, no smiles, but nasty husband and wife. Now you bake a damper loaf and I'll tidy up."

All the next day the smoke signals rose from beyond the horizon, the undulating ridges of the sand dunes, the areas of scrub, and the vaster areas of plain. Marie was now less ebullient but nonetheless she was happy and found a strange peace in her heart. At times she wondered how she could possibly have lived near a city for so long. Bony could hear her singing but so softly that the tune failed to reach him. Now and then he was assailed by doubts of the wisdom of having brought her to exposure to hardship, probably to grave danger, but the singing at the rear of the dray defeated the doubts.

The camels were becoming accustomed to doing without water every day, and were much more tractable. They thrived on the wait-a-bit and the mulga with a nibble or two now and then off the saltbush, so that dry camps could be chosen for their offering of dead wood for the cooking and the comfort of being in the lee of trees.

On the seventh day following departure from Merlee's camp they sighted a land mark which the chief at the last camp had made prominent on his dust map. It rose imperceptibly above the north-east quarter, blue-black as though washed by the ocean. Water had been promised at the foot of this rock having a flat top and roughly resembling a top hat. From this rock Bony would have to proceed due west in the general direction of Wiluna, and at another mark southward to Breakaway House.

It was toward late afternoon the next day that they reached Top Hat Rock. Bony was delighted and yet wary because such an outstanding natural feature would be of importance to the aborigines for the legends associated with it, equally with the store of precious water. It fascinated both desert travellers.

The Hat was based on a mound of rock covering many acres. The mound itself, Bony estimated, was a hundred feet to the summit, and the Hat rose to a further hundred feet. The crown must be convex for when it rained – if it ever did – water poured over its rim to score in the wall a deep runnel, and this mark zizzagged to the rock mound to overflow to a great but shallow crevice.

At their approach hundreds of birds rose from this crevice and many lean but hardy kangaroos fled away to sit straight to watch them at distance. Bony obtained the rifle and the dray went on. At the foot of the mound grew great sandalwood trees any one of which would have made ten or eleven tons of joss sticks. There were cabbage trees and wattles and thriving mulgas, and the wait-a-bits grew in great clumps. The ground about was massed with tussock grass which no fire had burned and which now was dry and brittle, and which caught the windblown sand at the lee of each.

The camp site Bony chose was backed by a clump of wait-a-bits forming a shield from attack at one side, and several mulgas on the other to which the camels could be neck-roped. The animals evinced no nervousness but were in position for water. Taking Marie with him, he scouted about in widening circles and nowhere found human tracks. The ground was churned by the feet of dingoes, emus, rabbits, and wild horses. They looked at the water in the crevice and shuddered. It was red with mud and partly covered with green slime. It must have been fed by a hidden cistern higher up the mound because the level coincided with the rock verge.

Having circled the entire mound, having watched the birds' behaviour, having sniffed and looked for smoke, Bony was confident that this place was theirs at least for the night. They had found a rock-hole of pure water, guarded against bird and beast by slabs of rock, and Bony considered it a little odd that the desert blacks would take the trouble, being indifferent to the quality of water.

However, the camels drank and drank their fill and were content to lie down at their protective trees and chew the now moistened cud. While Marie made a fire and chose the driest wood, Bony cut and dragged branches to them. He drew water from the protected rock-hole, bringing down to the camp a filled petrol tin and the bucket. This chore he did twice as the next camp would be a dry one, and while at the hole he could not see the dray or the camels in the alcoves of wait-a-bit scrub.

The sun was setting and above the backdrop of bush Bony

could see the rock towering above it. It was to the east of the camp and the prevailing westerlies had sandblasted the granite front. The monolith from this angle took on colour, at first a rose pink which rapidly deepened to flaming scarlet, and then as Bony and Marie watched, Marie exclaiming ecstatically the while, the sun went to bed and at the bottom of the Hat the scarlet faded into purple and slowly the purple rose to be in turn based on a growing band of indigo blue. They were thus watching this progression of colours mounting up the Hat when Bony witnessed at the base of the Hat upon the rock mound the appearance of one aborigine after another, till eleven were racing down the slope to the water filled crevice.

Each was entirely naked, being without even the pubic tassel. They were short and lean. Their bodies were caked with grease and sand dust. They carried throwing spears. They were like men crazed for water. Bony told Marie not to move. The fire was smokeless, merely a mound of red embers ready for cooking purposes. The wind came from the south, and thus desert noses would not smell them.

Bony ran to the end of the alcove, fell flat and edged his way round the bush to watch. The aborigines were now in the crevice water, beating themselves with wet hands, shouting when not scooping water into their mouths. Beyond them when they emerged and picked up their weapons, the scarlet was but a ribbon about the top of the Hat, the purple coming half way up and the rest all blue. The blue took the savages, and the flint tip of every spear was a blue star. One spear was pointed towards the crouching Bony, and as one man the eleven raced away in the opposite direction, running seemingly without effort, with the promise of never tiring.

The camels rose with startled grunts to stand on legs like springs. Marie vented a gasp of dismay, and Bony turned and ran back to her. She was pointing now, and following the direction he witness fifteen or twenty more racing upon them from the west, black midgets against the flaming horizon. Telling Marie to get under the dray, he waited with the rifle.

A minute later he could detect details against the sunset. These men were different. They wore the pubic tassel. They were more robust. Their spears were longer and they carried a throwing stick, notched to take the end of the spear and so cast further and with deadly accuracy.

Surprise gave way to astonishment when these men veered to pass the camp. They ran silently, not as fleet as they might but with the dogged tirelessness which could be maintained all day, or all night. From the other end of the alcove of bush Bony thankfully watched them running to the distant dunes, the sun filled western sky tinting their naked bodies. He watched them mount the sand dunes, saw them on the summit for an instant, watched them vanish on their hunt for the first party. The Hat was draped with mourning.

"Well now! We is still here, Bony. What was all that for?" asked Marie, and then without drawing breath asked if she could put the fire out.

"Oh no, my love," expostulated the chuckling Bony. "Put that damper into the oven, or we'll have no breakfast to-morrow. I'll make a billy of tea and we'll eat in the last of the daylight. That mob won't be back till to-morrow. They were not interested in us just now, and mightn't be if they do return. Cricky! There's a dozen 'roos coming to water. I must bag a couple of them."

The kangaroos approached cautiously past the camp toward the water, and after them there emerged low to ground, several shadows, the slinking forms of hunting dingoes. Bony bagged two of them. The 'roos were mystified by the shooting rather than frightened. They sat up on their tails and Bony killed three, for the elfin thought was with him that the second party would return and that a meat offering might avoid trouble. He went out and brought in the dingoes and the kangaroos which he hauled into the branches of a sandalwood tree.

CHAPTER FOUR

Ports of Call

Although it was improbable that the aborigines would attack during the dark hours of night, Bony sat with his back to the dray wheel, and the rifle across his knees, with the automatic in its holster slung from a shoulder. Behind him Marie slept soundly and only once reached for him through the spokes.

The two camels cat-napped, occasionally shaking themselves and clanging the bell strapped to each long neck. Strange noises came from the water-filled crevice: soft scuffling and the thumping of kangaroos, as a thirst crazed dingo darted among them with interest only in the water. At distance a pack of dingoes set up a howling which in the long past had caused migrants to think of wolf packs and similar enemies.

Into Bony's sky appeared the stars known to bushmen as the Three Sisters, and they told him it was after midnight. It was coolish rather than cold and no naked aborigine would be active until after dawn. Bony permitted himself to cat-nap, too, his sub-conscious keeping guard to warn if the camels became alarmed.

The night wore away and the dawn came, and Bony dozed on when ordinarily he would have wakened at the first dawn after a night's comfortable sleep. On waking his eyes encountered broad daylight, and he was aroused by the bells on the camels as they lurched to their feet expectant of breakfast.

There, one hundred yards from the camp squatted a naked aborigine, his head resting on folded arms based upon his knees. He had no spears that Bony could detect, and he was there on a courtesy call waiting to be invited.

"We have a visitor," Bony told Marie, gently waking her. "Come to ask after our health. Don't hurry. I'll replenish the fire."

There was no dressing for Marie had lain down under the blanket fully dressed. She crawled from under the dray, washed her face, combed her hair, and the permanent was losing ground. Meanwhile Bony had broken open the hot coals overlaid by ash and tossed onto them a supply of wood, and then taking up the rifle, for as host he might arm himself, he approached the squatting aborigine, calling when within twenty yards. He could observe no weapon near the man, nor a spear gripping between the big and second toes of a foot. The man sat up, then stood and waited for Bony to draw near.

He would be about thirty, in the prime of his life. He was well conditioned. For a desert aborigine he was not ill looking. He surprised Bony when he spoke in broken English assisted by much sign language. He raised his right hand, then his left to show that neither held a weapon, then he raised first his left foot and then his right to prove that his feet were weaponless. Bony advanced, and the aborigine smiled, saying:

"Blackfeller Boss say for whitefeller Boss come see in camp."

"What for?" pressed Bony, suspiciously, and suspicion was banished when the caller said:

"Blackfeller Boss all mate with Merlee."

"Goodoh! You work on station some time, eh?"

The aborigine shook his head, saying:

"Went up stock route for cattle. Brought a mob down to Wiluna. Whitefeller Boss learned me English. Long time ago, betcher."

"You bin Beaudesert?"

"Ya, Boss. We gettum cattle."

This decided Bony. He asked where the aborigines were camped and the visitor signed to the east side of the monolith, now rearing blackly against the rose tinted morning sky.

Bony signed him to accompany him to his camp where he lowered two of the kangaroos and proceeded to skin them, knowing that the hunting party would have no tucker. On a bag he carried a carcass, and the visitor carried the other over a shoulder. It was thus they arrived at Blackfeller Boss' camp to be met unceremoniously by eighteen gentlemen of the desert. Without their lubras to carry a firestick they couldn't be bothered so early to make a fire with a flint and tinder, and they fell on Bony's gift, stripped the carcass with the razor sharp flint spear heads, and fed raw. They were slightly advanced from the genuine wild blacks who would have torn at the meat like a pack of dingoes.

Whilst they breakfasted, Bony made a small fire with a match, and when satisfied his fire was burning brightly squatted beside it. Eventually there came to squat with him the ugliest, by white man's standards, aborigine he had ever seen. He was well past his prime, but not withered by age. He was deep chested, and the muscles of his thighs were as thick ropes. With him came a leaner individual and the man who called at the camp. All three were still caked with sand and dust into which they had burrowed for warmth.

They were presented with a stick of chewing tobacco, and with delight they chortled, chewed, emitted sighs. The ugly man grunted and said something to the former ambassador who translated:

"Blackfeller Boss say for you good whitefeller. Kangaroo goodoh. Bacco goodoh. You all goodoh with Merlee, you all good feller us blacks. When you come along camp?"

"I decided to stay here to-day. Feed up camels, shoot more 'roos and dingoes perhaps."

"Blackfeller Boss say all bloody right by him. You shoot 'em up. All blackfeller eat 'em up. Blackfellers drove 'roos to water and you shoot 'em up goodoh."

"Who does this water belong to?" asked Bony.

"Us blackfellers."

"What blackfellers you all chase last night at sundown?"

This took a little translating, but the answer came through the interpreter with unexpected bawdiness.

"Dirty black bastards come out of desert looking for lubras. Got close to us blackfellers' camp. Caught a lubra and she yowled, and we got after 'em. Speared four of 'em and others got away in the dark."

It was now Ugly Mug's turn to question. He spat with remarkable accuracy at an ant not yet limbered up by the rising sun, and the translator said:

"Blackfeller Boss says where for you go to next tribe?"

Bony smoothed the ground and drew a map showing his present position well to the east of Wiluna. He made a mark from this derelict mining town northward, saying:

"Canning stock route. Aim to hit it about here, then down to skirt Wiluna, then on down the Number One Fence and so to Breakaway House." Ugly Mug nodded and scowled, and Bony went on: "Tell him no want Yarco and White Feller Boss Gosford know I come this way. Say I want them think I came down stock route."

The Chief got this and grinned. The interpreter said:

"Yarco dirty black bastard. White feller Boss Gosford dirty white bastard. No good for blackfellers. All damn crook. Blackfeller Boss say for you to come on to camp. He tell next tribe and they tell next on the stock route, and they say for you come down the route from Beaudesert."

The conference ended shortly after this and Bony returned to his camp and Marie who had been waiting with some uneasiness.

The day was spent quietly. Bony pottered about drying his skins to prove his calling, and Marie washed underclothes and baked. At eventide the aborigines beat up the 'roos from afar and Bony shot a dozen. For the following two days they were escorted as royalty to Ugly Mug's main camp above a large soak-hole in a creek which apparently had not run water for a decade. And so the days passed, and their course gradually veered to the west far out behind the derelict town of Wiluna.

Meanwhile for Marie her home in Brisbane, her three boys and their wives, the delivery men, and the bills seem to recede swiftly into a past life altogether, to become unreal, and now and then she felt ungrateful to Providence who had given so much to life. Under the present circumstances often she felt guilty of being too happily content, too eager to push on and on into another adventure, and another experience she had tasted in a long ago existence.

Sometimes she caught her husband's approving glance and smile as she managed the brake, the camp chores, the cooking, and above all the camels she had come to love. They looked now for a crust of bread at the end of the day, or waggled their split upper lip in a make believe kiss.

Bony noted how in character she was becoming, wearing her old clothes without regard, walking in her elastic-sided stockman boots as though she hadn't worn shoes for forty years. She sang as always when on the move, and often practised upbraiding him for being a lazy, careless, good-for-nothing. Even put a sound shrillness into it making it sound genuine.

In his own way Bony was happy not only for this spurious freedom from police work. He was happy because his Marie was obviously so. For the first time perhaps he was made aware of what she had been deprived in her service to him in love and in her service to his career. He had conquered and raised himself high: she had surrendered cheerfully all along the line to push and help him. She reminded him allegorically of a duck kept in confinement for a long long time, and then released to take to the water, and like the duck, she was preening her spiritual feathers and becoming beautiful.

She was losing avoirdupois, gaining resilience in her legs, becoming less cubical and still retaining weight in the right places. He knew she was over fifty, but the layers of time were being surely stripped from her.

On the way westward they met a prospector who said he was known as Goldy Chops. This day they were dry camped on the verge of a broad-leaf mulga forest, and witnessed him approach accompanied by an aborigine wearing clothes, and three pack camels. The prospector apparently was joyful at meeting strangers, and whilst the abo unloaded the camels, he squatted with Bony over what should have been a camp fire. He laughed easily revealing so many gold teeth that his sobriquet was deserved.

"Makin' for Wiluna, eh?" he exclaimed, chewing hard. "Not much of a joint now the mine's shut down. Worked her to death they did. But she'll come again some time. Still a few blokes hanging around. You can get baker's bread and butcher's meat if you want. What's your target?"

His beard was brown and curly. His eyes were washed blue. The teeth dazzled Bony.

"Been following the route picking up skins," replied Bony. "Could do with a bit of horse breakin'. Aim to make down south along the Number One. Homesteads down a bit might want a breaker."

"Yair! You never know."

They talked of this and that, Bony avoiding mentioning Breakaway House and hoping Goldy Chops to would do so, when Marie went into her performance.

"What d'you mean sitting there all evening on your bum, and gassing your head off? What about bringing wood and making fire? I gotta bake and slave getting your tucker for you and all you do is gas."

Bony grinned at the visitor and he grinned back, stood, negligently waved and departed for his own camp fire which his abo assistant had started.

Bony gathered fire wood and in a moment had their fire going, and Marie to stand over him, arms akimbo as though continuing the upbraiding. She said, suppressing a giggle:

"How did I go?"

"Wonderful, my sweet. You are now performing perfectly. I could hear the snarl of the angry spouse. I am now learning how to be submissive, and so we ought to become good actors believing in our roles."

"Don't you think it peculiar we've seen no smokes to-day?"

"No. It was arranged with Ugly Mug to avoid signals excepting one to-morrow notifying an aborigine camped at the east end of a station property of a telecast. He'll be told to signal our coming from the north to those south of him, and so we go south right down to Breakaway House."

"Seems a long way round and a lot of fuss and bother?" opined Marie, and added: "Still there were those three policemen."

"As you say. We have therefore to be subtle, very subtle. Sorry you came?"

"If you ask me that again I'll really go to market."

Early the next morning Goldy Chops came to say good bye, and now Bony probed.

"You know the country down around Mount Magnet and Narndee?"

"Was there a few years back. Outstation of Narndee's now the old Gov'ment Camel Breeding Station." Goldy Chops twirled his beard and proceeded to fill a pipe. "Where you might get a bit of work would be at Breakaway House, this side of the Number One. They say the Boss is a nasty piece of work, but pays well for contract jobs."

"What about Narndee?"

"Blokes stationed at the Gov'ment Camel Station. It's called Dromedary Hill. Got a telephone there. Well, see you later."

That day Ugly Mug sent up his signal, and that evening camp was made a few hundred yards off from a well and yards. From a humpy of old iron and boughs there came an elderly aborigine wearing pants but no shirt who wanted to know from which direction they had come. On being told from the east – a hand wave in that direction – he departed for his camp, and the two lubras with a dozen children who appeared to inhabit it with him. He came again the next morning to say he had been 'speak 'um' with a man Bony guessed was Ugly Mug or his medicine man.

This fellow could be easily understood. He drew the ever universal dust map, advising Bony of the way, pointing out the wells to avoid going too far to the west to follow the Number One. Also he was able to give much information about

Breakaway House and its out-lying huts and wells.

Four days later Bony and his Marie looked down on the great house from which this property took its name.

CHAPTER FIVE

The night prior to this day had seen them camped at an outlying well at the eastern extremity of the Breakaway House Station. There was no hut. There were makeshift yards for horses, and a box like contraption to house the engine to pump water when the wind failed to move the wind mill. From this well there was a rough track bearing the marks of truck tyres, and thus Bony's camels followed this track. As they proceeded the ground became firmer, more flat, and more densely covered by the desert scrub.

Eventually they emerged from this scrub with astonishing abruptness to find themselves on the edge of a great breakaway and overlooking a flat-floored valley from two to three hundred feet below the average land level. Due to the scintillating sunshine distances were hard to judge, but the far side was probably five miles away. Here were no weathered residuals. Cover the valley with water and there were the coasts of a great sea inlet. The coasts were on uniform height and there were countless little bays and countless jutting headlands.

It ran roughly north-south and far along it to the south was Breakaway House which even at this distance portrayed notable outlines. One would not expect to find such a house beyond the 100-mile radius of a seaboard city, built by convict labour for the landed gentry in that far past era. Bony counted eight chimney stacks.

"We'll camp here for lunch," Bony decided. "That is our Mecca."

The track turned to follow the verge of the breakaway, and the camels were urged forward till the noon camp was chosen to give a bite to eat. They were not in such good condition as when they set out from Merlee's camp, but much more tractable.

The customary fire was lit and the customary tea made in the blackened billy, and then lunch of baking powder bread and salted kangaroo meat, during which they looked at the breakaway and the house which they were to investigate.

The grey valley floor was green polka dotted with saltbush, the larger old man saltbush, with blue bush and small areas of scrub larger than on the lips. There were areas, too, which sparkled whitely and redly with massed mica particles, the show windows of jewellers being brought to mind. Small white clouds lifted high the blue sky of matchless purity.

"It could be a State Governor's residence," remarked Marie. "All open, though. No high wall about it to keep the mob out. What are those white marks in the ground?"

"Could be cement paths. I was told that Gosfer gets about in an electric chair."

"Could be, Josh. What a place to find here."

"Glad you don't forget the Josh," Bony said, earnestly. "To forget and call me Bony could be fatal to success. You're looking fine, my snappish, waspish wife. Boots down at heel. No stockings. Skirt rented and mended. Blouse – what a blouse! Hair straight where it isn't bedraggled. Sand all over your face, and black eyes as hostile as bull ants."

"You're no Beau Brummel yourself, Josh. There's a patch coming adrift from your pants, your shirt hasn't been washed for a month. Your limp's become a fixture, and you want a shave as much as Robinson Crusoe. Look! There's two horsemen down there."

The riders were coming from the direction of extensive stockyards. They were halted by a gate in a cross fence, and having passed through urged the horses into an easy canter. They disturbed sheep that had been lying down, and as he could see no cattle, Bony surmised that the entire valley was given over to sheep.

Soon after being on the move again they came to a sharp decline down the face of the breakaway, and here Marie had to brake hard, and Bony walked with her at the rear in case the camels bolted. At the bottom there was a hut beside a well which could not be seen from their lunch camp. It was an ordinary one-room building of iron having an iron roof, but within was a table and flanking form, and the fireplace appeared to have been recently used.

There was a windlass over the well but no evidence of sheep watering here, and Bony decided to camp for the day and proceed to Breakaway House early the following morning. He took the camels from the dray, watered them at the well and hobbled them out to feed, and he was gathering firewood when the two horsemen appeared round an angle of the breakaway face.

He could now see that one was a woman, and the other a weathered man of middle age. The woman coolly looked from him to Marie standing in the hut doorway. Bony guessed her to be under thirty. She was a round faced redhead and her hair gleamed in the sunlight beneath the old felt hat. The man said, sharply:

"You have permission to camp here?"

"No. But as the sheep aren't watering I thought we could do no harm. Being a bit late in the day, we didn't want to get to the house until after finding out things. Where we could camp and all that."

"Where you come from?"

"Been up the stock route a bit. After dingoes and 'roos."

The man dismounted and by the reins led the horse to the dray into which he peered and thus could see the skins Bony had collected. He was neatly dressed, wearing jodpurs and Bony asked were he the boss.

"Manager. Where you making for?"

"Nowhere in particular," Bony replied. "Bit tired of being on the move. Any chance of a job here? Horsebreaking? Cattle work?"

"Could give you a bit of horse breaking if you're any good. None of the abos are."

"If he is any good he could break that filly for me," said the woman, hopefully. Her voice was remarkably clear, and now her blue eyes were concentrated fully on Bony who was nervously prodding the dust with a boot tip.

"We'll try him first, Miss Leonard." Then to Bony: "All right you can camp here to-day. I'll have a word with Mr. Gosper about the breaking. You turn up in the morning, and if it's okay I'll tell you where to camp and where to paddock the camels."

They rode away toward the house, and Marie waited for Bony to speak, but Bony went to the kneeling camels, commanded them to stand, and hobbled them to permit them to ramble where they would find feed. He spent the afternoon overhauling his skins and dingo scalps, and Marie washed in kerosene buckets and cooked a brownie with which she had never lost touch.

"I've been wondering how you would get along baking yeast bread," Bony observed whilst she was taking the cake from the rough iron camp oven.

"I learned at the Mission, and what I learn I never forget, Doubtful Face. D'you know anything about that woman?"

"She's the daughter of a younger brother who is said to have been a coast watcher in the Islands and was killed by the Japs. Something of a writer, and stays here for long periods to assist her uncle in writing his memoirs. It's all I know of her. To me she seemed pleasant enough."

"In love with that man she was with."

"So. I didn't notice anything."

"Being a man you're not supposed to."

"Well, I can tell you're in love with me."

"'Cos I let you. It isn't what a woman sees in another, it's what she feels."

"Then my powers of observation aren't as acute as I have boasted."

Marie laughed outright. She said:

"You don't boast as much as you used to. Put the billy on for a cuppa."

Later Marie expressed the hope that Breakaway House would have tinned milk at least in the store as she hated tea without it, and asked did Bony think the store would have clothes to sell.

"Almost certainly," he told her. "We'll trade the scalps and skins. I'm wanting new pants and your old skirt ought to be burned."

"Treating a poor woman so! You went and burned my city dress, and now look what you've brought me to. When are you going to tell me what all this is about?"

"A walkabout, as I said in the beginning."

"But you let out about Gosfer who owns this place. And other things, too. You're on an assignment, so out with it."

Bony's blue eyes withdrew from the eagle flying above a mob of sheep on the far side of the valley, and he looked at his wife.

"There have been moments when I've felt I ought not to have

brought you from home. One of them was when Ugly Mug's abos chased the wilder ones deeper into the desert. Here at this Breakaway House I'm not taking chances. We proceed slowly and with caution, and we must never forget to maintain our assumed characters.

"According to Constable Moody stationed at Mount Magnet, a change came over this place some two years ago. Twice a year he leaves on a tour of duty to all the outlying stations, accompanied by two of his trackers.

"One of his duties is to maintain a rough census of the aborigines living at or near a station, and in this he is assisted by the station manager, or owner, as the case may be. He came here two years ago, and found Gosfer very ill and the entire organisation disrupted. There was no cook and all the abos bar three or four old crones were away on walkabout. That is all bar a man called Yarco known to the policeman as head man of the work force.

"He found Gosfer lying on a couch in a darkened room and suffering from malaria which Gosfer said he had contracted when on a trip through New Guinea a year or so earlier. There no was need for worry or medical attention as he knew what to do, having quinine with him always. When the subject of the census came up Gosfer told the policeman he hadn't prepared it and would do so when the abos returned from walkabout and deliver it when sending a truck to Mount Magnet for stores. Further, the policeman could be easy in mind as Gosfer had sent for his niece and she could be expected any day. Looking back on that interview, the policeman thinks that although Gasper was undoubtedly ill, his welcome was far short of what it had always been.

"Not that Gosfer is a kindly character. He was stricken with polio when a young man and stubbornness rather than calm courage brought him back to the point of running about in his chair. He is irascible, a spasmodic labour driver alternating with long retirement to his study where he is said to be writing his family history. The history ought to begin with a convict ancestor thought to be one Elgin Gosfer, but he must have employed Mister Billy Goat to chew up the records."

"Mister Billy Goat!" echoed Marie.

"He devoted years of his life to tracing the history of the great families among the various archives, and removing all references to their origin. In America much effort has been devoted to prove the original ancestor was one of the Pilgrim Fathers. Our voyaging fathers arrived in manacles, and their guards and officers were all on the same level.

"Anyway, Mr. Gosfer is reputed to be unbalanced. By that I mean he is either generous or mean, either a recluse or a party man, and in later years either canny or foolish in business."

"Where do we come in?" asked Marie.

"The business angle to this Breakaway House has apparently slipped since the sacking of a bookkeeper about the time the constable couldn't get the census. Gosfer told the constable he had done this because the feller was lazy, and further that the niece would be taking over the books and secretarial work.

"The next time the policeman called at Breakaway House on a routine patrol, he found the niece there, and the place being run properly by a white stockman *a la* manager. A white cook had been sent up by a city agency. He got the census. There were several minor discrepancies but these he straightened out with the help of chief aborigine Yarco.

"Still later, down in Perth the wool and stock agency people were becoming worried over the affairs of Breakaway House, and they were in a cleft stick because Breakaway House was a very valuable account and they had to avoid displeasing Gosfer. It happens that one of their departments is the employment agency for supplying cooks and domestics to stations, and when Gosfer wired for another cook, they sent up one of their inspectors to find out how far Gosfer was down the road.

"He was here five weeks, then pulled out and travelled to Mount Magnet to catch the train. It seems that the truck was late and the feller had no time to call at the police station. The policeman wasn't there, anyway. The station master recalled him boarding the train, but he never reached Perth, and simply vanished."

"Any known reason?" pressed Marie.

"None what ever. Fine reputation with his employers. Family man with exceedingly good prospects. It isn't certain that he did board the train at Mount Magnet as the stationmaster cannot be sure of the man and from the inspector's photographs failed to identify him."

"And you think he might not have left Breakaway House?"

"It is a possibility, in view of the known fact that a previous cook was so bashed by an aborigine that he had to enter a hospital, all at Gosfer's expense as the insurance company wouldn't pay for the injuries received."

"Why was the man bashed?"

"He avers that the fight was forced on him by two aborigines at the instigation of Yarco. There should have been a prosecution but money averted that. What about another cuppa?"

Sources

Up and Down Australia: Short Stories

The Man Who Liked Work: "The Man Who Liked Work," *Life*, Melbourne, 2 January 1928, pp38-42.

My Money on the Rain: "My Money on the Rain: A Memory of Outback Days," *The Herald*, Melbourne, 23 June 1934, p32.

Mice and Men: "Mice and Men," *The Bulletin*, Sydney, 4 July 1934, p48; "Better Late Than Never", *Wings*, vol 2, no 7, 21 December 1943, pp8-9.

The Dream That Did Not Come True: "An Outback Marriage – and its Chains: The Dream That Did Not Come True," *The Herald*, Melbourne, 4 August 1934, p33.

George's Accommodating Brother: "George's Accommodating Brother," *The Bulletin*, Sydney, 26 December 1934, pp40-41.

Sunset Joe's Goanna: "Sunset Joe's Goanna," *The Australian Journal*, Melbourne, vol 71, pt 833, 1 August 1935, pp1024-1029.

The Grousers: "The Grousers," *The Bulletin*, Sydney, 27 November 1935, pp48-49.

Frozen Pumps: "Frozen Pumps," *The Bulletin*, Sydney, 12 February 1936, p30.

Why Markham Bought a Radio Set: "Why Markham Bought a Radio Set," *The Listener-In*, 18 August 1934, pp16-17.

Hullo, Mate! "Hullo Mate!" *The West Australian*, 26 December 1931; "The Galah and the Madman," *The Herald*, Melbourne, 9 October 1933.

Rainbow Gold: "Rainbow Gold," *The Sunday Times*, Perth, 29 January 1933, p28.

Mirage Water: Frederick Barmore, "Mirage Water," *The Australian Journal*, Melbourne, 1 June 1936, p781.

The Stalker of Lone Men: "The Stalker of Lone Men," *The Bulletin*, Sydney, 26 June 1935, pp46-47.

Laffer's Gold: "Laffer's Gold," *The Western Mail*, Perth, Xmas Ed 1932; Murphy F & Nile R (Eds), *The Gate of Dreams*, Fremantle Arts Press, 1990, pp81-82.

A Lovely Party: "A Lovely Party," *The Australian Journal*, Melbourne, vol 74, pt 868, 1 July 1938, pp872-879.

Golden Hills: "Golden Dawn," *Everyman*, vol 2, No 27, 1 August 1929; "Gold in Treasure Hills," Yots! p4.

The Demijohn: "The Demijohn," *The Bulletin*, Sydney, 3 June 1936, pp28-29.

A Waif on the Nullabor: Frederick Barmore, "A Waif on the Nullabor," *The Australian Journal*, Melbourne, 1 June 1936, p850.

Four Gold Bricks: Frederick Barmore, "Four Gold Bricks," *The Australian Journal*, Melbourne, 1 July 1936, p992.

Lady Stand Fast! "Lady, Stand Fast!" *The Australian Journal*, Melbourne, vol 71, pt 834, 2 September 1935, pp1168-1173.

Willi Willi: "Willi-Willi," *The Australian Journal*, Melbourne, vol 71, pt 835, 1 October 1935, pp 1336-1342.

Henry's Last Job: "Henry's Last Job," *The Herald*, Melbourne, 14 September 1939.

The Mover of Mountains: "A Mover of Mountains," *The Herald*, Melbourne, 14 October 1939, p19; "Mover of Mountains," *The Chronicle*, Adelaide, p64.

Henry's Little Lamb: "Henry's Little Lamb," *The Herald*, Melbourne, 5 December 1939, p18; *The ABC Weekly*, 1 November 1941, pp39-40.

Joseph Henry's Christmas Party: "Joseph Henry's Christmas Party," *The Herald*, Melbourne, 23 December 1939.

Pink Dick's Elixir: "Pinky Dick's Elixir," *The Herald*, Melbourne, 18 January 1940, p34; *The ABC Weekly*, vol 3, no 1, 29 March 1941, pp47-48.

The Vital Clue: "Vital Clue," *The Herald*, Melbourne, 19 January 1940, p10.

Where DID The Devil Shoot the Pig? "Where DID the Devil Shoot the Pig?" *The Herald*, Melbourne, 29 January 1940, p27.

That Cow Maggie: "That Cow Maggie," *The Herald*, Melbourne, 11 April 1940, p36.

The Great Rabbit Lure: "The Great Rabbit Lure," *The Herald*, Melbourne, 19 April 1940, p12.

Led by a Child: "Led by a Child," *The Listener*, 6 January 1934, p12.

New Boots on Old Feet: "New Boots on Old Feet," *The World's News*, 27 May 1939, p24; *The Herald*, Melbourne, 27 December 1939, p11.

Wisp of Wool and Disk of Silver: "Wisp of Wool and Disk of Silver," *Ellery Queen's Magazine*, New York, vol 74, No 6, December 1979; *Ellery Queen's Cruise Round the World*, Dial Press, New York, 1981; Knight S (Ed), *Dead Witness: Best Australian Mystery Stories*, Penguin, Ringwood, Vic, 1989, pp204-219; Latta D (Ed), *Sand on the Gumshoe*, Random House, Hornsby, Australia, 1989, pp167-180.

Breakaway House: "Breakaway House", *The Bony Bulletin*, No 31, February 1990, pp2-5.

Up and Down Australia Again: More Short Stories

Little Stories of Gallipoli: "Little Stories of Gallipoli," *The Argus*, Melbourne, 10 January 1916, p5; "Storyettes of the Great War," *Hampshire Telegraph and Post*, Portsmouth, 7 April 1916, p5; 14 April 1916, p5, 20 April 1916, p5; and "All Must Pay," *The Argus*, Melbourne, 8 January 1916, pp 15-16.

Under Shell-fire at ANZAC: "Under Shell-fire at A.N.Z.A.C.," *Hampshire Telegraph and Post*, Portsmouth, 7 April 1916, p5.

Drafts for Haig: "Drafts for Haig," *Daily Mail*, London, 6 September 1918.

The Miracle: *The Miracle*, Manuscript, Box 6, Upfield Collection, Baillieu Library, University of Melbourne, c1926.

The Water Witch: "The Water Witch," *The Novel Magazine*, London, vol 25, no 145, April 1917, pp94-99.

The Death Heralds: "The Death Heralds," *The Novel Magazine*, London, vol 26, no 151, October 1917, pp15-20.

The Head of the Revolution: *The Head of the Revolution,* Manuscript, Box 6, Upfield Collection, Baillieu Library, University of Melbourne, c1920.

The Murderers' Home: *The Murderers' Home*, Manuscript, Box 6, Upfield Collection, Baillieu Library, University of Melbourne, c1922.

A Desert Flower: "A Desert Flower," *The Australian Journal*, Melbourne, vol 71, pt 832, 1 July 1935, pp920-931.

Love and the Leopard: *Love and the Leopard,* Manuscript, Box 5, Upfield Collection, Baillieu Library, University of Melbourne, c1935.

The Bewildered Castaways: "The Bewildered Castaways," Melbourne, *The Australian Journal*, vol 74, pt 862, 1 January 1938, pp70-79.

A Man Who Dreamed: "A Man Who Dreamed," *The Australian Journal*, Melbourne, vol 73, pt 861, 1 December 1937, pp1638-1642.

Wandi and the Bilker: "Wandi and the Bilker," *The Australian Journal*, Melbourne, vol 73, pt 860, 1 November 1937, pp1477-1481.

Derhamboi the Makromme: "Dehamboi the Makromme," Melbourne, *The Australian Journal*, vol 74, pt 864, 1 March 1938, pp352-359.

The Black Squatter: "The Black Squatter," *The Australian Journal*, Melbourne, vol 74, pt 865, 1 April 1938, pp488-495.

A Storm in a Quart Pot: "Storm in a Quart Pot," Melbourne, *The Australian Journal,* vol 74, pt 867, 1 June 1938, pp794-802.

Bringing in the Outlaws: "Bringing in the Outlaws," *The Advertiser*, Adelaide, 8 June 1935; *The Herald*, Melbourne, 22 June 1935.

Charlie the Cook: "Charlie the Cook", Manuscript, R Blackmore, Victoria, c1925.

The Colonel's Horse: "The Colonel's Horse," *The ABC Weekly*, 4 January 1941, pp41-42.

Night of the Tin Cans: "Night of the Tin Cans," *The ABC Weekly*, 25 October 1941, pp39-40.

The Cairo Spy: "The Cairo Spy," *The ABC Weekly*, 5 July 1941, pp41-42.

Mis Oo-La La: *Miss Oo-La-La,* Manuscript, Box 6, Upfield Collection, Baillieu Library, University of Melbourne, 1941.

Joining up with Rafferty: "Joining Up with Rafferty," *The Australian Journal*, Melbourne, vol 70, pt 826, I January 1935, pp31-34.

Breakaway House (Revised): *Breakaway House,* Manuscript, BREA/MS, Upfield Collection, Baillieu Library, University of Melbourne, 1962.